A S ASON OF LEAVES

D1322572

Catherine Law

A SEASON OF LEAVES

preface

This paperback edition published by Preface 2009

10 9 8 7 6 5 4 3 2 1

Copyright © Catherine Law 2008, 2009

Catherine Law has asserted her right to be identified as the author
of this work under the Copyright, Designs and Patents Act 1988

Extract from *The Return of the Soldier* by Rebecca West
(p168) reproduced with thanks to PFD.

First published in Great Britain in 2008 by Preface
1 Queen Anne's Gate
London SW1H 9BT

An imprint of The Random House Group Limited

www.rbooks.co.uk
www.prefacepublishing.co.uk

Addresses for companies within The Random House Group Limited
can be found at www.randomhouse.co.uk

The Random House Group Limited Reg. No. 954009

A CIP catalogue record for this book is available from the British Library

ISBN 978 1 84809 0989

The Random House Group Limited supports The Forest Stewardship
Council (FSC), the leading international forest certification organisation. All
our titles that are printed on Greenpeace-approved FSC-certified paper carry
the FSC logo. Our paper procurement policy can be found at
www.rbooks.co.uk/environment

Typeset in Minion by Palimpsest Book Production Limited,
Grangemouth, Stirlingshire
Printed and bound in Great Britain by
CPI Bookmarque Ltd, Croydon CR0 4TD

*Dedicated to the memory of Gertrude Charlton and
all those who follow their dreams*

Prologue

Cornwall
June 1992

THE FLOORBOARD HAD BEEN SQUEAKING FOR MONTHS. Wincing as she knelt down, her arthritic joints creaking in protest, she coaxed the nails with the claw end of the hammer. Aged and rusty, they came out easily, like pulling a knife out of butter. The furrows in her brow relaxed. Irritation was replaced by satisfaction: one more tiresome chore – boringly regular in this old house – was dealt with. Lifting the small section of floor-board, she stopped. She caught a glimpse of what looked like paper in the gap between the joists. As she lowered her hand into the void, her fingers brushed the letters in their dusty grave.

Holding the envelopes in her hands, she was struck by a bright, soul-cleansing understanding. The letters were still sealed and were addressed to her. Many minutes passed as she stared at them: moments when she knew not the difference between happiness and grief; life and death. She knew he would speak to her again one day; she knew he'd let her know, somehow.

In her hands were his letters to her: unread, unknown, unearthed forty-six years after she had last seen his face.

How could it possibly be any other way?

Cornwall
September 1992

LEANING OUT OF HER BEDROOM WINDOW, ROSE PEPPER COULD SEE to the edge of her world. Beyond her garden wall lay the churchyard, where long grass between the graves was hazy in the Indian-summer light. Rising cheerfully above the crooked headstones sat the granite church, squat and small. She squinted. On one side of her garden was the post-war cube of the new vicarage and the cluster of stone cottages that made up the hamlet of Trelewin. To her right was the stile and foot-path that led to Pengared Farm. These days, the church was her boundary. What lay beyond was softened and blurred as if by tears, but really, she corrected herself, by geriatric myopia.

She rested her arms on the stone sill, feeling the residual warmth from the sun that had long moved round to the front of the house that faced the sea, its golden light sparkling like diamonds on the water. Her home, the Old Vicarage, had stood there on the cliff for a hundred years: granite walls and a Gothic facade withstanding all that the Cornish weather threw at it. If she cared to observe, she would see a century's worth of scars: rainwater stains, a leaning chimney, a loose roof tile here and there. *I have lived in this house for nearly half of its life*, she reminded herself, rubbing at the smooth stone sill with her fingertip. *And for three-quarters of my own.*

Her daughters often wondered why she chose to use this room at the back for a bedroom. After all, the great bay window at the front commanded the sea. But Rose knew what constituted a good view. The garden lay before her, shimmering. Butterflies bounced among frothing purple lavender; roses melted into one another like scoops of ice cream. Her eyes rested on the corner by the far wall where, under the spreading boughs of a cherry

3

tree, lay a patch of long glossy grass. The tree had been planted in the year after the war, and she had watched it grow. Every autumn, leaves fell from the cherry and covered the grass around its trunk; she never raked them up. Nettles flourished in this corner, for the butterflies, she conceded, and she allowed ivy to grow wild, crawling from the stone wall between the garden and the churchyard to tangle itself around the tree. Every year, the creeping ivy fingers reached further still. *I like this bedroom. I like this view*, she told herself. *I can keep watch from here.*

She used to be able to see so much further from the window: beyond the stile that marked the edge of the glebe, even to where the footpath snaked over the rise of the headland on the far horizon. She could, however, still make out the old letter box that once belonged to Pengared Farm. It stood, rusting on a pole by the stile, guarded by brambles. During the war, the postman only went so far, and it was up to Betony or Ted Cumberpatch to come and fetch their own post, walking the two miles across the headland from Pengared Farm to Trelewin. A lifetime ago.

From the cooking aroma rising up the stairs, Rose calculated she had about fifteen minutes' peace before she'd be called by her daughters for dinner. Lara was cooking chicken fricassee downstairs in her kitchen. It was one of Betony Cumberpatch's recipes 'which *always* work': a special meal before the three of them left tomorrow on their trip to Prague. That was Lara's thing: cooking. Her elder daughter Nancy's thing was finding fault. If Rose was to have her way, it would have been fish and chips from the village: so much easier when there was all the packing to do. But then Nancy would not have approved.

Rose sighed, squinting hard through the fading late afternoon light at the rusting letter box, remembering how, when she worked as the Cumberpatchs' land-girl, she used to reach in past cobwebs and snails for their post. She wanted to go down there now and grasp that stupid pole, wrench it from the ground and sling the whole thing over the hedge. She did not want a celebratory meal. She did not want the fuss. But ever since she had found the letters under the floorboards in the spare room, her life had become one big fuss. They were such innocent things: three simple brown envelopes. Krystof had addressed them so diligently to her at Pengared Farm, and yet they never made it to her. They only got as far as that cursed letter box for Pengared.

When she unearthed them – was it really three months ago? – there amid the dust between the joists, her tremendous shock, crumbling voice and darting fingers compelled her daughters to radiate towards her and fill her head with their voices and their concern. The trip to Prague was their idea. They coaxed her, and protected her; they tried to make it all right. But all she wanted was the peace and space to remember.

They were having an Indian summer in Cornwall. She smiled and leant a little further from her window, tasting the sweet, balmy air tinged with a tang of sea salt, watching the church tower bask in the afternoon light. In Krystof's language, September was *Zárí: the month that glows with colour*. How right he was. She kept his words alive, kept his memory bright. In the dark every night before she drifted off to sleep, the thoughts and words spinning through her head were in Czech.

It had been another warm day, the day of the haymaking at Pengared during the war, when she and Krystof had laughed deeply into each other's faces, their clothes stuck with seed heads, their eyes full of the low golden sun. He bent close to speak to her in his sing-song accent while the clack-clacking of Ted Cumberpatch's hay cutter pummelled their ears. Petals in the meadow rose like confetti. Krystof's scent and the vibration of his laughter sunk under her skin. And stayed there. That had been July. By the time September, *the month that glows with colour*, was over, he was gone.

'Mum? Are you OK?' Nancy walked in without knocking and eyed the unpacked suitcase on the floor, piles of clothes and an unfilled toiletry bag on the bed, the general melee of her mother's bedroom.

Rose kept her face to the window and the view of the church, willing treacherous tears to disappear; for her eyes to smile again.

'I'm fine,' she lied easily, picking up some knickers and throwing them into her case. 'There! Nearly done.'

Her daughter sighed without humour. She picked up her mother's pistachio-coloured cardigan from the bed, shook it out and began to refold it. 'I know how much you hate packing, so

I thought I'd better check up on you. Dinner will be ready soon. Lara's sauce is bubbling and the wine is breathing. Not sure if fricassee is right for such a warm evening, if you ask me.'

Nancy was a tall, handsome woman, who always knew better. She had strong, well-placed features and a habit of padding around the farmhouse at Pengared in one of her husband Mo's old shirts. Sensibly, once she'd hit forty, she cropped her thick dark hair into a choirboy style, although Rose thought it made her look like a beanpole.

Now Rose felt her daughter's dark, scrutinising stare.

'Look, Mum, are you sure about going to Prague? I'm beginning to think it's not such a good idea, going back after all these years. At your age? You seem all of a muddle recently. You seem so distant. Finding Krystof's letters has been a real blow, hasn't it? I wonder if it isn't all a bit too much for you. I was only saying to Lara just now, have we been hasty . . . arranging it so soon? But it seemed such a good thing to do, with the Wall coming down, and everything. Are you really ready to go back there?'

Rose was unable to answer, her mind felt disabled. Trying to distance herself from the letters, the trip, Krystof, she asked after Nancy's mother-in-law: 'How's Betony? I haven't seen her for a while. Still cooking her wondrous meals?'

Nancy was baffled. 'Of course she is. And a good job too. Mo hates my cooking. I let her get on with it. There must be some advantages to living with your husband's mother. That's one anyway. Ah, I see you've managed to pack *something*.'

Nancy stooped to the case and picked up the bundle, wrapped carefully in her mother's silk scarf. Rose's hand rose in reflex, like a cat's paw, to grab it back. She stood rooted, seething, while Nancy sifted the flimsy envelopes in her hands.

'I see. You're waiting until you get to Prague before opening them. I don't know how you can bear it. Just think of what lies inside these letters. The truth, I suppose. I can't see why you won't just rip them open here and now.' There it was: that little piece of her father Will behind her eyes. *His* handsome eyes. The desire to control, and then the panic when that control starts to slip. 'Don't you think you should open them now? Get it over with?'

'Not at all.'

Rose could not look her daughter in the eye as she reached for the letters with a surprisingly steady hand. Cradling Krystof's letters, so fragile, so *light*, she noticed how they were disintegrating at the folds, a little torn. Like me, she thought. His looping hand was off-centre, the inked postmark, *Praha 9 June 1946*, fading. Once again, her mind was lame. She could not bear to think. She wrapped them tenderly back up in the scarf and stowed them in a corner of her suitcase.

Nancy would not take her eyes off them. 'I still can't believe my father stole them. You reckon he took them from the old letter box and hid them? I wonder what made him do it? I'm so sorry, Mum.' Nancy sat on the bed with a flump, a great sigh rushing forth. Her large hand, as red and calloused as any self-respecting farmer's wife's should be, swept back through her cropped hair. 'What a bastard.'

Rose was struck by how vulnerable her hard-faced Nancy was for a fleeting moment. She said, gently, 'You have no need to apologise for something that man did. For someone you never knew. Something so long ago . . .'

She sat down at her dressing table, herself breathing a monumental sigh, catching Nancy's eye in the mirror. It seemed far easier than face to face. 'You're right. I have always hated packing,' she said lightly. 'I feel so *useless*, packing. Drives me mad. I mean, this hairbrush . . .' She picked it up and used it to smooth her bobbed grey hair behind her ears. 'Should I pack it now? No. I will still need it in the morning. I can't bear the boring minutiae of it all. Packing a suitcase always means an end of something. It means I have to *think*.'

'Look, I'll help you. I'll do it for you.' There it was, the controlling streak rising to the surface of Nancy's skin: Will Bowman manifesting again, and again.

Rose flinched. 'No, thank you, Nancy. I can manage. I am not feeble and decrepit yet. Even at *my* age.'

She turned once more to her reflection, and pondered. 'What is it they say? You know you're getting old the moment you look in the mirror and see your mother staring back at you.'

A sixty-seven-year-old woman was staring back at her. She saw a high forehead, softly lined, her features fading into one another, becoming less apparent. Her eyes – still as green as a cat's – had kept their pretty almond shape, even if they were a little hooded. She was unable to wear eye make-up any longer but her hair was still glorious. Thick and glorious. Her land-girl friend Meg had once told her it was as red as a fox's tail. An American GI had told her she was a real-life firecracker. Now, all the colour was gone but the grey still glowed warm from the odd auburn hair that stayed with her and refused to leave.

She glanced out of the window at the turning season's gilding of the countryside, blurred before her eyes. Now she was here, in the autumn of her life. Realisation hit her with a jolt of sadness: she had always thought that, by now, she'd be in Prague once again; living, laughing, loving. Walking beside Krystof across the Charles Bridge.

She shook away the image, telling Nancy, 'But of course my mother never made it anywhere near this far. Poor dear Mother . . .'

Nancy was uncharacteristically quiet, her eyes softening momentarily in sympathy.

'Well, the years are certainly passing,' said Rose, rallying. 'Look at my scar. I hardly notice it now. I've carried that round with me since I was seventeen. What's that – fifty years! And now, good heavens, it's all but faded away.'

Nancy peered over her mother's shoulder at her reflection and shook her head.

Irritated, Rose said, 'There, see? That crescent-shaped mark on my cheek.'

Nancy shrugged. 'It's so small I've never really noticed it. It's always been part of your face. It's not important, Mum.'

Rose pressed her lips together. Nancy didn't know how wrong she was.

Lara called up the stairs, her voice reaching them like a snatch of tune. 'Dinner's ready, come on, you two.'

Nancy put her hand on her mother's arm. On reflex, Rose drew away and then, ashamed, tried to make amends by leaning closer.

'Before we go down,' said Nancy, oblivious to her discomfort, 'I just wanted to remind you that Cringle Cottage is always ready for you if you want it. If you want to leave this old place, put it all behind you, and start afresh. Don't worry, it hasn't been left to rack and ruin since Meg died. Mo's been painting it. Whitewash everywhere. He's fixed the roof and the chimney doesn't smoke any more, he's tested it.'

Rose glanced again out of her window, her eyes darting in protection of her thoughts, worried that Nancy would read them.

'I like this house.' There was the lie. 'It's been my home for so long . . .'

'But Mum, this huge old place . . . the running costs, the heating bills. You're rattling around in here. Oh, I know it's lovely in the summer but . . .'

'There was a time,' Rose suddenly laughed, walking out of the bedroom, 'when you couldn't wait to get your hands on it. Both of you, seduced by the pictures in glossy magazines. Lara sorting out my kitchen and bathroom; putting in the roll-top bath. You doing up the hallway, fixing those floor tiles . . .' They were now at the top of the landing looking down on the large square hallway below. The floor was Victorian mosaic in black, terracotta and cream.

'And now you want me to leave it all behind,' Rose chided.

'We loved it as kids,' mused Nancy. 'This rambling old place with its cubbyholes and dusty corners: a perfect playground for us. But things are different now.'

'But you never knew about—' Rose stopped and shook her head. 'Nothing,' she said, forcing another laugh. Her daughters had never been aware of the chilling, draining emptiness of the rooms once their playing was over and they were tucked up in bed; the creeping loneliness that followed her solitary figure upstairs every night.

'It's just a thought, Mum,' Nancy was saying. 'After the shock of finding Krystof's letters. We could put this place on the market; I'm sure you'd make a good profit. Live in Cringle Cottage. You'd be five minutes from me, Mo and Betony, not half an hour's walk over the headland. It could be a project, keep you occupied.'

'At my age?' Rose tried to make a joke.

'On the market' meant surveyors, buyers, people who would prod and poke. The longer she held out, the less likely she'd have to face it. The longer she could protect her daughters, and herself.

With Ted, his brother Hugh and now Meg gone, her secret remained with just herself and Betony.

'Don't know why,' said Nancy, standing at the top of the stairs, 'but I always feel uneasy walking around this landing. Maybe I fell as a child.' She stopped and her eyes burrowed into Rose's. 'Did I hurt myself? Did I fall down the stairs? There's something odd about it. Some strange memory. It's funny what lies buried in the subconscious, isn't it?'

Rose's hand gripped the banister. She dared not answer.

'Did I hear Nancy mention the *project*?' cried Lara, her bright face greeting them as she peered over her shoulder whilst energetically draining the veg over the sink. 'Don't you think Cringle Cottage is perfect for you, Mum? Keep talking, while I finish this. I don't want to miss out on anything.'

Rose stopped at the kitchen threshold, her spirit draining clean away, her eyes filled suddenly with Krystof's face. His deep-grey eyes now belonged to Lara, the joy for life that surrounded her like a halo was his. He was standing there: his face behind Lara's eyes. Even the way her fair fringe fell over her forehead.

'Nothing has been decided,' Rose said, her voice weary. 'One thing at a time, please, girls. My, that smells good, Lara. I can't wait.'

She felt them both back down; they knew not to press her.

'Go through to the dining room then,' Lara said cheerily, 'and I'll bring the starters.'

'Come here first,' Rose said, holding her arms open. 'Both of you,' she added quickly.

Her daughters stepped forward and she hugged them together. Why was she always struck by how unalike they were? What did she expect? Their fathers had been as different as heaven and hell. She had tried to bring them up as equals; tried not to have a favourite. But with Nancy, Rose's guilt worked its mischief in so many ways. The secret about her father, Will, which she would take to her grave, had built an invisible wall between them. Even now, married to her old friends Betony and Ted's son Mo and living at the farm where she herself had once lived and worked. Nancy seemed as far away as ever.

In the kitchen, Nancy's embrace was stiff with pent-up frustration. Lara just fell into her arms, pressing her face into her mother's cheek.

'So, which area did you live in, Mum?' asked Lara as Nancy poured the coffee. They had cleared the dessert plates and continued to sit at the dining table, French windows open to the garden. Beyond the wall, the church shimmered like pewter as the sun went down.

Lara was leafing through a book open before her on the cloth. Rose stared at it, feeling her lip curl with distaste.

'What on earth is that?'

'The guidebook I bought,' Nancy answered, affronted. 'Of course, I'm pleased I arranged this trip when I did. It says in there that September is the best time to go, according to the weather graphs. Not too hot, not too cold. It will be good to go before the crowds descend. Just think, all those Warsaw Bloc countries opening up to us now. I think we'll be some of the first Westerners to get there since the Wall came down.'

Rose cringed at Nancy, who was being a know-all. 'I won't be needing a guidebook,' she said.

'But think how much has changed,' Nancy pressed on. 'We're talking nearly fifty years. The Communists booted out. The Prague we lived in then has all but disappeared.'

'I hope to God some aspects of it have.'

'Well, of course, all the important things will still be there: the Charles Bridge, the Old Town Square, that amazing astronomical clock,' Nancy reeled off the tourist sites, 'but the atmosphere will be different, the *people* will be. You forget that I can't remember any of it. I will be discovering it for the first time for myself. I can't tell you how helpful it's been corresponding with those students at the university. They're very interested in our case. When I last wrote they agreed to meet with us one afternoon, did I tell you?'

'Our case . . . ?' Rose felt Nancy was racing ahead of her.

Lara, flicking through the book, raised her head. 'I'm glad we're going. This is just what I need.' She looked at her mother. 'Oh, I know the trip is for you, Mum, of course, but now my divorce has come through, I want to focus on myself and have a nice little holiday. It will help me forget a little, while hopefully it will help you remember.'

Rose was desperate to change the subject. 'So, Lara, have you heard from Greg recently?'

'No, which is a good thing,' retorted Lara. 'Last time I heard, he was still a shit. Anyway, I don't want to talk about him. This is about us. And our quest . . . our case, as you put it, Nancy. Now let's see, where is the university? Oh, I see, right by the river. I take it the students will help us find my father.'

Rose's stomach balled up into a hard stone. She held her breath, trying to stop the eruption of a huge uncontrollable sob. Prague surfaced in her memory: bells rang out over the fairy-tale spires and red-tiled roofs; the majestic castle presided from the top of the hill; the insides of churches dripped with gold; birds circled the river in the light of the setting sun. And then the deep-freeze of winter when the river lay cold and stiff under the arches of the Charles Bridge. The air did not touch her bare flesh for months and birds fell frozen from the sky.

She saw Lara's face, struggling to show empathy, looming towards her.

'What happened, Mum? Will we ever know? The letters will tell us, won't they?'

Rose rested her head in her hands. They'd been through all this before. It was beginning to get her down.

Nancy shook her head at her sister.

'No, no, Lara's right, Nancy.' Rose sounded very old and very tired. 'I'll tell you what I remember. The letters can wait.' She took a deep breath. 'Krystof's house was opposite a monastery in the *Stare Mesto*, the Old Town.' She waited as Lara eagerly turned pages, tracing columns of text with her finger. 'It was a tall house. Built of stone. Crumbling stucco. Truly beautiful, faded and grand. It had been in Krystof's family for a century at least.'

'How many floors?' asked Lara.

She counted on her fingers. '. . . three, four. But we had to give them up to the Communists. They put us in the attic, crammed in we were: Krystof, Babička, Nancy and me.'

'Oh, Babička! The old lady,' cried Nancy. 'How funny that I should suddenly remember her. She was Krystof's granny, wasn't she?'

'I wonder what else you will remember?' said Rose. 'We were there for less than a year, you know; you were very young. You had your second birthday there in June 1946, just before we left.'

Nancy swept her pensive eyes over the photographs in the guidebook. 'I keep having snippets . . .' she said, 'flashes in my head, just like with the landing here at home. I remember there were a lot of stairs in the house in Prague. And in my mind, narrow streets. And Babička; she had rather large, wrinkly hands and long white hair. I also remember crying . . . the cold.'

Rose swallowed hard. 'Do you remember Krystof?'

Nancy wrinkled her nose. 'Hardly. Hardly at all.'

'He was a father to you.'

For less than a year. That's all we had.

Nancy was blunt, defensive. 'I don't remember.'

Rose was incensed. Nancy was quick to apologise when she didn't have to, for her own father's cruelty and madness. For someone she never knew. But she would show no contrition for not remembering Krystof.

To distract herself from her anger, Rose looked over at Lara.

'You've taken to wearing your hair in a ponytail.'

'Do you like it?' Lara flicked her hair. 'Since my divorce, since I got rid of Greg, I want to feel young again.'

Rose said, 'It's just how you wore it as a child. What traumas we had, trying to get a brush through it.'

Her ponytail would swing behind Lara as she ran, Rose remembered. Every day, she had wanted Krystof to see his daughter run; her hair bouncing; her smile a mirror of his.

Am I the only person, apart from Betony, left alive who remembers him? thought Rose with a jolt. She looked at her two daughters who were both waiting on her every word, eager to hear more about their life in Prague.

'The Communists were taking over,' she went on. 'It began to get dangerous, and, soon after your second birthday, Nancy, Krystof and I decided we had to leave. You know all this. I don't see why I have to go over it all again.'

'But you've never really told us. Not properly,' persisted Lara, not hearing the warning crack in her mother's voice. 'Why didn't Krystof come with you?'

Rose rested her thumping forehead on the coolness of her

hand, shielding her eyes, which were screwed up tight with pain. She whispered, 'He couldn't. He simply couldn't.'

Rose could not sleep. Usually the night sounds of Trelewin soothed her, but tonight she lay with her eyes wide open against the darkness. In the silence of her bedroom she listened to the small hours marked by the chimes of the church clock and Krystof's voice saying over and over, '*Ruzena*, I will follow.'

She replied, '*Následujte mě* . . . follow me.'

Three years ago, she had watched the Wall come down on the evening news. She saw the joyful people jumping on graffiti-splashed chunks of mortar; she saw their ecstasy and their open arms as, like a surging tide, Easterners piled through the gaps. She wondered and dared to hope. Now he will contact me. He knows where I am. He must reach me here.

But she didn't know that his letters had already reached her and had been sleeping – crumbling – for forty-six years under her floorboards. He might phone, she had thought. Funny to think they had never spoken on the telephone. His voice. Oh, to hear his voice again. She could not remember it.

The bedroom window was open and right at the edge of her senses, the waves of Trelewin cove below were breaking and receding on the sand. She found herself smiling in the darkness, remembering how Krystof had never been able to fathom the beauty of the sea, how he had marvelled at its vastness, its freedom. How he had cried with joy that it existed.

She knew what she would do with his letters. Once they had got their taxi from the airport into Prague; once they had been dropped off at the hotel, unpacked and had a light refreshment; once her daughters had consulted the guidebook and decided what to do first, she would leave them. She would take a tram to the river. She'd find a spot where she could see the Charles Bridge downstream. Perhaps she would watch the water tumble over the weir, or count the statues on the parapets. Then she would fight her cold fear and bury it deep inside. She'd take the bundle of letters and gently unwrap them. She'd take her life in her hands. Using her handbag-sized magnifying glass, she would carefully check each postmark, check each date. And one by one, in the order which Krystof sent the letters and in the order that

Will Bowman concealed them, she would slit each envelope open and read . . . and read . . . and read.

She drifted, holding on to that rare glimmer of anticipation in the darkness. Her fear fading. At last, the truth . . . their truth.

A tap on the door, gentle at first. She thought she was dreaming. But then it grew urgent. Rap rap rap. The bedroom door opened.

'What? What is it?' she hoisted herself upright against her pillows. 'Is that you, Nancy?' Of course it wasn't Nancy; Nancy never knocked.

'No, it's me.' Lara's tall, slim figure in a white nightie slipped into the room, quickly shutting the door behind her.

'What's the matter?'

'Oh, Mum, I can't bear it. Switch your light on. Switch it on!'

Rose fumbled in the dark.

'Please, switch it *on*!'

'Lara, whatever . . . ?' She peered at her daughter as the sharp light from the bedside lamp hit her.

Lara was panting, her rosebud mouth the shape of an 'O'. Her grey eyes, Krystof's grey eyes, wide and tearful. Her blonde hair fell over her face, shielding her, but Rose saw and smelt tension, and fear.

'Lara, it's two o'clock in the morning. Whatever is the matter?'

Lara was hiding something behind her back. She bit her lip as she carefully brought her hand round, clutching what looked like an old stained towel. The towel was wrapped around something dead and heavy. She placed it on her mother's lap and it sank into the bedclothes.

'Lara?'

'You tell me what it's doing here. I can't believe it was there, right there in the cupboard.'

'Why were you looking in your cupboard at this time of night?'

'I wasn't. It was earlier. Just before I was going to sleep. I wanted to find my old walking boots to take with me. The cobbles of Prague are hard on one's feet, apparently. Instead of my boots I found this disgusting thing. I haven't slept at all. Mum, what's it *doing* here?'

Rose picked up a corner of the towel and carefully pulled it to one side. The weight of the object sat between her knees.

It felt vaguely familiar to her, like the weight of someone's hand. Willing her tired eyes to focus, she pressed her fingertips into the towel and found cool metal. She ran them along the length of it until she touched the smooth wooden handle, her finger alighting on the trigger.

'It's Krystof's gun,' she breathed. 'Oh, God, I'd forgotten . . . since you girls left home, I have just shut doors and left things to the dust and mice. Oh, Lara. What a shock for you. I'm so sorry.'

'But what's it doing in the cupboard?' Lara shrieked, shivering by Rose's bed.

'I doubt it's loaded,' Rose said, remembering, with a thrill of pleasure, the crack of the bullets as she fired them off one by one. She gazed down at the pistol as if it was an old friend: a Model 24, standard Czech armed forces issue. It was quite a dinky thing: a short, fat muzzle of dull metal, a gleaming wooden handle. It used to fit in the palm of Krystof's hand, and it slipped inside his coat pocket with ease.

'You've got to get rid of it!' hissed Lara.

A strange, sweeping lethargy filled Rose's limbs. She touched the pistol tenderly. 'You know, Lara,' she whispered, 'I am so sorry about this. Of course, I knew the gun was here, somewhere in this house, but it had slipped my mind, like a lot of things do these days. Yes, it is a horrid thing. But believe me, Lara, it means a lot to me. It was the last thing your father touched.'

'You mean, he really *is* dead? He died using it. Did someone shoot him? Was he shot dead?'

'No, no . . . what I meant to say was: he had been carrying the gun . . . before we parted. I can't explain to you . . .' Her eyes slipped sideways to Krystof standing on Prague station concourse as her train pulled away.

'But it's a *gun*. And you're just sitting there!'

Rose was weary. 'Lara, I can't get worked up over this. I can't let myself. I have been through so much, that the sight of this gun right now is really not having an effect on me. Not the horror that you expect me to feel. I'm sorry about that.'

She watched her daughter's open, incredulous face close down with fear.

'Well, you must be made of concrete then,' Lara snapped.

'Maybe I am.' Rose wrapped the pistol back up in its grubby towel. 'Tomorrow, before we leave, I'm going to take this thing and throw it into the sea.'

'Good.'

'But for now, it is going in the bin.' She reached out and tossed Krystof's gun into her waste-paper basket.

Temporarily satisfied, Lara retreated to the door. 'Do I tell Nancy?'

'Do what you like.'

On this, Lara returned and sat by her mother's feet.

'You're so calm, Mum. I don't understand.'

'I don't either. Concrete, you see.' She managed a smile. Inside her chest her heart was turning itself inside out, and her agony was beginning to register on her face. She could barely manage to keep her voice smooth and motherly. 'But right now, Lara, you are going to sleep, and so am I. We have a long day tomorrow.'

Lara glanced towards the waste-paper basket. 'I don't know how you can sleep with that thing in your bedroom.'

Rose looked at her daughter in sorrow. *You don't know your mother at all*, she thought.

She said, 'Goodnight, Lara.'

Lara crept towards the door. 'You don't have to throw it into the sea, Mum. Not if it was the last thing my father touched.'

Rose switched off her light and lay in the darkness listening to her thoughts: '*Skutečný* . . . and *skutečný* . . .' and marvelling at how the words for truth and reality were the same in Czech.

A light aircraft droned across the sky. She stared towards her bedroom ceiling, imagining the plane's flight as it passed overhead in deep darkness, unusually low on its path along the Cornish coast to Plymouth airport. She was grateful to the unknown pilot for breaking in and stopping unpleasant thoughts from spiralling towards unimaginable horror, the horror, truth and reality that she was keeping from her daughters and from herself.

But then her concrete heart tripped over its beat and the sound of the plane's engine turned a fresh page in her memory.

Planes in the sky, flying a steady path. Planes in the sky, a whole squadron. Planes in the sky, a bank of them seven miles wide, like a great storm approaching. Sharp-eyed navigators looking down on the English countryside, at the line of the coast and the treacherous, white breaking waves. Planes in the sky over Plymouth docks: battle-black, shiny nosed Dorniers with a heavy cargo to offload.

And there she was, down in the street. Tiny Rose, trapped by the rain of bombs, trapped by the fire; trapped in the air raid with Will Bowman.

She sank deeper into her bed, helpless to the memory, wretched with it all.

The night of the raid was the night that changed everything; changed the truth; changed the reality of what Rose Pepper was to become.

PART ONE

Cornwall
January 1943

One

CIGARETTE SMOKE BURNT HER EYES AND SEEPED INTO THE very weave of her clothes. Standing patiently in the Anchor pub, down at the Plymouth docks, Rose reluctantly breathed in the fug. The noise and the beer puddles and the dim light from 40-watt bulbs sapped her spirit. She wanted to be outside. She wanted to be home in her parents' back parlour listening to the Light Programme on the wireless. It was nearly bedtime. It was quarter to eleven and last orders had been rung out. Surely she could go home now? Her legs itched under her nylons, courtesy of Will and his nudge-nudge contact. No, it looked as though he was getting in one last round.

The crowd jostled, grew noisier, realising their drinking-up time – and their farewells – were closer than they had thought. Able mariners on leave were clinging drunkenly to their mates. Girls with nervous, watery eyes waited for a last goodbye, or wore bright red lipstick as a banner of bravery. A group of privates was singing 'Tipperary'; in a corner, an officer was kissing a WVS girl.

Everywhere Rose looked she saw a uniform: the Tommy khaki and forage cap, the voluminous fatigues of the mariners, the buttoned-up and commanding Air Force. She felt a patter of pride in her chest; very soon even she would have a uniform of her own. Will's Air Raid Patrol get-up was not quite as endearing as the forces' issue: baggy overalls and a black tin hat with a luminous white 'W' on the front. He was exempt from active service because of his chronic asthma but still did his bit. He was the hero of the air raids, so he told her – all rotas, buckets and stirrup pumps – and her parents thought he was wonderful. But she often had to stifle a laugh when he called in to see them on his rounds: the hat was far too small for him perched there on top of his large, handsome, humourless face.

His fingers gripped hers now as he paid for his beer and a port and lemon for her. He leant aggressively on the bar, his elbows clearing the way. When he was agitated or determined, his wheezing grew louder and she could hear it now as she waited, overwhelmed by the bulk of his broad back, her face near the wool of his coat. He did not ask what she wanted to drink. She did not want anything. All she wanted was to be at home.

Disappointment nagged at her as he pulled her behind him through the pub and sat her down at a corner table. She watched while he stood and laughed with a band of Tommies, clapping his hands on backs as if they were old friends, ignoring her. Her shoulders sank; she felt small. *It's the war*, she told herself. *I'm bound to feel down from time to time. I should count my—*

'What's that face for?' he interrupted her thoughts, pulling out a chair and perching beside her. 'Just some old chat with the boys. Looks like you need a little trip. How about in the spring, Rosebud, I take you up to town? The raids on London have stopped now. We could do with getting away from this Luftwaffe dumping ground. How does tea at the Ritz take you? The building's steel-framed, you know. Safe from bombs. We could stay the night. Live it up a little.'

'Will! What are you suggesting?' She was indignant and blushed furiously. 'What would my parents say?' The thought of spending the night with him was bizarre. She could barely envisage it, let alone look forward to it.

He supped his beer, leaving froth around his mouth. 'Sylvia and George like me.' His confidence at using her parents' first names irritated her.

'Have you forgotten?' She mustered a good-natured smile. 'I start my training next week and my duties at Pengared Farm in March. There's no time for a trip to London, Will, however much my parents like you.'

He put his large hand flat on the table and gave her an unnerving stare. She undid her coat and slipped it off her shoulders. Cold sweat clung to her back like an uncomfortable cloak.

'You're not still serious about this Land Army lark, are you?' He was incredulous. 'I can't quite see it, if you ask me. All that muck and manure. Far too much like hard work for a nice girl like you.'

'I'm used to early mornings at the shop,' she said, hating the defensive note in her voice. 'I lift sacks of flour, tins of stuff.'

'What, with old Mrs Brown and her black-market butter under the counter and her firm hand on the ration books? You don't know you're born, Rosebud. You wait until you're up to your neck in muck, breaking your back. It's not all chirping birds and haystacks, you know.'

'I want to do my duty.'

'Ah, now, Rosebud.' His fingers grabbed hers and he pulled both her hands towards him. He began to play with her engagement ring, allowing the chip of diamond to flash weakly in the dim light. 'I'd say it was your duty to marry me.'

A year ago, she would have giggled. Handsome Will Bowman – the senior clerk at the Western bank, with his bachelor maisonette and sleek Ford car – was going to marry her. Now, in the Anchor pub down by the docks, feeling tired, hot and wretched, and longing to be home chatting to her mother, she extracted her fingers from his.

'We've talked about this, Will,' she said patiently. 'We must wait for the war to be over. And then of course, you know . . .' She paused, lowering her eyes. 'When it's all over, I want to go to college. I want to be a journalist.'

'You mean learn typing and shorthand? I'll say it again, my Rosebud. If we are to be married, won't all of that rather get in the way?'

She felt his finger press under her chin and he made her look at him. He dipped his head and gazed at her from under long lashes; his blue eyes melting momentarily.

'I remember when I first saw you, Rosebud,' he said, holding her hand, 'when I gave your dad a lift back from the bowling club. In your school uniform, you were, doing your homework.' His fingers tightened. 'And then your mother invited me in for tea on a run of Sundays. She knew what was going on, did Sylvia. She's not blind. She saw the looks you gave me. The looks I gave you.'

Yes, Rose remembered the pulse of pleasure at the attention from this man of twenty-eight, when she was a mere girl of sixteen. She remembered the lightening of her step as his Ford pulled up outside and the flutter of butterflies when he asked her father's permission to take her to the picture house.

23

She squinted now through a curl of cigarette smoke blown their way from the next table. A trickle of worry made her mouth twitch.

'What's that look for, Rosebud?' Will's face hardened again and he shrugged, turning away from her to survey the room again. 'Something tells me you'll always be a shop girl. What's the use of college? A land-girl first for a month or two, until Churchill and his cronies get their act together. And then of course, Mrs Bowman. So, what's the use of it all, when there'll be babies to look after?'

Her mouth gaped and her face stiffened in shock but Will did not notice. She watched as his eyes explored once more, resting on the slim back of a Wren near the bar. Something sank into her, then, a strange understanding. Was it the way his eyes darkened, became more shielded? Was it the way the Wren turned her head, her red-lipped smile making it all the way round to him?

'Is that her?' hissed Rose, leaning over the table. 'Is that her?'

Her hands clenched into fists. She wanted to throw her drink over him.

'What are you talking about?' He turned reluctantly towards her. His face closed down, his eyes searching for a way out. He was caught. His tongue licked his top lip where beads of sweat were brightening.

'Will. Answer me.'

'Let's not do this here, old girl. Not in front of this ship-load.'

'Mrs Brown was right,' she whispered, her voice thick with anger. 'She *does* look good in her uniform. All smart and tucked tightly in. Mrs Brown saw you. Kissing that *girl.*' She took a sip of her port and lemon to counter the dry wooliness inside her mouth. The drink felt like hot bile in her gullet.

Will pushed his face close to hers. 'If you must press me, then all I can say is, there's a war on. Things like that happen all the time. And Mrs B is a nosy old cow.'

'Two minutes ago, you wanted me to be your wife.'

'Look, poppet, you're jealous. A smart uniform, proper war work. Dangerous times. She was probably drunk. I know I was. I took her for a walk over the Hoe. Probably missing her fiancé or something. I was probably missing you. You're not too free with your kisses these days. To be honest, I can't remember the last time we got friendly. It doesn't really matter, does it, Rosebud?' He took up her hand again and pressed it to his lips.

She knew that he was right: it didn't really matter. The war changed everyone. You hardened to it. Took it on the chin.

'I give them no encouragement, you know. Now look at me. A lot of the girls, they get sexy, missing their men. Terror does it to some people. They meet a nice fellow like me and with the blackout down, and everything, they get fruity. You can't blame them, Rosebud.'

Them? He said *them*.

'So, how many *have* there been?' she snapped, snatching her hand away. She began to twist at her finger, digging her nails under the gold band. Her teeth were bared in anger as she pulled off the ring.

'Don't you dare.' Will's breath was sharp, his wheezing rattled. He grabbed for her hand.

'Why don't you give this to her over there? I certainly don't want it,' she cried.

'Don't do this to me. Forget all this rubbish. It means nothing. You and I are going to be together. You know it.'

'I know nothing of the sort, not now.'

Will drew his shoulders back. Even sitting down, his body was like a wall to her. 'Your parents won't hear of it.'

'Leave them out of it. How dare you!' She held the ring out to him; her fingers trembled. 'This has just confirmed everything. I had my doubts and now I know. So thank you, Wren,' she gestured out to the crowded pub. 'Thank you, countless girls from all over Plymouth. I don't love you, Will. So take your ring back, please. It's over.'

Will glared at her, and she felt the full force of his anger as he took the ring, brandishing it back at her. His face drained, his lips curling over his breath.

'It's not true. You do love me. Silly little girl. Grow up, will you? So I kissed a couple of girls. One or two little indiscretions and now this. You need to pull your socks up and remember how lucky you are. After all, who is going to love you . . .'

His words failed, drowned by the sudden haunting wail of the air-raid siren. The whole pub reacted as one, tipping back chairs and jostling for the door. Rose stood up and was instantly carried along in a wave of shoulders and elbows. Will disappeared in the crush. All around her voices shouted in agitation or were timorous with quiet fear. 'God, I can't bear that sound!' 'Someone put a sock in it!' They all knew the drill. The navy lads would run to their stations, back to the docks in perverse eagerness to be part of it. Air-raid wardens would clap on their tin hats; firemen would stand by their pumps, eyes raking the sky; policemen would blow their whistles, ineffective in the melee. The rest of them, if they had any sense, would head for shelter.

Rose was on the pavement, the ominous drone of the siren filling her with utter dread. The blackout in the streets by the harbour was intense. There were no friendly lights, just white search arcs needling the sky over Plymouth. In the intermittent light she could make out the dark bulk of the surrounding hills, the quiet, cowering suburbs. She crunched up her shoulders as the crowd dispersed into the darkness, not knowing which way to go. Footsteps retreated down the cobbles. A weird calm settled in the air. The sky was empty – and silent.

Will's hand closed around the top of her arm, tight like a tourniquet. She jumped. 'Come with me, Rosebud,' she heard his voice in the dark. 'Let's get to the shelter before the fireworks begin.'

'Leave me alone.' She tried to shake herself free. 'I'm going home.'

'Don't be ridiculous.'

An ARP warden strode round the corner, eyes stern under his black hat, a torch sharp in their faces. 'Oi, you two fools,' he bellowed, 'get in the bloody shelter. Jerry won't wait for you to stop your canoodling, you know.'

'Don't worry, mate,' Will's voice was suddenly light and friendly. 'It's Bowman, St Budeaux division. Just sorting this out.'

'Ah yes, Bowman. Shelter's down Tobacco Street. That way. Get there quick, I would. We're in for a bloody night of it.' The warden hurried on.

Rose twisted her arm. He held her fast.

'Now listen to me.' He shook her. She smelt his beer and his hair cream; sensed his familiar, menacing face close to hers.

'I will not. I'm going home.'

'You stupid girl. Listen to me!'

Rose shuddered. Faint at first, and then expanding by the second, came the awful rumbling of the bombers. A heavy, broken throb curved over the sky and put a hard lid on it, trapping her down there on the dark pavement. Anti-aircraft guns on the hills overlooking the Sound began their retort, aiming into the night, thumping into her spine. Ack-ack. Ack-ack.

'What use are they!' she screamed, sickened by the noise. 'What bloody use are they?'

And then, the inevitable. The invisible bank of planes let loose their bombs and they began to stream down, whistling like black, deadly rain.

She felt the first crump deep inside her body as the dockyard exploded and the hard cracking noise split her ears. Another cluster of mines, then another: so precise, so steady. The noise and the violence were all she knew: above her head and in the earth beneath her feet. She collapsed against the pile of sandbags by the pub wall. The smell of burning reached her instantly. Three years into the war and she never got used to the terror. She knew it could be any street, any building, any one.

A voice yelled down the street, 'God help us! The docks are under fire. Not again, God, not again!'

Someone replied, 'Bastard Jerry's getting good at this. Knows the bloody way by now.'

Will leant over Rose, making her stand up. Her legs would not straighten. Her knees were water. He pushed her against the sandbags. Her heart rapped in her throat.

'This isn't over between us,' he hissed into her ear. 'Raid or no raid, this isn't over.'

'I'm not scared of you, Will.' But as she looked into his eyes with the air on fire behind him, fear instantaneously dried out her mouth.

Another stick of bombs fell, this time right at the end of the street. She crumpled again into shock, stuffing her fingers in her mouth as shrapnel fell in a shower, sparking off the road. A belch of pressure pressed down on her head as the houses on the corner blew out their guts, dust and smoke billowing. Flames poured like water over windowsills and doorsteps. Her hearing was blasted away.

'Get away from me, get away!' she screamed into his face as

noxious fumes grazed her throat, making her gag. He grasped her arms and hauled her upright.

'Take the ring back,' he yelled, gripping it in his fist. 'Take it back, and tell me you love me!'

He hit her in the face. She screamed and cowered, retching up sticky port and lemon through her dry, twisted throat, her hand over her cheek where the ring had cut her. Her body folded in half. Her knees hit the pavement hard.

Half inside her body, half outside her body, Rose was alternately carried and then marched down steep steps into the confines of a tunnel. Down, deeper down she went, propelled by the strong arms that trapped her, held her up. Her ankles twisted painfully, her grazed knees buckling, stockings torn to shreds. Her shoes scuffed without mercy on the floor.

She leant against a crude brick wall under a low ceiling. On reflex, she dipped her head to sit on a slatted bench, shuffling along to make room for others. Slowly, with every breath of smoky, stale air, her senses returned to her. Dark figures loomed in the shelter; some leant forwards, blocking their ears, others held children, constantly soothing. The sound was muffled, as if under water. Somewhere, down there in the gloom, the blonde Wren might also be sheltering. At the other end of the tunnel they were singing 'Run Rabbit Run'.

Rose squinted at the glow of a lantern at the edge of the darkness. There was the hiss of a Primus stove. Someone was making a cup of tea.

The seat beneath her shifted and thumped; the earth was flinching from the crump, crump of the bombs. Someone yelped in shock. Then someone else laughed. 'Bad shot, Jerry!' Her nausea returned as she was suddenly aware of Will jammed up against her, his heavy arm around her shoulder.

A woman sitting opposite her in a knitted wool hat leant forward and said, 'You hit your face, darling? Shall I take a look? Blessed blackout. Or was it shrapnel? Bit of a war wound, I'm afraid. Damn those Nazi bleeders. Here, have a cup of tea.'

Rose held out her shaking hands for the steaming cup. Her arms ached, her head felt as if it had been cracked wide open. Tears fell as she tried to place her quivering lips against the rim.

Will's bulky body both shielded and trapped her. Along the tunnel someone was praying. A clear, firm voice rang out, 'Under the shadow of thy protecting love, O God our Father, we compose ourselves for sleep. Above and around us are dangers, but thou art nearer than all the dangers. And we are not afraid.'

We are not afraid. Rose sat up. 'My parents!'

Will's arm tightened. 'They have their Anderson,' he said into her hair.

'But they don't know where I am.'

'They know you're with me. They know you're safe with me.'

She collapsed slowly back against his side. She was exhausted, sullied. She wanted to take off all her clothes and throw them away for they were dirty and encrusted with fear. But then, squander bug, she chastised herself. That would be wasteful.

Will's fingers tipped her chin up to face him. He avoided her eyes and looked, instead, at the cut on her cheek.

'Just a scratch,' he told the woman opposite, speaking over the top of Rose's head. 'She'll be all right in a day or two.'

'Might leave a scar though,' replied the woman. 'And such lovely skin she has. Never mind, lovey, something to remember this night by. And what a bloody night it is too. We're the lucky ones down here. Can't imagine what it's like for any poor bastards left up there. Count your blessings is what I say.'

Will laughed briefly with the woman and Rose felt herself drift away. After an age, there was a merciful, unbelievable silence from the streets above and then the all-clear rang out. The singing changed to 'White Cliffs of Dover'. Voices began to chatter, rising in hope and perseverance.

Will whispered in her ear. 'Here, Rosebud, we mustn't lose this again.'

She opened her eyes, shook herself awake and looked up at him. His face softened into a smile. He slipped the ring back on her finger.

Two

A CORNISH MORNING IN SPRING: A SUN-BRIGHT WATERY SKY WITH the breath of sea on the breeze. Rose stood at the side of the lane, her shadow long and her suitcase set down next to her regulation Land Army shoes. Hawthorn hedges rambled vertically, worried by a chilly breeze; two or three slate roofs peeked out above. Behind them was the square granite church tower; between them a blue slice of the sea. She wriggled her toes, relishing the ability to stretch her legs and breathe fresh air after her two-hour bumpy ride on the bus from Plymouth. The driver was revving the engine, ready for the off. She called to the conductor, who was leaning against the side of the bus, stoking his pipe, 'Is this Pengared? You said "Pengared next stop". Which way's the farm?'

The man clamped his pipe in his teeth, glowering at her. 'This is Trelewin, miss. We don't go any further than this. Pengared's over that way, two miles across the headland, is all. There's no lane to it that'll take a vehicle like this. No hardship for folks around here to walk it, but looking at your face, seems a bit of a hike, doesn't it? I suppose you hoity-toity Devon town girls aren't used to a bit of walking. You're in the real country now. You're not at some college, learning how to milk off a pretend cow with a bag for udders.' He bared his teeth, sucking his pipe. 'I've seen it in the *Daily Record*. Bloody ridiculous. How are you going to cope up at the farm?'

Rose opened her mouth to answer him, to remind him about what she and the rest of Plymouth had had to cope with: air raids and burnt-out lives. But her voice was drowned out by the bus driver's insistent revving. The conductor hopped back on and, belching fumes, the bus negotiated a three-point turn on the triangle of tarmac in the centre of the hamlet. Off it roared, with a sarcastic wave of the conductor's pipe, and she was left to the silence of Trelewin.

She pulled out her letter from Mrs Pike, district commissioner, South Cornwall Land Army Division.

Your employers, Mr and Mrs Edward Cumberpatch, expect you to arrive on 15th March 1943, at 09.00 hours sharp. I suggest you take the earliest possible bus from Devonport and disembark at Trelewin. To reach Pengared Farm, you must take the footpath by the Old Vicarage, past the church. Follow the path for a mile.

Mrs Pike was right about many things, Rose thought, *but she was wrong about the mile if the conductor was to have his way.* She crossed the tarmac and found the footpath beside an old empty house. Huge blank windows veiled by ivy were like mournful staring eyes; the chimney stacks a little wonky. Altogether it looked a rather sorry sight.

Brushing along the path through nettles and brambles, Rose was grateful for her thick Land Army socks and breeches. Birds in the trees were chattering, building their nests and winding down their early chorus. The graveyard between the old house and the church was quiet and sleeping, peaceful in the new spring sunshine. She spotted a tin letter box on a post, with rusted lettering on its side, *Pengared Farm*, and felt her first duty was to check for Mr and Mrs Cumberpatch's post. The box was empty. Snapping the little door shut, she felt the eyes of the old house on her back. Hurrying along, she was soon over the stile, away from Trelewin, climbing higher and higher across the open headland.

Her case grew heavier and her shoes began to pinch even though Mrs Pike had assured them all that they'd soon wear in. She stopped to rest, undoing the buttons of her greatcoat to feel the breeze on her neck. Her shirt and tie made her feel proud and professional. On her head was clamped the cowboy-style hat. *Don't forget the hat, girls. Rather snazzy, isn't it? It's very becoming and shows you mean business.*

Halfway up the bright and breezy headland, the footpath split and Rose paused again to take in the view. Behind her she caught a glimpse of the roof of the old deserted vicarage and Trelewin church above the treetops, and in front of her, bursting at her with its fresh, salty breath, was the great expanse of sea. A path disappeared into ferny undergrowth down to the sand and grey wire of Trelewin cove. *We'll fight them on the beaches,* Mr Churchill had boomed. Rose shivered. The water looked so peaceful and innocent, but she knew full well that under the waves out at sea U-boats cruised in stealth and silence. Sitting at a hurried breakfast with her parents that morning, she'd heard the BBC man on the wireless say that since the beginning of the year, twenty-seven merchant vessels packed with food and munitions had been torpedoed into the icy Atlantic.

Her mother had switched off the radio, not wishing to hear bad news, and Rose had wondered if she'd ever seen her mother sit through a bulletin. Thank God none of them knew of anyone at sea, or in North Africa or Singapore. Her father was too old, and had already done his bit in what he called 'the last lot'. She had no brothers. And Will, of course, was exempt. Rose picked up her suitcase. She didn't want to think about Will.

'Don't worry about us, Rosie,' said her father as she boarded the bus at Devonport earlier. 'Your mother and I will be fine. We have Will to look after us. He'll keep popping in on his rounds to keep us in the know.'

She had felt a tingling in her nose: suppressed tears. 'But the raids, Dad,' she'd said. 'I'll be so worried.'

'The skies have been quiet since January, since the raid on the docks.' Her father hoisted her suitcase after her. 'I think Hitler's got another agenda. He's had bad news from Stalingrad, and Egypt and the desert are keeping his hands full. He's not going to care about little old Plymouth, now, is he? Will will keep us safe. And we have our Anderson.' His tall frame stooped slightly to peck her forehead.

Her mother, nervous and frail through lack of sleep, stood on tiptoe to kiss her cheek. 'Take care, Rosie,' she said.

Rose had watched her mother press her rouged lips together. She never went anywhere without her lipstick. She said it was her armour.

Standing on that bright clifftop above the sea, Rose was seized by a new thought. It was spring, a new year: surely the war couldn't go on for much longer. Here, at Pengared Farm, among strangers, making new friends, working in the fields that rolled to the sea, she was suddenly free of that grinding fear that had enveloped her for years. She could escape the war. She could escape Will. She was doing her bit for the country and was free at last of all the things that choked her.

And her parents had their Anderson.

She checked her watch, grasped her suitcase handle and headed for Pengared.

Nestled there in the valley was a little group of buildings: cowshed, stable and barn with its great door propped open. Hens strutted in the yard. Across the way was the old rambling farm-house. Yellow clouds of lichen bloomed over the ancient slate roof; tiny casements were tucked under the eaves. Rose breathed in the scent of hay, the green whiff of cows as she unlatched the five-bar gate and entered the yard. In a flash she was surrounded by a terrific commotion as two sheepdogs bounded from nowhere and streaked past her legs with a slashing of tails and tap of doggy claws on the cobbles.

And then, too late, she noticed the sign on the gate: *Do not open. Please climb over.* She called, 'Here boy, here boy,' but was ignored as the dogs ran this way and that out in the rutted track. They snuffled, tongues flicking from the sides of their mouths in an ecstasy of freedom. 'Oh, go your own way, then,' she muttered, but looked round in embarrassment to see a young woman with curlers in and a topknot scarf rushing towards her from the house.

'You let them out. You let them out. Oh, now what? They never come to me. They never do what I say. Mutt! Jeff! Heel! You see, it's no use. They don't listen to me.'

'I'm so sorry. I didn't see the sign. I'm Rose Pepper, from the Land Army. Not a good start, is it? I'm afraid I'm no good with dogs either.'

The woman barely looked at Rose. 'Not a good start, no. He's been waiting four weeks for the likes of you. That Pike woman promised us months ago. He's been ticking the days off on the calendar. Wants to put in a complaint. He's not pleased on the Land Army and he's not going to be pleased on this either. Mutt! Jeff! Whoever you are! Blast you, wretched dog!'

Rose set her suitcase down and quickly undid the latches.

'Don't unpack here. They'll savage it!'

'Biscuits. Mother packed me biscuits.' She rummaged under her clothes. 'Saved her coupons for me. This might just do it.'

Rose opened the tin and in a flash, two wet noses prodded at her fingers, snapping up the biscuits.

'Oh, you wasted good biscuits. Now these dogs are spoiled as well as stupid.' The woman latched the gate behind them, aiming a kick at the one leaping up, resting his muddy paws on Rose's arm.

'Perhaps the sign should say, *Don't let the dogs out whatever you do,*' Rose said, shaking either Mutt or Jeff off. 'I'm awfully sorry. Is Mr Cumberpatch or his wife at home?'

'I'm Mrs Cumberpatch.'

Rose looked at the woman full in the face for the first time and extended her hand. Instantly, the woman's eyes flicked to her cheek. 'That looks nasty. How did you get that then?'

Rose touched the scar on her face with a nervous finger. 'During the blackout. Walked into a door. So clumsy.'

'Have you tried lanolin to fade it? Sheep's fat, you know. Old wives' remedy. Folks round here swear by it. I've got a jar in the cupboard.'

Mrs Cumberpatch was certainly *not* an old wife. She was a stick-thin girl, a shade older than Rose, with bony wrists, huge blue eyes and a smooth open face like Olivia de Havilland on the cover of the *Radio Times*. Even in her apron, curlers and headscarf she had a pure, still beauty.

'Come on.' She picked up Rose's suitcase and marched off across the yard with the two dogs snuffling after her. 'I'll show you in. Meg the other one is with him out on the top field. Sowing barley. It's going to be a long day. By, he did need you a month ago. Ah, here's Mo.'

Mrs Cumberpatch dropped the case on the step and bent to pick up a grubby toddler who was making his escape from the kitchen. His chubby arms and legs looked like soft uncooked pastry, scuffed with dirt. His cheeks were brick red and his eyes a cloudy blue. A toothless smile nearly split his face in two.

'What a beautiful babe.'

'He's our Mo. Maurice really, but we call him Mo. You need to be back in your playpen, don't you, boy? Pity he looks like a caged animal in it. Say hello to . . . em . . .'

'Rose. Rose Pepper.'

She followed her employer into the kitchen, where the smell of fresh baking bread made her sigh.

Mrs Cumberpatch jiggled the baby up and down on her hip. 'I see you're missing your home-baked bread. I expect the stuff you buy in Plymouth isn't up to much.'

'We haven't had a good loaf in months.' Her mouth ached for it.

'I bake every other day. We had a store of wheat left over from last year. Home Office don't know about it, mind. This year he's doing only barley. Orders from on high. They want us to break up the meadow next year for sugar beet. First time in four hundred years, he reckons, it would have been ploughed. That's the war for you. I was conceived in that meadow. That's why my mother called me Betony. After the meadow flower. Have you got your ration book?'

Rose handed it over and Mrs Cumberpatch put it in the dresser drawer. 'We have our own butter. And eggs. I expect you're used to just one egg a week on the ration. Not healthy, I say.'

'My parents keep chickens, so we do all right.'

Rose thought of her father and the pleasure in his eyes as he tapped the top off a rare boiled egg on a Sunday morning.

'I sell them down the village through Jack Thimble. Black market and all that but who's going to say anything? They all want their fresh eggs.'

'Jack who?'

'You know, Jack Thimble. The grumpy bus conductor.'

'Oh, yes, I know Jack Thimble.'

'He's only cross because the Yanks commandeered his new bus. He was hopping mad. Hasn't cracked a smile since. Come upstairs. You'll share with Meg. Hope you don't mind, but I can't help you if you do.'

Betony Cumberpatch hooked Mo onto her hip and clomped up the dark stairway at the far end of the kitchen. Rose followed her along a dim landing with walls the colour of mustard and a strip of worn carpet on the boards. 'Bathroom's in there. One bath a week, of course. And the lavvy's outside. Ah, I see from the look on your face, you're not used to that sort of thing, are you? You're an indoor-toilet type of girl, I can tell.'

They went up another narrow stairway into a stuffy bedroom under the eaves. One of the twin beds was made up with a neat counterpane and a patchwork quilt; the other was unmade, strewn with socks and a pair of knickers. On the headboard were pasted pictures cut from periodicals: Clark Gable, Frank Sinatra and Fred Astaire.

'We need you girls,' said Betony. 'His brother's in Malta, far as any of us know. He's sore about it. Worried sick, if you ask me. The sky caved in when Hugh said he'd enlisted. I say it was either that or wait for the call-up. But then it touches everyone, doesn't it? He's been in a permanent bad mood since. You'll get used to him.'

'You mean Mr Cumberpatch.'

'Yes, my Ted. Call him Ted. He doesn't like high-talking Mr this and that. And you must call me Betony. Like I said, my mother fell for me in Pengared meadow. Funny how I ended up marrying a Cumberpatch and came to live here. But then you should see Ted. Anyone would want to marry him.'

Betony bumped Mo onto the floor and he instantly set off, shuffling on his fat nappy. 'Meg works like a carthorse,' she said. 'Can't fault her. You . . . you look a bit thin. Although you are tall. How strong are you?'

'I have my paperwork here.' Rose pulled out her official form signed by Mrs Pike. 'It tells you everything you need to know about my capabilities. Everything I've been trained in: ploughing, milking, hen work, pig farming . . .'

Betony wrinkled her nose: 'I don't . . . I can't. Show it to him if you like, but he'll not be interested. He'll want to *see* what you can do. Bits of paper drive him crazy. All that red tape and Home Office claptrap. I'll make a cup of tea, and you can have some soup and bread. And then you have to get started. You best hurry. They're expecting you – oh! Look at that sparkler. What's his name?'

Betony held the tips of Rose's fingers, admiring her engagement ring.

'Will. Will Bowman. He's back in Plymouth.'

'Navy?'

'Not in the forces, he's . . .'

'Reserve occupation?'

'No, he's in the bank.'

'Can't do without him, can they? Must be very important.'

'He's exempt. He has a chest condition. But he does do his bit, he's a . . .'

'Ah.' Betony's face fell blank. She plucked Mo from the floor and left the room.

Rose turned to her suitcase and began to unpack, hanging her dress in the wardrobe by Meg's clothes and folding her aertex shirts in the spare drawers. She took off her engagement ring and hid it in the pocket of her dressing gown.

She pulled her overalls over her breeches and jumper.

'If you're going to be a land-girl, Rose Pepper,' she said to the wall, 'you'd best get started.'

In the kitchen, she hurried her soup and sank her teeth into the delicious bread, while Mo, on the loose again, crawled around her legs and bumped his head on the chair. Betony stood next to her on the threshold of the kitchen door, pointing the way.

'Go across the yard. Over that gate. Follow the path by the meadow, my meadow. Keep going. See that line of trees; that's the path that leads to the top field. You can't miss them. They'll be waiting, so hurry.'

Rose appraised the farm buildings as she scurried across the yard. They were patched and re-patched, tired and worn but clean and cared for. Mutt and Jeff bounded after her, sniffing her heels, while the long face of a chestnut mare watched her from a half-open stable door. The horse's eye was rolling and white; yellow teeth gurned at her. She heard Betony call after her, 'That's Blossom. Ted's mare. You'll get used to her.'

'I don't want to try,' Rose muttered to herself, remembering the donkey that had kicked her in the stomach on Par Sands when she was eight.

Her stride had purpose but her ears rang with nerves. Her stomach was plummeting down to her new boots. Here she was in her overalls, a newly trained land-girl with Mrs Pike's paperwork to prove it and yet she felt like an impostor, a hoity-toity Devon town girl, as she skirted Betony's meadow on her way to her first job-of-work.

The air around her was full of the fresh breeze from the sea. Bare hawthorns rattled, their little buds in waiting. Catkins shivered and blackbirds hopped in the dirt. She spied dunnocks springing from their hideaways at the tread of her boots and skimming away across the brown, sleeping meadow. Young wild daffs opened their yellow faces in the hollows of tree roots. Her ears pricked to the rumble of an engine and in automatic fear she tilted her head to the sky, wondering if she'd see a lone Messerschmidt. But then, she saw the green army truck with a rounded bonnet and a yellow star on the door trundling along the top road.

'The Americans!' she cried in relief, her strides growing longer, not knowing how to shake off the pleasure of seeing the truck. They were their saviours, here to help. Rose felt them very welcome.

'Hey, Ginge!' came a woman's cry over the hedge. 'Stop gawping at the Yanks and get a move on! We're waiting. Oi, over here!'

There, beyond the gate of a freshly turned field, was a girl in overalls with her hand cupping her mouth, shouting, 'Oi!' With her was a man in a trilby and a youth lounging against the trailer.

'Yes, Ginge, I mean you!' The girl, mouth bright with lipstick, was puffing on a cigarette, her eyes like little blackcurrants snapping up and down as she examined Rose's frame. Her dark curls were encased in a topknot scarf, while Rose's hair was being whipped by the wind, puffing up all round her face. In her haste to leave the farmhouse and not keep them waiting, she'd forgotten her scarf.

'Hello, I'm Rose Pepper,' she piped up and, not daring to undo the gate, began to climb over.

'Well, put up the flag, I'll tell Winston,' said the girl in a rolling St Ives accent. 'She's arrived.'

The man stepped forward. 'Now, Meg, there's me being rude and you being rude, and only one of those things I allow, so simmer down, girl.' He looked at Rose. 'Good afternoon Landgirl Pepper. Ted Cumberpatch.' He held out his thick-palmed hand. 'This here's Meg, you might have guessed, and Joel here helps out.'

The lad, head down and hands in pockets, scuffed the turned sod with his boots.

'His mother is desperate to keep him out of it,' Ted said to Rose, 'so we work him hard, say we need him more than we do. But of course, when it comes down to it, when he's old enough, in the end, he'll have to go.'

The boy straightened his shoulders, and turned his head away.

'Anyway, Ginge,' announced Ted, 'we needed you a month ago.'

'So everyone keeps saying. But as I explained to Mrs Cumberpatch, I couldn't have been here any sooner, really I couldn't I've only just finished training. I have all the paper-work . . .'

Ted smirked, dismissing the very idea with a wave of his hand.

She continued, earnest, 'Well, I'm here now, and eager to get on with the job.'

Meg gave her a slow handclap.

'Show some manners, Meg,' grumbled Ted. 'And you, come here.'

Rose obeyed, stepping forward and watching nonplussed as Ted unknotted the scarf from around his neck.

'Here, lovely, use this on that wild-fire hair of yours. It's already driving me mad.'

Flushing, she took the scarf, still warm, shook it out and turned her back on three pairs of staring eyes to encase her hair. Immediately more disposed, she felt confident and fit for work.

'Thank you,' she beamed, ignoring Meg's sardonic smirk.

She put Ted at anywhere between thirty and fifty. Lines ran deeply from his nose to the corner of his mouth and over his forehead, carving up his weathered, handsome face. His shock of russet hair was clamped tight by his trilby that had seen better days and his body was sheer weight of muscle, with solid legs planted in the soil. She wondered if he was not too blustery for the fragile Betony, but had no doubt where little Mo got his looks from.

'Right, as you know, Ginge, we're here to sow barley. And now we have our full complement,' he nodded at her, 'we can begin.

Here, Joel, you get the shovel. You, Meg, start filling this sack. I'll get Ginge started.'

Rose followed the others and grabbed a stomach-shaped canvas sack. Joel climbed up into the back of the trailer, stood on the huge pile of silvery seed and began to shovel it into the sack that Meg, cigarette in the corner of her mouth, held wide open for him.

'Well, well, Meg,' said Ted, scratching his chin to hide a smile. 'I was wondering if we'd got the timing right.'

Joel sniggered, losing his concentration, missing Meg's sack with his shovel-load.

Meg's face was a picture, her dark eyes flicking sideways to Rose. 'Yes, Ted. What is it they say?' Her sack was full and she moved away, stamping her cigarette butt into the soil with her heel. 'What *is* that old country lore you keep spouting? Something about when it's a good time to sow barley?'

'Yes, Meg, what *is* it?'

'I know,' she crowed, impatiently. 'You can't sow barley until the soil is warm to your bare backside.'

Joel blurted a laugh, his eyes smarting, his neck red beneath his collar.

Ted said, 'Now Meg, I'm glad it was you who said that, and not me.' He turned on Rose. 'Well, Ginge, I know it's your first day and all, but we need to test it for sure. How about it?'

Rose looked from Meg's sharp, mocking eyes to Ted's crinkled half-serious face to the boy covering his mouth with a grubby hand. Her voice was strangled with indignation as she said, 'I am quite sure that is not the official method of assessing when the soil is ready for barley. Not in the way we were taught at Plymouth anyway. What would Mrs Pike say, I wonder.' She paused, took a deep breath and caught Ted's eye. She began to laugh, getting the joke. 'All right, Ted. I'll do it,' she said. 'But only if you show me first.'

Rose trudged up the vast top field with the heavy sack of barley seed across her shoulder, and then she trudged back down again. With every third step she dug her hand into the bag, pulled out a dusty handful and broadcasted it with a wide swing of her arm.

'Sweep it. Sweep it. Keep the rhythm!' Ted yelled at her. 'Keep to your furrow. Keep going, Ginge. And remember where you've already been, for Gawd's sake.'

Her arm was screaming, the muscles burning, but when she tried to swap arms she could not get the action right. She was breathless, the seed dust was getting into her lungs and her boots were caked with heavy Cornish soil. She stopped for a moment watching Joel and Ted proceed across their section, the sun slanting behind them. They looked like soldiers advancing into battle, regimented and determined, just like the ones in the jerky reels she'd seen of the Great War. Just after the whistle blew.

She wiped at her eye.

'Too much for you, Ginge?' Meg called out.

'Got something in my eye,' she shouted back. 'Just taking a breather.'

'Well, don't spend too long on it. We've got barley to sow.'

'I think I've kept up quite well.'

'Not really,' bellowed Meg. 'The rest of this bit's yours!'

Rose stared, dismayed at the area she still had to cover.

'Well, onward and upward,' she muttered, her heart not in it. How could she do this, day in day out? She was utterly beaten. Her back was throbbing and stiffening up by the minute. Her arm felt numb and useless as if it no longer belonged to her. How could she have imagined she could ever be a land-girl? Will was right.

'Ugh!' she breathed. 'Damn him!'

'What was that?' Meg called.

'Just wondering if there was a chance of a hot bath tonight.'

'Not on your life. Saturday is bath night. There won't be any hot water. And remember, Ginge, whenever there is, I go in first.'

'How did I guess?'

Meg stopped and looked across at her. 'Hey, do you like the way this field has been turned?'

'It seems fine to me . . .' Rose wondered what she was getting at.

'I did it. All by myself. Finest, straightest furrows Ted's ever seen. Can you plough? Oh, no, don't tell me, you have the paperwork to prove it.'

'I like to plough. I can drive an Allis.'

'Whoopie. I used Blossom to harrow and roll it. Hitched her up like in the old days. Saved on petrol. Bloody glorious it was.'

'Is she easy to handle?'

'Absolute nightmare!' Meg laughed. 'Oh, I see that's not good news for you, Ginge. Maybe you should ask Ted to keep you away from the horse, if you're that scared.'

'I'll do whatever is required. I'll do my bit.'

'Yes, yes . . .' Meg waved her away.

Rose returned to the trailer for more seed, her eyes streaming from the cold wind on the exposed hillside. Her nose was red and her lip wobbling. Ted met her there.

'Right, Ginge, that's enough. I think you're through. First day is always the worst, and I don't want to kill you straight away. You're no good to me dead. Finish now. Go back to the house. Bet will have some tea on.' He peered at her. 'Well done, Ginge.'

'Thank you, Ted.' She bit her lip, determined not to cry. She mustered her strength. 'Ted, can I ask you something? Can I ask you not to call me Ginge?'

'Sorry, my lovely. But it's up here now,' he tapped the side of his head. 'Don't worry, you'll get used to it. Like you'll get used to all of us.'

The cool spring day drifted into a cold spring evening. The lamp was lit in the kitchen and Mo was tucked safely in his cot upstairs. Betony dished out mutton stew and potatoes at the table by the warmth of the black lead range. Rose was ravenous, made delirious by the smell of it. She fell on her plate.

'Hold on, greedy,' hissed Meg at her side, giving her a sharp dig with her elbow. She nodded towards Ted and Betony who were saying grace, eyes closed, mouthing a prayer.

'You'll learn, Ginge,' said Ted when they had finished, filling his tankard with a froth of bottled ale. 'Every evening we say a prayer for our Hugh. Last we heard he was in Malta. We all say something private.'

'Who will you pray for?' asked Betony, as she tucked into her meal.

Rose straightened her shoulders. 'No one in the forces, I'm afraid – as you know . . .'

Meg turned on her: 'Oh, don't be *afraid*. There's no need to

42

be *afraid*. You should be grateful you have no one out there. I wish that was me.'

'Her fiancé is in the bank, in Plymouth,' said Betony. 'Sorry, Ginge, I can't remember his name.'

Meg piled in. 'Is it war work? Is he a top dog? Can't do without him, can they?'

Weakened by Meg's energy, Rose said, 'He has an important job in the bank, yes. But he is also exempt on medical grounds. He has asthma.'

Meg tutted and put her angry face close to Rose's.

'Asthma? *Asthma?* My little brother Bertie lied about his age. Joined up at the start. Went over with the BEF. Got a bullet through his back in the fiasco that was Dunkirk. Didn't kill him, though. He drowned in two inches of sea water. His mates tried to help him, but it was chaos. Bleeding chaos.' Meg was screwing her napkin up in her fists.

'I'm sorry,' said Rose.

'No, you're not, you're relieved. Your fiancé is safe. My Bertie is under the mud in some French field. Will they bring him back when all this is over? Who knows? Who cares? I know Whitehall doesn't.'

'Hush, Meg,' Betony whispered, glancing at Ted's stricken face.

Meg sank back in her chair. 'Sorry, Ted, I do go on.'

Ted looked up, beaming a false smile along the table. 'Hugh writes when he can. That lad is certainly seeing the world. He's going to have a hell of a suntan when he gets home. Can't believe it really, what ordinary lads like him get to do. The places they see. He's seen our Mo just once in all his life. But he'll come home.'

Betony rested her hand on her husband's arm. 'That's more like it.'

Rose felt uncomfortable witnessing the mutual compassion in their eyes.

She piped up, 'My fiancé, Will, is an air-raid patrol warden.' But no one seemed to notice.

Aware of Meg prickling at her elbow, she tried again, 'Meg, I'm sorry for your loss.'

Meg turned her currant eyes on her, wet with unshed tears. And then she gave her a crooked smile, putting a forkful of stew in her mouth. 'This war touches everyone, doesn't it. Just you wait until it's your turn.'

The attic bedroom was cold, damp and stuffy.

'Do you mind if I open the window?' Rose asked.

'Yes, we'll freeze,' said Meg, taking off her clothes and throwing them on the floor. She stood in her brassiere and knickers, her strong thick-set body throwing statuesque shadows on the wall. The blackout blind was drawn and the small oil lamp gave off an insipid yellow light. The sloping ceiling seemed even lower and the beds were islands on the inky floor. Meg's face was a white oval against her black curly hair.

'Hey, Ginge, is that a war wound then?' She pointed at Rose's face.

Even though she was so bone-tired that she felt as if she had been run over by Jack Thimble's bus, Rose gave in to her constant need to be courteous. 'If you mean my scar ... yes. It's nothing, really. I was caught in an air raid with Will. The last big one we had, back in January. He was off duty that night, but helped people to safety. Flying glass. I got caught by flying glass.' She sat down on her bed, amazed at how easily the lies tripped off her tongue. And how difficult it was proving to get her story straight.

Meg turned off the lamp and the deep silence of the night enveloped the pitch-black room. Rose fumbled with her clothes and felt her way into bed. She lay her head on the cold, unfamiliar pillow, imagining her own fresh linen and silky eiderdown back home. Hot tears began to soak into her hair.

'Hey, Ginge,' came the whispered voice in the darkness.

Rose's shoulders tensed in agony. She heard the bed next to her creak and groan as Meg shifted herself. Oh, leave me alone.

'Oi, Ginge! I just want to say ... the war does terrible things. Terrible things to us all. Losing Bertie has made me rotten. I'm a bit of a piece these days.'

Realising that this was a mild apology, Rose mustered some strength to ask, 'How do you mean?'

'The Yanks,' whispered Meg. 'I just can't have enough of them. It's my way of coping, I suppose. You wait. Next village hop at Polperro and we'll go.'

'Really, Meg. I'm engaged.'

'Oh, I know that. Do you love him?'

'Well, really. I don't think I have to explain myself to you, do I?'

'Listen, Ginge. At dinner. You hardly defended him, did you? He doesn't get your blood racing, does he? If someone said what I said to you about the man I love, I would have let them have it. I insulted him and his work. I don't know any different, do I? He could be an amazingly brave man. But you said nothing.'

The silence in the bedroom pressed down on Rose's ears.

'I don't think you do,' Meg said.

'What?'

'*Love* him.'

She opened her mouth to speak, but could not.

'We'll leave it now, shall we?' came Meg's satisfied voice. 'Can't wait to show you my Yanks. They're such gentlemen. All *Hi* this and *Ma'am* that. They dance like Fred Astaire. They give you ciggies and gum.'

Rose rallied. 'I don't smoke.'

'How did I guess? Then they take you for a walk, wrap you up in their coat and give you something else too!'

'Meg, really,' she tried disapproval.

'Shush! Listen a moment.'

In the dark, Rose cocked her head.

'There they go,' giggled Meg. 'Drives me mad listening to that when I haven't had any.'

'Goodness!' Rose cried, horrified but fascinated at the same time. 'I thought they weren't at all suited.'

'Oh, they are. She's the backbone of them. Without her he'd crumble. He can't cope without his brother. But she gives him heart. They are truly in love. God, listen to me. I'm letting myself down saying soppy rubbish like that.'

Rose pulled the covers over her head to try to muffle the intimacies from the marriage bed downstairs. Her thoughts drifted home, and then to Will. Were she and Will ever in love? Were they ever backbone and heart for each other? Would she crumble without him? Her indignation began to recede, only to be replaced by a cold bite of emptiness.

Three

ROSE WAS SHAKEN FROM HER SLEEP BY THE RATTLING ALARM CLOCK. The attic window was a cold pale square and she was warm and surprisingly comfortable. A few weeks on at Pengared and the lumpy mattress had begun to mould itself to her body. She lay for half a minute, wiggling her toes, enjoying the quiet moment and knowing that Meg, too, was wide awake, waiting. Then she had to move.

Back went the covers, and bare feet touched the rug over the chilly lino. On went shirt, breeches and jumper, her fingers feeling for buttons. At the washstand she splashed her face with cold water and let out her usual cry of shock. A proper wash could wait until after breakfast. She wrapped her hair up tightly while Meg moved with equal speed. Not a word was spoken, not even a good-morning grunt. No one spoke until hot tea was poured in the kitchen.

Downstairs by the warmth of the stove, they sat at the table holding their steaming mugs and taking slices of toast provided by Betony.

'How did Mo sleep?' Meg asked Betony once her tea had sunk in.

'Oh, very well. I didn't tell you, Mrs Thimble's evacuees have nits.'

'Ew, keep them away from me.'

Rose piped up, 'Is that Mrs Thimble, wife of Jack the bus conductor?'

She was ignored.

Betony went on, 'And she caught one of the townie blighters stealing a pot of jam. She told them "We don't steal things in the country," and the little tyke said "Balls".'

'Cheeky beggar. Cockney?' Meg asked.

'Of course,' said Betony.

The two women dipped their heads and giggled while Rose continued to nibble in silence on her slice of toast, sighing with relief when Ted came in, stamping his feet and bringing with him his masculinity and the chill of the dawn.

'Cows, Meg,' he announced. 'I've just brought them in.'

'Who's to help me?'

'Joel is already there.'

Meg gave Rose a smug look. Ted never asked her to help with the milking, even though she had been given a merit by Mrs Pike. She longed to be inside that shed with the soft-faced sleepy cows, the humming of the cooling machine, the smell of silage and cud, Joel painstakingly sluicing the gutters. The nearest she got to the milk was rolling the churns down the track to the stand where they were collected by the cart. If Ted ever got round to asking her, she knew she would have lost her touch by then.

'Yard, Ginge,' he said. 'Then see to the hens. You can muck out once the milking's done.'

'Yes, Ted. Then what?' She hoped for some tractor work, hauling bales of straw, perhaps. She loved being out in the fields, high on the headland.

'Later on? Hoe the sugar beets. Meg, the Allis needs an oil change.'

There was another look of triumph from Meg.

'Breakfast in two hours,' said Betony, stoking at the grate. 'Oh, Ted, didn't you need Blossom for something?'

'Oh, yes. Meg, when you've finished the milking will you harness her, please?'

Rose felt her shoulders sink with relief. At least she did not have to go anywhere near that horse.

Ted said, 'Fine animal. Such a steady worker.'

'Part of the family,' Meg muttered to Betony. 'Treats her like an aged maiden aunt.'

Rose picked up the heavy yard broom and felt creeping discontent as she bent her back to the mess of straw and dung stuck to the cobbles. She swept and sweated, then bent to shovel the muck into her barrow. Shades of green, yellow and brown merged into a pungent mess and her restlessness transformed into pain across her shoulder blades.

Wheeling her third barrow-load to the muck heap she paused to rest. Her hands were red and chapped, her nails black. She watched Meg, over the way, languidly urging the herd back out to pasture, tapping a stick gently on bony hips.

Meg noticed her. 'Your engagement ring won't look so nice now, will it, on those hands. Anyway, stop preening, Ginge. You can get started in the cowshed now.'

Irritated, Rose called back, 'I always do the henhouse before breakfast, to get it out of the way.'

Meg shrugged and went on her way.

Rose opened the door to the henhouse to let the chickens out onto new straw that she had strewn for them in the yard. They emerged from their quarters, jerky head forward, twitching and changing direction. 'Go on, ladies, go on.' Rose used the toe of her boot to nudge the reluctant ones. 'Mucky little devils.'

Then she stooped to the small door in the side of the hut to collect the eggs still warm from the hens' bottoms. This was her favourite part of the day, but also the briefest. She carefully placed the precious brown eggs in Betony's wire basket, took them to the kitchen and put them on the dresser. Then she took a deep breath.

Hen dung was far worse than cows' could ever be. On her knees with her head and shoulders stuck right inside that musty little shed, the stink of it reached right down to her stomach, sending a queasy rush back up her throat. She took up the small trowel and began to scrape the splattered hen muck from the perches; some of it crusted, some of it still wet. Feathers floated in front of her face and she dared not breathe in case they got stuck up her nostrils. Even though she held her breath she could taste the smell. It stayed with her all day long.

At last, she shuffled back out and hollowed her back around her two hands, rubbing her knees, ready for a good wash and some breakfast. She saw Meg amble back from the pasture in the hazy morning sunshine and head to the stable. By the time Rose had put away her tools, she heard the metallic clop of Blossom's hooves on the cobbles. Meg proceeded across the yard towards her, holding the leading rein like a natural horsewoman. Rose moved to one side.

'She's really quite harmless, Ginge,' Meg trilled. 'I don't know what all the fuss is about. She's an old lady, really. A gentle old lady.'

'A cantankerous old lady.'

'She can sense your fear. You're making it worse standing there like that. Why not be friendly? Go on. Be brave. Stroke her nose, I dare you.'

'I'd rather not, I told you, I . . .'

Suddenly the roar of an engine ripped across the sky. Rose ducked, glancing up to see blue and red circles on the underbelly of a Spitfire as it thundered towards the sea. Blossom – spooked by the plane – jerked her head, rolled her eyes and flattened her ears.

Meg clung to the rein, her arm stretching as Blossom yanked in terror. She yelled, 'A dogfight! My first dogfight!'

'Is there another plane? Did you see a German?' Rose spluttered, her own fear escalating as the horse grew more and more agitated.

Suddenly, stamping the cobbles and her eerie whinny rising in pitch, Blossom wrenched her head from Meg's grasp and reared up. Hooves pummelled the air over Meg's head. The horse's body, now perpendicular, all but blocked out the sun.

'Steady girl, steady!' came Meg's cry. 'Oh, my God, steady!'

Through the explosion of hooves and the animal's awful noise, Rose saw that Meg was frightened. In one dreadful moment, the animal's heavy chin cracked down on Meg's face, sending her reeling to the ground. Meg clutched her nose and tried to shuffle backwards in the dirt.

Without a moment to think, Rose stepped forward and reached towards the horse. The rein was flying around like a whip but a calm voice inside her head told her to grab it. She tugged it down in one deft movement, placing her hand flat on Blossom's nose.

The horse snorted and foam flew in Rose's face but she kept a firm grip. She spoke the same calm words out loud that she could hear inside her head. Finally, Blossom stood still, her sides heaving like bellows. Meg scrambled to her feet, her nose bloodied.

'There wasn't another plane, damn it!' Meg cried, craning her neck towards the sky. 'He must have been answering some scramble, or mayday, or something.'

Rose snapped with a surge of anger. 'Is that all you care about? Plane spotting? Trying to wave at the pilot? You could have been *killed*!'

'What do you mean, *killed*? It's only old Blossom.'

'I couldn't have controlled her for much longer. What if she'd gone wild?'

'But she didn't, and you did all right. You *did* control her.'

Meg reached forward to stroke the animal's nose and asked, 'Have you got a handkerchief for my nose?'

'Here, take this. Keep it.'

'Thank you. And sorry.' Meg bit her lip. Her voice had a humble ring.

In silence, as a team, they walked Blossom back to the stable and gently led her into her stall. They shut her in.

'Best stay in there for a bit,' Meg said to the horse. 'Got to keep calm, old lady.' She looked across at Rose. 'You know, when I used to do the henhouse, I always put a dash of cologne on a scarf and tied it round my nose and mouth. Helps with the pong.'

'That's a good idea. It doesn't half smell.' Embarrassed by Meg's humility, Rose couldn't look at her. She gazed at Blossom instead. 'She still looks a bit loopy. She certainly had a fright.'

'So did I,' said Meg.

Rose felt the force of Meg's dark eyes on her.

Meg said, 'But you saved it, Ginge.'

'I did, didn't I?'

They smiled at each other across Blossom's shoulders as the horse lowered her head to the hay in the manger.

Even in the darkness of her sleep, Rose heard the planes. The gnawing drone came from the back of her dream, driving forwards until her eyelids opened to agonising reality. She sprang awake and crouched on her bed, frozen. Fear flashed like a beacon inside her head.

'They're not after us, they're flying too high.' Meg was beside her, lighting the lamp. 'Must be Birmingham, Bristol or

Plymouth.' Meg peered at her in the gloom. 'God, sorry Ginge, I didn't think ... but they are heading that way. Come on. Quickly.'

Ted was knocking on the door, a huge dishevelled shadow. 'Get going, girls. Get down those stairs. We never hear the blessed siren out here, when the wind's the wrong way.'

Meg grabbed Rose's dressing gown and wrapped it round her. On the landing they stopped for a moment to look east. The night was deep dark navy blue.

'Nothing tonight, thank God,' said Ted. 'Sometimes that horizon glows like a sunset.'

Even so, Rose groaned with fear, with utter helplessness, as Meg pulled her down the stairs. They found Betony crouched under the kitchen table with Mo snuffling, blissfully oblivious, in her arms. Betony's eyes were huge and her face grey with fear, but it softened the moment she saw Ted.

He pulled the ring on the trapdoor in the flagstones. 'Down in the cellar. Come on, all of you.'

They bent double to take the stairs down into the dank space. Rose's ears filled with the sound of her own fear as she remembered the shelter in Tobacco Street, the bulky presence of Will beside her, the metallic taste of panic. In the raids, she thought, when we go underground, it's as if we are burying ourselves alive.

Ted lit the lamp to reveal the Cumberpatch shelter: a cosy den with two battered old armchairs among the barrels and boxes, and a square of old lino over the earth floor. He got the little Primus going for tea, while Meg tucked a blanket around Betony and Mo in one of the chairs.

'Sit down, Ginge,' she said, pointing to the other chair.

'I'm fine. I'll sit on the floor.'

'No, no, I'll sit on the floor. You look done in.'

All was silent now that they were below ground, but Rose's hands were still shaking. Meg made a spot for herself at her feet and sipped the tea that Ted poured.

'The animals, Ted?' blurted Rose. 'What about the cows? Blossom?'

'Didn't know you cared so much about the old girl,' came Meg's voice, soft in the half-light of the oil lamp. Rose felt Meg's warm hand on her knee.

'I can't do anything for them, can I,' Ted replied. 'That's what's so frustrating. Being totally at those bastards' mercy. But as soon as we get the all-clear, I'll be up there to check on them. You can come with me, if you like. Put your mind at rest.'

Betony yawned. 'We get past worrying. We can only save ourselves, in the end.'

'Must bring it back for you, Ginge,' said Meg, turning on her side on the floor, making a pillow out of a blanket and curling up to doze. 'It never gets any easier, does it?'

'Ginge,' said Ted, peering at her in the gloom. 'Buck up. You can telephone home in the morning. By the look in your eyes I think you need something stronger than tea. There's not much left but here goes.' He poured two small tots of whisky into chipped cups.

She threw it down her throat.

'That better?'

'Not really, but it helps.' Tears of gratitude stung her eyes.

Ted cleared his throat, settling himself on a box of apples. 'We've been a bit tough on you since you arrived, Ginge. All of us. Wartime has made a hard master out of me.'

'I'm getting there,' Rose said, mustering a little strength to quell her fear. She glanced up at the low ceiling festooned with shadowy cobwebs, wondering where the bombers had been heading.

'You've been through a lot,' said Betony, lifting her head up to listen. 'You've had to live through all these raids. I'm sorry. I realise your parents might be in the thick of all this now, and your fiancé—'

'He'll be out doing his rounds,' she interjected.

'Ah, you see,' said Ted. 'Not a complete shirker then.'

'Oh!'

'He's playing with you, Ginge,' said Betony, lowering her voice to a whisper. 'And Meg admits she has been particularly awful to you about him. But I think you know why she's like that, why she's a little defensive dynamo. Her brother – well. You know about her brother. She's still hurting.'

Rose glanced down at the sleeping Meg, wondering how it was she could drain herself of all her energy so quickly and let herself go. She smiled; the whisky was working. She said, 'She tells me that's why she likes the Yanks, and they like her.'

Ted raised an eyebrow. 'We know what she's like. And you, Ginge, we're getting to know you. You two are chalk and cheese. You don't mind Ginge really, do you?'

'It makes me smile. So there. Makes me feel . . .'

Ted teased her. 'Singled out, picked on? *Special?*'

'Oh, yes, very special.' She laughed.

Betony's voice was tired and thin. 'So, you and your fiancé . . . when are you getting married?'

Rose sat upright. 'Oh, I don't really know. When the war is over, I want to go to college. So not for a long time.'

'You don't want to rush things, do you, Ginge.' Ted looked at her. It was not a question. 'You sound relieved . . . about not getting married straight away.'

'Do I? Oh, dear.' She tried to sound breezy, feeling the whisky warm her bones. 'Well, my parents *will* be safe, tonight. My father built a magnificent shelter in the garden. It's a plain old Anderson but he dug it really deep. Will helped him, actually. Dad used sandbags round the entrance and painted it nice and white inside. There's two bunk beds. It's a bit of a squeeze. Being tall, I'm forever bumping my head. We get the stove going, just like yours. When the raids were really bad it became a routine. As soon as Dad got home from work, Mother would do a quick supper and it would be out to the shelter with our hot-water bottles and a thermos.'

'That night you were caught in the raid,' said Betony. 'Must have been terrifying.'

'Tough, isn't it, girl,' said Ted, and Rose suddenly laughed out loud.

'It is rather,' she said.

'That's better,' said Ted.

She rested her head on the back of the chair, satisfied. She felt safe with the Cumberpatches; she felt her friendship with Meg had been validated. The whisky made her head swim in delicious sleepy waves.

In a mere moment, Rose was awoken by a frantic ringing of the telephone and a trample of feet over her head. Heart pounding, she leant forward to see a square of daylight above her. It was morning and she had been fast asleep in the cellar.

Betony was calling her to the phone. She shook herself free of her blanket, rushed up the steps and through the trapdoor. The receiver was lying on the stand in the hall. She stopped herself. She did not want to pick it up. She glanced through to the kitchen where Betony was busying herself with Mo, turning discreetly away from the hall doorway to give Rose some privacy. She did not realise how hard she was holding her breath until she lifted the heavy receiver and held it to her ear. Her knees gave way when she heard her mother's voice.

'Thought we'd better call, darling. Surprised the line's not down.'

'Oh, Mother, are you all right?' Tears squeezed through her screwed-up eyes. She pressed her hand to her throat as she listened to the voice crackling over the line.

'We're fine. It was a light raid. Will came round especially this morning to check on us. They were just dropping off after Bristol. Poor old Bristol. Just some damage by the docks, but nothing like we had in January.'

'And Dad?'

'Yes, yes, we're all fine. Will not so. He's missing you, we can tell. He sat and had tea with us. Says he hasn't had a letter from you in weeks. He says he wants to visit. See the farm for himself. See what's keeping you from him.'

Her mother's voice sounded rather accusing. Rose's stomach dropped. This was her life now and it felt delicious to be away from him. The thought of him here at Pengared was astonishing. She brightened, and told her mother, 'I spent the night in the cellar with everyone. Ted, Betony, Mo and Meg. I had my first taste of whisky.'

'Don't tell your father,' her mother pretended to warn her. 'How is it being a land-girl?'

'Fine, hard work, but fine.' She was beaming now as she glanced through to the kitchen where Betony was slicing yesterday's bread for toast and Meg was pouring the tea, their convivial chat warming up now it was obvious that Rose's family was safe.

'Come home and see us soon, darling,' said her mother and Rose opened her mouth to reply, but the operator interjected and their three minutes were up.

She stood for a moment in the hallway and then, suddenly remembering, put her hand into her dressing-gown pocket. It wasn't there. Somewhere between the attic bedroom and the cellar floor, her engagement ring had been lost.

It will turn up, she told herself and raced upstairs to dress.

Four

FROM THE ATTIC WINDOW IN THE EARLY EVENING, ROSE SAW A shimmering haze of silver-green over the top field. As if overnight, the barley she had helped sow on her first day was springing out of the red soil. The weeks had spun quickly past, the season had changed and she was part of life at Pengared Farm.

She missed her parents and sometimes longed for home, but she knew that as soon as she arrived at Stanley Crescent, Will would be there, taking her hand as if it belonged to him and kissing her chastely on the cheek. She knew her parents would smile on them as they took tea in the parlour. And in private, she knew that he'd take her in his arms and beg forgiveness for what happened on the night of the raid. He'd stare into her eyes, turn it all around and make her feel small and sorry.

'Stop dreaming,' said Meg behind her, 'and help me with my buttons.'

Meg turned her back so that Rose could do her up. Everything about Meg was circular, from the polka dots on her red dress to her dark eyes, black curls and large, round bosoms. Rose felt flat-chested, boyish and a frump by comparison. Out of work clothes and in dresses the difference between them was even more acute.

'What's the matter with you?' Meg scolded. 'You can take that look off your face. We're going dancing, remember. We're supposed to be enjoying ourselves tonight. And whether you will or not, I am going to have a jolly time, so you might as well smile and be done with it.'

'Oh, it's just this dress,' Rose said, smoothing her hand down her dark blue frock. 'I should have brought my best dress with me, but I didn't think I'd be going *dancing*. This one is so old-fashioned, I've had it since I was fourteen. You look so wonderful. So bright and pretty. I feel like a granny.'

'Enough of that, the blue suits you. Brings out your eyes.' Meg reached forward and undid one of the buttons at the neck. 'That's a start.' She spun Rose round to face the mirror and scrutinised her. 'What sort of colour is your hair, anyway? It's not a carroty red, is it?' she mused, and took up a brush. Rose's hair was thick and straight with a little wave at the tip. 'I think it's your best feature.'

'My mother says it's Titian.'

'It's what?'

'After the great artist. This red was a colour he always used.'

'You're so damned educated, Ginge,' laughed Meg. 'And I bet the GIs will love it. That's it. You're smiling now. Yes, I would say it's an autumn red, a foxy red. I don't know Titian but I know what a fox's tail looks like. And look at that face.' She carefully rolled up two locks of Rose's hair and pinned them around her forehead. 'You might like to borrow Betony's curlers once in a while. There, now the Yanks will see more of you. They'll die for that skin and those freckles.'

'Do you think so? I hope not. I don't want to encourage anyone.'

'What are you saying, Ginge? That you don't want to meet anyone new? Even though you don't love the incredibly brave and dashing Mr Will Bowman?'

'Did I *actually* say that?' Rose felt swamped by the emptiness again and glanced shyly at Meg.

'No, you didn't have to.'

She felt ready to confide. 'Did I tell you, he had an indiscretion with a Wren? Mrs Brown, the lady who runs the corner shop, told me, and he didn't deny it. I saw her in the pub and it was so obvious.' That Wren was always going to be there, she knew, just as she sensed her in the air-raid shelter; always there, somewhere in the dark.

'Ugh, Wrens. They're the worst. You should have broken it off there and then. Why haven't you, for goodness' sake?'

'I tried to the night of the raid. He wouldn't have it.' The sudden truth of it made her relax. 'I'm thinking about ways of telling him, next time I'm home. I really am.'

'*Thinking* about it? Then you're halfway there,' Meg teased.

'It's just that my parents like him so much.' She looked at Meg's exasperated expression. 'But I'm going home next weekend. It's best I do it face to face. I'll do it then.' The thought of it left her cold.

'I think you're too kind.' Meg was cross. 'All he needs is a *Dear John*. He'll understand. There's a war on. Anything could happen. You've moved on with your life. You're here with us. You've changed these last few weeks. You don't love him. Now come here.' She opened her compact and handed it to Rose. 'This stuff is new. Helena Rubinstein. Sounds rather fancy, doesn't it? Grumpy Jack got it for me. Covers all sins.'

Rose picked up the little white sponge and gently used it to dab creamy powder over her scar. In the soft evening light her face glowed and butterflies grew excited in her belly.

'Come on, Titian beauty,' said Meg. 'I can hear Ted grumbling from here.'

In the evening half-light, squeezed into the front seat of Ted's old truck, they drove along the top road to Polperro, the fishing village beyond Trelewin. Rose was squashed up against the door while Meg was pressed against Ted. Every time he changed gear on the steep lanes, his hand accidentally brushed her knee and she giggled.

'Quiet, Meg,' he warned. 'It's not what you think. I am a happily married man as well you know, missy.' He peered through the mud-splattered windscreen. 'I must say, it's a fine evening for this abomination.'

'Whatever do you mean?' Meg pretended to be indignant.

'Those Americans and you girls at this shindig. It's so bloody obvious. It will be like a cattle market. And as for you, Ginge, remember I think highly of you, and you're spoken for.'

Rose kept quiet. She glanced sideways and, blushing, caught Meg's scrutinising eye.

'Oh really, Ted,' said Meg, pulling the hem of her dress down, 'now you've put the thought right into my head.'

Rose watched hawthorn blossom falling like gentle snowflakes on the bonnet of the truck. Beyond the hedgerows, crops burgeoned in the fields sloping down to the sea.

'Hey, Ginge.' Meg dug her in the ribs. 'When this bloody mess is over, I'm going to drive the Allis tractor along here. I'm going to drive it all the way to Polperro and get myself a drink. What do you say? Are you going to come with me?'

'Of course I will. I can't wait for this awful war to be over.'

'What a lark we'll have, trundling down these country lanes with no worries about petrol rationing or being bombed.'

Ted grumbled, 'Something tells me we're all in for a long wait for that day.'

'Oh, a girl's got to dream,' sighed Meg.

Ted pulled up at the top of the village street.

'This is as far as I'm going,' he said. 'Polperro's far too steep for motors. You're on your own now.'

'Good,' said Meg. 'Seeing us with you will put the fellas off.'

'You girls be careful,' he called after them as Meg slammed the truck door shut. 'I'll be in the Sailors' Arms, ready to go at eleven. Sharp. Any trouble, you know where I am.'

'You won't leave without us,' Meg said.

'Be late and you'll see.'

'Good old Ted,' said Meg, linking her arm through Rose's. 'He had to dig up one of his petrol cans buried in the orchard for tonight. Betony persuaded him. At least he gets a night out at the boozer for his trouble. I like it when he goes all big-brother-ish on us.'

'He is kind,' Rose said. 'We could have caught the bus, I suppose.'

'Oh no, the farm truck has much more style.'

Laughing, they clipped down the cobbled hill past rows of whitewashed fishermen's cottages. In Polperro harbour, fishing boats bobbed in the sheltered water; beyond the gap in the sea wall the water was a balmy blue, as the sun danced its way down the horizon.

Rose sighed, 'How lovely it is here.'

'Never mind *lovely*,' Meg retorted. 'We're not here for the view. This is what we're here for.'

Meg pulled her up some steps into a tin-roofed church hall and through the door under a fluttering Union Jack. Pushing aside the blackout curtain, they paid their pennies and walked into a chattering crush of people.

'Oh, my goodness,' Rose said in Meg's ear as they stepped into the throng, feeling the heat, breathing the cigarette smoke and absorbing the swing of music. 'A real band! I've never been to a dance like this before.'

'Are you joking?' cried Meg, raising her voice, and using her hips to push her way through. 'Hasn't Will Bowman ever taken you dancing?'

'He doesn't dance.'

'Why doesn't *that* surprise me?'

She had to shout for Meg to hear her. 'There was once a dance at my parents' bowling club and they had a gramophone in the corner. But this – goodness me!'

'Oh, Ginge, welcome to the world!'

And what a wonderful world it is, Rose thought as they pressed through the laughing, surging mix of khaki and blue, punctuated by floral dresses of village girls and land-girls out of uniform. The rhythmic brass and relentless drumming broke over her in a soft, rocking wave; so different from what she listened to on the cosy wireless in her parents' parlour. Here the music was raw, insistent, live. She caught sight of a banner over the stage: *Polperro welcomes Hank Ancourt and His Band*; another one said *South Cornwall Munitions Benefit*.

'This lot are stationed round the headland. I saw you gawping at them the day you arrived. They've brought their own band with them, the lovely Yanks,' cried Meg, her face rosy with excitement as she waved at the conductor, Mr Ancourt himself, and winked at the trumpet players. 'I've never seen the brass so big.'

The lights were strung with red, white and blue bunting, the stage was draped with a huge Stars and Stripes and the floor in front of it was bouncing with dancers. Girls' hair swung, dresses swirled and men turned deftly on their heels. The American GIs, British sailors, Wrens, Auxiliaries and Polperro villagers all bobbed, twirled and jived to the muffled trumpets and infectious beat, their bright faces transfixed with pleasure.

Rose was mesmerised. She wanted to stand there and watch all night, not miss a moment. Suddenly, the music stopped. Everyone stood still, waited a beat and then shouted,

'Pennsylvania six-five-thousand!' A moment later they all took up where they left off. Rose clapped her hands with joy. 'Oh, I love it! I love it!'

Meg was tapping her arm, nodding to someone coming up behind her.

'Hi, girls, care for a drink?' A close-cropped red-necked GI elbowed his way to them.

Meg looked him up and down. 'Yes, please, don't mind if we do. Two beers, please.'

'Lemonade for me,' urged Rose, her smile frozen.

'No, Ginge, not when it's being bought for you,' hissed Meg.

The GI brought the drinks over to their table. As he set them down, Meg gestured towards Rose. He took the hint and grabbed Rose by the hand. 'Care to dance, ma'am?'

'Go on,' said Meg. 'I'll guard your beer.'

She assented for she didn't know what else to do. He was tall and thick-set and instantly her face was pressed close to his scratchy lapels. She cautiously lifted her chin to look at his corn-fed face.

'Private Solwell, ma'am. From Ol' Kentucky.' He beamed down on her. 'Raised in the wild, beautiful bluegrass state. Then before I know it, shipped out across the sea to fight for Uncle Sam. Gotta help you guys over here. Gotta kick those Jerry butts. You'all dance good, ma'am.'

'Pleased to meet you. I'm Rose Pepper, from Plymouth,' she said. 'Thank you, but it's you. I don't dance *good*. *You* dance well. You're leading. I don't know what to do.'

'Are you flattering me, ma'am? Wow, would you look at the colour of your hair. Where have I seen that colour before? Why I know, on the feathers on our little old rooster back home.'

'Well, thank you, I'm sure.'

She tried to keep up with him, shuffling her feet as best she could, wishing she had learnt how to dance. She glanced over her shoulder and saw that a pretty blonde girl was sitting in her seat, leaning close to Meg and chatting in her ear. The song finished and everyone on the dance floor stood still to clap.

Kentucky bowed. 'Thank you, ma'am, you'all enjoy your beer.'

'Oh, he was so polite,' she told Meg, 'but I really can't dance.'

'This is Mabel Cole,' said Meg, and the blonde girl gave Rose a quick smile. 'She's over at Hunter's Farm. She's lonely, never gets out.'

'Got my eye on that big fella,' said Mabel, tucking a cigarette between her lips and smoothing her red dress over her skinny hips. 'Might just see if I can bag myself a big fat Yank.'

'That's my girl,' laughed Meg.

Mr Ancourt on the stage tapped his baton for silence to count in the next tune: 'One, two, you know what to do . . .'

Another man appeared by the table and Rose felt another pair of hands – this time small and sweaty – take hold of hers.

'You like Glenn Miller?' This GI looked Italian, short and dark. He moved in close, smelling of beer.

She smiled politely. 'Yes, I do. My parents like him, so I . . .'

'You a land-girl, huh?' He pulled her out into the melee of the dancers. 'Do you know any haystacks nearby?'

From their table, Meg and Mabel giggled, digging each other in the ribs and nodding fierce encouragement at her.

'I beg your pardon?' Rose had to shout over the music.

The GI moved her closer to his barrel chest and pressed his wet lips to her ear. 'I said, do you know of any haystacks where we could . . .' His hand slipped down to her bottom and his whiskers scratched her neck.

'How dare you. I'm not that sort of girl,' she cried, pulling away and spotting his wedding ring. 'And you're married!'

'Oh, I'm married all right. Little lady is sat at home right now in Queens, New York, New York. But I'm here, you're here. There's a war on and a great big pond between us. Give a guy a break! You care to sit down with me, ma'am?'

She glanced over her shoulder to where he was indicating and saw that Meg and Mabel had been cornered by two GIs. Meg was sitting on one man's lap, supping her beer and arching her back, showing the tops of her stockings, while Mabel was running her hand inside the collar of the other's shirt.

'No, thank you,' Rose stuttered. She tried to extract herself, but his damp hands clamped tight to her hips.

'My, you're a tall girl. I love it that you are. My, what a lovely long neck, just right for nibbling, and hey, I'm just about level with your titties. Just right for—'

'Leave me alone.' She wrenched herself away and walked off

with a straight back, head held high to sit down in a corner, away from the dance floor. It was spoilt now. The GIs were being fresh with the Wrens, the sailors were groping the land-girls and she watched them with a strange mixture of envy and loathing.

Next to her, a couple were holding hands sedately across the table. The woman was in a Wren's uniform, and Rose, catching her eye, felt her stomach flip in misery at the memory of Will's misdemeanour.

'Oh, don't look so affronted, love,' said the Wren, glaring at her. 'No need to get prissy and look down your nose at them. They're here to help us. Couldn't do it without them.'

'I know that,' she snapped. 'I know that full well. I just wish they wouldn't take advantage. They start off all polite, and then they . . . misbehave.'

'"Misbehave",' the woman mocked her. 'You bring it on yourself. After all you came with *her*.' She nodded to where Meg was sitting on a lieutenant's lap, her face being devoured by his moustache. 'They think you're the same as her. By association. Tough luck, Miss Snippy.'

'My friend is only being like that because she is in mourning.'

'We *all* are. But we don't *all* behave like that.'

Rose stood up and made a bid for the door. Pushing aside the heavy black curtain, she slipped out of the fuggy dance hall into the caress of the sweet night air. She loved the music, she loved to dance, but she could not cope with the attention, with the slipping of morals. She knew that Meg would say, just as Will had, 'There's a war on.'

Relief swept over her as she began to walk down the dark street, drawn by the stillness of the sleeping harbour, leaving the noise behind her. Her footsteps clipped on the steep pavement, past blacked-out windows, towards the water.

The sun had long set but the sky was still light in the west and the harbour walls were lapped by inky water. It was a bright night, a bombers' night. A little breeze brought a chill to her and she stood still, wrapping her arms around herself, wishing she'd brought a cardigan. The music inside the church hall faded in and out and she relished the silence of the seafront, the breath of the sea. In that peaceful, empty moment she suddenly sensed someone watching her. The man was reclining on a bench, feet propped up on the harbour wall, hands in pockets, uniform hat pulled right down over his nose. She turned her back on him to look at the fishermen further along the quay, stowing their nets in the pinprick of light from their shielded lanterns.

The stranger spoke out of the darkness: 'A beautiful night. Such a perfect English night.'

She glanced back, wondering if the man was talking to himself, and then demurely fixed her eyes on the line of fishing boats.

'And you the perfect English rose.'

In one swift motion, he sat up on the bench and removed his hat.

'I beg your pardon?' she asked, suddenly nervous.

'The perfect English rose, if you don't mind me saying.'

His accent was heavy, definitely European. She tilted her head to hear him better. She could not place it: he hissed his 's's, his voice rose up and down like a song, he emphasised the wrong syllables. Confused, her mind reeled to the dawn watch, the Home Guard, the constant warnings about Nazi parachuters.

'Oh, my God,' she blurted, 'you're not a German, are you?'

He leapt to his feet, crying, 'Jezus-Maria! What an insult. You have actually sworn at me.'

She was horrified as he sprang forward, his face young, open and utterly shocked. She muttered a quick apology and turned to go.

He cried after her, 'Please. I did not mean to shout. Do not leave. Do not go away.'

'Tell me who you are then!' she blustered through fear and embarrassment.

'Don't be frightened. Please. I am a Czech soldier. I am Czech.' He fumbled in his top pocket for his papers. 'Captain Novotny. 29th US Regiment. I am taking the air, just like you.' He took a step towards her. 'Far too hot in there. All those people. I don't really like their music. Not like our *own* music at home. All those – you people say – Yanks. It's too much for me. So *noisy*.'

She strained to hear if the fishermen were still there, wondering if they could come to her aid, but all she could make out were their boots ringing on the cobbles as they made their way home.

'I came down here to be near the sea,' he said, revolving his cap round and round in his hands. 'Back home we are land-locked, so, being here in England, I can't take my eyes off the water. And if I can't see it, I love to smell it. And if I can't smell it, I love to hear it. It gives me peace, possibility.'

He moved closer towards her, and on reflex she turned away.

'No, no, please,' his voice was soft. 'I said please not to go away. Please, English rose. I'm with the Americans.' He pointed up towards the hall from where strains of 'Moonlight Serenade' eased out into the night. 'But I can see from your face that that is perhaps not a good thing. What I mean is, I am stationed with them, but I am not *like* them.'

Her shoulders relaxed as a soft breeze from the sea lifted her hair. 'But I do have to go,' she insisted. 'It sounds like they're playing the last songs. The love songs.'

'Ah, you don't like that?'

Rose watched him, suddenly trusting him enough to tell him, 'They make me want to run to the ladies and hide. I can't bear it. All the sentiment. All the "We'll meet agains". This bloody war.'

'It makes you sad. You have a love somewhere out there?' He swept his arm wide.

'A love?' Her mind went blank. Of course, there was no *love*. 'No, nothing like that.' She stifled a laugh and turned away. 'Well, goodnight.'

'Please, don't go. Not yet!' he implored her.

Rose looked at his face more closely, her eyes adjusting to the darkness. He was fair-haired and his face had a creaminess, a freshness. His eyes were deep grey and issued a pure light; his smile was bright and open.

'Please? Dance with me?' he asked.

She laughed. 'Here?'

'Why not? We can do whatever we want.'

'But that's what they are doing in there. *Whatever they want*. And taking advantage, using the war as an excuse.'

'Ah, but they are doing it with their bodies, not with their souls.'

She waited as this expression sank into her consciousness, and then, feeling a sense of peace settle inside, she surprised herself and stepped forward into his arms. Gently, he took her hand in his own soft, cool palm. His fingertips were tender on the centre of her back. He barely touched her as he swayed her to the music drifting down the street. She felt the muscles in her jaw relax, her shoulders drop and her feet become light. She felt as if she could dance, *really* dance.

'Just one moment of bliss,' he mused, his strange voice a caress, mesmerisingly close to her ear. 'Our own moonlight serenade.'

She listened to the music, wanting to know more.

'Did you leave someone behind in Czechoslovakia?'

'I left everything behind.'

Suddenly understanding his immense sorrow, Rose held his hand tighter as they danced with light, sensitive steps on the cobbles. The slow, swaying music became part of the night, mixing with the noise of roosting gulls on the rooftops above and the chopping splash of the waves on the steps below.

She turned her head and smiled into his eyes. 'You don't have to use the word "English" when you address me.'

He cocked his head, half amused, half puzzled.

'You called me an English rose. But my name is – merely – Rose.'

His eyes shone as he understood. 'I knew it. Such beauty, like the flower,' he whispered, and then corrected himself. 'I'm sorry, Miss Rose. I am being very forward for a Czechoslovakian officer and gentleman. What I meant to say was that you do look lovely tonight.'

'Thank you.' She accepted the compliment with grace. 'But I think I still look like a land-girl.'

'So? I do not think that is a problem, even if it was true.'

She waited a few more bars of the music. 'And you? We haven't been properly introduced.'

'My name is Krystof. And, as I was saying before, I am from Czechoslovakia where we have no sea and I can't take my eyes off . . .' he winked at her and let his gaze drift with mock reluctance over her shoulder, '. . . the sea.'

Laughing, she told him, 'I know a lovely cove near the farm where I work. If you squint past the wire and imagine children playing in the rock pools, it's heaven. I like to think of it as my cove, that I am the only person who knows it's there.'

'Ah, but you have just told me . . .'

'. . . and the sand is so soft between your toes.'

'I have never felt sand between my toes!'

'You should.'

'I will, with you at your cove.' He glanced towards the sound of voices outside the church hall. 'Looks like the dance is over.'

They stopped and she felt herself drawn to look into his eyes. She waited, mesmerised by his kind, open face as he looked back at her.

'Hey, Ginge,' came Meg's whooping cry, as she skipped down the steps, hanging onto the arm of yet another GI. 'Time to go or we'll turn into pumpkins.'

Mabel was hoofing up the street with a man in uniform, throwing back her head in laughter.

Krystof asked her, 'What is this "ginge"? What is this "pumpkins"?'

'That's my friend Meg, and I won't introduce you, if you don't mind. I have to go. It was lovely to meet you.'

'You cannot go, Rose. You haven't told me where you are staying?'

His hand rested on her elbow and gently pressed her flesh. She did not want to go.

Meg's urgent cry broke the spell. 'Come on, Ginge – let him go. Ted's taxi service to Pengared is awaiting. Mustn't make him mad. He's a grumpy enough old sod any day of the week,' she told the GI, who by now had lost interest.

Rose looked at Krystof. 'She's a good girl, really.'

'You live at Pengared. I think I know it. Is it close by the camp? These Cornish names. They are difficult for me. Do you mind if I . . . ?'

She felt a gentle flipping under her heart, a warmth in her veins. 'No.'

He bowed and stepped back into the shadows. 'Until next time, English Rose.'

Five

IN THE MORNING, ROSE GLANCED OVER AT MEG. SHE WAS STILL FAST asleep, her pale face scrunched into the pillow and her dark curls a tangled cloud around her head. As Rose opened the bedroom window to let in the fresh air, Meg rolled over and begged for water.

'Never again?' Rose asked her.

'Never again,' Meg muttered, reaching for the glass. 'Tell Ted I'm poorly, will you? I can't do the cows. I'll make it up to you. Promise.'

'At last,' Rose teased her, 'a chance to milk the cows.'

After tea and toast with Betony, Rose got up from the table, pulled on her jacket and headed out into the bright sunshine.

'And where do you think you're going?' Ted called across the yard.

'To collect the eggs, as usual, and see to the hens. Why, do you want me to do the cows instead,' she asked eagerly, 'seeing as Meg is unwell?'

'That girl better haul herself out of her bed and quick!' he called up in the direction of the attic casement, knowing Meg would hear him. 'No, I'll see to the milking.'

'What, then?' Rose asked, downcast.

'Don't look like that, Ginge. I'm giving you the morning off.'

'What?'

'The morning off.'

'Are you sure?'

'Stop procrastinating, Ginge.' Ted nodded towards the farmyard gate. 'You're keeping him waiting.'

'Oh, goodness!' She stopped short with a tremor of excitement. She had not seen Krystof there, leaning on the gate, his peaceful face soaking up the sunshine. The dogs pattered around their side of the gate, their noses pointed towards him, their tails thrashing with pleasure.

The stranger from last night had sought her out, just as he had said he would. Trying to compose herself, her heart racing, she hissed at Ted, out of the side of her mouth, 'Are you really sure, about the morning off?'

'I want to know if *you* are sure, Ginge,' he said, gravely. 'I'd like to know what your fiancé might think of this.'

Rose lowered her head, biting her lip. 'We'll go for a walk. What's the harm in that?'

Ted growled, 'Go quickly, before I change my mind.'

She glanced again at Krystof who was waiting patiently for her. He gave her a sleepy smile. She thought quickly, 'Ted, can I take the dogs?'

'If you must. If you feel that will break the ice, give you something to talk about, help with your romance, then yes.'

She threw him a dark look as he strode away across the yard, laughing and waving his hand to dismiss her. Then she heard the casement rattle and a dishevelled Meg leant out.

'Yoo-hoo, Ginge, I knew it!' Meg cried, her eyes dark slits in her white face. 'When I saw you with him, dancing by the harbour, I knew it!'

Rose blushed and pressed her finger to her lips. 'I'm surprised you can remember anything about last night.'

With a schoolgirl giggle, Meg slammed the casement shut.

Rose waved at Krystof to wait and hurried back to the kitchen to grab the dogs' leads from their hook. She suddenly realised why Betony had been grinning at her across the table.

'Did you know he was there? All this time?'

Betony nodded in response, her eyes shining. 'He was there at first light. Asked Ted if he would allow you the time off; permission to take you for a walk. Said something about the cove, or the sea, or something. Permission was granted.'

In the yard, she hooked the leads onto the dogs' collars, feeling the energy of their quivering sides and twitching shoulders. They were being surprisingly obedient: they sensed escape and they had never forgotten her biscuits and lived in futile expectation of more.

'Heel, Mutt, Jeff.'

The dogs obeyed, trotting beside her as she walked towards Krystof, both leads in one hand. She felt a strange stew of confidence and butterflies fluttering in her stomach. Her eyes never left Krystof's face. Had everything she had felt when they danced and held each other and looked into each other's faces been in her imagination? Had he felt it too?

He took off his cap, a deep smile curving his face, his head gently nodding. Suddenly, deep down, she realised she had been expecting him.

She reached for the latch on the gate.

'No, wait,' he cried. 'Look, look at the sign. You should not open the gate. It says so. See, I am good at English. I can read the sign. Look!'

'It's all right,' she said. 'That only applies when these two are loose in the yard. But now they are on the lead, and under my control, they are far better behaved.'

The dogs trotted around the gate as she opened it.

'Like so many things,' he said.

She grimaced. 'What on earth do you mean?'

'So many things are in your control.' He glanced at her for her reaction.

'Hardly many things. I can count only the dogs at this precise moment.' She looked at him. 'I hope you are not suggesting that *you* are in my control. That would be inappropriate and, anyway, it's far too early to be saying that sort of thing.'

'Early? It's eight o'clock in the morning. In farming, that is not early.'

'I mean—' She stopped, yanking the dogs back. 'Ah, I see, you are teasing me.' Her blood settled in satisfaction as she watched the pleasure break over his face.

'You don't mind, do you?' He laughed.

She walked in one wheel rut and he walked in the other. Mutt and Jeff trotted between them on the strip of green, occasionally tangling their leads until Krystof took one of the dogs and made him walk on the other side of him.

'Are you taking me to your *cove*?' he asked, saying the word carefully.

'That's where I'm going so . . .'

Sunlight dappled through trees and a lacy froth of blossom

grew on spiky hawthorn hedges. She heard the panting of the dogs and the crunch of their boots on the ground, the peace of the day.

'English springtime,' said Krystof, watching the benign blue sky, with the occasional puff of white cloud, arching overhead. 'Is very beautiful.'

'You remembered where I lived, then?' she asked, feeling shy. Her earlier bravado, boosted by the distracting dogs, was fading fast.

'I forgot at first,' he said. 'These Cornish names tie me in knots. But all I had to do was ask some of the platoon. They remembered you from the dance. The fiery redhead, someone said, the firecracker. But *Ginge*? That's what your friend called you. Not sure I like that name.'

'I'm not sure either.' She smiled and hooked her leg over the stile. 'But part of me finds it endearing.'

They walked up the footpath that snaked over the headland. Gulls were swooping, their calls keening overhead.

'The sea cannot be far away,' he said. 'The birds always stay close. It's like they are keeping watch over us.'

She noticed that their footsteps were in rhythm, their strides the same length.

'I hope it is acceptable for me to call on you.' He looked at her, just as she caught his eye. 'I have a morning pass from my commander. Your boss didn't seem to object. I hope you don't mind.'

'Mind?' She pondered on it, smiling at the formality of his words. 'When I woke up I was thinking how much I wanted to show you the cove. I was thinking how strange it must be for you not to have seen the sea until you came here. I was thinking that your English is very good. And that my Czechoslovakian is non-existent.'

'I have been with the Americans for nearly four years, so I have picked it up, as you say.'

'Well, that might not have helped you as much as you'd like,' she teased.

They reached the brow of the hill and the sea suddenly broke before them: the rolling waves, the expanse of grey-blue that was not quite yet a picture-postcard colour. A salty breeze ruffled the clifftop grasses. She bent down to let the dogs off their leads and they sprang forward, ears flattened, tongues snapping at the corners of their mouths.

Krystof fell to his knees. 'Oh, the agony,' he cried out, laughing at himself. 'The agony. The beauty. Look at it. See how far it goes. It's enormous. It's as big as the sky.'

'Are you feeling unwell?' She laughed with him.

'Take me there. I want to touch it.'

She led him to the footpath that took them down to the cove. Soon enough, gravity began to propel them into a cave of shady hawthorns and they were enveloped by a tunnel of green and silence. Their trousers were wet from brushing past curling ferns. Ahead, the dogs crashed through the bushes, emerging now and then as a flash of fur and wet nose. The sound of the sea was muffled by the undergrowth and all she could hear was Krystof breathing behind her. But then, she turned a corner and the cove was before her. It was perfect, her cove, sheltered by cliffs and dotted with miniature rock pools washed by a friendly tide. Krystof cried out, 'Oh, my God!' as he heard the first rolling whoosh of the waves.

He ran over the smooth wet sand, dodging rock pools and the wave-licked boulders, his boots crunching scattered shells. He stopped abruptly at the twists of wire strung between wooden props following the shoreline like an ugly scar.

'I want to go in. I have to touch it.' He hopped on one leg to loosen a boot and then fell onto his backside as he struggled to pull off the other, sock and all.

'Krystof! Are you mad? What about the wire?'

She caught up with him. Beyond the barbed wire, waves, spent and bubbling with a trace of foam, hissed towards them, making the sand perfectly smooth.

'You think I haven't breached tougher wire than this?' Krystof called to her. 'This is as bad as Jerry wire. Useless. I dug this sort of stuff out of the desert with a spade. It might try its best to keep *them* out, but it won't keep me in.'

He took off his shirt and rolled up his trousers. Rose let out a short burst of laughter and then clapped her hand over her mouth. She had never before seen a man without his shirt on. Not her father, nor Will. She definitely did not expect to see Will like that before they were married. And yet here was Krystof, naked from the waist up as if it was the most natural thing in the world.

'You're not going to go over?' she said, with a shake of caution. 'There may be mines.'

He stopped and looked carefully at the sand. 'No. No mines.'

'But the dogs might try to follow. I don't want them hurt on the wire. Ted will kill me.'

'Don't you worry about them. That one is sniffing in that pool. The other one is licking that rock.'

She did not bother to look round to check. She could not pull her eyes away from Krystof. His skin was creamy, smooth, not a mark on it. Pink nipples sharpened by the breeze nestled in downy golden hair on his chest. Rounded muscles defined his arms.

He stepped back a few paces, judged the distance and then pelted to the wire. She squeezed her eyes shut as he sprinted past her and heard him yell with joy as he breached it in one bound. He plunged into the water, kicking great plumes up with his legs.

'Be careful,' came her feeble voice, but she gave up chastising him and began to laugh.

He stood to attention, facing her, saluted and fell backwards flat into the water. The splash obliterated him and he came up floating, his feet like a rudder. He tipped his head backwards and drank a hard mouthful of sea water, which he spouted like a whale.

'Keep your mouth shut!' she called.

'I can't stop laughing!' he called back and then shouted out in Czech.

'What did you say? What are you saying? Tell me. It's not good manners to speak in a foreign language when others around don't speak it. How do I know you're not being rude to me?'

He sank under the waves and leapt up like a glistening dolphin. 'I said, "You don't know what this means to me." And, "I love the sea like I love my mother." And, "Why can't I live like this for all time?" And, "How is it that you aren't in here with me?"'

'Because I – because I can't jump as high as you.'

He stood up and waded back to shore with powerful strokes

of his thighs. His trousers clung to him like a second skin, his hair was swept back like a marine god. She forced herself to look at his face, which glowed with pleasure as he gazed back at her through the wire.

He reached out and beckoned her towards him. She saw his chest expanding rapidly with his breathing, but his face was still, his eyes concentrating on her. She stepped forward. The wire was as high as her shoulders. She stared at it, at its twisted violence, so rusted and vile, dividing them. And then she looked beyond it to Krystof.

'*Polib me*. Rose,' he said.

'What was that? I told you, Krystof, you'll have to speak English.'

'I said "kiss me". Kiss me. Say it, Rose.'

'I'm not going to say that! Who do you think you are? You be careful.' She tried to sound cross but it wasn't working. Krystof's smile grew wider and wider. 'You know what your GI mates said to you last night. I'm prickly, remember. Fiery.'

'No, this wire is prickly. Will you jump it?'

She laughed. 'I can't, Krystof. It's impossible. You'll have to come back.'

'Can I kiss you if I come back over?'

'Oh, I'm not sure that I meant *that*.'

He reached his fingers over the wire and held them towards her. She copied him, tentatively stretching. Their fingertips touched. His fingers felt warm. They felt *right*.

She realised she was holding her breath. 'Come back over, Krystof,' she whispered.

He turned from her and walked back into the sea.

'Where are you going?'

'I've got to get further back. There's not as much space this side.'

He waded, dug his heels into the wet sand and then sprang forward. She clapped her hands over her eyes; she could not watch. His wet trousers would weigh him down. He did not have enough space to run. He might not make it. She heard a lot of splashing and a yell and then Krystof was in a ball in the sand at her feet, clutching his bare foot.

'Just a scratch.' He was rolling over. 'I'll live. For a bit. Then gangrene will set in.'

She yelped in panic. 'Let me see.' She knelt down and took his foot in her lap. He lay back on the sand, groaning.

His foot was strong and wide, the hierarchy of toes beautifully proportioned. His skin was perfect. 'There's nothing! There's nothing here, you rascal! You're play-acting.' She stood up, dropping his foot. 'It won't wash with me!'

He stayed where he was, lolling on the sand as if he was sunbathing. '"Rascal"? "Wash with me"?' he called. 'What are you saying, English Rose? What are these strange words? I merely wanted you to touch my foot. We've touched hands, now we touch feet.'

Rose gazed at him, liking the way he found joy in every little thing; liking the way his eyes shone at her, laughing with pleasure; liking the rush of bliss surging through her body. She had to shake it off. She had to remind herself: she was engaged to be married.

Abruptly, she turned from him and walked towards a boulder to sit down. Krystof ran after her and sat next to her. Mutt and Jeff joined them and sat either side, like statues, surveying the waves. Sensing a change of mood, Krystof sat quietly, squeezing out his trouser legs to make watery indents in the sand.

'What is it about the sea, Krystof?' Rose asked, eventually.

His eyes squinted, as if he was peering beyond the water, beyond the landmass of Europe, all the way to Czechoslovakia.

'Imagine growing up in a country where the sea is a fable, a fairy tale. We can only dream of it. Never see it or smell it. It is how pure oxygen would smell, I imagined.'

'It's lovely here. So peaceful.' She glanced shyly at him. 'It's lovely by the harbour at night.'

'Such a moment,' he said, equally shy. 'When I sat there last night, that was the first time I had been truly close. Oh, of course, I see glimpses from time to time as we go about our Ops, and on a ferry over from France. But to just sit still and watch it, listen to it in peace. The sound. That push and pull.' He looked at her. 'It's like breathing.'

She loved to listen to his voice. She wanted him to stop talking for he was making her feel light-headed. She wanted to rest her head on his shoulder.

'Why are you quiet, Rose?' he asked. 'I am sorry I teased you. Sorry I asked you to kiss me. It wasn't correct of me, was it?'

Rose jolted, realising she hadn't minded at all. 'I'm just thinking . . . thinking about a lot of things.' She sighed and looked out at the cove, seeing everything anew. Her life had changed so much in the past few months. 'This is my first time away from home,' she said. 'Breaking my back on the farm, making friends with Meg the hard way. Overcoming my fear of horses.' She laughed. 'Oh, yes. I have come a long way. And here I am, my first morning off, after my first proper grown-up dance, larking about at the cove with a Czechoslovakian soldier I met only the night before. Who would have thought it?'

Krystof turned to her and touched her face with his hand. '*I* would have thought it,' he said gently. 'It's your adventure, Rose. Your life. All these things are good things. Your new friends. Your new experiences. It's only just beginning.'

His touch surprised her; drew her to him. There was an unexpected warmth, a tugging in her belly and she found herself wanting to sink into the deep grey depths of his eyes. She felt delicious desire between them, pulling them together. He enfolded her hands in his own – soft and strong – and leant his face towards hers.

'Krystof!' she squealed, flinching back. 'I'm engaged to be married!'

He recoiled, looking at her in confusion, disappointment flickering through his eyes.

'I see. I did not know.' His voice was calm and serious. He looked down at her hand. 'But you're not wearing a ring. I assumed you were . . . actually . . . not engaged. How silly of me. It is wrong of me to assume.'

She twisted her fingers together on her lap. 'I'm sorry. So sorry. I lost the ring. I have been engaged a year,' she rattled on, desperate to explain. 'His name is Will. My parents like him. They think he is wonderful . . . He is twelve years older than me. Friend of the family. But truth be told . . .' She felt peculiar, crushingly disloyal, but not to Will. She had deceived Krystof by coming here to the cove and being with him, laughing with him, when she was promised to another man.

'Oh!' she cried with sudden bitterness. 'This bloody war! Three long years and we thought it might be over by the first Christmas. But it just keeps spreading further and further. It's enormous. I just want it to end.'

'The war, Rose? The war?'

'Yes, of course the war. But also . . .' She looked at Krystof, knowing that he understood her. 'I left home because I wanted to do my bit, to get away from the raids. I wanted peace. I wanted to *do* something. But really, I wanted to get away from *him*. I miss my own bed, I miss my home, Mother and Dad. But I don't want to go back. To face him.' She looked at Krystof. 'You're right. I just want it to end.'

He turned his face away from her.

'Listen to me,' she muttered, ashamed, 'ranting on about my silly little worries.'

He sighed and stood up, keeping his eyes fixed on the horizon. 'We all have our own stories, our own troubles. It has been a long, hard journey for me to be standing here, talking to you.'

Humbled, she asked, 'What happened to you, Krystof?'

She waited, rubbing the velvety ears of one of the dogs, while he stared at the wire. And then he told her how angry he felt when the Germans invaded in March '39 and Czechoslovakia fell, and Britain did not declare war. Turned a blind eye.

'The Nazis took our uniforms, our munitions, our dignity,' he said. 'They changed the map without asking anyone. I couldn't believe it when my commander surrendered, but it was orders from our government.'

'You were *ordered* to give up?' she asked.

'But a band of us from my regiment weren't going to have any of it. We struck out and crossed the border to join the Polish army. But when the Germans invaded in the September – and the war proper declared – we headed off again while the borders were still open. I rode a motorbike; someone had an old truck.

'He made it to Paris, crossed the Channel on a ferry, arrived in London.

'I went straight to the War Office to offer my services, and they stationed me with the US army.' He stopped to pick up a shell and gazed at it, turning it over in his hands like a piece of treasure. He sighed deeply. 'Over the years, Rose, I have watched the Allied failures. First the Sudetenland, then Prague, then

Poland, then Dunkirk, the fall of France. *That* was the worst day, wasn't it? How much lower could we go? But I was at victorious El-Alamein and now I see a change. We're getting stronger . . . Something *new* is happening . . .' He stopped and looked at her.

'You've come through so much, Krystof. I feel ashamed at bombarding you with my so-called troubles.'

'I've come through so much, but now all I see is you and your little frightened face.'

'What about *your* family? The people you left behind?'

'We live on a farm near a village, not far from Prague. We have a farmhouse there and a townhouse in the city.'

'And now?'

'I can only guess that they are tolerating the Nazi regime and the puppet government; tolerating Hitler and his vulgar accent on the radio. My country has been dismembered, but my family still has to run their farm, work in the fields and tend the animals, like you do. But I have no idea, really. I have no idea where, what . . . anything.'

'Nothing?'

'Only silence.'

Rose bit her lip and pressed her face to the dog's head. 'I'm sorry, Krystof.'

His voice brightened. 'I think that if I picture them there at the farm – my mother, father and brother, Tomas – then they *will* be there, happy and healthy.'

'I do the same with my parents,' she said, feeling the connection between them enveloping them like a warm embrace.

'They would love to know you, Rose. I know they would. One day, perhaps, they will.'

She watched his face as he put his hand over hers and, again, felt the warmth of his body close to hers. She sighed and closed her eyes. She waited. Her breath caught inside her, the sea whispered beyond the wire. This was their moment. Forget Will. She would deal with Will. All she knew was Krystof.

The moment passed and she opened her eyes. Of course, he didn't want to kiss her, not now he knew she was engaged.

But Krystof was peering over her shoulder, towards the top of the cliff behind them.

'There's someone there, watching us,' he said. 'No, don't turn round yet.'

She stared towards the top of Trelewin cliff. The silhouette was unmistakable; the stance she knew so well.

'Oh, God, it's Will,' she cried. 'Why is he here? How did he know?'

'Will? Your fiancé Will?'

She felt inexplicable panic rising fast. 'We'd better go.'

'Why on earth, Rose? Why should we go? We have done nothing wrong.'

She looked at him. 'You wanted to kiss me, remember?'

'But I didn't.'

'Oh, God.' She wrung her hands. 'You stay here, I'll go up.'

Krystof looked at her. 'So I see. It was your day off. You were to meet him here anyway. You are playing with me. I am a fool.'

'No, not at all. No, Krystof. I can't believe he's here. I never thought he'd just turn up. Oh, goodness. What shall I do?'

'All right, then, we go up the path together. We have nothing to hide. And anyway, Rose . . .' He stopped her in her tracks with the tone of his voice. 'You said you wanted to finish with him. Perhaps this will help.'

'But not now, not like this. This isn't how I . . .'

'Why are you so agitated? Why are you so . . . frightened?'

'It's nothing. Nothing. Just the shock of seeing him here, and here I am enjoying myself with you – oh!' Her hands fluttered. 'Get the dogs. Where are the dogs?'

'Here, here they are.' Krystof's voice soothed through her panic. He bent to the animals and clipped on their leads. 'There, they are safe now. They are with us and they will behave.'

She looked at him standing there, so generous, so calm. She knew that she loved him.

'Come on, Rose,' he said, 'I will escort you up the path.'

Will's face was frozen. He did not say a word and yet his eyes spoke to her. They were hard, like Cornish granite. Uncompromising. His shoulders were set; his arms rigid by his side. At his feet was set a wickerwork hamper, which she recognised from home. It was her mother's.

'Will!' She tried to call gaily, but her mouth was dry, her words failing as she fought for breath from her walk up the steep pathway. 'What a surprise! I had the morning off so I . . . I didn't know you were coming. How did you find the place? Did the bus conductor tell you? Oh, what's his name. Can't remember. Jack, that's it. You can't mistake old Jack.'

'I motored here and parked by the church.' Will's words were measured and even, his mouth a grim, set line. 'Used my precious petrol. Wanted to surprise you. Looks like I've had a bit of a surprise myself.'

Rose glanced at Krystof behind her, whose face was a picture of composure.

'Er, Will, this is . . .' she began.

Krystof interjected, 'Thank you for showing me the cove, Miss Rose.' He stood to attention and saluted. 'I bid you a very good morning. Good morning to you, sir.'

Without catching her eye, he turned on his heel and marched off towards Trelewin church.

Will stared after him for an age before turning on his heel and picking up the hamper. He began to walk over the headland in the opposite direction to Krystof, towards Pengared. Rose, in confusion, felt obliged to step in beside him.

It was a long, drawn-out minute before Will spoke again. 'Showing Slovac conscripts the sights, are we?'

She panted, still out of breath. 'He dropped by the farm. He's stationed nearby. He had never seen the sea.' She paused, feeling a sting of anger. 'And he is Czech, not Slovac.'

'Is he indeed?' Will stopped and looked down at her, as if he would laugh at her. 'Well, he can look at the sea all he wants. He doesn't need a female companion to do so. He does not need my fiancée to do so, does he?'

'He's a long way from home, he . . .'

'So he's lonely. A lot of people are these days. Just like my Wren was out on the Hoe.'

'No, no!' she blurted in all truth. 'No, it's not like that at all!'

Will appraised her, his smile patronising. 'Not sure I understand what you mean by that, little Rosebud,' he said, 'but we can forgive each other these trifling matters. He's gone now, back to his barracks, no doubt. Just like my Wren. Long gone.'

He took her hand, and she bit her lip for his flesh felt cold and inhuman compared to Krystof's. She mustn't think of him. She must concentrate on Will. This was her chance to face him and be strong.

'I have some news for you,' announced Will, suddenly bright and cheerful. His change of demeanour at the snap of a finger tripped her up, made her brace herself. 'That's why I came by today. I wanted to see for myself what draws you so strongly to this blessed, out-of-the-way corner of the county. I wanted to see what keeps you here, preoccupies you, and stops you coming home to visit your parents – and me. I wanted to see what prevents you from picking up a pen and writing to me. Once, it has been, Rose. Once in two whole months.'

'Will, I have been so busy. The farm . . .'

'Ha, I see that the Yanks are based nearby, with the other foreign soldiers, but I will skirt over that. And, yes,' he gave a perfunctory scan of the bay from their vantage point on the headland, 'it is pretty enough here, but can't we do something about these blessed dogs?'

Mutt and Jeff, trying hard to be obedient on the lead, were snuffling around the bottoms of Will's trousers and, Rose noted, were now curling their lips to show their teeth.

'Here, give me the leads.' Will took them from her hand and marched the dogs over to a fence where he promptly tied them up and left them there, straining and yelping in surprise.

'Stay, boys,' called Rose, feeling sickened by Will's reaction, but knowing it was best for them if they did what they were told.

'That's better,' said Will. 'Shall we sit?'

He produced a blanket and shook it out over the grass. Rose perched herself gingerly on the edge of it as he opened the hamper.

'I thought we'd have a picnic, Rose. This is what folks do in the country, isn't it?' He unpacked a thermos, some sandwiches wrapped in paper and two slices of cake. 'Your dear mother made this for us. But then she knew it was going to be a special occasion. Me coming to surprise you. And look here. Champagne!'

'Goodness,' said Rose. 'How did you get hold of that?' Then she caught his eye.

'Don't ask,' he said, knowingly.

Embarrassed, she glanced back towards Trelewin and where Krystof had been heading. The pathway was empty. Wherever Krystof was, she felt she was still walking beside him. Her shock at her feelings silenced her.

Will pressed on, popping the cork and splashing champagne into two tumblers.

'It's far too early in the morning for champagne,' she said.

'Not when you have something to celebrate,' he countered, 'like we do.'

Confusion made her mute.

'Did you ever notice the old house over there?' Will persisted. 'Between those trees? Trelewin, is it?' He passed her a brimming tumbler.

She found her voice. 'If you mean the house by the church, that's the Old Vicarage. It's derelict, I think.'

'Not so much of the derelict, if you please,' he said. He lowered his voice to effect intimacy. 'Anyway, I want us to celebrate, Rosebud. To put all our troubles behind us.' She saw him glance at the scar on her cheekbone and watched his eyes ineffectively shield his guilt. He said, 'I want us to make a fresh start. I feel we are equal now, what with my little indiscretion and now yours . . .'

'Will, I haven't—'

'Shush. Come on, Rosebud,' He stretched out on the blanket, sipping his drink. 'Come and lie beside me.'

'I'd rather not. It's still rather damp.'

He laughed. 'I like that in you, Rose. You're so demure and proper. It's rather endearing.' He patted the blanket. 'But do lie down.'

'I really don't want to.' She bristled, sitting upright and hugging her knees. She sipped the champagne and felt it would choke her. 'The thing is, Will, that recently, since I've been away, I've been thinking—'

'Now stop right there, Rose,' Will interjected, 'and *think*, instead, about this! Remember that old house.' He pointed back towards Trelewin. Rose gazed at the peaceful view; the treetops; the seagulls circling over; the spot where Krystof disappeared. 'You'll never guess what. I've just bought it. For us. For you.'

Rose's head jerked forward. 'You what?'

'For you and me, my dear. Our marital home. Thank good-ness for this war, I say, for I got it dirt cheap with help from my employers at the Western bank. Staff mortgages are such a good perk. The agent showed me round. One quick look was all I needed.' He got up, knelt by her and gripped her shoulders so he could peer into her startled face. 'Your mother tells me you love this place, the farm, the countryside, so I was thinking only of you.' His voice was like syrup. She thought she was going to be sick. 'We can get away from Plymouth, live a real country life. We can zip around the lanes in my Ford. Visit your parents of a Sunday. Perfect.'

'Oh, Will no . . .' Her voice cracked with shock. She shook her head.

'And next weekend,' he blundered on, draining his glass of champagne, 'when you're home, we can tell your parents. Name the day. Make it official. Well, they know so much anyway. They know about the house. They know I'm here today. I wanted to get things moving. So we can start our life together. Just look at you, Rosebud. Country air agrees with you. I can see a flush on your cheeks, a spark in your eyes.'

But her cheeks were crimson with embarrassment; the spark was unshed tears. She searched desperately for a way to tell him it was over, but how could she now? She had planned to tell him at home, next weekend, with her parents close by. Home, where she felt safe. But now, she realised, her parents were in on this: the Old Vicarage, the picnic and the champagne. Right now, she wanted to run away from them all. Set the poor, whim-pering dogs free, and run away.

Her throat constricted with frustration. 'Will, I really don't think that—'

'Oh, do stop talking, Rose,' he said, 'and kiss me.'

'Will, I think you've drunk too much . . .'

'What rubbish. It's only a bit of champagne.' He leant over her, his breath fired with alcohol. When she flinched away, he grabbed her hand to pull her back.

He stopped. 'Where is it?' he asked, his voice cold again. 'Where's your ring?'

'Somewhere safe, in my bedroom,' she lied. 'You don't want me to lose it around the farm, do you?'

Irritated, he picked up the bottle and refilled his own tumbler.

'Have some more champagne, will you?' he snapped. 'You're cold as ice.'

'I have to get back to work. Ted only gave me the morning off.' She wanted to stall him, change the subject. Get away from him. 'This has all been very nice, and I'm very grateful . . .'

'Oh, you and your blessed work. I'll make you late, they'll sack you and then you can spend all your time with me. Come and lie here!'

She flicked his hands away, stood up and brushed off her trousers. 'Really, Will.' She looked down at him. 'I think you're a little drunk. What would my parents say?'

'Oh, yes, mustn't upset the in-laws. I can't wait till next weekend,' he said, his voice suddenly sing-song with anticipation. 'To see their faces when they know you'll be mine. We will truly be together. Man and wife.'

Rose knelt by the hamper and thrust the picnic back in, tipping away the rest of the champagne. Panic made her fingers shake but inside she felt a hard core of reserve return.

'I'll show you the farm if you like,' she said.

'Oh, yes, Rosebud. The little farm.'

She felt proud as she opened the gate to the yard and shut it firmly behind them, letting the dogs off their leads.

'What a ridiculous sign,' he said.

'It's so the dogs don't get out onto the track.'

'Surely the dogs should be tethered at all times.'

In the face of his rudeness, she began to chatter. 'We have a small herd of Friesians. Over there, in the stable, is Blossom the mare.'

'Looks like that horse is ready for the knackers.'

She soldiered on. 'There's the apple orchard. The blossom was lovely. We have three pigs and a flock of smelly hens. And there, on that hill, is the crop of barley that I helped sow on my first day.'

He barely glanced at the field before fussing with his shoes, which were immersed in a muddy puddle the colour of khaki.

'Bloody muck,' he mumbled.

'I won't lie, it's hard work,' she said. 'Ted, the farmer, works fifteen hours a day. His brother Hugh was called up. That's why they have us, Meg and me.'

He was barely listening. 'Well, you won't have to do it for ever.'

She felt a sudden pang at the thought of no longer being at Pengared.

Reluctantly, she said, 'Come into the kitchen and meet Betony. I'm sure we can have some tea.'

As she pushed open the kitchen door, she saw Betony slicing bread on the dresser, her back to the door.

'Well, Ginge,' Betony said, facing her shelf of white plates, 'and how was your walk with your young man? We were a bit taken aback by it, I must say, but as long as you're happy. We were only just saying how nice and handsome he looked. What a surprise, what a lovely—'

Betony turned her head and her words failed. She peered beyond Rose's shoulder to the tall dark man behind her. She held the bread knife skywards, her other hand gesturing inanely. 'Oh,' she said. 'Oh. Oh.'

Rose stepped forward, her voice rising as she tried to sound normal. 'Betony, I'd like you to meet my fiancé, Will Bowman.'

'Oh,' Betony said again.

Meg barged through the door to the stairs, calling, 'Ginge is back! She's back, she's back, with the man of her dreams!'

The shocked silence that stilled the air inside the kitchen was broken eventually by Meg's giggling. 'And here *he* is! Pleased to meet you. Heard so much about you.'

She held out her hand to shake Will's, her other hand keeping her dressing gown together. 'Please excuse me, I have been rather indisposed this morning. But it is lovely to meet you at last, Will Bowman. We've heard so much about you.' She flashed Rose a glare from her currant eyes, her bright face breaking into laughter. 'Give me a moment, I'll just fix myself up. Be right back.'

Will's confusion was modified by an unsightly leer as his eyes rolled over Meg's curves pushing at the folds of her dressing gown. 'No need to on my account,' he said.

Betony cracked teacups and plates into each other as she set them on the table. 'Tea anyone?' she squealed. 'Bread and butter?

Fresh this morning. I've been busy while that young sloven Meg...'

Will stared openly around the Cumberpatchs' frugal kitchen, finding everything he saw there amusing: the dull walls, the scrubbed table, the dusty light shades, the old stone sink. Rose watched him take in Betony's slender back as she bent to collect some better crockery from the dresser, his eyes resting for far too long. She watched him smile to himself until, suddenly, he caught her looking at him and swiftly came to her side.

'We've been having a romantic time,' he gloated to Betony, putting his heavy arm around Rose's shoulder. 'A champagne picnic out on the headland. We're celebrating!'

Ted opened the back door and stomped his way in. Rose watched his face twitch in confusion as he walked forward automatically to shake Will's outstretched hand.

'Welcome to Pengared, Mr er...'

'It's Will,' insisted Betony, right in Ted's ear. 'Will Bowman. It's Rose's fiancé.'

'Did I miss something? Did I hear you say you were celebrating?' asked Meg, coming back downstairs in her work clothes.

'We've had champagne out on the headland,' Will boasted again, sitting at the table and accepting a cup of tea from Betony, while everyone else pulled up a chair. 'Do you good people know the Old Vicarage at Trelewin?'

'Of course,' said Betony. 'It's been empty for years.'

'Not for much longer. I've bought it. I and my lovely wife-to-be will soon be living there.'

Betony leant towards an open-mouthed Ted. 'He means Ginge,' she whispered.

'Jeepers, Ginge!' cried Meg, her voice loaded with meaning. 'I can't keep up with you!'

Rose stared at her, begging for some help.

'Well, our Ginge here is a dark horse,' said Ted gruffly.

'We'll be neighbours, my good man,' Will went on, 'and this little lady will no longer be a land-girl. No longer up to her elbows in all this muck. She'll be my wife. A banker's wife. How very grand.'

'You'll miss it, won't you, Ginge? You'll miss the farm and

everything that goes with it.' Ted directed his meaning at her and she lowered her eyes under his scrutiny.

Her shoulders sank as the drowning sensation returned; the disappointment radiating from her three friends around the table only added to her misery. Tears stung her eyes as she lifted her steaming cup to her face and she caught Betony looking over at her with a barely perceptible shake of her head.

Six

UPSTAIRS IN THE ATTIC, ROSE DUG HER FINGERS INTO POCKETS AND opened drawers. 'Oh, where is it? Where is it? I can't remember the last time I saw it. Oh, Meg, I can't finish with him if I can't give him back the ring,' she wailed.

Meg rolled over on her bed where she was reading a curling paperback for the second time. 'Yes, you can.' She peered at Rose through her dishevelled curls. 'You're not having second thoughts, Ginge?'

'It's just that he gets so *cross*. And I can't bear it.'

Meg said, 'You won't have to bear it for much longer if you tell him straight. Anyway, you're making him sound like an old school teacher who's going to tell you off. Although from the look of him the other day, I'd say more like a head boy. Very handsome. Quite a man. Bit of a spiv, really, but I'm sure he carries his ARP uniform off very well.'

'Oh, Meg . . .'

'Just think, Ginge. He's quite a catch. Good job. Exempt from service. "Likely to stay alive", as my mother would say. And that lovely big old house at Trelewin to rattle around in together. There you go. Couldn't be simpler.'

'Stop it.'

'I know. We *all* know. He's not right for you. You're not in love with him.' Meg's gimlet eye bore right through her. 'I just want you to bear that thought in mind when you see him this weekend and tell him it's over once and for all. And that he can keep his stupid house.' Meg sat up. 'We all hated him, by the way.'

Rose ignored her. She knew the truth and she was beginning to panic.

'I'll just have to say I forgot it in my rush to get the bus.' She wrenched open yet another drawer.

'You've already looked in there,' said Meg. 'And there you go again, thinking of ways to explain yourself. Just tell him to get *knotted*.'

Rose snapped her suitcase shut. If only it was that easy. As easy as shutting a case, as putting a lid on it. But she was going to have to open up a Pandora's box when she got home: undo a year of misguided feelings, unravel Will's plans for their future, untangle all of her parents' expectations of her.

'Are you ready, miss?' asked Meg. 'I'll walk over with you. There might be some post. I've nearly finished this book and I can't read it for a *third* time. I'm hoping mother's sent me a package from St Ives.'

Outside in the yard, as they lifted the suitcase over the gate they heard the clatter of a bicycle on the stony track. Skidding to a halt in front of them, the messenger, all of fifteen, in peaked cap and cycle clips, hopped from the saddle.

'Telegram for Cumberpatch,' he announced, his ruddy cheeks raw against his milky skin and his uniform far too big for him. A boy doing the job of a man – one more upshot of the war.

'I'll take that,' said Meg, scribbling in the ledger and sending the boy on his way to trudge back up the track. She hooked her leg over the gate. 'Funny how bad news manages to get here quickly, while my spy novel might be languishing for days in that post box at Trelewin.'

Rose followed her back over the gate. 'Heavens, Meg, you don't think—?'

'It's War Office. Official stamp, look.'

'It might be Hugh.'

'It most probably is.'

Crestfallen, they dragged their feet back across to the house and into the kitchen. Betony's smile and exclamation of 'What have you forgotten, Ginge?' fell away as she saw their expressions.

'A telegram?' Betony choked on the word. Her red-knuckled hand reached for it. 'God. No.'

She slit it open, her head shaking. Her eyes scanned the flimsy chit of paper. 'I can see *Hugh* here . . .' She began to cry. 'But I can't see anything else. I can't . . . you know I can't.'

Rose stepped forward, her insides twisting. 'Here, give it to me.' Her hand juddering as she read the telegram in one breath. She sighed. 'He's fine, Betony. He's fine.'

Betony snatched back the paper. 'Fine?'

'Yes, yes. It just says he's coming home. He has leave.'

Betony screwed up the paper, fresh tears springing from her eyes, her face contorted.

'God damn it!' she cried. 'If only I didn't have to put myself through this every time.' She raced from the kitchen, calling 'Ted!' over and over. 'Ted! Ted!'

He must have heard from inside the barn for he came running, throwing his pitchfork to the cobbles. They met in the centre of the muddy yard and he understood straight away. He gathered Betony tightly, pressing her to him, rubbing off her tears with his muddy hands. He grabbed the screwed-up telegram and tossed it aside.

Watching them, Rose felt confused momentarily and then immediately realised why. Jealousy. Ted and Betony loved each other. They needed each other. She wanted what they had and she knew she'd never have it with Will. Her mind drifted to Krystof, walking away from her over the headland.

Meg dug her in the ribs. 'Come on, let's leave them to it. They don't need us around.'

They hurried over the headland, each taking turns to carry the suitcase.

'I can't believe he bought it,' Rose said as they walked along the path next to Trelewin church. The Old Vicarage sat there beyond the wall, blank-windowed and cold in the sunshine. 'Look at it. It's monstrous.'

'Oh, Ginge, you're so hard done by.' Meg was rummaging in the Cumberpatch post box by the stile. 'How can you be so ungrateful? A huge house to make your own, when other people's are being bombed to rubble. Married soon? Children on the way? A perfect life.'

'Will you stop teasing, Meg.' Tears of frustration stung her eyes. 'I can't bear it.'

Meg put her hand on her arm. 'I'm just winding you up to set you on your way.'

Rose surprised herself by laughing. 'Well, instead, can't you just mind your own business?'

Meg laughed. 'You know I can't do that for nuts!' She caught her up in her arms and kissed her cheek. 'Now go see your parents. Have fun. And stay strong. Think of your perfect stranger. Think of Krystof! God, I can hear the bus. Hurry! And tell Jack Thimble I need some stockings.'

The bus rumbled across the bridge over the Tamar into Devon, leaving Cornwall and Pengared far behind. From her seat near the back she could see Plymouth spread out below her. The bombed-out docks of Devonport were identifiable by their misshapen buildings and smoke curling from long-smouldering fires in the rubble. Somewhere down there was the Anchor pub. The building had survived, that much she knew, but how much of her old life remained since that awful night? Enveloping the hilly city was peaceful Plymouth Sound as smooth as a piece of glass. Four grey destroyers slept at anchor.

She caught Jack Thimble's surly eye and he came along the gangway, banging his hips against the backs of the seats to steady himself as the bus turned a corner. He leant over and told her, below the chattering of the other passengers, that he'd have something for Meg on her return journey.

Alighting at North Prospect, she walked along streets that no longer existed. Terraces of solid granite, built a hundred years ago, were as they should never be seen: with their guts hanging out, front doors dangling, possessions ragged and scattered. Rose felt sad that she was used to it. How *normal* the horror was these days. A fireplace was suspended midway up a wall, curtains swung at a window with no floor beneath it, a window frame lay intact on a mound of smashed bricks.

Rose's mother had told her that most people had been moved on, but she caught sight of a woman, hollow-eyed and stooping, washing her front step. Behind the doorway was a jumble of rubble and twisted joists, a dusty sofa and a battered bed: there was no house.

'Good afternoon.' The woman stopped her mopping, her dish-cloth dripping filthy water onto her slippers. 'Post's still being delivered up and down here where they can, lovey. I don't want to miss out on letters from my boy, do I? Postie's got to have somewhere nice to put them, hasn't he?'

Rose stared at the woman, who was nearly cross-eyed with fatigue. 'It does look nice,' she lied. 'You've done well to keep it so.'

What she wanted to say was that it looked pathetic and degrading. If this was the British bulldog spirit Mr Churchill was booming on about, then he could keep it.

'Can't be much longer, can it?' muttered the woman, bending to her filthy bucket. 'Then my boy will be home.'

'Let's hope so.' Rose walked on. *Keep smiling through*, they all sang. Hope was so tenuous, she decided. But it was the only thing that kept them all going. She thought of Krystof and how far he had travelled to keep hope alive and suddenly a weight lifted from her shoulders.

She began her climb up the hill to St Budeaux and its leafy avenues of semi-detached houses, all built the year she was born. Her parents were the first people to own their house. This comforted her: her home was as old as she was and her parents would always be there. And here she was: Stanley Crescent. Sight of the road sign lifted her with joy. Hope returned.

But first, there on the corner, was Brown's the grocer's.

She pushed the door and heard the familiar tinkling of the bell. All was quiet inside: Mr and Mrs Brown must be out back. The light was dim because they used oil lamps. Polished wood shelving reached to the ceiling, arranged with a meagre display of tinned food: National Household milk, oven-baked beans and custard powder. Mrs Brown liked to arrange her packets and tins in fancy patterns, so that Sunlight soap might sit alongside Woppa peas. Anything to brighten her, or her customers', mood these days, Mrs Brown would say. The counter was washed down and ready, the parquet floor worn in all the familiar places. Potato Pete and Oxo advertisements on the wall advised Rose how to cheer up her vegetables, and subsequently, herself.

'Be with you in a moment,' Mrs Brown called from the back.

Rose breathed the warm smell of the shop and remembered her happy mornings here, checking ration books, weighing flour from the tub, slicing bacon and wrapping it in paper, carefully arranging packets of dried eggs in the window to emulate Mrs Brown's artistry. She heard a footstep.

'Rosie, my lovey.' Mrs Brown was an energetic woman with

sparkling eyes behind horn-rimmed spectacles and streaks of grey hair poking out from under her headscarf. She stepped forward to peck Rose's cheek, rubbing her hands down her white overall. 'Lovely to see you. Look at your flushed cheeks and your uniform. Ooh, you do look the part. Proper land-girl. Farm work doing you a power of good?'

'It is, Mrs Brown. I'm home just for the weekend. Thought I'd drop by on my way. How's Mr Brown?'

'Taken poorly. Nerves, poor devil.' Mrs Brown bit her lip and shook her head, lowered her voice. 'Doctor's given him tablets. He says he can't take it. When North Prospect got the worst of it last time, I tell you, he'd had enough. He got blown to hell at Passchendaele, as you know, and now it's happening all over again. It's the noise he can't stand. He built the deepest Anderson in Plymouth in our back yard but he won't go in it. Reminds him of the trenches. Says the damp seeps into his bones. Doesn't want to die like a rat in a hole.'

'Oh, Mrs Brown.'

'First time he's opened up in twenty years. It's brought it all home. Those men that went through it in the last lot, well, they don't want to start reliving it again, do they.' The shopkeeper paused, her worried eyes far away. 'Listen to me go on. It's not as if we're the only ones, is it? And you, my Rosie, how have you been? Have you preferred being . . . away from it all?' Mrs Brown lowered her chin and stared at her over the top of her specs.

'In a way,' Rose said brightly, 'but I miss Mother and Dad. Getting a bit homesick. The work is hard, but the family is very nice, I—'

'What about being *away*?' Mrs Brown wanted her to understand.

'Yes, yes,' she said, understanding full well. 'Being away has helped enormously.'

Mrs Brown's eyes shot to her left hand and they gleamed some more when they spotted it was naked.

Noticing her, Rose lifted her voice. 'Now, what can I get Mother? What might she be needing?'

Mrs Brown took her cue to bustle back behind the counter. 'There's not a lot here, lovey. But if you want to treat her, how about some carob?'

'Doesn't have quite the same ring to it as a nice box of Milk Tray, does it?' she laughed. 'Even so, I'll take it.'

'Two shillings, lovey, and I must say,' Mrs Brown pressed the change into her hand, and let her sharp eyes penetrate, 'I'm so sorry for what I told you about Mr Bowman and the Wren on the Hoe. About me seeing them, and all. But I felt I had to. So difficult under the circumstances. But I see, clever girl,' another glance at her hand, 'that things have moved on and turned out for the best. They always do. Mr Brown said—'

'Thank you, Mrs Brown,' Rose broke in to stop her. 'Everything is fine.'

As she strolled along Stanley Crescent, the pleasant scene of bay windows, tiled roofs and gables unfolded before her. Garage doors and garden gates were all painted to match – deep green or navy – and flowers bounced in the breeze behind low garden walls. She focused on the spot where her house would appear from within the curved street and averted her eyes from the reminders of war: white lines painted on lampposts and along the middle of the road, tape criss-crossing everyone's windows. The warm air spoke of a perfect summer's day and above red chimneys arched a cloudless sky. At last, she saw her bedroom bay. One window was open and her net curtains fluttered. She began to hurry and in one breathless moment she was standing at her own front door with its small window depicting a ship in full sail, unaware of the tears streaming down her face. She rapped the door knocker, too caught up to find her key at the bottom of her bag. Home. She was home.

Suddenly she was gathered into the hallway. Her father, in his sleeveless sweater, her mother in her apron, pulled her to them both, crushing her tight.

'Where've you been, girl? Where've you been?' Mr Pepper growled. 'How are the yokels? How is that damn farm?'

'It's damn fine,' Rose laughed, brushing at her tears. 'They call me Ginge. I don't like it, really, but they *are* lovely. Oh, Mother, have you a hanky?'

'Honestly, you *never* have a hanky.' Her mother rummaged up her sleeve and they all clutched one another and laughed, both women wiping tears, her father blowing his nose.

'*Ginge* indeed,' said Mrs Pepper, tapping her own red hair. 'I wouldn't have it if I were you.'

'They're good people. I'm settling in well.'

'Your hair is new,' said Mrs Pepper. 'Are you rolling it differently?'

'Meg taught me. Meg is the other land-girl.'

'Oh, yes, and what's she like?'

'Where do I start?' she laughed.

They walked through to the back parlour where the French windows were open to the garden. 'Don't get too settled there at the farm,' said Mrs Pepper, trying to mask her trifling jealousy. 'This is home, remember.'

'How could I forget.' Rose's insides settled as she looked around the familiar room: the pair of chairs by the tiled hearth, the standard lamp behind her father's chair, the small curve-backed sofa now a little worn on the arms. There was mother's knitting basket with half-finished 'socks for soldiers' bundled inside, and this week's copy of the *Radio Times* next to the radiogram. This was humming gently with a swing tune. Mother had drawn the blackout curtain at the window as far as it would go to let in all the sunlight.

'How long have you got?' asked her father, stepping towards the sideboard where he set out three tiny glasses. 'A toast, I think. Rose deserves it. Look at her in her gaiters. You look damn fine, girl.'

'I've got two days,' she said, not wanting to think of her journey back already. 'Today and tomorrow. I'd better get the last bus.'

'That's not really two days, is it,' observed her mother, sitting down in her chair. Beneath her careful smile, Rose saw she looked weary.

'Well, we're going to make the absolute damn best of it,' said her father, bending to the cupboard. 'I know it's in here somewhere. Where's the sherry? We've not touched a drop since you went. And we've got a smashing dinner today, haven't we, Sylvia.'

'Oh, yes, Rose. Dad wrung Emily's neck specially.'

'Dad!'

He said, 'Well, she hadn't been laying well. And it is a special occasion, after all. Roast chicken, your favourite.'

Her mother said, 'And first-crop peas out of the garden. None of your tinned stuff. And Will is coming for tea.' Her eyes brightened. 'Then everything will be complete.'

An immense silence filled Rose's head. 'I'll just take my bag upstairs and get changed. I'll be back down for sherry.'

As she went upstairs and opened her bedroom door, her smile returned. How wonderful it was to be back there. Her bed was made up with fresh sheets and her pink satin eiderdown. On the window seat beneath the fluttering curtains sat her old rag doll, while her little ornaments had been dusted and perched in their usual places on the mantelpiece. Her best brushes and combs were laid out on the kidney-shaped dressing table and the rag rug over the linoleum had been washed. Not a thing was out of place and she thought briefly of Meg and her mess. Meg was welcome to that attic room tonight.

Setting her bag on the Lloyd Loom chair by the bed, she went to her wardrobe and took out her Sunday best dress with its pretty print and puffed sleeves. She took off her uniform and put her dress on. The silkiness of the fabric felt strange against her skin after the stiffness of her shirt and breeches. The bodice had tiny shell buttons all the way down and it fell in flattering pleats over her bust. She caught sight of herself in the mirror and decided to take the dress back to the farm with her. She wanted Krystof to see her wear it. Smiling, she pressed her hand to the place on her arm where he had touched her to say goodbye, just before he walked off across the headland. Her heart began to tap delightfully at the thought of getting back to Pengared and seeing him again.

'Rose,' called her mother up the stairs. 'Dad's found the sherry.'

'Hurry up, though,' he added. 'There's not much left.'

Bless them, she thought. *They see the changes on the outside, but have no idea how much I have changed inside.*

Sipping her thimbleful of sherry, Rose followed her father through the French windows and down the concrete steps.

'Look at my rose beds,' he said. 'Fine cabbage patch they make now. Cabbage roses, you could say – ha! And see the leeks and potatoes? They're doing well. We'll have damn good runner beans, too, come August.' He pointed to the canes that strutted along the garage wall, dazzling with red flowers and alive with bees.

She looked around the garden which had once rambled with roses, lupins and hollyhocks and that, for three years now, had been turned over to vegetables, the chicken run and the great hump of the air-raid shelter right in the middle of the lawn. Her father had certainly dug it deep, with the help of Will, she conceded, and had even fitted a proper wooden door instead of the sacking like the neighbours.

'I see you've managed to sow grass seed over the top of the Anderson, Dad,' she said. 'It'll make good camouflage.'

'Damn sure it will,' he said, glancing up at the sky. 'Sorry about Emily, Rose. But Jessica and Martha have lived to scratch another day.'

'Do you think they miss her?' Rose squatted down by the chicken coop to peer through the wire. Now a bit of a farmyard fowl expert, she noticed the remaining Pepper hens did not seem to be doing well. What scraggy specimens they were, she thought, compared with the plump hens of Pengared.

'No, but they'll probably smell her cooking,' laughed her father, nodding towards the kitchen door through which Mother could be heard moving pots and pans around.

'Probably not so much meat on her, if she's anything like these two. Are they laying all right?'

His face straightened. 'Not too well. Not well at all. That's why Emily's in the pot. Haven't had an egg in weeks. Have had to put up with that ruddy dried stuff in puddings again. I know your mother tries her best to drown out the awful tang. How I long for a sizzling fried egg.'

'I should have brought some from the farm,' said Rose. 'If only you'd told me the hens weren't laying.'

'I shouldn't complain,' her father went on, 'when so many people make such sacrifices, like those poor devils in the Atlantic. But it's those little things.'

Mother emerged from the kitchen with a dab of flour on her face.

'Lunch won't be long.' She linked her arm through her daughter's. 'Yes, you *do* look well, Rose,' she said, as if to answer her own private worries.

'It's all that good country air and good country cooking. Not that your cooking isn't—' Rose stopped herself as her mother's face flushed with confusion and her eyes filled with tears. 'Here, Mother, let me.' She wiped the flour gently off her mother's cheek. 'Has it been tough here, these past few months?'

Her father cleared his throat. 'Yes, yes, it has. The raids just get you down. There's fewer of them now, though. Jerry's giving us a break. Shouldn't complain.'

'North Prospect is a right mess,' observed Rose.

'But don't you worry about us,' said Dad. 'We soldier on.'

She was aware of her mother scrutinising her. 'Your scar hasn't faded, has it? What a dreadful night that was. I'll never forget it. We thought we'd lost you.'

Mr Pepper said, 'But thank goodness for Will.'

Her mother said, 'He'll always be my hero, the way he took care of you that night.'

Rose turned her face away.

'At least you feel safer now, out on the farm,' said her mother. 'And you're doing something for the war effort. Makes you feel good, doesn't it, doing *something*.'

'Just like old Emily did,' said her father. 'Come on, I want to listen to the one o'clock news.'

'I don't,' said Mother. 'It's always bad news.'

Rose said, 'Sit here in the sunshine with me for a bit, while Dad's inside. Then I'll help you serve dinner. Are you all right?'

'Yes, yes,' said Mrs Pepper, sitting on the step and hugging her knees. 'Your father keeps it that way. He's very strong.'

Rose tipped her head back to look at the clear blue sky. 'What a beautiful day,' she said. 'You'd never imagine what menace can rain down on us from up there.'

'You must never worry about us,' said her mother, pointing to the air-raid shelter. 'That thing is good and solid.'

'It's safe once you're in there, but I do worry. At Pengared I'm out of harm's way, a bit cut off. I feel frustrated. You seem tired. Everyone I meet is tired. Even poor Mr Brown is having trouble coping.'

'Having a funny turn more like,' said her mother. 'But you know who keeps me sane? Will. He pops in here every other night on his ARP round, checking we're OK. Quick cup of tea and off he goes into the blackout. Like I said before, our hero. I can't wait for you two to be married. How happy I'll be.'

Rose saw the tiredness briefly lift from her mother's face and felt a thud of dread in her stomach. And then, to sully the summer air even more, a grave, precise voice issued from the radiogram as her father turned the volume up. He came excitedly to the French windows to say, 'Reports are just coming in. They've blown up the dams on the Rhine.'

'There,' said Mother, triumphant, 'another victory for our boys. It'll be over by Christmas.'

Rose caught her father's eye and sighed, 'Where have I heard that before.'

Dipping her head under the kitchen mantle, she stirred thick gravy on the front hob, while her mother carved up Emily on the drop-leaf table, plucking at the meat with her fingertips and throwing the bones in a pot for next week's soup. They worked round each other, used to the narrow room and to the glaring heat of the coal boiler that shared the hearth with the cooker.

It was a fine meal, Rose conceded, as she took the plates through to the front room: new potatoes roasted in chicken fat, fresh peas from the garden and little pieces of Emily smothered in gravy.

'Here's the wish bone, Rose,' said her father, linking his little finger around one of the prongs and reaching across the table.

Rose squeezed her eyes tight and tugged on the bone, thinking girlishly of Krystof, finding herself clutching the larger piece.

Her father said, 'Now your wish will come true.'

Her mother poured water into glasses. 'And I think we can guess what she wished for. Don't be shy, Rose. We know you so well. We know how you feel about Will.'

Rose looked down at her plate. Her mother's food was suddenly unpalatable. Her stomach slopped with a wave of nausea. She tried to swallow some water. It did not help.

'I'm sorry, Mother, Dad,' she said, her voice caught in her throat, 'but you don't know how I feel about Will. And neither does he.'

She stared at the tablecloth while her parents carried on eating, their cutlery chipping away at their plates. It was as if they'd not heard her.

She lifted her eyes fearfully, first to her father's and then her mother's face. 'I don't love Will,' she said, louder, 'and I don't think I ever did.'

Abruptly the sound of eating stopped. Her father put down his knife and fork. 'What's this, Rose?' His head was cocked, his face blank. 'What are you telling us?'

'I've met someone else,' she blurted, shocking herself with the utter joyful truth of it. 'He's a Czech soldier. He fought at El-Alamein. I met him at a dance, well, outside a dance. On Polperro harbour. We've had just moments together, but he is—'

Her mother's cutlery crashed on to her plate. 'Oh, but Rose! *Someone else?* What about Will? How could you do this to him?'

'Now, Sylvia,' said her father, putting his hand on his wife's arm, 'let Rose speak. Let her tell us what's going on.'

Her mother roared, 'She doesn't know what's going on! Rose, you've just been taken in by the romance of it all. A brave soldier. Yes, I'm sure he's very nice. But Will? How could you? He's brave, too. I know he's not in the firing line, but my goodness he is out there every night the bombers come over.'

Rose tried to find some strength to face her mother's distress. 'But Mother, he—'

'And so dependable. He is *here*. After the war, what will happen to this Czech chap? He'll have to go back. He can't stay here. But Will will be here. Will has always been here. We've known him a long time. You can't do this to us!'

When her father spoke, his low voice was like a soothing balm, far below the pitch of her mother's. Rose found herself listening. 'You know the war makes everything uncertain, everything so messy. It's all been magnified. This dashing soldier, of course he's appealing. But by the same token, your feelings for Will . . . surely you regard him. You like him? In such uncertain times—'

Her mother interjected, 'You're a fool to let him go for some fly-by-night squaddie who'll be gone in a few weeks. How long have you known him? A day? A week? You've known Will since you were at school. Will is your future, your life. What are you *thinking?*'

Rose watched aghast as two angry spots of colour tinged her mother's pale, drawn cheeks.

'Mother, with respect,' she said, 'I have done nothing but think about this since . . . since I started at Pengared. It's not so much to do with the man I've just met. It's to do with Will and me—'

'I can't talk to you any more.' Her mother began to scrabble for a hanky, turning her face away, her shoulders slumping. She looked frail. The front of her apron was slack and stained with gravy. Through her sobs, her voice lifted to a wail. 'Is this is how you want to be? Be a fool. Be a silly war bride. Be like those stupid girls hooking up with the GIs. Don't you see . . .' She rounded on Rose, her plate pushed to one side. 'When there's a war on, you need something strong in your life. You can't do much better than Will. He's even bought you that house over at your beloved Pengared, Trelewin, wherever it is! You can take that look off your face, you ungrateful girl.'

Rose found the look in her mother's eyes disturbing.

'Yes, yes,' Mrs Pepper went on, 'we know all about it. He told us. How excited we were for you. Your very own house in the country. When all this is over and the men come home, there won't *be* many left for you to choose from. Think of all the poor girls who have no fiancé, no husband. Think yourself lucky!'

'Oh, Mother, I know I'm lucky.' Rose heard a shrieking edge to her own voice and tried to control it. 'I have a wonderful home here with you and Dad. But don't you see, you have both been plunging on pell-mell with the idea of Will and I getting married. You *love* the idea. It would make *your* wishes come true. But I feel so utterly trapped and helpless. You don't understand. I don't love Will. And if I don't love him,' the shriek returned, 'there's no future.'

'*Love!*' her mother spat the word into her hanky and stood up with a harsh scrape of chair legs over the parquet. '*Love!*' She left the room, her footsteps quickly retreating up the stairs.

Rose's father carefully placed his knife and fork together next to his uneaten food and pushed the plate away. The silence was a barrier. She felt as if all the air had been sucked out of the room. How could her mother be so scathing about her being in love? She peered at her father's face. Did this mean her parents no longer loved each other? Was loving someone the *wrong* thing to do?

Her father cleared his throat, and spoke wearily. 'Your mother is trying to protect you. She thinks the world of Will, and believes he will be right for you. With all the horrors going on these days—'

'Doesn't she want me to be happy?'

'She wants you to be safe and content. Not chasing a dream which, let's face it, could be dashed and broken in an instant.'

'But how could she be so scathing about being in love? Is that it? Is that how it is with her?'

Her father's eyes narrowed. 'Oh, she loves – deeply. She tells me every time the sirens wail that she wishes she did not love us. The *both* of us. Because of the pain.'

Rose felt the hairs on her scalp rising to hear her father speak this way.

'The night you were caught in the raid on Devonport, she knelt on the floor of our shelter and prayed for you. She believed you would be safe with Will, and she was right.'

Rose opened her mouth to interrupt. She wanted her father to know the truth of what happened that night: the truth about the Wren, what Mrs Brown saw on the Hoe, and what happened in the wild darkness outside the Anchor pub. She touched a shaking finger to the scar on her cheek. Then she looked at her father's earnest face and sank back.

His eyes were watery and his hands kept touching his mouth. He said, 'I think your mother's view is that if you don't love, then you won't get hurt.'

'Dad, I can't let this bloody war change my life . . . take over my life . . .'

'But it does. It did for me in the last lot. I came home broken. But when I met your mother, she transformed me.'

'Because she *loved* you.'

She saw a shadow of joy move over her father's face. She brought her hands together over her cheeks, realising then that she was crying. A weary sigh escaped her. 'Oh, Dad, if only you met Krystof . . .'

Her father broke a smile. 'Ah, so he has a name.'

*   *   *

Rose tapped on her parents' bedroom door. 'Mother? Mother? Are you awake? I've brought you a cup of tea. Can I come in?'

On hearing a murmur from inside, she quietly opened the door and stepped into pitch darkness.

'Why have you pulled the blackout?' She moved with care towards the window, just able to make her way by the daylight from the landing behind her. The contrast with the sunny parlour downstairs was acute: the very brightness, thought Rose, that her mother had insisted on for her arrival.

'Shall I open the curtain, or put the lamp on?'

Her mother's voice croaked from the bed. 'Open the curtain. Let in a little sunlight. That's right. I've got such a headache.'

Rose placed the cup and saucer and box of carob on the night-stand and sat gently down beside her mother, who was curled up on top of the candlewick bedspread.

'Did you sleep?'

'A little. What time is it?'

'Just after three.'

Her mother hauled herself up and sat against the headrest. 'What's this?'

'My gift to you, with my first wages. They're not real choc-olate, though.'

'That's lovely.' Her mother's voice was soft now but with an edge of pain. She took a sip of tea.

Rose said, 'I've cleared the plates. The food will keep for tomorrow.' She waited. 'Mother, I'm sorry . . .'

'What's he like then? This brave Czech soldier?' There was a thin smile on her lips. Her hair, as fiery as Rose's own, was dishevelled from lying down. Rose reached forward to gently smooth it over her ears. 'Thank you, dear,' said her mother. 'Do I look a fright?'

'No. Never.'

'That's one thing this war won't do, turn us all into frights and slovens. Now then. Your brave soldier.'

'I can't say he's *mine*, exactly,' Rose said shyly. 'As I told you, we've only had a short time together. Moments, in fact. But meeting him has made me realise that I don't want to be with Will.' She held her mother's stare. 'But I'd love you and Dad to meet him. He is Captain Krystof Novotny, now stationed with the Americans near Polperro.' She felt her voice lift with pride. 'He was in the Czech army, but left when Germany invaded. He managed to get to Poland, but then when the Germans invaded there, he—'

'No, no. Not his potted history,' her mother interrupted. 'I'll hear that another time, from himself, no doubt. I want you to tell me about *Krystof.*'

Rose faltered. What did she really know of Krystof? How could she explain to her mother that when she looked into his eyes, she *recognised* him; that she saw herself there? How could she describe how the briefest of his touches felt as though his body was part of her own? That to see him walking away across the headland, leaving her with Will, was like having knives dragging in her stomach.

She wanted to tell her mother, he is a wonderful sportsman, someone I can trust, someone I can talk to, someone who makes me laugh. But she could not, for she did not know these things. But she *knew* him.

'Mother,' she said, wiping away gentle tears of pleasure, 'I don't know him – I just *feel* . . .'

Her mother leant back against her pillows, her face ashen and her voice croaking when she finally spoke. 'We were blind, I suppose. About Will. We wanted the best for you, our lovely Rose.'

'Oh, Mother.'

'I truly hope you will be happy. I truly hope your captain will make you happy.'

'Will you give me your blessing?'

'I will.'

She bit her lip. 'And Will?'

'Put him out of his misery. Perhaps he will be able to relinquish the house. Perhaps there are ways around it. Maybe he hasn't signed the contract yet?'

Rose flushed with guilt, then hated herself for it.

'He's expected at four,' said her mother.

'I'll feel so much better when I've told him, once and for all.' Rose blew her nose and began to gather her strength together. 'And it will be wonderful that you and Dad will be here to support me.'

'Oh, no, dear,' said her mother, and Rose felt her palms wash with an icy sweat. 'While I shut myself up here in the dark, I decided that your father and I will take a walk to the bowling club. Leave you and Will in peace. Poor man. He needs his privacy at such a time. And to be honest with you, after all this upset, I don't think I can look him in the eye.'

Rose heard Will's knock at the door. As she walked along the parquet, drops of sweat inched down her spine like goading, disappointed fingers. There he stood in shirt, waistcoat and tie, with his trilby shading his eyes, holding a bunch of roses as if he were a matinee idol. Her mouth went dry.

'Ah, Rosebud. Hello, my love,' he beamed. 'May I?' He stepped past her, planting a peck on her check and tucking his hat onto a coat hook, before marching off down the hall, calling, 'Hello, George. Hello, Sylvia.'

'My parents are not at home,' she said, reluctant to close the door now that he was standing in the hallway, filling it up.

'Oh?' He stood looking at her.

'They've gone to the bowling club to meet some friends. Such a nice afternoon, they—'

'So I've got you all alone? Clever little Rosebud.' He moved towards her, proffering the flowers. 'These of course are for you. I can't tell you what lengths I went to, but let's just say I had to pull a few strings. Ask no questions. Roses for my Rosebud.' He cocked his head to wait for praise.

'They're lovely,' she uttered a perfunctory response. 'I'll get a vase.'

'Not just yet.' Will took the flowers back from her and tossed them onto the sofa. He caught her hands, splaying her fingers with his own so that they were intertwined. His fingers were so much bigger than her own. Didn't he realise how much this hurt her? She winced, glancing at the flowers, wanting to busy herself by putting them in water, wanting to do something, anything but this.

His eyes danced over her face and down her body and she cringed under his gaze.

'Now, Rosebud,' he said gravely, 'I have a lot of apologies to make to you. The flowers are just the start of it. It's been a long week. Each day I have longed to see you. Now we can talk properly. I think our little picnic last weekend was not a complete success. Those awful farming folk weren't very welcoming, were they? At last we're on our own.' Will sighed dramatically; he spoke reluctantly. 'I was jealous of your Slovac soldier. No, no. Don't say anything. Can you believe it? The reason why I was jealous is because I love you—'

'Will, I—'

She lifted her eyes to his face while he swung her arms, fingers still linked, in an attempt to be playful. A strange grin fixed his jaw. Fear coiled inside her chest.

'I love you, Rosebud.'

'I'll just make some tea.'

His face dropped and he held up her hand, peering at it in an exaggerated fashion.

'Still no ring?'

'Silly me. I took it off last night for my bath, put it somewhere safe. In my rush this morning, I must have forgotten it. I nearly missed the bus.'

'Silly Rosebud.'

She watched him as a mouse would watch a kitten.

'Did you say something about tea?'

She found she could breathe again. 'Yes, yes. You sit down. Switch on the wireless. Dad has left his paper. Or go in the garden if you like. Mother put out deckchairs.'

'No, I'll help you. I'll put the flowers in water.'

Confused by this uncharacteristic offer to help, she found him a vase in the sideboard and went into the kitchen. Will was right behind her. She quickly gave him the vase and turned to the hob to light a flame under the kettle.

'Forget the flowers,' he said, dumping them on the kitchen table this time, 'it's you I want.'

He stood close behind her, his hands on her hips. She felt his hot breath all over her hair.

'I hope you're pleased with the house,' he whispered. 'We'll arrange for you to look around before long. As soon as you can stop that silly work at the farm, we can be married, make it our home. Just think, Rosebud, I got it for a song. But the real value is so much more, don't you think? The real value is that it is ours.'

'It's rather a large house,' she muttered, flinching her shoulders away from him. She fiddled with the tea cloth, wringing it through her hands. She could not face him. 'Will, I'm not sure. I want to tell you . . . I . . .'

'Such a pretty dress,' he said. 'I always liked you in it. First time I saw you, down at the club, you were such a bright young thing. Sweet sixteen. And now . . . I can't quite believe my luck. Soon to be mine.' He ran his knuckle up her spine and rested it on the nape of her neck. He lifted her hair to plant a kiss behind her ear.

'Stop it! Please, Will. Not now.' She turned to face him, wanting to cry. She'd been flattered by this man, once. This handsome man who'd singled her out.

'Come on, Rosebud, we've made up now. We can put all those things behind us.'

She gritted her teeth. 'Well, I can't put the night of the raid behind us.'

He ignored her. 'Here we are, with the house to ourselves. Don't tell me you didn't plan this. Persuaded your parents to go out, so we could be alone. I knew you'd surprise me one day. Little minx.'

Anger flashed like searchlights from her eyes.

'How dare you say that! It was my parents' idea that they go out because they know I—' She steadied herself. 'They know I have something I wish to say to you.'

'Not the Wren again.' He let out a laboured sigh. 'I thought we'd got over that.' He pressed his thumb to her scar. 'I thought we were even, Rosebud.'

She gritted her teeth. 'Please don't call me that.'

'What does *he* call you then?'

'Who?'

'Your little Slovac.'

'Nothing. He doesn't . . . He's not . . .' She trailed off, biting her lip, looking anywhere but at Will.

'Those country folk,' he said. 'That Meg girl. They all knew, didn't they? They all knew about your fancy man. That's why they looked so shocked to see me. What a fool I am.'

He rested the weight of his hands on her shoulders. Sweat prickled her skin, irritating her. The sun through the kitchen window was strong and the heat from the hob with its simmering kettle intensified.

His voice was distant and formal, like a radio announcement. 'You and me, Rosebud,' he said. 'There's nothing that can beat us. No silly Wren. No silly Slovac. They're both passing fancies. Let's put it all behind us. Let's get married.'

Her head was level with his shoulder, his body loomed over her. Will's strength was like a wall she could not climb. The hot hissing of the kettle was boiling in her temples. She felt rage, a need to defend herself. She wanted to be free.

Why had she once found him so attractive? Why had she agreed to have him take her out? Why had she let it go this far? He broke into his schoolboy smile and dipped his head, looking at her from under his eyelashes. He was trying to be the Will she first knew. Her stomach turned.

She reached up to her shoulders to push his hands away. He resisted and then she saw him look into her eyes.

'You are so cold, Rosebud,' he said. 'I've always thought it. Ice cold. Frigid.'

And then she knew. When she first met Will Bowman, and in the weeks that followed, someone else had inevitably been there, too. Side by side, cracking jokes, clapping hands on backs, digging out the shelter, whistling old tunes, lifts in the car, a drink at a country pub, watching the bowls clicking away on the green. Always there to give her a few more shillings for the picture house, a wink and a time to be home by. And now her father was not here. He'd left her to it and his absence hit her hard. The truth of it was, she had only liked Will in the first place because she associated him with her father.

'Will,' she said, as plain as day, looking up at his grinning, sheepish face, 'I have been trying to tell you for so long. And if I don't get it out now, I'm going to go mad. I do not love you. I am breaking off our engagement once and for all. I want you to leave.'

His eyes narrowed to two pinpricks.

'We've been here before, haven't we?' he leered. 'You tried this in the pub back in January, but I made you see sense.'

'This time, Will, it's real.'

He looked down his nose at her, appraising her as he would a column of numbers in his ledger at the bank.

'Why the sudden change?' He suddenly sounded weaker, like an old man.

She braced herself. 'No change. I have never loved you.'

There was silence. Then a sharp intake of breath. Without a word he picked up the flowers on the kitchen table and thrust them at her, tearing into them in childish frenzy. As she lifted her arms to shield her face from the thorns and stems, he yelled in anger, slung the roses to the floor and crushed them under his heel. She cowered, crouching down as he loomed over her. The kitchen seemed to empty of all sound. He bent down and held her shoulders like a vice, his face close to hers and his tortured, chesty breathing spluttering over her. He held her, possessed her. 'How dare you,' he snarled. 'After everything I have done.'

A sudden shriek pierced the air, like a screaming, scalded cat. He released her and backed away. She slid to the kitchen floor and instinctively curled up, her hands over her ears, trembling with terror as the screaming persisted. 'A raid? A raid?' she whispered through a dishevelled hank of her hair. 'Is it a raid?'

He leant down, pressing his face to hers, using his thumbs to rub away her tears from under her eyes. 'You silly, silly girl.'

She looked into his angry eyes and garnered dignity to hiss at him, 'Get out.'

He walked away, down the hall, slamming the front door behind him like an explosion.

After some moments, she pulled herself up: her body shaking, her limbs shivering and her head still full of the wailing. She collapsed onto the kitchen chair and placed her face flat on the table, feeling cold sweat wash over her scalp.

She gingerly lifted her head to glance towards the hob. There was no raid, there were no bombers. The kettle was just about to blow its top.

She slept in her bedroom, curled up on her eiderdown. Breezes through her window cooled her shocked, exhausted body. When she awoke, she could hear the rattle of the grate. Her parents were home. It was teatime.

Later, she sat in the parlour next to the wireless. The French windows were wide open to the June evening and the dusk light was soft and pure. Her father stood watch for a while, peering up at the darkening sky. All was quiet. Mother put down her knitting and implored him to sit with her. She read a book while Dad flicked through the *Radio Times* and turned to the Light Programme.

'It's that lovely Glenn Miller,' sighed her mother, closing her eyes to listen.

Rose watched the smile relax her mother's tired face and then smiled across at her father. She was veiled by peace, lulled by the radio.

'What a beautiful evening,' she said. 'I wish it would never end.'

'It must, of course,' said her father, catching her eye. 'I'm glad to see you looking so happy. I hope all is well.'

'All is well, Dad.'

She didn't want to say any more. She didn't have to.

Presently, he shut the blackout curtain and lit the lamp. She made her sleepy way to bed, leaving her parents downstairs in the yellow glow of the parlour, amid the clicking of knitting needles and the hum of contented conversation.

Rose fell into bed and hugged her pillow. Outside a gate creaked and a neighbour rattled a bicycle up a path. She thought of her own blossom-covered lane, and valley green with spring. She began to tremble with delight. Utter, unimagined delight. She willed herself back to Pengared, and to Krystof.

Seven

WITHOUT HESITATING, ROSE STOOPED TO BLOSSOM'S GRAZING MOUTH and hooked the leading rein onto the harness. She waited patiently while the horse shook out her mane, stamped her hoof and finished her mouthful.

'Not so much of a *night*-mare now, are you?' she told the horse. 'You old softy.'

Shadows were melting from the corners of the pasture as the short summer night evaporated into dawn. The sun had already slipped above the eastern horizon, making lanky shadows of Blossom's legs, its warmth a prediction of the glorious day to come.

'Walk on, old girl.'

Voices reached her from Betony's meadow as she made her way down the bridleway.

Long grass billowed over a good four acres, sprinkled with a mosaic of buttercups, cow parsley, daisies and the ubiquitous purple betony. Tiny waking butterflies fluttered upwards from the grass and, under the hedge, blackbirds hopped for worms. In the trees around her, birds carolled in little gangs. Over in the corner, Joel was sharing a cigarette with Meg, while Ted, oiling his mowing machine, gave her a welcome salute. As she walked Blossom through the air still holding the cool of the night, she sensed the age of the meadow and she sensed the generations who had been here before her on such summer mornings, ready to make hay.

She helped Meg harness the horse to Ted's cutter, speaking deeply into Blossom's velvety ears, which were pricking this way and that.

'What's she seen, then?' Meg looked over her shoulder. 'Who's the old girl seen? I don't wish to make a bad joke, Ginge, but It's That Man Again.'

'What? Oh, goodness. Krystof.'

He was ambling across the meadow, knee-deep in wavering grasses, sleeves rolled up and army cap tilted to the sun.

Ted called out to him, 'Good of you to help out, Captain Novotny! We need all the hands we can get today, but don't you go distracting any of my workers here.'

Rose felt herself blushing furiously as she caught Krystof's eye and then looked away. She was delighted, and surprised. When she dared to glance back at him, she saw that his shirt showed the outline of his shoulders; shoulders she had already seen naked. She bit her lip. On his arms, hairs were made golden by the rising sun. Suddenly, overwhelmingly, she was shy of him. It had been two weeks since the dance at Polperro, two weeks since their walk to the cove, and so much had changed. She felt her life was starting over. And now that he was unexpectedly here, in Betony's meadow, possibilities opened before her like a long, wide valley. She felt a warmth settle inside.

Meg leant over and whispered in her ear, 'At ease, soldier.'

Krystof smiled, equally shyly, and said to Ted, 'Good morning, sir. I told my commander, haymaking is war work. He gave me a day pass.'

'Good morning.' Meg bounded over to Krystof, all smiles. 'Here, tie this string around your trousers. You too, Ginge.'

Krystof asked, 'What is this for?'

'Stops the mice climbing up your legs,' Meg trilled. 'They're driven mad by the cutter as it gets nearer and nearer them in the long grass. Then, whoop, up they go. A safe haven, so they think. Worse are the rats. Could give you a nasty nip or two.' Meg raced off to have another quick cigarette with Joel.

Catching one another's eye, Rose and Krystof duly bent in unison to tie the string just below their knees. She felt a giggle rise in her chest and glanced at him. His shoulders were shaking as he tried not to laugh, all thumbs as he fumbled with the string.

'Sounds like a Gestapo torture method to me,' she chuckled.

'*Moc to bolí*,' he said.

'Excuse me?'

'It hardly bears thinking about.' They joined with laughter, their eyes connecting.

'Why are the men in shirts and waistcoats?' he asked her sotto

112

voce, struggling to control his mischief. 'Why is Ted wearing a battered old hat?'

'It's the great British way. Ted and his trilby,' she said through a bubble of laughter. 'Well turned out whatever the occasion.'

'I'd better keep my cap on.'

'It's not a competition, Krystof.'

They laughed out loud, their heads close. She felt his fingertips on her arm. 'It's good to see you again, English Rose,' he said.

Ted called, 'Right, you lot! You, Joel, keep Blossom's head straight. Watch her, make sure she keeps a steady line. You three, start raking behind the mower. Meg, your extra task is to keep us all fed and watered.'

'And what will *you* be doing, Ted?' Meg teased.

'Well, I'll be in the driving seat, of course. Like I always am.' He sat himself on the little seat of the cutter perched above the blades between the two spindly wheels and took up the slack on the reins. 'Right, last time for Betony's meadow. Get up there!'

Blossom's harness jangled as she plodded forward and the clack-clacking of the mower began.

Meg handed Krystof and Rose a rake each.

'What did he mean by "last time"?' asked Krystof.

'Orders from the Min of Ag,' said Meg. 'The meadow is to be ploughed for sugar beet or turnip next spring. Need to feed people, more than animals.'

'But it hasn't been ploughed for four hundred years,' said Rose, watching Ted and his machine advancing along the hedgerow.

Meg said, 'Don't get all sentimental, Ginge. There's a war on.'

'What about the cows? They need to be fed.'

'Not if they're dead they won't. Next spring, slaughterhouse for the lot of them.'

On the hillside, Ted's gentle black-and-white cows lowered their heads to pasture. So much was expendable, thought Rose. So much lost. Animals. People. Expendable.

Meg was watching. 'Don't go all misty on me, Ginge. Come on, bend to it.'

Standing alongside Krystof, she did as she was told and began to swing the wide head of the rake over piles of grass that had fallen in the cutter's wake. She relaxed, breathing the

113

green-scented balmy air, while petals from flower heads mown along with the grass clouded her view across the meadow. She absorbed the perfection of the day, caught in a capsule of time, watching Krystof surreptitiously out of the corner of her eye as he concentrated, with serious face, on raking and turning the cuttings. He glanced at her and on they worked together. Every so often inexplicable giggles would rise into the air. Piece by piece, Betony's meadow fell.

'How many days' work do you think, captain?' called Ted from his cutter as he clattered past.

'Two, I'd say.' Krystof stopped to rub his back and flex his fingers.

'You know your farming, sir, don't you?'

'I have a farm in Czechoslovakia!' he called back.

'Need to get a crack on,' cried Ted. 'Won't be many more days like this left.'

Something in Ted's tone made Rose stare after him. 'He doesn't just mean the fair weather, does he?' she said to Krystof. 'He means the end of a way of life. In so many ways.'

'But a new beginning also,' smiled Krystof. 'Change is good, remember.' He came near her and put his hand on her waist. 'Is everything all right, Rose?'

She gazed at his face, nodding slowly, aware of the firm warmth of his hand through her cotton shirt. 'Yes. Indeed it is,' she said.

She was solemn, hoping that he understood. She looked into his eyes, as the air once again filled with chaff and petals. The scent of the earth, the honest work of the day filled her body with satisfying vibrations.

Sensing his sorrow, she said, 'Your farm will still be there.'

'You're right. The Germans still need hay and cattle, so it will be. And one day you will see it, Rose.'

'I'd love to,' she whispered.

His kiss was so light, like a feather on her lips that she barely noticed it but, as she turned back to her rake, she was left with a delicious scooping in her belly.

Meg called out, 'Oi, you two. No slacking!'

Ted reined Blossom in on the stroke of twelve and Meg led her to the shade in the corner so the mare could drink long and hard from the trough. They all rested by the hedge, knowing that Betony was on her way with the lunch pail and a flask of tea. Meg spotted her near the gate. 'Yoo-hoo! Over here! We're parched and starving.' Then she jumped up to attention, shielding her eyes. 'My, my. *Hello*, soldier!'

Rose squinted to see Betony strolling into the meadow cradling a milky-skinned Mo. With her was a man in khaki.

'Dear Christ! It's Hugh!' cried Ted, throwing down his hat and running across the meadow, kicking up chaff along his way. As he greeted his brother in an enormous embrace, they appeared as one silhouette under the sharp sun, joined instantly by Betony and Mo.

'How wonderful,' Rose breathed.

'Indeed it is,' said Meg. 'I wish I had my compact on me. How do I look, Ginge?'

'Fine, Meg,' she said, appraising the wild curls escaping her friend's topknotted scarf and her dungarees cinched tightly in at the waist and clinging to her rounded bottom. 'You're bound to be a hit.'

Meg laughed and licked the corner of her hanky to wipe her face.

Hugh Cumberpatch was a younger version of Ted, a little taller and a little leaner. His face had been tanned by the Tunisian sun, making his smile brighter than anyone else's, yet his eyes looked tired and dazed. He strolled over and saluted Krystof, instantly recognising rank.

'So you're with the Americans, then, sir?'

'For my sins, sergeant,' said Krystof. 'They're a good bunch. A brave lot. Seems like there is a bottomless well of new recruits waiting to swell the ranks. It's good to know you've got that behind you.'

Betony spread the blanket over the mown grass. 'That's enough war talk,' she snapped.

'Sorry, Bet. God, I've missed you.' Hugh hugged her and planted a sloppy kiss on her cheek.

Betony poured tea and began to hand around doorstep sandwiches.

Hugh was fumbling in his top pocket. 'Before I forget. Rose Pepper? You're Rose, aren't you? I have a letter for you. I checked the post box on my way. Old habits and all that.'

She took the letter. It was from her mother.

'I'm Meg Wilson, by the way,' chimed in Meg, leaning forward to shake Hugh's hand. 'That's Meg, experienced land-girl, a real all-rounder.'

Rose slit open the letter. Her mother wrote:

Dad and I are both well . . . Jessica and Martha have started laying again, possibly, Dad says, as a last-ditch plea for clemency . . . Mr Brown has been taken away in an ambulance . . . The runner beans are the best ever . . . Will has visited; he's not himself, fairly distraught. But he's bravely trying to forget you . . .

Rose sighed and glanced over at Krystof sipping his tea and listening to the others' chatter.

Will is a good man. I do hope you will be happy with your soldier.

'Oh, crumbs,' she said out loud, and then smiled across at Krystof's anxious face. She mouthed to him, 'Every-thing-is-all-right.'

Please visit us once the harvest is done with.

She folded the letter away.

Hugh said, 'Midday on the first day, Ted? We'll have to do better than this. I'm going to fetch out my old scythe from the barn. See if I can't help you out a bit.'

Meg squealed, 'I'll come with you,' and, waiting a beat for Hugh to raise an eyebrow, trotted after him. Ted held back until they were both well out of earshot, halfway across the meadow, before saying, 'Well, he has been in North Africa for a year.'

Joel, lazing quietly over by the hedge, began to chuckle and sing, 'One man went to mow, went to mow a meadow.'

At five o'clock, with the sun slanted long and golden across the meadow, Ted surveyed the work.

116

'Good job well done, everybody,' he said.

'I'll finish the last square by hand,' said Hugh, brandishing his scythe.

'Wait a moment,' said Ted. 'My shotgun's propped by the hedge.'

Rose watched while Ted cocked his gun and trained his sights on the edges of the remaining section of standing grass.

'Rabbit pie for supper,' sang Meg, clapping her hands. 'Run, rabbit, run, rabbit run, run, run!'

'We'll take Blossom back,' said Rose. 'She doesn't like the guns.'

Krystof joined her to lead the weary horse up the hill to the pasture.

Here, in the shade of a hazel tree, she unharnessed Blossom and rubbed her sweaty sides with handfuls of grass, while Krystof gazed down at the view, the farm nestling in the crook of the valley, the headland beyond, the cluster of trees and granite crenellations of Trelewin church.

'England slumbers,' he said with a heavy sigh.

Rose let Blossom canter off and watched her dip her long head and fall gracefully to her knees, rolling on her back to scratch away the ghost of the harness, grunting with pleasure Intermittent pop shots from Ted's gun echoed around the hills. Blossom was oblivious but Rose saw Krystof flinch.

He said, 'It doesn't seem right to hear that out here, on such a day. The rabbits, cornered like that. Driven crazy, to certain death. *Muj Boze*, Ruzena! Am I losing my nerve?'

'Not losing your nerve, just being normal.' She scooped her hand into his. 'Would you like to walk to the cove?'

They strolled down the bridleway, hand in hand. The pressing of his flesh against hers was right and good. Her excitement began to bubble.

'What's this place?' he asked, pointing to Cringle Cottage, snug in a fold in the valley. Green mould was encroaching up its once-white walls, helping it blend with the garden around it.

'That's the old gamekeeper's cottage,' she said. 'It's empty. Ted doesn't know what to do with it.'

'Could just do with a bit of care and attention,' said Krystof. 'Would make a lovely place to live in peace time when all this is over. What do you think, Ruzena?'

'Ruzena?' she asked.

'Yes,' he said. 'Everyone else seems to call you anything but your real name so I thought I'd try. Ruzena is Czech for Rose.'

'I like it,' she said.

'Better than Ginge?'

She rested her head on his shoulder. 'Much better.'

As they passed by the house, she said, 'Do you mind awfully if I change? I feel as if I could grow potatoes under my fingernails. I want to stop being a land-girl for a few hours.'

Up in the attic room, she stripped off her work clothes, smelling her own fresh sweat and finding rings of grime round her wrists and ankles and the back of her neck. She took off her scarf and brushed the dust out of her hair. Pouring water into the bowl, she splashed her naked skin to wash away the toils of the day. Outside her window she heard more splashing and saw Krystof holding his head under a torrent of water from the pump.

Clean and refreshed, she put on the dress with the tiny pearl buttons and brushed her hair again until it shone, letting it fall to her shoulders. She eschewed her face powder, preferring the glow of her cheeks and feeling the warmth of a day in the meadow seeping deep into her bones.

Drowsy, but light-footed and a little frisky, she walked by Krystof's side over the headland and down the steep, shady path to Trelewin cove.

They slipped off their shoes and ran barefoot across the baked sand to their rock. They rested in silence, enjoying the peaceful breathing in and out of the waves. Beyond the wire, the water shimmered like a million diamonds.

'You will love Praha – Prague,' said Krystof.

'I will?'

'And Prague will love you.'

'Tell me all about it.'

She got down from the rock and stretched out on the dry sand. It gave way like a feather bed. He joined her and she rested her head against his crooked arm, looking up at the sky. Their fingers entwined and she closed her eyes to listen to his melodious voice.

'Before all of this, before all of this *war*, our country was a beautiful republic. It was a golden era. Such prosperity. We Czechs love our land. It is celebrated everywhere in music and art.' He rested his chin on the top of her head. She listened to him drop his consonants, making his 's's sound like 'v's. 'You think I don't like you with dirty hands,' he chuckled, 'but we Czechs love our land-girls. They appear on posters advertising beer and on biscuit tins, with rosy cheeks, frothing tankards and wheat sheaves.'

She felt him pause to think.

'But now, who knows what's become of them all? I can't bear to think of jackboots tramping through our countryside, tramping across the Old Town Square.'

She gripped his hand and pressed it to her lips.

He said, with bitterness, 'The enemy is too big, too vile for me to deal with on my own. At first I was wild with hope, ready to jump any wire for freedom.' He pointed to the barbed defences on the beach. 'But now, I think, what is the use? So much sacrifice,' he went on, except there was no 'c'. 'So much *sacrif-y*. And what for, Rose?'

Suddenly, she was angry. She lifted her head. 'For you and me, Krystof, and for our families, and our countries. Don't give up. I need you to be strong, and then I can be.'

'Brave Rose,' he said, gazing at her frown. He tried to rub it away with his fingertips and then pushed a strand of hair from her eyes.

Lying close to her, he plucked tiny shells from the sand and rested them in a row along her arm. She gazed down at them: each delicate, fragile shell had a tender pink interior.

'You are not allowed to move, Ruzena, or they will fall off.'

'But you're making me all sandy,' she pretended to complain. 'It's all going up my sleeve.'

'Ah, but when you find the sand later, it will be something to remind you of me.'

'I won't need reminding.'

His kiss found her mouth, and she folded her body against his, breathing deeply, taken aback by the dizzy rushing in her head.

'Goodness,' she breathed.

Krystof gathered her hands together, planting kisses over her face. 'Really?'

'Oh, yes. Really.'

She felt the delicious weight of his body on hers, the delightful brushing of his lips down her neck.

Presently he whispered, 'I can be brave if you are. I can go on, if you can.'

'We'll see it through,' she said.

'We, Ruzena?'

'Yes, we.'

'Are you truly . . .' he dipped his head shyly, '*free*?'

'I am,' she said, understanding him without him having to say another word. 'It's over. I told him.' She smiled at Krystof's happiness. Smiled into his continuous kisses. 'And,' she went on, 'Mother wants me to visit after the harvest. Will you come too? I want you to meet them. I want them to meet you.' She saw his happiness double before her eyes. And then a shadow fell across his face.

He sat up and held her close. 'If I can get a pass, of course I will come. But everything is tightening up. We are to start training. Mock battles on Dartmoor. It's very serious. We are even using live ammunition. It's leading to something, Rose. Even Monty came back to give us a talk. Real rousing stuff. The Yanks cheered their heads off. They're ready for anything. Oh, *Jezu*, I shouldn't be telling you this, but I have to share everything with you. I need to, Ruzena.'

She felt tears sting her eyes. 'Don't tell me, Krystof, I don't want to know.'

She sat up and let him rest his head on her lap, holding his head with her hands, pushing her fingers into his hair. When he gazed up at her, she saw herself reflected in his eyes. She saw her life in those grey depths, everything her life was going to be.

'Time is pressing,' Krystof said, reluctance dragging his words. 'Time I was back at base.'

They stopped at the gate to the farm, watching Mutt and Jeff bounding over to greet them.

With a catch in her voice, she asked, 'When will we see each other again?'

'Soon. I'll tell my commander that there's a harvest to bring home. Although, as I said earlier . . . it will be more and more difficult . . .'

She pressed a finger over his mouth. 'Don't speak. I don't want bad news.'

He wrapped his arms around her and she felt his heart beating. They held onto each other. There was no need to speak.

Eventually he glanced over her shoulder. 'I know you don't want to hear bad news, so do you want to hear something funny instead?'

She pulled back to look at his face. He was grinning.

'Always,' she said.

'Look behind you.'

She started to giggle. Across the yard, Hugh was gingerly opening the barn door. Glancing left and right, he gesticulated into the darkness behind him. Out came Meg, tugging at her trouser belt buckle, tufts of straw clinging treacherously to her curls. They both trotted off in different directions.

'Oh, Meg Wilson,' tutted Rose.

Krystof laughed. 'Oh, Sergeant Cumberpatch.'

Eight

ROSE WAS WRAPPING UP THE FIRST CROP OF APPLES IN NEWSPAPER and arranging them in rows on the shelves inside the shed, when she heard – and felt – the rumbling. The ground beneath her feet vibrated and the misted pane of glass in the shed window rattled. Even the onions hanging from the rafters overhead quivered on their strings. Ducking outside into the yard, she spotted a convoy of heavy khaki trucks, their canvas roofs flapping, swaying along the top road.

'If I'm not wrong that's Fourth Division, Ginge,' called out Ted, leaning on his pitchfork by a pile of hay outside the barn. 'On manoeuvres, as they say. Wonder where they're off to?'

She squinted to the brow of the hill, seeing the familiar US army star on the door of a truck.

'I wonder,' she said, shielding her eyes from the low September sun. She swallowed hard. What about Krystof's division? A coil of fear plummeted through her, turning her feet cold. She shivered, even though the farmyard was warmed by golden slanting light.

She and Krystof had barely seen each other since the day of the haymaking; just snatched, precious moments over a long, hard summer of toil. This bothered her and her mother's words echoed: 'Fly-by-night squaddie.' But Rose resolutely ignored them. Tomorrow they were going to spend the day at home with her parents; and then her mother would see how it really was.

Rose turned her puzzled face to Ted. 'I wonder what's going on?'

'Perhaps this man can tell us,' said Ted, looking behind her.

Silhouetted against the sunlight was a familiar figure, scaling the farmyard gate.

'Krystof!' she cried, running over to him. She hugged him, pressing her face into his uniform. 'You're a day early. *Tomorrow.*

My day off is tomorrow. Did you get the day wrong? They're expecting us then. I doubt Ted will let me go today, there's too much work to do. He needs some bales of straw hauled to the top pasture and Betony wants me to help her with the plums . . .' She stopped when she glanced up and read his eyes. 'What, Krystof? What is it?'

He would not look at her. 'I have eighteen hours.'

'Until what?' Her voice gurgled in her throat.

'Until I go. The leave I had authorised for tomorrow has now been brought forward to today. Today is my embarkation leave.' He glanced up at the line of army traffic on the horizon. 'It is us next. This is it.'

She had no idea she was crying until she felt his fingertips gently wipe away her tears. The time had come, the time her mother had warned her about. She looked Krystof square in the face but he avoided her eyes again, glancing at Ted and back at the brow of the hill. She held his chin with her hand and drew him towards her.

'I told you I didn't want bad news,' she said evenly.

She heard a footstep behind her.

'Ted?' she asked, turning to face her employer.

'Don't even ask me,' he said. 'Just go.'

Krystof had parked his staff car on the top road and so she hiked with him up the track in silence, clasping his hand as if she never wanted to let it go.

'Come on, Ruzena. I'll take you for a spin.' He tried to sound cheery, but she heard a new tone in his voice.

The main road was congested with army traffic so they motored down the twisting tunnel of back lanes to Polperro. Raucous squaddies packed the village pub, drinking away their last day. Krystof went in on his own and brought their shandies out to the sea wall where they had first met. They sat with their back to the sun-warm granite and listened to the slap of the waves below them. She tasted her drink and it was bitter.

'We can have some ice cream soon,' he said.

'I don't want ice cream.'

Presently, he said, 'Perhaps some cockles with vinegar instead. I tried them once. Didn't like them, but if you want them, we can have them.'

'Krystof, I don't want cockles.'

Rose bristled, feeling a torrid mix of despair and frustration grinding through her head. She fixed her jaw and tried to ignore it, but with each moment that passed, she felt her spirits weaken. Each moment was wasted. Each moment took them closer to his departure.

Krystof sighed deeply, gazing around the busy little harbour. 'That's where I watched you walk down. That's where I saw your flaming hair and your neat dress and your rather wonderful ankles. That's where I saw your cross little face and flashing green eyes. This is where it all began,' he said. 'But, Rose . . . No, look at me, I said look at me. This is not where it ends.'

She glared at him, then admitted, 'Krystof, I'm scared.'

'It is a shame that I cannot meet your parents tomorrow,' he said. 'I have to leave at dawn.'

'Well, I'm not going home now,' she snapped. 'Ted won't give me more time off.'

'Surely he will let you have one more day. Oh, Rose, they're expecting you.'

'I can't go.'

'You haven't seen them in months.'

'I really can't go.'

'Are you sure, Rose?'

'I don't want to go. They'll say . . . *I told you so*. There – it's horrible, but they will. I'll have to tell them you've gone. I can't bear it.'

'Wire them, at least,' he said, reluctantly. 'Tell them you can't get the time off. They'll understand. The post office is at the top of the hill.'

'I'll tell them it's war work. Not that I swapped my day off to spend it with you. They wouldn't understand.'

'Your parents are still unhappy about you breaking it off with Will.'

'I really don't want to talk about it.'

They fell silent in mutual misery.

'This was not a good idea, coming here to Polperro,' muttered Krystof, looking around him. 'It's too crowded. I want to get away from all these people.'

'They've all got the same idea,' she said, her voice jaded and sad. 'They're all snatching their moments. Look, there's that girl. What's her name? Mabel. She's with a squaddie boyfriend, looks like.'

She pointed out Mabel Cole, the girl from the dance, who was sitting in the beer garden, her bright yellow hair glowing in the sunlight amongst a sea of khaki.

'Oh!' said Krystof, peering over. 'She's with Vaclav. He's in my company. He's from Moravia. Hey, Vaclav!'

The soldier looked over and waved and Mabel, on seeing Rose, gave a giggling salute, clutching his arm.

'Isn't it so sad,' she squealed. 'They're all going.'

Rose looked at Krystof. She whispered, 'I can't bear it here. I just want us to be alone.'

'We both know where we want to be,' he said. 'Let's go back to the cove.'

She popped into the post office and quickly sent a telegram home, trying to explain, but knowing the short, sharp words would hurt them.

'I'll go home soon,' she promised herself. 'I'll make it up to them.'

They lay on his jacket on the sand by their rock and she rested her head in the crook of his arm.

'How many times have we actually seen each other, I wonder?' he asked.

'Not that many,' she said, wistfully counting them off on her fingers. 'The first time at the harbour, then at the cove, the haymaking . . . there was that time when I was cycling into Polperro on an errand for Betony and your company marched past. I nearly rode into the hedge to get out of the way. I didn't dare look for you in case I got you into trouble.'

'Oh, I saw you,' he said, caressing her neck. 'I saw you wobbling off down the lane.'

'And there was a time during the harvest. I was on the back of Ted's truck and your staff car zipped by on the other side of the hedge.' She remembered how her back muscles had been fizzing, her shoulders burning in the sun and how her stomach clenched with desire when she saw the merest glimpse of the back of his head.

'I don't remember that. I am sorry. That is one time I have missed. I am so sorry. Ruzena, Rose. So sorry.'

He spoke into her mouth, punctuating his words with kisses. She tasted her own tears. His arms formed a shield around her but, even so, the dangerous outside world kept crashing into her thoughts. Her throat quivered with suppressed rage as she looked up at his face.

It was chilly now at the cove. The wind was rising. Drops of blown rain and sea spray peppered the sand and yet the sun still cast a mellow light, making sharp shadows of the rocks and cliffs.

'Summer is over,' she said. 'Our glorious summer is over.'

'This should be a beautiful time,' said Krystof. 'September – our *Zárí* – is "the month that glows with colour". Did you notice the leaves in the hedgerows? How they are beginning to turn? How the sun shines across the land?'

'The way you speak, it's so beautiful,' she said. 'But I want it to be summer again. Not September, the autumn. Always our summer. Always.'

He held her tightly and pressed his face to her neck. She felt his warm tears soak into her collar.

'How can this be?' he asked, his voice muffled and broken. 'How can this war be like this when you are here with me. And I am here with you. I love you, Rose. I cannot leave you.'

She shuffled around so she could look at him, holding his lovely face in her hands, feeling her own strength rise as his faded. 'Krystof, you won't leave me. You'll never leave my side. Not while you are loved by me.'

'How can I go out there and shoot a man dead?' he cried. 'I can't do that when I have held something as beautiful as you like this in my arms.'

In her head, her voice said, *but you will have to*.

She stopped him speaking with a kiss that took her own breath away.

'I love you, Krystof,' she said when at last he allowed her to pull away, 'and I will wait for you. I will wait for that day when you come strolling back to Pengared Farm, and climb over that silly locked gate, with Mutt and Jeff yapping around your ankles. I will be waiting.'

* * *

The sun was sinking into an inky sea as they made their way back up to the farm. Over the headland, gulls began to roost, their cries absorbed by the swelling sound of the waves. The blackout was already down in Trelewin.

'Five times,' he said to her as they reached the stile. He hopped over and turned to help her, his hands firm on her waist. 'I can't believe it, Ruzena. I have only seen you five times. And I feel like *this*? What an incredible notion. Sorry, that didn't sound how I wanted it to. My words aren't working properly. I don't know what to say. Or how to say it.'

She sat on the top rung of the stile and gazed down at his face. A surge of courage pulsed through her veins.

'It's hard for me to find the words, too,' she said, 'but the fifth time isn't over yet. I want to be alone with you, tonight. We still have the night. You don't have to be back at base till dawn.'

'Oh, Ruzena . . . are you sure?'

They strolled back along the rutted track. 'I want to tell you something. Will once invited me up to London, and suggested we stay at the Ritz. I was horrified, worried what my parents would think. And, quite frankly, it turned my stomach.'

She glanced at his puzzled face.

'It made me feel sick.'

'Ah, I see.'

'But now, my God, with you it is a whole new world, a whole new feeling. To be honest, I don't care any more what my parents think about you and me. And I wish we could have the Ritz.'

They reached the gate and began to climb over, their shoes snuffled by the excitable dogs.

'But, Krystof, what I am trying to say is, we have the barn,' she said.

He stopped her, holding both her hands. 'Ruzena, I wish I could offer you more than the barn. I mean . . . Hugh and Meg . . .'

'But it doesn't matter to me.'

'Do you think we will get straw in our hair?' he asked.

They laughed gently, leaning forward to touch foreheads.

'Wait here a moment,' she said. 'I need to fetch something from the house.'

Rose went upstairs and pulled the blanket from her bed.

Downstairs in the kitchen she wrapped bread and cheese in a tea towel and cut a large slice of apple pie. Betony, making her first batch of jam with plums from the orchard, watched her in silence. Mo gurgled from his high chair.

'Take this,' said Betony, handing Rose a bottle of her elderberry wine.

'Are you sure?'

'Are *you* sure?'

Rose told her, 'Never been more so in my whole life.'

She found Krystof waiting for her in the hayloft high up under the rafters where the last of the sun spun threads of gold through gaps in the roof tiles. She trod the precarious rungs of the ladder, gripping her wrapped bundle of food with her teeth. He bent down and relieved her of it, smiling in the honey-warm light. In one swift movement he lifted her and settled her on her feet on the dusty boards. She breathed the earthy fragrance of grain and wood, the freshness of new hay, and the scent of Krystof's skin. She left him to open the bundle while she began to arrange some straw bales and covered them with the blanket.

He watched her closely for a moment, then cleared his throat. 'Ruzena, we will not be lovers tonight,' he said.

She paused and glanced round. His face in the shadows was soft with love and an unusually deep contentment settled within her. She knew he was right, and it pleased her.

He went on. 'I don't want us to be like Hugh and Meg. I want it to be right. I think we should wait. I think we should be married.'

'Married?'

She knelt down and carefully laid out the bread and cheese, the pie.

'What are you thinking? What do you say to that, Rose?'

Her hands shook as she pulled the cork from the wine. 'I am lost for words. It's like a dream.'

'But do you want to?' He sounded worried, his voice edged with pain.

Rose sat close to him, cross-legged on the floor. 'More than you'll ever know,' she whispered, her heart pounding. 'I am finding it hard to cope with this. It's like all the best things and all the worst things rolled into one. And on top of it all, the world outside is conspiring against us. Dedicated to keeping us apart.' She took a deep breath. 'But I say, damn it all. Let's drink to us.'

He took a swig from the bottle and then handed it to her. '*Na zdraví*. Cheers, my Rose.'

'You need to ask my father's permission,' she said, relishing the sweet wine as it warmed her inside. 'If we want it to be right *and* proper.'

'Can we use Ted's telephone?'

'Oh, the line isn't working. It's been down for days,' she said in frustration. 'Nothing is ever straightforward, is it? But when I next go home – soon, I hope, I'll tell them the news. Can we get a special licence? What do people do in these circumstances? It must happen all the time these days. Can you get special leave?'

'You told me to tell you no bad news,' he said, 'so I cannot answer your questions. But I will try my best to get something arranged.'

She whispered. 'I can't believe you won't be here tomorrow.'

'I'll be *somewhere*,' he whispered back. 'Dartmoor or Salisbury Plain . . . but always with you.'

In silence, in the warm loft, fragrant with hay, they drank the sweet wine and ate the bread and cheese. They sat facing each other under the low sloping ceiling and when the bottle was finished, the laughter began. She felt low, slow giggles rising from her belly and out through her mouth in a steady stream. And when her tears began to flow, he stopped them with a look. Tears were replaced by more laughter, deeper and warmer than before.

As chilly midnight approached, she grew tired and sank into the hay bed next to his warm body.

'I can hear stars singing,' she whispered sleepily.

She entwined her fingers into his, marvelling that his little finger was the same size as her ring finger.

'We will watch the stars in Czechoslovakia. The night skies are clear and wide on my farm,' he told her. 'I will take you there. You will meet my cows, horses, my family.' He pushed her hair behind her ears. 'How are you going to manage, leaving your parents behind?'

She thought of her home, her parlour, her parents sitting alone; she wrapped up that image and stowed it away.

'But *we* will be a family,' she murmured.

Gradually the night shadows shifted and a grey dawn crept over them.

She slept for just one hour inside his arms; a twitchy, nervous sleep. She felt his lips pressed to her forehead the whole time, his arms like a great cradle.

And then, as the sun inevitably rose, he pulled himself away from her. With no word, he put on his boots and jacket. He was being ripped from her. She tried her best to smile through the silent tears raining down her cheeks.

As he lowered himself down the ladder, she stared with disbelieving eyes at the sight of his face, his eyes soft with adoration, disappearing below the edge of the loft floor.

Nine

THE COLD WOKE HER. SHE DID NOT HEAR THE SIREN WAILING OVER the headland from Trelewin; it only reached them at Pengared if the wind blew in their direction. Her dream had been of Krystof: he was walking away from her in silence with autumn leaves falling around his face. And all she kept saying was that she wished it was summer.

A month had passed since he left, and she'd had one letter. He could tell her nothing of where he was, or what he was doing. His voice, his words, were utterly miserable. The letter was short, but laced through with love. Whole sentences were blocked out by the censor's pen. She had cried when she read it, great fat tears of frustration. Now she stood in Meg's shoes; now she knew what it felt like to have someone 'out there' amid the excruciating uncertainty and looming danger. How could she possibly bear this? Her mother was right about not wanting to love. It hurt too much.

She shivered on the landing with Meg, staring out of the window into the night. The horizon towards Plymouth was red with flame. Meg put her arm round her shoulder.

'Come on, Ginge, it will be fine. Let's get to the cellar and make Ted heat us some warm milk.'

Huddled in the darkness, Rose imagined her parents sheltering in their Anderson and a twinge of guilt twisted her gut. She still had not been to visit them. With the end of the harvest, work was frantic on the farm and Ted could not spare her. The last free day she'd had she had spent with Krystof; that precious day filled her waking hours and haunted her dreams.

In the morning, dazed and sleepy, she sat at the kitchen table to sip her cup of tea. She thought about the day ahead and felt weary: she had to see to the hens, turn the apples in storage, sweep the yard; she might give Betony a hand with making plum jam using their combined sugar rations.

Each raid became more difficult to bear and she felt her spirit washing away from her bones. When would it ever end? When would she see Krystof again? What was he having for breakfast? What was *his* day going to hold for him? She reached for another slice of toast, hoping it would give her strength.

'Oh, my goodness,' Betony exclaimed, stopping by the trapdoor to the cellar. She bent down to pick something up. 'Goodness gracious.'

Rose turned to catch sight of her engagement ring held delicately aloft between Betony's fingertips.

'You've found it?' She was aghast. 'Good God!'

'It was there, stuck between the floorboards all the time, Ginge. Well, I never.'

Betony handed her the ring, then turned towards the sound of rattling bicycle tyres along the track. Rose, fearfully following her gaze to the kitchen window, wrung her hands together. On reflex, she slipped the ring onto her finger.

In the yard Ted called out, 'Ho there!' and then Rose heard his long strides across the yard. There was a snatch of conversation between farmer and messenger. Betony kept herself pressed against the table; Mo was banging a spoon on his high chair and Meg was still upstairs, so Rose felt it was her duty to go to the back door, open it and ask Ted who the telegram was for.

She stood on the kitchen step, feeling the chill of the October morning on her hands and the tip of her nose. Ted was walking towards her, his face unreadable, his eyes like two pinpricks of darkness in an ashen face, concealing what he knew was typed on that flimsy strip of paper in his hand.

'What, Ted?' she asked. 'What is it?'

He kept on walking towards her, and when he reached her, he stretched out his hand. She felt his palm on the back of her neck, cupping the base of her skull.

'What, Ted?'

'You know a Mrs Brown?'

'Yes, yes, the corner shop. Oh, dear. Poor Mr Brown. Has he finally succumbed?'

'I don't know about that, Rose.'

She flinched in shock and fixed her eyes on Ted. *Rose?* He'd called her Rose.

Betony was at her elbow. 'Get her inside.'

She let herself be led back into the kitchen, and she allowed them to seat her at the table.

'Oh, dear, Rose,' Ted sighed.

Misunderstanding and suddenly irritated, Rose snatched the telegram from his hand and unfolded it. *House destroyed. Stop. Come home. Stop. Marion Brown. Stop.*

Rose folded her hands around her waist and rocked back and forth. 'Whatever does she mean, the silly woman,' she said. 'I wouldn't describe it as a house. It's a shop with a flat above. More a maisonette, I would say. Why does she want me to go home? Has something happened to Mr Brown? Has he actually *died* this time?'

She looked up at Ted and Betony. They stood over her, their hands on her shoulders. She asked them, 'But why would Mrs Brown want me to go . . . ?'

She felt her face stretching and tingling, as if a mask was being laid over it to shield her from the two faces that filled her view; their twisted brows and watery, staring eyes.

'Oh, Ginge,' whispered Betony, 'you need to go home.'

'But why should I? I don't want to. I want to stay here with you. I have to see to the hens, sweep the yard. Ted, you've got to let me sweep the yard. I must do that. I must. I can't go home. I can't go. Not now.'

She bent her head and stared at her lap. Her fingers twisted inside and out, tangling themselves. Her ring dug into her flesh. It seemed strange to be wearing it after so long. And yet the ring took her back to a time when she was engaged to Will Bowman; back to a time when her flesh wasn't churning with sickening horror; when panic wasn't rising like cold vomit in her throat; when the ground wasn't rocking under her feet.

Meg's anguished face appeared suddenly close to hers. 'Come with me. We'll pack a few things.'

Rose let herself be guided like a child up the stairs. She sat on her bed, staring, her mouth agape, as Meg rummaged in her drawers.

'Do you want this jumper? These socks?'

'I can't do it.'

'These knickers? Where's your hairbrush?'

'I can't do it.'

Meg looked at her, aghast.

Rose said, 'I don't want to pack. I don't need anything. I don't care. Why would I need a hairbrush?'

Downstairs, Ted was pacing the kitchen, his face white.

'Petrol's run out. I am so sorry. I've used the last can. I can't even take you as far as Trelewin.'

Meg took her hand. 'Come on, I'll come with you to the bus stop.'

Rose shook herself free and reached for a jar of Betony's plum jam from the dresser. Meg looked at her, puzzled. Rose told her, 'I promised Mother I'd take some home.'

Ted ran his hand over his face and through his hair; Betony stared but said nothing, burying her face against Mo's soft cheek.

Fallen leaves were scattered in the bus's wake as it picked up speed along the top road. Jack Thimble eased himself down the gangway towards Rose, his face set and surly. She rummaged in her purse for a shilling to find she only had a five-pound note. She proffered it with a shaking hand, knowing he got cross when passengers did not have the right change. He scrutinised her face, his eyes narrowing. When he did not respond, she pulled out the jar of jam from her bag and offered him that instead.

He shook his head, reeling off her ticket anyway, keeping his puzzled eyes fixed on hers. And then he seemed to understand. He reached into his breast pocket, pulled out a silver flask of brandy and offered her a nip.

Everything was normal. Stanley Crescent curved ahead of her, the houses neat and homely. On the road there was a scattering of shrapnel over which two schoolboys were picking for souvenirs – this was usual on any day of the week. Rose felt a blinding rush of relief as she stopped outside her house; relief that made her knees buckle. Mrs Brown was losing her marbles, just like her poor husband. Her home wasn't destroyed. It looked absolutely fine.

The police rope around her garden wall was fluttering in the wind. She walked straight through it, plucking at it and tossing it aside. From the pavement behind her, she heard a know-it-all voice shout, 'You can't go in there, love. It's too dangerous. ARP has cordoned it off for a reason, you know! Oi!'

There was something different, however, about the front door: it had sunk a little into the ground. And the window with the ship in full sail had a great crack through it. She felt an unsteadiness in her stomach, like sea-sickness. An instinct told her to use the side gate and go round the back.

As she reached the end of the passage by the garage she sensed a strange smell: a smouldering; a damp rotting; something bad. Her mother's enamel colander lay in the vegetable patch alongside a dented tin of milk, discarded among her father's charred cabbages. It was as if the soil was belching out random bits of rubbish. The chicken coop was a tangle of wire and singed straw; she spotted the brown corpse of a hen, feathers lifted by the breeze.

She stood still, pondering over what she saw, what was left of the garden, not able to take it in. Then she glanced at the house. The back of it was missing. It looked like a doll's house with the walls folded back, all ready for a little girl to play. She almost smiled; except what little girl would want to? Under the gutted roof, the bath was suspended and water spurted from broken pipes. The black and white bathroom tiles looked as pristine as ever and yet the wall they were attached to was bulging like a distended stomach. Her parents' bed was shattered into sticks, lying on the parlour floor; pages of the *Radio Times* flicked over and over, as if being read by the wind. Every single object was coated in thick grey dust. Like ashes, she thought. Her eyes widened as she stared into the wreck of her home; the jar of Betony's jam that she'd been clutching for her entire journey slipped from her hands and smashed onto the ground.

'What a waste,' she trembled, staring at the sticky, oozing mess that had splattered her shoes. 'What an utter waste.'

She looked up, expecting her parents to walk out of the rubble of the back parlour and tell her not to squander good food. To tell her everything was all right.

'Come on, Dad,' she whispered, her throat beginning to clamp tight in agony. 'Come on, Mother, I'm here now.'

A crater gaped open where the Anderson had once stood. The twisted corrugated-iron roof fanned out from it like the petals of a bizarre flower. Her shoulders stiffened as she stepped tentatively over what was once her garden, the place she used to play. *It's all right,* said her father, *we have our Anderson.*

In the pit lay one of her mother's shoes: brown with a stacked heel and a polka-dot bow. It was her best shoe, and looked as good as new. They must have been at a party for the evening, coming home for cocoa and a bedtime programme on the wireless. They must have dashed out here when the siren blared.

Around her, leaves fell, stripped from the trees in her neighbours' gardens. She tilted her head to look at the sky and wished it would blow away. She wished that the sun had not risen, that this day had not happened.

She was lost and alone; her world was broken. Her childhood gone. The little girl who would play with the doll's house no longer existed. She wanted to throw herself into the pit and find her parents; find her life again. Her body began to shake as if it was being sawn in two.

There was a voice behind her, by the garage: 'Like I said, I told her.'

Then someone called out, 'Oi! You shouldn't be here, miss!'

She turned to glare at them. 'I don't care what you say,' she screamed. 'This is my home. This is my parents' house. Get off my property.'

There were two men, both in some sort of uniform. But then, she thought, these days everyone wore a uniform.

One of them said, 'It's not safe, love. You have to leave. If you'd just come with us, someone will make you a cup of tea.'

'Tea? Tea! Did you hear what I said,' she hissed, her teeth clenched. Her eyes misted over. 'Get out!'

Another man stepped forward. 'Leave this to me, Reg.'

This person came close to her and, through her half-blind, confused eyes, his frame seemed familiar.

'Dad?' she said.

'Oh, Rosebud.'

She let him come near her; she let him stand close. His wide shoulders in black overalls seemed to shield her. His arm went around her, ducking her face away from the worst of it. She looked up into Will's eyes. They were bright with shock.

He said, 'We took your parents away this morning. I am so sorry.'

'But where are they? I want to see them.'

'It's best you don't.'

'I was supposed to come home . . . weeks ago . . . after the harvest . . . before . . . But I didn't, and . . .'

How quiet it was in her garden. As Will held her, she watched each leaf as it fell, innocently, twirling to the ground.

She began to cry, and pieces of herself started to break off. Parts of her life were scattered all over the ragged bombsite. She tried to breathe. She couldn't believe her heart was still pumping. Why was she still alive? And why was her blood moving in the wrong direction?

Clutching her mother's shoe, she kept her eyes on Will's sleeve, assimilating his presence as something she was used to; something from her past.

'We need to leave now, Rosebud,' he said. 'Let the authorities deal with it.'

She concentrated on his nickname for her. How in the past it would irritate her. Now it was all she could do to keep herself together and to be able to put one foot in front of the other.

She heard her own voice as if through fog. 'Will, wait.'

Picking her way back to the pit, she pulled out her mother's other shoe. Will took off his coat and put it round her. She let herself be led through the gate and back to the street.

A woman in glasses and headscarf appeared, and it was many frozen moments before she realised it was Mrs Brown.

She heard her say, 'Darling Rosie. What a dreadful shock. Will you come home with me? I have a spare bed now Mr Brown's in hospital. Come on, lovey. You need a brandy.'

And she heard Will say, 'She's coming home with me.'

And 'Oh!' from Mrs Brown.

But she wasn't listening. She was shattered, empty of all thought or feeling. When Mrs Brown put her concerned face into her line of vision, she simply copied Will: 'I'm going home with him.'

His Ford was waiting, gleaming at the side of the road. He settled her into the passenger seat. She heard disembodied voices through the window.

'At least give me your address, Mr Bowman, so I can keep in touch.'

'Rose will be in contact with you, no doubt, when she feels able.'

'Well, she knows where I am. Poor love.'

'Thanks for your concern, good day.'

When he got into the car beside her and pressed the starter switch, Rose's senses filled with memory: happy motoring, trips to the picture house.

'I'll take you back to mine, Rosebud,' he said.

She could not answer him; she could look neither left nor right.

As the Ford pulled away, a khaki car drew up behind it and a figure jumped out, waving frantically.

Will glanced in his rear-view mirror. 'I see the army is here. Perhaps there's an unexploded bomb,' he muttered, crashing up into second gear.

How could she possibly comment? Hot tears spilled from her eyes and streamed down her face. Her head was churning, trying to stop the dreadful thoughts, the awful truth from reaching her consciousness. She could barely hear what Will was saying, or indeed see where she was going.

Will's bachelor maisonette had one gas ring, tatty curtains and a smell of damp, but Rose had never seen anything as welcoming as the single bed in the narrow brown bedroom. She'd never felt anything as soft and supporting as she slumped onto it, her head against the clammy pillow, and as Will lifted her legs from the floor to the bed. She longed for sleep, for obliteration. He pulled off her shoes and let them clump onto the floor. He held a glass of brandy to her lips and she took a nip, the fumes stinging her nose.

'Second one today,' she said, and had no clue why.

He pulled up a patched eiderdown that smelt of mothballs and folded it over her shoulders.

When she opened her eyes it was dark. She'd woken in the

same position she'd fallen asleep in: curled up and stiff. She began to shiver. The blackout was down; she had no idea what the time was. The door to the room was ajar and a triangle of light slanted across the lino.

She heard the striking of a match against its box and thought that she was home and that Mother was lighting the ring under the kettle. And then, reality. She unfurled her legs and shuffled to the door.

Will was sitting in his armchair by the gas fire, under the dim 40-watt bulb. He was smoking and reading; the radiogram babbled in the corner. The cigarette was a Player. Her father smoked them, but only outside and only when her mother was out. She closed her eyes to hear her father say, 'Put that damned cigarette out, boy. Sylvia's home. You'll get us both into trouble.'

Will looked up and closed his book, turning the cover away from her. He switched off the radio.

'Ah, Rosebud. You've surfaced. Just listening in on the Krauts,' he said. 'Tea? Toast?'

He moved towards her, head cocked on one side, which she read as sympathy. He put his arms round her and she wondered how she'd got there.

'How are you feeling?'

'Cold,' she managed, 'so desperately cold.'

He told her to sit by the fire while he sliced bread in the kitchen. She didn't want to sit so she tried to follow him but the kitchen was too small for them both. He sent her back out, giving her the job of toasting bread in front of the gas flame while he poured the tea.

Squatting in the half-light, on the rag rug, she noticed the book cover was in German in a black gothic typeface. She held the toast as steadily as she could, feeling detached, as if she was watching herself in a film.

'Here we are, Rosebud.' He gave her a cup of tea, made her sit in the armchair and began to spread marge on the toast.

She took tentative sips as he stared at the ring on her finger. She saw a settling of satisfaction on his face.

'I knew it, Rosebud, I knew we couldn't be parted for long. I can't tell you how wonderful it is to see you wearing my ring. That silly argument we had, all that shouting. I never knew you had it in you. But I'm learning about you. From now on, we'll build on it. It's all in the past now.'

He sat on the floor by her feet and passed her a slice of toast, which she numbly munched. Reaching for her hand, he turned the ring on her finger.

'And now *that's* back in its rightful place. And so are you.'

A memory made her pull her fingers away from him.

He looked her over. 'Time you went to sleep again. Shock does that to a person. It's nearly midnight anyway. You need to sleep.'

She felt the cold reach her belly where it squatted; her insides began to shiver. 'If there's another raid,' she said, her mouth dry, 'leave me here.'

'Don't be silly, Rosebud. Oh, you are in dreadful shock.'

The reflection in Will's shaving mirror was not the girl, Rose, but a woman she did not recognise. She had grey skin and eyes wide with an agony that she had yet to understand.

She splashed water on her face but this merely reminded her that she was still alive, and cold. She dressed in his pyjamas, rolling up the legs and sleeves so that they fitted.

He was arranging a pillow and blanket on the sofa, wearing a pair of pyjamas identical to hers. In another life she might have laughed at the sight of them both dressed the same.

Instead, she asked, 'What are you doing?'

'I'm tired too, Rosebud. I'm turning in.'

'Will you sleep in there with me?'

He froze and looked at her, a brief shadow of triumph crossing his face.

'Whatever you want, Rosebud.'

'But leave the light on out here.'

'You well know that's wasteful. As an ARP I must warn you. My governor would say—'

'Please leave it on,' she snapped.

She lay in the narrow bed, facing the wallpaper, and peered at the swirled pattern with the attention of a cat and with eyes dry and wide open. She made herself small and allowed Will to move in behind her, his body like a dam that would prevent her spilling out of the bed, and out of herself. He made a warm prison for her. His hand found hers, drawn as always to the ring on her finger.

'I am so sorry about your parents,' he said. There was a crack in his voice; an emotion she had not heard from him before.

'Please, don't talk,' she said.

Suddenly, Krystof was holding her hand. He was laughing and singing, surrounded by sunshine with hay in his hair. She felt a smile stretch her face. In the next breath, it fell away. The summer was over. Krystof had left her, walking away through falling leaves. Gone to war. Lost to the great, vast war. And this . . . This is the life she had expected, what her parents had always wanted. In Will's bed. Will taking care of her.

Water was gurgling in a pipe somewhere and the bedside clock ticked too fast. Will's asthmatic breathing was laboured and hot in her ear. She wanted to block it out and remove it all. But then what? There was simply nothing else.

She turned her head to the sound of the breathing. She kissed him. She shuffled her body round to face him, hearing his grunt of surprise. He was soon finished with kissing. As he entered her, the pain blinded her to everything. It eliminated her life and all that had happened to her. And for that moment, and all the quick moments that followed, she felt no other pain. It was like mercy.

It was over, and he released her.

'I knew it, Rosebud,' he whispered to her in the semi-darkness. 'I knew you'd one day be mine.'

Ten

IN THE DULL MORNING LIGHT, WILL SAT BY THE RADIOGRAM IN HIS shirtsleeves with his tie draped loose around his collar. He ate toast with his mouth open, slurping his tea. Rose stood watching him from the bedroom door. She felt empty: no emotion, no spirit.

'Just off to work, dear,' he announced, glancing at his watch. 'Life goes on. And thank goodness it does. It's the best medicine. You'll be all right here on your own, won't you? Perhaps you could do a bit of shopping. You can use my ration book for now, until you can get yours sent over from the farm. And don't buy anything frivolous like butter or sugar. I can get hold of all that, remember.'

She stared at him, barely listening, thinking how awful his table manners were. Her neck began to stiffen with shock and her ears filled with a rushing pressure. Cold realisation crept into her consciousness as she leant against the doorway. The squalid horror at what had happened to her parents began to replay itself in her mind's eye with grinding, agonising certainty.

Will glanced at her. He stood up, brushing crumbs from his trousers on to the floor and walked over, wrapping his arms around her. 'How about I go to the town hall at lunchtime, Rosebud,' he breathed into her ear. 'See if I can set a date. After last night, well! Let's see if I can make an honest woman of you.'

She flinched with shock and whispered into his shoulder, 'But my parents?'

'It's what they would have wanted, you know that.'

His use of the past tense forced hot tears to splash down her face.

'But where are they? I – I want to see them.'

'Oh, Rosebud, believe me. You wouldn't want to.' He drew away from her and she looked up into his eyes. They were opaque with a memory; an experience that he would not share with her. She looked away.

He said, lightly, 'So, what will you do today?'

'I – I could do a little housework,' she muttered, looking around her.

'Well, whatever you do, don't go round to Stanley Crescent. You're not fit to. It'll only set you back.'

'But I want something . . . something . . .'

'Believe me, before you arrived yesterday, I had a good look around. I picked over what I could. I found some papers, your birth certificate, but really . . . it's such a mess. The voluntary services are probably clearing it now.'

'I – I have my mother's shoes . . .'

'There you go! What's left there now is only fit for the scrap heap. We'll start afresh in our new house.'

'Our new . . . ?'

'The Old Vicarage. It's high time I moved us out to Trelewin. It's all there waiting for you.' He held her tightly and she felt a little warmth trickle through her body.

'Trelewin?'

'Yes, the house is still mine. I just knew, *just knew*, it would only be a matter of time before you were.' He went on: 'The bank has agreed to a transfer. I had already applied in the summer, hoping we'd be able to start our life together. And I can register with Polperro ARP. Keep the buggers happy . . .'

But she wasn't listening to him. Her head filled with the sounds of the sea, the seagulls over the cove, the hissing of the water through the wire. The old, empty house would be her sanctuary. She'd be close to Pengared; back near her friends; away from her destroyed life in Plymouth. And away from whatever Will remembered seeing in the pit at the back of her home in Stanley Crescent.

Mrs Brown came knocking. 'I saw Mr Bowman in the town yesterday,' she trilled as she bustled in, 'and he told me your news, Rosie.'

'News?' Rose asked, distracted. 'Oh, the wedding.' She took no pleasure in being a bride-to-be.

Rose put the kettle on the hob in Will's bachelor kitchen and sighed with weariness. It had been nearly two months since that dreadful day when she returned to Stanley Crescent. She felt lethargic and sick. Was this what grieving did to the body? she thought. She had no energy left for her visitor, however kind she was being. She realised she had not seen Mrs Brown since the funeral. Her chattering made Rose think of happy days behind the counter, going home to her mother and dad. She felt herself clench her fists.

'This is *exactly* what you need, my girl, after what has happened,' Mrs Brown settled herself in one of the chairs by the hearth. 'A fresh start. A new life. And I'm so glad that you have managed to . . .' she lowered her voice, 'concede to an understanding with your fiancé. Forgiveness goes a long way, I say.'

'Forgiveness?' Rose asked from the kitchen, undoing a twist of tea and spooning it into the pot and thinking, *You've changed your tune*. 'What do you mean?'

'Oh, your mother told me how much Mr Bowman adores you, how he hated you being away at the farm. But then, when you had your *falling out* in the summer . . .'

'You knew about that?'

'Your mother told me, God rest her. She told me you threw him over – which I wasn't at all surprised at – but that he was distraught. Of course, I never told your mother that I saw him down at the Hoe with that *woman*. That would have made her see him differently, that's for sure.' Mrs Brown paused, then whispered, 'I know I did.'

If only Mother and Dad had known about the Wren, thought Rose. They would have been glad to see the back of Will. But what did it matter now? What did any of it matter?

'So, you forgave him, Rosie. Good for you. Now you can start afresh.' Mrs Brown shivered. 'Oh, no, I won't take off my hat and coat yet, thank you, dear.'

Rose set down two cups of tea and fired up the gas fire. Overwhelmed with tiredness she rested back in the other armchair and took a sip of tea. Nausea swam up her gullet.

'Sorry, Mrs Brown,' she said, swallowing gingerly, 'but I think the milk in the tea must be off.'

'Nonsense.' Mrs Brown sipped her own cup. 'It's fine. Now, something tells me you need some new clothes, seeing as your house and everything is . . .' The woman stopped herself and bent to her shopping bag. 'So look what I've got here.'

Rose barely glanced at what Mrs Brown was doing. She pushed her cup of tea away; the smell was revolting.

'Don't turn your nose up. It's good curtain material from the church bazaar. If I can't get you in order, then what can I do? Now with Mr Brown stuck in the Royal, I need some company. You're like the daughter I never had. And now, I'll try to behave like a mother.'

Rose's stomach contracted. She turned her face away and bit her lip.

'Oh, sorry, Rosie. Don't listen to me wittering on.' Mrs Brown pulled out some brown woven material and a handful of silk. 'Look, I've even got a scrap of parachute for the trimming. I could fashion a corsage from this.'

'A corsage?' Rose tried to sound interested.

'For your wedding suit. This is perfect.'

'Oh, the wedding . . .' Drowsiness washed over her, blocking out the enormity of the impending date.

'Now, now, we can't have you living like this, living in *sin* with Mr Bowman for much longer, can we?'

'Oh, I . . . ?' Rose blushed. 'He sleeps on the sofa.' It had not occurred to her what others might be thinking. All she had wanted was somewhere to stay until it was time to go back to Cornwall.

'Bless you,' Mrs Brown smiled. 'You are such an innocent. Come on, let me measure your waist. Stand on this chair.'

Rose obeyed.

Mrs Brown wrapped the tape around her waist. 'Ah, twenty-five.' She wrote the measurement with a stub of pencil.

'Oh,' said Rose, 'I've put on weight. Must have been Betony's lovely cooking. Except I haven't had the pleasure for nearly two months now . . . since I've been . . .'

Her mind slipped to Betony, Pengared and Meg, and the calling seagulls over the cove.

'It will be nice for you to be back near the farm, away from here,' Mrs Brown chattered on, her eyes darting around the mean flat, resting on the stained lino and patches of damp on the walls. 'And a good steady man like Mr Bowman will soon set you straight. It's what you need right now, Rosie. In the circumstances.'

Mrs Brown tapped Rose on the bottom to indicate she should get down from the chair. And what were those circumstances? Rose wondered. Soon to be Mrs Bowman, living in a pretty hamlet by the sea; away from the raids; shielded from the war. But her parents were gone, and so was . . . Suddenly, she clenched her hands into fists, desperate not to cry. Oh, God, Krystof was gone. Their love and their summer were a lifetime ago. He had been sucked away into the war, just like her mother had said he would. And here she was, allowing herself to be pulled away from him in the other direction. Mrs Brown . . . Will, conspiring to drag her away from him. Surely, if she had the strength to fight back, surely there was a chance . . .

'My dear, no tears, please,' Mrs Brown cried, putting her arm round her. 'But of course you can cry. You're a bride, after all.'

The woman handed her a handkerchief and Rose began to mop her face, her wretchedness adding to the gripe of sickness in her stomach. She rested her hand over her waistband, hoping to soothe herself.

Mrs Brown glanced down, and then hard into Rose's face.

Rose watched the scrutinising, short-sighted eyes behind the spectacle lenses roam over her features.

'Oh, dear. Oh, my dear. I wonder. Do you think you might be . . .'

Rose was irritated and wanted her to leave her alone. 'Goodness, Mrs Brown . . . what now?'

'Wrong side of the blanket, they say, but never mind, there's a war on. It must happen all the time these days. Just no one talks about it.'

'What on earth do you mean?'

'Why didn't I think of this before! You're expecting, my dear. Look at your face . . .'

Rose held the handkerchief over her eyes and began to shake her head.

'That's right, dear, have a good cry.' Mrs Brown began to thrust her sewing kit back into her bag. 'No wonder you're rushing to get married before Christmas. And I've got my work cut out to get this suit made. But don't worry. I'll have it run up in no time. Chop, chop.'

Rose pulled down the blackout to the darkening afternoon, switched on the dim lamp and sat at Will's desk to write three letters. The first was to Mrs Pike, district commissioner, South Cornwall section, to explain that she was leaving the Women's Land Army now that she was to be married. Then she wrote to Betony and Ted, trying her best to explain. She wrote that events had overtaken her; her parents' deaths had shattered her, and that she would not be returning to work now that she was to marry Will Bowman. At least, she told them, she'd be close by at Trelewin: the sweetener that she used to convince herself. She finished with a note for Meg, hearing, already, the exasperation and protestation ringing around the Pengared kitchen.

And then she heard the sound of Will's key turning in the lock downstairs. She stood up and smoothed her housewife's apron, trying to brighten her expression into one a prospective bride might wear.

'Hello, Rosebud, what are you up to?' asked Will, throwing down his coat and briefcase. He glanced at the letters on the desk. 'Ah, good, you're letting the country folk know. About time, too. They'll be wondering what's happened to you, these last two months. Although I hope they don't think that it'll be open house at Trelewin. I'd rather those yokels weren't living in our back pockets to be honest with you.'

He dipped to the gas fire and turned it up a notch. 'Christ, it's cold out there and the air's choking with coal smoke. Anyway, I've brought something home to warm us up: two tins of Californian peaches. But perhaps we'll save them for Christmas Day in our new home. Only three days to go, and only two until our wedding,' he crowed. 'Am I the luckiest man alive, now I have you, Rosebud?'

She declined to answer him. 'Mrs Brown came back again today. She's going to make me my wedding suit.'

'Don't go getting any ideas about inviting that busybody,' he said. 'We'll pick witnesses off the street. We don't want any fuss, do we?'

'She's being very kind,' ventured Rose. 'I had nothing, and she's gone to so much trouble.'

'Good, good. I'm sure you'll look a picture.' He walked over, wrapped his arms around her and caressed her bottom. 'And I can't wait to take it off you again, once we're back in our new home. Once you are Mrs Bowman for sure. Once you are mine, Rosebud.' His bristly chin scraped her neck.

She struggled, pushing him away. 'None of that, please, Will.'

He pulled back but still held onto her, laughing down into her face. 'Ha, Rosebud, I always knew you were a traditional girl. Rather conventional, if you ask me, but I think we're both the same, deep down. Sleeping on the sofa has done me a power of good on the anticipation front. Just you wait until our wedding night. Then you'll see how much I really love you.'

There was a sharp look in his eyes, just as there had been in the kitchen at Stanley Crescent.

'Thing is, Will,' she peeled his hands away, 'I have some news for you. Mrs Brown suspected . . . I hadn't been feeling at all well . . . I think I'm . . . I am . . .' She began to cry.

'No, really! You're . . . ? You're pregnant?' he exclaimed with a triumphant whoosh. 'Well, *ain't that a kick in the head!* A father. I'm to be a father. I *am* the luckiest man alive.' His jubilant smile stretched wide. Then he stopped smiling and glanced at her, taking in her crumpled face, her incessant tears. 'Hold on a moment, Rosebud. Is it mine?'

'Of *course* it is!' she bellowed, pulling away from him and rushing from the room.

Sitting on the edge of the bed, Rose rested her head on her knees and covered her ears. She wanted to block out Will, block out the baby, block out her shivering terror.

Will knocked on the door.

'Hey, hey, I'm sorry,' he cooed, coming into the room to sit next to her on the bed. He kept his distance. 'That was uncalled for. I shouldn't have said that. Look, I'm a rotter. I'm the cad who gets butter from under the counter and nylons at the pub. And those tins of peaches are going to cost me a favour or two, I can tell you. But I am here. I love you. And we're going to have a baby.'

His words made her jolt with disgust. How her father had hated the black market. How a little bit here, a little bit there was all very well, but it was criminal and an insult to the merchant sailors who risk their lives in the Atlantic. If only her father had known *that* about her fiancé. She looked at Will and felt her lip curl.

'Sometimes I think you hate me,' he said, his eyes searching her face. 'I admit. I'm selfish. I was an only child, you see, and my mother spoiled me.'

'I am also an only child.' Her voice was small. 'I was . . .'

'And I will look after you, like I promised your parents.' He wrung his hands, his face twisting pitifully. 'I'll never forgive myself for kissing that Wren. I'll never forgive myself for my behaviour on the night of the raid . . . and what happened to your face . . .' As his fingertip reached to touch her scar, she flinched her head away.

'But you are still wearing your ring.' He tried again, plucking at her left hand and holding it up to kiss it. 'After all we have been through, will you ever forgive a pathetic man like me? There's a big house in the country waiting for you, Rosebud. All you have to do is marry me, and we'll be happy.'

She looked up at him through her streaming tears. 'You insulted me,' she whispered. 'You think the child might not be yours.'

'I was thinking of your fancy man. Wondering if you . . .'

'What do you know? You know nothing about it!' She knew she had wanted to sleep with Krystof that night in the barn; wished she had. She felt too weary, too sick to speak.

'Look, Rosebud. You have to understand. Those men are gone. That camp near Polperro has been cleared for three whole months now. The Division has moved on. To Salisbury Plain, perhaps. To the New Forest? Who knows what Churchill has in mind for them? We civvies are mere mortals compared to them. He will be a hero, your fellow. All we can do is sit and watch it all happen. And try to get on with our own lives.' Will's voice was plaintive, persuasive. 'It's the war, Rosebud. He would have had to have gone sooner or later.'

Abruptly, Rose stood up and dashed the tears from her eyes. She wanted to escape, leave this sordid flat and contemptible man behind. But something in the corner of the bedroom caught her eye, made her stop. There in the shadows lay her mother's shoes with the polka-dot bows.

'I need to clean them in time for the wedding,' she said. 'They're still filthy.'

'I'll do that. Allow me,' Will leapt up.

She held up her hand. 'No!' she cried. 'Let me do something for myself.'

Sheepishly, he handed them to her and she slipped them on. They fitted perfectly.

She heard her mother's voice, ringing through her head, scolding her, pleading with her. *You're a fool to let him go for some fly-by-night squaddie who'll be gone in a few weeks. Will is your future, your life.*

How right she was, thought Rose, gazing down at the shoes on her feet and then glancing at Will's bland, confused face. This is my life.

The first person Rose saw as she left Plymouth Town Hall a married woman with Will was Mrs Brown, waiting in the drizzle on the steps with her shopping.

'I just had to stop by on my way home to see you married,' Mrs Brown called from under her umbrella. 'I've got no rice to throw, but never mind. It would make a bit of a pudding in all this rain, wouldn't it? Congratulations! You look wonderful. Lovely suit, if I may say so. Lovely hat.'

Rose responded on reflex. 'Thank you, Mrs Brown. Thank you for coming.'

As Will turned to shake the hand of the man he had collared to be a witness, Mrs Brown beckoned her over to share her umbrella.

'Are you straight off to Cornwall now, Rosie?' she asked.

'Yes. There's no wedding breakfast. None of Will's family seemed to have been able to make it, and my . . . Well, my friends aren't here. Just you, Mrs Brown. I'm glad to see you. You have been such a help to me since . . . I can't tell you how good you have been.'

'Oh, hush. Anyone would do the same. Don't forget where I am, now, will you?'

'I haven't asked you: How's Mr Brown?'

'Still on medication. I don't think he'll be out for a long old time.'

'How are you managing at the shop?'

'I've taken on a young girl. Just like you, she is. Her first job . . . but enough of that . . .'

Rose's mind drifted to the time when all she had to worry about was stock rotation and ration books.

Mrs Brown chattered on. 'Oh, Rosie, I have to mention. Not sure how important it is but I completely forgot to tell you. You know on that day you came back, that dreadful day after the raid.'

Rose felt the woman's thin hand close tightly over her own. She said, 'Yes, that awful day . . .'

'Well, that army chap, who pulled up in the car, you know, before you drove off . . .'

'I don't remember anything about another car. I didn't know anything about an army chap.'

'Poor love. Of course. I'm being insensitive. You've probably blotted it all out.' Mrs Brown pressed her hand on Rose's forearm. 'But this army chap . . .'

Rose suddenly brightened. 'But I do remember. Will did say something about an unexploded bomb, and the army. What's happened? Was there another bomb?'

'No, no. I know nothing of another bomb. Gracious, I hope not, anyway.' Mrs Brown gritted her teeth and shivered. 'I won't mention that to Mr Brown or he'll go right under. No, this army chap, well, he wasn't English that's for sure . . .'

Rose stiffened. 'He wasn't . . . ?'

'No. He was foreign,' Mrs Brown said with a trace of disdain. 'Not sure where from. Ah, look at your face, Rosie. More tears. You do make a lovely bride. So emotional, so beautiful. How are things . . . ?' Mrs Brown's eyes dropped to Rose's belly.

Rose felt her mouth dry up and tried to swallow. 'But wh- what did he say, this *chap*?'

'Oh, him! He said he was sorry. What for, I don't know. To be honest I couldn't understand a lot of what he said, being foreign. He was speaking so fast that he was rather garbled. Sorry he was too late, or something. He'd heard about the raid the night before. He seemed to know who you were. He'd motored all the way from somewhere in the west country that morning. Of course, they can never tell you, can they. I told him there and then that he needn't have bothered as you were being taken care of by your fiancé. That you would be safe with Mr Bowman. And he sort of . . .'

'Oh?' Rose pressed a hand to her throat.

'He sort of looked crushed. There, that's a good word: *crushed*. There he was, leaping out of his car full of beans, full of authority. Looked good in his uniform, if I remember rightly. And then, when I told him that you were going home with your Mr Bowman, he sort of *wilted*.'

'But what did he *say*?' She tried to focus on Mrs Brown's eyes and not her rain-splashed glasses.

'He said he had to be on duty that evening. Eighteen hundred hours, whatever that means. Colonel's orders. Threat of court marshal. I said, well, bully for you, or something. I was a little overwrought, you must understand. It had been a dreadful day.'

'But I don't understand!' Rose broke down, her head collapsing into her hands. 'It was . . . it was . . . He was there? He was at Stanley Crescent? He came to find me?'

'Was it important, Rosie? You'd gone with Mr Bowman. I thought . . .'

'But you didn't *think*! Why didn't you tell me before!' She shook her head violently, wanting to scream.

Her sobbing brought Will to her side.

Mrs Brown backed off, telling him, 'I'm sorry, I seem to have upset Rosie.'

Through a wash of tears Rose saw Will glare at Mrs Brown.

'I suggest you take your tittle-tattle elsewhere,' he barked. 'She's had enough to deal with already, don't you think? It's our wedding day, for God's sake.'

'I was only trying to . . .'

Standing on the town hall steps, Rose's loneliness was complete. The drizzle chilled her ankles, seeping into her bones.

Will handed her a handkerchief. 'Silly woman, that Mrs Brown. What is she thinking of?' His arm was heavy around her shoulders. 'Shush, come on, Rosebud, that's enough. Dry your eyes. We'll soon have you safe and warm. Let's get in the car.'

Rose stared up at her husband's face, and realised she didn't know him at all. She could barely remember who she was.

Eleven

THE RAIN FOLLOWED THEM ALL THE WAY TO TRELEWIN WHERE THE Old Vicarage stood in its dripping garden, its windows blank and unwelcoming. Paint peeled and bubbled on the front door and moss carpeted the stone steps. Rose shivered in the hallway while Will fetched their suitcases from the car. She heard him swear as he unbuckled them from their perch above the spare wheel. She didn't want to move any further, to open the doors to the rooms of her own house. The stairs rose in front of her into the darkness. Her nose twitched at the smell of unlived-in spaces, undusted nooks, the aroma of mouse.

She braced herself and took some tentative steps across the hall, her mother's – *her* – shoes clipping on uneven Victorian mosaic tiles, and opened a door to the kitchen. Light through a row of windows emphasised the dust on a table, the grime on the shelves which had rows of hooks for cups, pans or whatever a housewife might want to tidy away. A range sat in the hearth and beside it was a wooden dresser, not unlike Betony's. Rose peered around at all the things that she could clean and polish. Reaching over the stained sink she pushed open a window and let in some damp air. She stuck her head in a cupboard and did not baulk at the stale smell inside. All she could think of was how she could clean it, clean all of it, with lemon juice and vinegar, just as her mother had shown her.

'There you are, *Mrs*,' Will called, and a nerve stiffened in her head. 'What do you think of the place? Just think, if we hadn't had that silly argument in the summer we'd have been in here months ago. It would be all ship-shape by now, as those navy blighters say. Well?'

'I – I quite like the kitchen,' she said.

'Well, could do with a lick of paint. And never mind these

old loose tiles out here in the hall. I'll soon cover them up with lino. They'll be good as new. Easier to clean, too.'

'I don't mind cleaning,' she said. 'Let's leave the tiles. I'll get them restored once the war is over.'

'If you like, but I think it's a waste of time,' he said. 'God, I didn't realise quite what a dump this place was. But never mind. Like I said, I bought it for a song.'

He came close to her and rested his hands on her shoulders.

'Have you recovered from earlier, Rosebud?' He sounded as if he would expect nothing else.

'I – I feel a little better,' she lied.

'I want you to take care of yourself and . . .' he placed a hand flat on her stomach, 'now there's to be a little one, you have to think of him as well. You have made my happiness complete, Rosebud. Look at your face. It's all been a bit too much for you, hasn't it? I could kill old nosy Brown. If she hasn't caused us enough trouble. Still, we won't have to see her again. Come on, look in here.'

He ushered her through a doorway into a large room at the back of the house. In a former life, it would have been a grand sitting room; there was a fine mantelpiece and French windows that opened onto the terrace. Beyond the low garden wall, clothed in ivy, lay the church, squat and grey in the rain.

He said, 'I'd forgotten how close we are to the church. Once the war is over, they'll start ringing the bells again. I hope it doesn't bother us. If it does, I'll soon let the old vicar know. There's his new house over there. You can just see the roof. Pity he left this one in such a state.'

Will forced the latch on the French windows and they opened with a creak. The dank day entered the room in a blast of chilly air. Rose gazed around at the brown lino, the scattered, worn rugs, the dusty pine cones arranged in the hearth, thinking, Where can I start in here?

And then, chattering voices drifted over from the footpath beyond the garden wall.

'Oh, oh,' Will said, none too pleased. 'Looks like we have visitors. Already!'

'Goodness, it's Betony and Meg. How wonderful!' Rose clapped her hands with joy.

Will's face revealed his displeasure. 'You've cheered up all of a sudden.'

'But I haven't seen them in so long!' She rushed to the front door, impatient to say hello.

Betony and Meg crunched over the gravel, carrying a cardboard box between them, red-faced and soaking but smiling with pleasure.

'Ginge! We heard you'd arrived!' called Meg.

'How?'

'We have our spies. Didn't you see the bus earlier?'

'Mr Jack Thimble?'

Meg said, 'The very same. Told his wife. She told us. We know everything that's going on. Hello again, Will. How are you? I hope you carried her over the threshold?'

Will was watching their approach with narrowed eyes. 'Not in her condition, I wouldn't. Anyway, that's sentimental old rubbish. Carry her, indeed.'

The two women looked at Rose. 'Your condition? You mean to tell us, Ginge . . . ?'

'It's very early, I . . .'

Betony's eyes pierced Rose's for an uncomfortable moment, but then her voice brightened. 'Well, that's wonderful news, Ginge. We must help you get settled in. You must be worn out.'

Rose saw a glance of confusion between her two friends as she ushered them through. They set the box down on the kitchen table.

Betony said, 'Here's your first supper in your new house. Stew and dumplings, still piping hot and all packed in straw. Just return the casserole when you've finished.'

'Oh, this is wonderful. Your own recipe?'

'But of course.'

'Heaven.' She hugged them both in turn while Will leant against the doorpost, tapping out a cigarette. 'We should have a drink to celebrate,' cried Rose, feeling the trials of the day lifting a little. 'Don't we have a bottle of sherry somewhere, Will?'

He shook his head.

'We're so pleased you've come back,' said Meg to diffuse the silence. 'After all that happened, with your parents, we weren't sure you'd come back. We were so shocked and so sorry, Ginge.

And now here you are, married and expecting. It's all so sudden. Such a *surprise*.' Meg's eyes were wide with the question, *Why?*

'I know from your letter that you've left the Land Army but would you like to continue to work at the farm? Light duties of course, until the baby comes?' asked Betony.

'I'll do the hens for you,' said Meg. 'Say you'll come back.'

'We'd love to have you. You can help in the house,' said Betony.

'No wife of mine will ever work,' piped up Will Bowman, sucking on his cigarette.

Betony ignored him. 'I'm going to start knitting,' she said, 'little booties and jackets. Just you wait.'

'Oh, I've missed you, Ginge,' said Meg, hugging her. 'Those early mornings aren't the same without you to be grouchy with. And you used to shield me from that bear with a sore head called Ted.'

'I miss that bear,' Rose chuckled and then stopped, clapping her hand over her mouth. 'Good God. It feels so strange to laugh. I haven't felt like laughing in such a long time.'

'That's why we're here,' said Betony.

'Come on, show us round this big old house, then.' Meg linked arms with her.

Rose said, 'I haven't even been upstairs yet, so we can discover it together.'

Will cleared his throat and they all looked around. Rose had forgotten he was standing there.

'I think it's best you ladies leave us to ourselves now. We've got a lot to do. Lots of unpacking, we need to get settled.'

'Oh, but, Will . . .' Rose said.

Meg narrowed her eyes.

Betony was flustered. 'Of course. So sorry. We just thought . . . Well, there's some veg in there, and the last of the plum jam. And my apple pie. We'll go, then. So sorry to interrupt.'

Meg piped up, 'Come over for Christmas dinner.'

'Oh, yes, do,' said Betony, her eyes shining. 'Not much as usual, but Ted dispatched a chicken yesterday. It will be lovely to have you.' She added reluctantly, 'To have you both.'

Will's hand rested on Rose's shoulder as he stood behind her. 'Thank you, but I want us to have our first Christmas dinner here alone.'

Rose said, 'But Mrs Brown gave us a hamper. We've got . . .' and then stopped herself. She went on, 'Yes, thank you anyway, Betony. Will Hugh be home?'

Meg chipped in, 'No, but he's quite safe in Italy. The Jerries are retreating up the country. He's guarding Italian towns as opposed to attacking them. He is very well.' She eyed Will Bowman with distaste; he was looking at his watch. 'Come on, Betony,' said Meg, 'let's make tracks.'

'*Ginge*,' Will said, opening doors off the upstairs landing, tutting and then closing them again. 'Why do they have to call you Ginge? It sounds so awful. And, not least, rather unflattering.'

'I . . . I didn't like it at first,' she said, following him and peering into rooms behind him. 'But then it grew on me. It's their special name for me. They all had to grow on me too. My first few weeks there were—'

'That's right,' he snapped, opening the door on a dreary bathroom, 'but you don't like me calling you Rosebud, do you?'

'You still do, though, don't you,' she retorted.

She opened a door onto a room at the front of the house to be confronted by a double bedstead in the middle of bare floorboards and a bay window offering an uninterrupted view of the sea. The grey water was choppy and smudged by the rain. White foam raced in towards the shore.

'Ah, ha.' Will came up behind her. 'This, my dear wife, is to be our bedroom. And this is my wedding present to you. The bed frame is second-hand, but the mattress brand new. Our marriage bed. Doesn't it look luxurious? Aren't I kind to you? And the view, how wonderful in the summer, hey, Rosebud? Think of us waking up to that.'

'My goodness . . .'

She couldn't look at him, dreading having to share herself with him. At the maisonette she had managed to stall him, for the sake of appearances, but now the reality of sleeping with him left her cold.

She said, unconvincingly, 'What a lovely surprise.'

'Come here, then.' He pulled her towards the bed. 'This is why I wanted the snooping locals gone. I want you all to myself.'

'Will, the baby?'

'Someone told me it was good for it. Now come here, like a good wife.'

'But Will, I'm so tired. It's been such a long day . . .'

'Well, think of it this way. We don't have a sofa yet, so this is where I'm going to sleep. You'd better get used to it.'

'Will, really, I don't think . . .'

'That's it, lie here,' he said. 'I'm going to make you smile like a bride should.'

Twelve

THE RAIN FELL FOR THE REST OF DECEMBER, AND THEN IN JANUARY the air grew still and the sodden earth froze hard. The countryside fell quiet in the grip of the chill, and not a soul walked by the Old Vicarage at Trelewin, let alone knocked on the door.

Shivering in pyjamas, jumper and socks, Rose scraped ice from the inside of the kitchen window to let in a little more of the grey dawn light. She stooped to the range and began to rake the ashes and coax the banked-down coal into flame. Using both hands, she hauled the heavy kettle from beneath the scullery tap and set it to boil for tea. She waited, peering through the patch she'd made on the glass, then, in one hot motion, was horribly sick into the sink. She cried with every retch as she regurgitated whatever her tired body was anxious to rid itself of. After washing the mess away, she pressed her hot forehead against the cold porcelain.

She picked up the bread knife and began to saw the loaf angrily, so that the knife scored the board again and again. If only he'd got there sooner. If only he hadn't had to go. If only she'd been stronger. But how could she have been? She had no idea what she was doing.

She watched through the window while the tea was brewing. Outside was silence; no one would ever guess a war was raging from the stillness of the scene before her. Beyond the garden the graves were fuzzy with frost, the long grass between them broken and dead. Through the naked hedges she could see the post box for Pengared – her only link with the outside world. He might write to her, yet. Write to her at the farm. Stop it, you fool. She clenched her fists to her stomach. You are married and pregnant. He has gone.

Will came down the stairs in his suit and tie, whistling, and she turned automatically to the door to greet him in the way he expected her to.

'Ah, Rosebud, I forgot to mention. I have to work late tonight. Something's come up at the bank.'

'Oh? What?'

'The auditors are in.'

'How late?'

'Put it this way, don't wait up,' he said.

She turned away. Another long day and evening alone in the house stretched before her. Loneliness shrouded her with its heavy, oppressive cloak.

Will crunched off over the gravel to catch the bus to the Polperro branch of the Western bank where he had been transferred. As the sound of the engine died away, Rose dressed in old trousers and a jumper, longing for the cosy wool of her Land Army uniform that she'd had to send back to Mrs Pike. The kitchen was the warmest place in the house, but she forced herself to venture out into the other rooms and keep herself busy.

In the sitting room, for some company, she switched on the radio and immediately turned the dial away from where Will always left it: hovering over Berlin. She was too late for the daily 'Broadcast to Housewives' but the friendly voices of the Light Programme drifted out as she swept the carpet, thinking how ridiculous the small pieces of furniture from the maisonette looked in such a large room.

She decided the place needed brightening up. Dragging Will's box of books in from the hallway where it had been since the day they moved in, she took the books out and, one by one, dusted them off and lined the shelves: *British Songbirds, Jane Eyre, The Shell Book of the Countryside, Nicholas Nickleby*. At the bottom of the box were some novels in German; she remembered Will telling her it had been his favourite lesson at school. She flicked through a dog-eared poetry book: *Des Müllers Blumen*. Will's schoolboy pen had translated it: *The miller's flowers. Tränenregen: showers of tears*. How pretty the language seemed on the page, she thought, compared to the raging broadcasts of Mr Hitler's speeches.

Thrusting her hand into the depths of the box, Rose pulled out a copy of *Mein Kampf*. She shrieked as if it had bitten her, dropped it back in the box and shoved the box back out into the hall. Suddenly, she was struck by a memory: Will reading it on the first night she stayed at the maisonette. She shook her head to banish the thought before the full awful scale of it fell like a cold axe through her skull.

Checking the time, she went to the kitchen window. Sure enough, Meg appeared by the post box, thrust her hand in and pulled out a letter. By the way her friend's head drooped, Rose could tell the letter wasn't from Hugh. She tapped energetically on the window and waved, but Meg neither heard nor saw her.

Dejected, she wandered back into the sitting room and switched the radio to the World Service. As she listened to dispatches from Burma and Guam, she watched the dead, cold day through the French windows, refusing to brush away the tears that coursed down her cheeks. She had already cleaned all the rooms they lived in; tomorrow there would be nothing else to do. People got depressed in the war, of course they did. But they soldiered on. Her mother used to tell her, *There is always someone worse off than you.*

The baby fluttered inside her and she thought of the dark, empty weeks that lay ahead of her. Despair rose to the surface of her skin like a rash.

A week later, waking up more weary than when she had gone to bed, Rose pulled herself out from under the covers, leaving the snoring bulk of her husband behind. Last night, she had managed to dissuade him once again from what he half-jokingly called his 'conjugals'. She felt satisfied that she had only complied three times since the first night at the maisonette and, then, felt mildly foolish for counting. Her swollen belly had become her shield, her excuse, and she patted it as she made her way downstairs in the cold darkness.

As soon as Will left for work, she dressed and waited in the kitchen, clutching a cup of tea to warm her fingers. Was it possible that the morning was infinitesimally lighter than the one before? She peered out into the gloom, desperate to spot the tiniest of green shoots poking through the leaf mould. What would this rambling garden reveal? Snowdrops and daffodils? *Father's favourite flowers*. Her hands shook and the cup thumped back down on the table.

It was Pengared post-box day, and soon enough, this time, Betony appeared. Rose stood at the window, ready to wave and shout, willing her friend to glance at the house. Surely she'd see her; surely she'd come and visit this time? Oh, why was Will so rude to them? Surely they'd still come and see her? She watched open-mouthed as Betony picked up her post, turned her slender back on her and disappeared down the footpath.

Rose could bear it no longer. Throwing on her coat and hat, she ran out of the house, crunched over the gravel, turned sharp left, left again, and plunged down the footpath.

'Betony!' she called, breathless, her feet like lead. Her stomach swayed below her belt. 'Betony!'

The full force of the icy air hit her as she reached the headland and began the steady climb, the cold scorching her throat, sweat drenching her back. 'Betony!'

At last she heard her and turned. 'Oh, Ginge! It's you! You shouldn't be running!'

Rose flung herself towards her friend, desperate to hug her but instead doubled over with a cramp like a vice in her side.

'I-so-wanted-you-to-visit,' she spluttered. 'I-am-so-alone.'

'But we didn't know what to do,' Betony wailed, putting her arm around her. 'Ted said we can't impose ourselves, better leave it for a bit. I must say, your husband didn't make us feel very welcome.'

'I'm-so-sorry-he-was-so-rude-I've-been-going-out-of-my-mind.' Rose straightened up, catching her breath. 'That house. It's deadly. So cold.'

Betony smiled. 'But now you're very warm. Look at you.'

'I had to escape. I saw you, and I ran!'

Betony peered at her, her placid face twisting with concern. 'You shouldn't be running. You shouldn't be *escaping*. Come back with me to Pengared for the day. It's so good to see you. We felt we couldn't come near you. You had such an awful shock, with your parents. You disappeared, and we just didn't know what to do.'

Rose turned her face to avoid her friend's gaze and devoured the view. They had stopped by the path that led to the cove. The trees and undergrowth were dank and dead; the gunmetal sea cold and still. White-winged gulls swooped over it like scattered pieces of handkerchief. Rose began to shiver.

Betony linked her arm. 'Come on, let's get going.'

They began to walk. 'Joel's gone,' said Betony. 'He's been called up. I bet his poor mother thought that four years ago when it all started she'd never see the day. Thought it would all be over by the time he was old enough. Something's going on, I know it. Have you noticed, even Polperro is empty of men now?'

'Really? I haven't been out at all.'

'Oh, Ginge, what have you been doing?'

'It's been too cold. Too awful.'

They fell into silent agreement until Rose managed a wry smile. She said, 'I suppose there are some men left in Polperro: there's certainly a bank clerk.'

'You mean . . .' Betony laughed. 'That's my old Ginge.'

'What have you there?'

'Two letters,' Betony said, 'both from Hugh. One for Meg. One for us. But I wish . . . I wish I could stand here and read ours for myself.'

'Let me help you,' Rose said. 'It's no good people just reading things out to you all the time. Let me teach you.'

Betony flushed crimson. 'Would you? Ted has tried, but he's very impatient, bless him. I'm just too embarrassed to ask anyone else. But you, Ginge? You will help me?'

Mutt and Jeff had not forgotten her; they bounded over as soon as Rose and Betony scaled the farmyard gate, snuffling Rose's hands in search of those elusive biscuits.

'Where's Meg?' she asked.

'Over at the meadow,' said Betony. 'Here, take her letter. Careful as you go, it's still icy.'

As Rose picked her way across the yard, Ted strode towards her. Without a word he enfolded her in one of his huge hugs, his silent greeting speaking more to her than words could. She felt herself collapsing inside.

'Thank you, Ted,' she said and went to find Meg.

There she was, in the corner of Betony's meadow, cranking

the starter handle of the Allis tractor, wild curls snug under a knitted balaclava and overalls belted above her rounded bottom. She looked up with a scream of delight.

'I knew it! I knew it wouldn't be long before you came back.' Meg ran to Rose, embracing her fiercely. 'You can't keep away. Oh, look at you. You're blooming.'

'I don't feel as if I'm blooming.' It was a relief to hear Meg's familiar chatter.

'Ooh, sorry. How are you feeling? Oh, Ginge, what ever *happened*?'

She swallowed hard, trying to be brave and find the right words. 'Krystof went to war,' she said, 'and Will was there for me.'

'But Ginge . . . surely Krystof . . .'

'Will is my husband.'

Meg's sharp eyes were unforgiving. 'Your husband made it very clear he did not want us to visit you.'

Rose distracted her with the letter. 'This is for you. Hugh.'

Meg snatched it gleefully and hugged herself. Her joy was physical as she danced around, ripping open the envelope, her eyes twinkling as she scanned her lover's words. 'Oh, he's fine. Eating pasta, drinking coffee. He's arranged his leave. At last! Oh, Ginge!' Meg skipped and hopped around her. 'We're getting married!'

'Meg!' Rose hugged her, feeling her friend's excitement, feeling the crispness of her own jealousy. 'When?'

'Beginning of June. I'd better go and see the vicar at Trelewin. I'm going to become a Cumberpatch.'

'Ted and Betony have a letter from him, too. I expect he's broken the news to them. They'll be so happy. You are so happy! I wish . . .'

Meg stopped her jiggling around and looked at her. 'You *were* happy, Ginge. Remember the dance, the haymaking? I am so sorry for your parents. We've not been there for you, to help you through it. But you left us, Ginge.' Meg held her and Rose, resting her head on Meg's shoulder, felt her friend begin to sob. 'But we'll stand by you now.'

Meg extracted herself and wiped her face with the backs of her hands, leaving dirty smears. 'Hey, look at me.'

Rose smiled quietly, but wished she, too, could cry.

'That's better,' said Meg. 'A smile. I must say, that scar of yours is looking angry today. Must be the cold. Isn't it bitter? So, are you going to help me today, or what?'

'I can try.'

Meg cranked the starter handle on the Allis and the spluttering engine broke the silence of the morning. She stepped up into the tractor seat. 'Come on, Ginge, you're not an invalid.'

Rose climbed up and slipped in beside Meg.

'Now, you haven't forgotten your promise to me, have you? I'm driving this contraption all the way to Polperro when this is all over, and you are coming with me.'

'Just try and stop me.'

'That's my girl.'

'Where's Blossom?'

'Being a lazy arse in her stable.'

'Glad to hear it. And the herd?'

'Gone to the knacker's.' Meg looked at her. 'But don't you dare get sentimental, or we'll all go mad. Now hop off a moment and sort out the ploughshare.'

'Are we really going to do this?' asked Rose, climbing back down. 'Are we really going to break sod on Betony's meadow? First time in hundreds of years?'

'You bet. Orders from above. Or should I say Min of Ag. Help me get her steady. Line her up. Here we go.'

The throbbing engine grumbled and the huge iron wheels began to roll forward. Rose pressed her foot on the plate of the ploughshare attached to the rear of the tractor and the silver blades made their first cut through the virgin earth.

She climbed back up, forgetting for a moment that she was carrying a baby.

'Woah, are you all right, Ginge?'

'Fine,' she said, feeling her belly swing and the vibrations shudder her bones. 'All the better for seeing you.'

Meg began to sing, '"Wish Me Luck As You Wave Me Goodbye"'. And waved at the meadow around her. 'Bye bye, meadow.'

How different it looked in the cold, pewter light of the February day. How far removed from last summer's golden days when they all bent their backs to make hay in the sunlight;

when Krystof leant in to pluck the seed heads from her hair, his fingertips leaving trails of ecstasy over her skin.

'It's the end of an era,' said Rose, feeling tears of defeat sting her eyes.

The tractor rumbled on and, strip by strip, the cold red earth was turned by the plough. Betony's meadow was no more.

Thirteen

ROSE AND BETONY SAT SIDE BY SIDE IN THE LAMPLIGHT OF THE WARM
Pengared kitchen, while Mo played quietly under the table.

'My third lesson,' said Betony. 'You're so patient.'

'It's the least I can do. You've been a great friend to me,' Rose
replied.

Betony sighed. 'People think I'm stupid. That I never went to
school. They don't realise – I just can't see the words. They're
like strange patterns. I can't remember them.'

'You've done well so far. I'll be with you every step.' Rose
picked up the old book that Betony had found in the
cupboard. *The Return of the Soldier*. 'Is this the book you'd
like to try?'

'It belonged to my mother,' said Betony. 'She was a great reader.
She did try to help me, but it was no use. I must be daft in the
head.'

'Come on, now, I'm not going to hear of it. Take a deep breath.'
Rose flicked to the first page. 'My goodness, I know this book.
My mother had it, too.'

And where was that copy now? Turning to dust on a scrap
heap somewhere?

'It was written in 1918. And here we are, just twenty-odd years
on and going through the same thing again.' Rose swallowed
hard. 'And I think of poor Dad and how he lived through
Flanders, and then it came to this . . . a bomb in his own back
garden.'

'Oh, Ginge,' sighed Betony. 'Will it ever end?'

Rose drew a brave intake of breath. 'And I know the story,'
she said, pressing on. 'This poor man, this soldier, loses his
memory because of what happened in the trenches. Shell shock
we call it now, don't we? They used to call it "hysterical fugue"

What a funny expression. And when this soldier comes home, he is so affected that he doesn't recognise his own wife.'

Betony was watching her closely, with her head cocked to one side. 'Go on,' she said.

'Right,' Rose said. 'Take a look at the first paragraph. Start here.'

'*I* – no – *If*,' read Betony, her cheeks flushed, her finger following the letters, her tongue protruding. '*If he* – *If he had* . . .'

How young she looks, thought Rose. How I have missed her and Meg and Ted. I should never have . . .

'Good, Betony,' Rose roused herself. 'Stay calm. Remember to breathe. Hear the words in your head before you say them.'

Betony slowly began to read, plucking at the words with her lips, and setting them free from the page: '*If he had been anywhere interesting, anywhere where the fighting was really hot . . .*'

'Have you been practising?' asked Rose, laughing.

'*. . . he'd have found some way of telling me instead of just leaving it as "somewhere in France". He'll be all right.*'

Rose felt the smile freeze on her face, her scalp tighten as she listened to her friend's tentative voice. She grew colder and colder with shock.

Betony sighed. 'How sad, and I haven't even got past the first page. It is the same thing all over again, but this time round, it's us, isn't it? We all know about the waiting. The not knowing.'

Rose could barely speak. 'I don't think this book is appropriate to read at the moment.'

'Why, Ginge?'

Rose couldn't look at her.

Betony ventured, 'Is it because, possibly, you are thinking of *your* soldier? Are you afraid to talk about the return of *your* soldier?'

Rose slowly lowered her head and rested it on the table. Mo, still playing underneath, put his little hands on her knee and she glanced down into his rosy face. He was astonished by the tears that flowed silently from her eyes.

'I'm sorry, Mo,' she whispered to him. 'It's all right, Mo. There's nothing wrong with me.'

Betony said, 'Yes, there is. Something is *very* wrong. Talk to me, Ginge. I want to help you.'

Rose lifted her face with a sudden surge of anger. 'There's nothing you or anyone can do to help me. This is all my doing. All my fault. He is gone for good. He won't be *returning*. Not after what happened.' She tugged at her maternity blouse to emphasise her stomach. 'Not after *this!*'

Betony fidgeted with the book, turning it face down on the table. She said quietly, 'Of course, we all want to know why one moment you had finished with Will Bowman, and were in love with Krystof. And then, the next thing we hear, you're married and expecting.'

'It's just what happened, so you will have to get used to it!' cried Rose. 'My parents would have been very happy!'

Ignoring her fury, Betony said gently, 'Krystof came here, Ginge, asking for you.'

Her body jolted. 'What?' Her voice croaked, '*When?*'

'On the morning after the raid, but you'd already gone with Meg to catch the bus. He'd heard about the air raid, had set out at dawn from Salisbury, had taken the staff car. He was already in deep trouble with his colonel, he said, but he had to find you. He was due back on duty in two hours. He was never going to make it. He had already been threatened with court martial. They call it desertion and they don't take it lightly.'

Rose's mouth hung open, a pressure building behind her eyes.

Betony said, 'He told me he had a marriage licence. He wanted to find you, and marry you that day. He was taking a huge risk but hoped, eventually, his colonel would sympathise.'

'A licence?' Rose repeated, as if it was the first time she'd ever heard that word.

'A special marriage licence. He said he was sorry he had not been in touch. Impossible, he said. Oh, Ginge.'

'He came to the house.'

'Oh?'

'He came to Stanley Crescent. But I didn't see him. Mrs Brown told me on my wedding day. *After* I was married.'

They both fell silent, overwhelmed by the wretched irony.

'We thought that perhaps he had found you, and that you got married,' said Betony. 'But then the weeks passed. Next thing we knew, we received your letter. Oh, if we could have done more, we would have, but we didn't know where you were.'

Rose's despair began to crush her. 'I was in shock. My parents . . . my home . . . I had no idea. This is worse, so much worse,' her voice rang with bitterness. 'It's beyond repair.'

'But not now, now you know he loves you, wants you?' asked Betony. 'Did you marry Will because you doubted Krystof?'

Rose gritted her teeth. 'What did it look like to him? Seeing me go off like that, with Will. Krystof was AWOL. On the brink of *desertion*. And I do that to him. He saw me with Will. I betrayed him. He won't be returning to me now.'

'Now, Ginge, come on.'

'No, Betony, I know you mean well, but I can't keep pretending. This is my lot. Look at me. I have ruined Krystof's happiness. I have ruined my own.'

Betony bit her lip, shaking her head. 'I don't know what to say.'

Rose dried her tears on her sleeve, trying hard to rearrange her face into an expression of normality. 'I betrayed my parents, too. I was supposed to visit them that day in September, remember? But it turned out to be Krystof's last day here. His embarkation leave. And I chose Krystof.'

'You weren't to know.'

'But I chose Krystof. And now I am paying the consequences. I never saw my parents again.'

Betony swallowed. 'And what of Will?'

'As far as Will Bowman is concerned, us getting married, having a family; it's what my parents would have wanted.' A defeated calm returned.

The clock on Betony's mantel ticked in the hollow silence; Mo gurgled and shuffled around their feet.

When Rose spoke, her voice cracked with anger: 'Is that the time? I must go. I have to get back to cook my husband's supper.'

She made a meat pie with scrag end from the Trelewin butcher, adding turnips to bulk it out. It was not as good as her mother's. *Your fingertips are too warm to be a good pastry chef, Rosie.* But it would have to do.

The key turned in the front door and a blast of cold air reached her across the hall and around the kitchen door. She tilted her head to look up at the ceiling, hoping that gravity would force the constant tears back into her eyes.

'Something's cooking.' Will's banal voice rang out as he hung up his coat and stowed his briefcase. He poked his head around the door. 'What delight have I got to look forward to tonight?'

Rose cut into the pastry and slopped two portions onto plates, adding boiled cabbage stalks and a dab of mashed swede.

'We never did make it to the Ritz, did we, Rosebud,' said Will, loosening his tie and rolling up his shirtsleeves.

They sat at opposite ends of the kitchen table. The congealing food swam before her as she tried to focus on her plate.

'Maybe we will, one day,' he said. 'To celebrate our first anniversary. Your birthday. The birth of our first child.'

First child? Were there going to be more? She lifted her knife and fork. They felt as heavy as lead.

'Not eating, Rosebud? Not feeling well? We can't waste . . . I was going to say *good* food, but let's just say *food*, shall we?'

She pushed her plate aside, the pressure behind her eyes escalating with every pulse.

Will forked chunks of meat into his mouth. 'Old Jones, the ledger clerk, got all patriotic in the staff room today, listening to Churchill's latest on the radio. Something about the Jerry retreat through Italy. I soon shut him up when I told him that I had expected us all to be speaking German by now. He went all "Land of Hope and Glory" on me. Then got really shirty when I told him I already did speak German, thank you very much. He got so het up he started spitting on my newspaper. Disgusting man.'

She watched him prise some gristle out of his teeth.

'You're looking rather blank, Rosebud,' said Will. 'You must remember Jones. He's the one they brought back from retirement because all the young clerks were called up. Our best boys go, and I'm stuck with stinky Jones and his halitosis.'

She covered her eyes with her hand and let out a cry of despair. Tears rained onto the table.

'Oh, Rosebud. Jones isn't that bad.'

She heard the scrape of his chair and felt the shadow of his large presence standing over her. Her body flinched; she dared not look up.

'Why are you crying?' he asked. 'Are you thinking of your parents? I'm sorry, Rosebud. So very, very sorry.'

The unusual softness in his voice made her glance at him. He pulled up his chair and sat close to her. He was being kind. She had to tell him. If she didn't she'd choke.

'Krystof . . .' Her sobs asphyxiated her, her shoulders jerked. She wrung her hands. 'I'm thinking of Krystof.'

'Oh, oh.' He raised his eyebrows, satisfaction relaxing his face.

'We missed each other by minutes.' Her words were strangled. 'I should have married him. Not you.' She looked Will square in the face, bracing herself for one of his slaps.

Will sat back in his chair and surveyed her; he waited patiently for her to catch her breath, rummaged in his pocket for a handkerchief.

'Well, I know that,' he said, unfolding it and gently handing it to her, his voice tender and deep. He gazed at her through his lashes. 'I have known that all along.'

'You knew?' she blurted.

'I have been thinking about it a lot recently,' he said. 'I've noticed how unhappy you are.'

'I just . . . I just feel . . .'

'You know what, Rosebud.' He remained respectfully distant while she tried to dry her eyes, blow her nose. 'We need to put that right. We need to mend this . . . constant moping and crying.'

His words set off another torrent of tears.

'Now, now. Shush now.' He paused, pretending to mull it over. 'I think you should go to him. I take it he's at Salisbury? I will drive you there myself. You can track him down. Have your fling, Rosebud. Get him out of your system.'

She gaped at him in disbelief, tears dripping off her chin. 'How can I? I'm married to you.'

'I am doing this to save our marriage. I'm doing this for you. An affair with him will help you see.'

She shook her head. 'See what?'

'That it wasn't meant to be.'

'I don't understand.'

'Go and have your pleasure with him. But remember, Rosebud. When it's all over, when it's run its course, which it will, I will be waiting for you.'

She looked down aghast at her swollen belly. Shame engulfed

her; her parents' scolding voices rang through her head. Ghosts flickered at the sides of her eyes. She was a disgrace.

'An affair?' she asked, still incredulous. 'What about the baby? I can't. I can't go to him like *this*!'

'Exactly,' said Will. 'This is the hand you've been dealt. It's harsh, isn't it? So difficult, these days, for everyone.' He sat back and shrugged. 'It's your choice.'

She guardedly looked at his face and was surprised to see it remained placid, his eyes brimming with patience. He took her hands and drew closer to her, entwining his fingers through hers. She winced.

'Time to move on, Rosebud. Time to start a new life. Time to think of the little one.' He placed his palm intimately on her stomach.

She turned her head away, not wishing to face him.

'He's gone,' Will whispered.

She felt a quickening, a flinching, of the little body inside hers.

And what has become of me? she thought.

Fourteen

WET SPRING SLOWLY UNFOLDED INTO TRANQUIL SUMMER. THE SKY over Trelewin grew wider, bluer, and leaves returned to the trees around the churchyard. With each passing week, Rose's stomach grew heavier and tighter, and she retreated behind it, shutting out everything that lay beyond the farm, the village and the headland. This house, this life, was to be her world now.

She stood at the bedroom window at the front of the house and, shivering, watched the sea. The air felt cold for June. A blustery wind was fretting at the waves, forming white horses all the way out to the horizon. Treetops were whipped into a frenzy and dark clouds sailed across the pewter sky. A summer storm was coming. She thought of Meg and Hugh's wedding tomorrow and shrugged off a taunting spasm of envy. She hoped the storm would pass.

She crossed the landing to the back of the house and went into the nursery. Earlier that week she'd painted the walls and put flowery curtains at the windows. Betony had given her Mo's old cot and promised her the pram. Now, wiping the cot down, she became breathless, feeling the weight of her sleeping baby pressing deep into her pelvis. She wanted to feel hope and excitement, but these emotions chided her. Poor little thing, she thought, tracing a finger over her stomach. I will try to love you.

She left the nursery and went into the small room that her husband called his office. I expect this needs a dust, she thought and looked around at his typewriter on the paper-strewn desk, the piles of books, 78 records, ashtrays, old radio sets and tangled wires and aerials. *Why does he collect such rubbish*, she thought.

The window was open a chink, so she pushed at it in order to close it properly and a gust of wind whistled through, blowing the papers off the desk and scattering them all over the floor.

Sighing, she stopped to pick them up, feeling her baby shift in protest.

'What on earth?' she muttered out loud, realising that she was holding a photograph of the Wren from the Anchor pub. It had been coloured at the studio: all blue eyes and red lipstick. Rose exhaled in shock. 'I don't believe *this*.'

Then, perversely, she smiled and bent again to pick up the papers. The picture did not hurt her; she could not care less.

She sat down at the desk, glancing with curiosity at the ream of paper in her hand, and began to leaf through the typewritten pages. A little ticking clock inside her began to speed up: they were all typed in German.

'It's all very interesting, Rosebud,' Will had told her, when he tried to explain why he listened in on Radio Berlin. 'It's good to *know* your enemy, isn't it? And the book by the man himself? He has some fascinating ideas. Give him that. A great leader of men. Some would say Mr Hitler has *charisma*. You've seen the thousands, the millions who follow him. They can't all be fools. The fact that I have read his book is nothing for you to worry about. Nothing at all.'

A chill gripped the back of her neck as she turned over the cover of a pamphlet hidden among the papers. Her teachers had always told her she was good at languages and, here, even though she'd not studied German, she could read the words *Kristellnacht* and *Jüdisch*. The chill reached her bones and froze the blood inside her heart. It was Nazi propaganda against the Jewish people. She didn't need a certificate from school to understand what it meant. It was in her hand; right under her nose; in her house. She was as guilty as . . . with a shout of surprise, she dropped it and was on her feet, reaching up to the shelves, her fingers flicking over the books, alighting on the spine of Oswald Mosley's *Tomorrow We Live*. Another man with *charisma*. An Englishman imprisoned for being a Fascist. The baby thumped inside her belly.

She tugged at a file next to the book and a sheaf of postcards fell into her lap. Some were tattered, some pristine; all showed naked women. She saw blonde hair, arms aloft, legs apart, faces glancing over perky shoulders; flesh upon flesh, and swastikas. One of them was wearing an SS hat. She groaned with revulsion. They fell through her fingers, littering the floor.

'Dear God,' she cried, pressing her hand to her forehead. 'How did he get hold of this stuff? What is it doing here? Why didn't I *know*?'

Frantic now, she opened the drawers, plunging her hands through pens, paperclips, the trappings of an ordinary office, knowing with every laboured breath of panic, that this was no ordinary office. She found an envelope stuffed with banknotes; she counted, two hundred, three, *five*. And in another envelope, a letter from Sir Oswald Mosley's office, responding to Mr Will Bowman's congratulations on his recent release from prison.

What was she doing here with this man? Who was she living with? Sickening guilt forced her to sit down. Why had she not seen this? Why did she turn a blind eye when she unpacked the book all those months ago? On top of waves of disgust, lurched fear. He hurt her before. He might hurt the baby. She wrapped her arms around her stomach, feeling for the first time an essence of motherhood: the will to protect her child. But there had been clues all along and she'd chosen to ignore them. How on earth could a bank clerk afford a mortgage on a house like this? Even if he had been given special rates. And the black marketing? Nylons, tins of peaches and bunches of flowers were all very well. But where did it end?

She looked with loathing at the stuff she had unearthed. She wanted to burn it. But she knew she must put it back. Her hands trembled – felt as if they weren't her own – as she shuffled everything into place as best she could, making it look as it did when she first chanced upon it. And then she left the room, firmly shutting the door as the storm outside began to rattle the windows.

The picture of the smiling Wren was the least of her worries.

Fifteen

ROSE COULD NOT SLEEP WITH THE BULK OF HIS BODY LYING BESIDE her. Her flesh protested, her stomach grinding.

At half past five, she crept from the bed. The sky was lightening with soft purity as she let herself out into the garden. The church floated before her, its grey walls glimmering as the colourless light of the June dawn increased. She walked barefoot across the lawn to the low wall and climbed onto it, hauling her baby-stomach with her. Sitting with her back to the house, her naked toes touching the long grass in the graveyard, she noted that the weather had changed for the better: the storm was over.

In the garden, unruly roses were radiant against a tangle of leaves; honeysuckle was ripe with fragrance. She listened to the birds rouse themselves, in treetop and on chimney pot, to pipe in the day. Was it really nearly a year ago that she had been up this early, ready to mow Betony's meadow?

Later on, struggling into the maternity dress that she had rummaged from Trelewin church jumble sale, she heard Will open the bedroom door behind her and walk in.

'Oh!' She turned her back, not wanting him to see her body. And then, to distract him, said, 'Your best shirt is ironed; it's hanging in the wardrobe.'

He sat on the bed, staring at her.

'It's been so long, Rosebud,' he said. 'I can't wait for that baby to get out of you, so I can . . .'

She picked up her hairbrush and sat at her dressing table to do her hair, her fingers shaking. 'What – what a lovely day for the wedding,' she managed. She felt his eyes boring into her spine as she listened to the many seconds of silence.

'I don't want my shirt. I came up here to tell you to stop what you're doing, because we're not going.'

She made herself turn to look at him, her eyes wide and perplexed. 'But she's my best friend. How can I not go?'

'Just say you're ill; something about the baby. We're not going.'

'But it's Meg's day.'

He shifted his eyes to the side when he spoke. 'You will get overemotional and distraught. She'll have her parents there.'

'No,' she corrected him, 'only her mother. Meg lost her father many years ago. And I told you, she lost her brother Bertie at Dunkirk. So her brother won't be there either.' She swallowed and said bravely, 'What is the real reason?'

'I'm only thinking of you,' he snapped and then looked peevish. 'Anyway, I want to stay here and tune in. There are some interesting reports coming through on the radio.'

'All you think of is yourself and that blessed radio.' She faced him, trying not to reveal her rage. Her anger was edged with fear of him and of what she'd found in his office yesterday. 'You're not thinking of *me* at all.'

'Yes, I am, dear Rosebud.' He stood up and came towards her. His hand rested on her shoulder as he looked down on her.

'Are you tuning in to Berlin again?' she asked, terror making her heart thump.

'Might do, there's a lot going on.'

She shifted her shoulder so that his hand dropped away. 'Well, you do that. In the meantime, I am going to my best friend's wedding. You, Will, can do what you like.'

He took a step back and sat on the bed. 'You seem different today, Rosebud.' His voice had a childish whine. 'Something's changed.'

She turned away again, defensively. 'Must be because of the baby.' Then she lightened her voice, lifting it into a half-laugh. 'But no need to worry. You never wanted to go to this wedding anyway. Don't forget, the day will be overrun with the locals.'

She gave him warm smiles until, satisfied, he shrugged and left the room.

Alone again, she doubled over, clutching herself, her stomach churning with a stew of dread.

*　*　*

At midday, Meg walked into Trelewin church on the arm of her mother. The bride's curls were trapped in a chignon, with a few spirals escaping to frame her face. Above her, the stained-glass windows captured rays of sunlight and she looked serene as she stepped beneath their illumination. Rose watched Meg walk by holding the bouquet of ox-eye daisies which she had gathered from the verges on her walk over from Pengared. She looked beautiful and grown-up in a white satin suit; saving her coupons had been an obsession.

Hugh waited for her by the altar, leaning on a walking stick, a legacy of a booby-trapped mine in Italy. His eyes sparkled in his sunburnt face and his medals stood out against the khaki. Bride and groom greeted each other with such a wondrous delight it forced tears from Rose's eyes.

The vicar began to intone, his voice thin in the hushed church. After the signing of the register, Meg and Hugh sat side by side, holding hands as Betony stood up before everyone, looked the congregation in the eye, opened the Bible and began to read: '*When I was a child, I spoke as a child, I understood as a child, I thought as a child: but when I became a man, I put away childish things.*'

Rose, immensely proud of her friend, met Betony's smile, twisting her handkerchief in her lap.

The guests followed the laughing bride and groom out of the church into the quiet shimmering afternoon and trooped back across the headland to the farm. Betony had set up a table in the dappled shade of the orchard and spread out the wedding breakfast of stargazy pie, lettuce, smoked ham, bread and marge, and a sponge surrounded by piped mock cream.

'We could have had real cream if we'd kept the herd,' said Betony, pouring out glasses of her elderberry wine.

'And real butter,' said Ted. 'But worse things happen.'

He'd strung Union Jack bunting along the edge of the table and set up his wind-up gramophone nearby. Guests sat themselves on rugs and chairs brought out from the house and barefooted Mo pattered on a carpet of pink clover, taking sips from lemonade cups and eating other people's cake. Rose watched quietly from a comfy rocking chair, her stomach swollen before her, nibbling on bread and marge.

'Ladies and gentlemen.' A ruddy-faced Ted stood up and cleared his throat. 'Boys and girls. I am offering my apologies for this speech before I start as I am not very good at speaking, unlike my gentle and surprising wife,' he raised his glass to the blushing Betony, 'whose words in church were an absolute blessing. Now, as is so blatantly obvious, we are here to celebrate the wedding of my little brother Hugh – brave soldier that he is, I heard him say he'd rather take on Rommel any day of the week – and his beauteous bride Meg.' There was a ripple of laughter and applause. 'What has not been so obvious is their love for each other which has grown slowly and matured like a good wine, since they first met nearly a year ago, and since their first roll in the hay.' Ted gestured to Meg who was laughing unashamedly. 'With apologies to Mrs Wilson. Sorry, madam. What I am trying to say is that, against all odds, in the face of dreadful adversity, not least Jerry's landmines – up yours, Mr Hitler – it seems my little brother and Pengared's stroppiest land-girl have found their way to true love. And I hope it is a lesson to us all.'

'Hear, hear,' someone called. Everyone cheered and clapped.

Ted said, 'Raise your glasses to the bride and groom.'

There followed a brief silence. Then Ted said, 'And here's to the King, to us all. And to absent friends.'

Rose sipped her lemonade, Ted's words tearing into her. She was pulled apart: the joy she felt for Meg stamped on constantly by envy and grief. This is how it should have been, for her and Krystof: married at Trelewin church and then here at Pengared surrounded by their friends.

Everyone went back to eating and drinking and the chattering voices blurred into one. The afternoon stretched languidly on. Insects bumbled among the ripening plums and the light constantly changed as the sun moved across the sky, making her world hazier by the moment.

Meg's smiling face came into view. 'Come with me, Ginge.' She pulled her to her feet and led her away from the orchard and down the track where the open faces of wild roses festooned the hedges above banks of pungent cow parsley. Threads spun by invisible spiders sailed across the blades of grass, catching the afternoon light. Cornwall, nearing the end of a warm June day, was paradise, full-blown and ready to expand into the languidity of a long, hot summer.

They stopped and leant on the gate to Betony's meadow where, in place of the waving grasses of last year, rows of sugar beet stretched to the far hedges.

'We did good work here, didn't we, girl?' said Meg.

'It doesn't look as pretty now, does it?'

'Trust you to notice that. Times have to move on, Ginge. We all have to.'

The hairs on Krystof's arms shimmered in the afternoon light; the cutting machine whirred and clicked, punctuating their laughter; his kiss lingered on her lips.

'I think I'm stuck in time,' Rose whispered.

'Oh, come on,' said Meg, 'you have your baby to look forward to.' She linked her arm and marched her further up the lane. 'That's what I want next. Mr and Mrs Cumberpatch are proud to announce . . . I thank God for that stupid Jerry booby trap. Sent him back to me sooner, didn't it. And with that limp and stick, he looks quite distinguished, doesn't he. This way, Ginge, I wanted to show you our wedding present from Ted and Betony. It's just down here.'

The hedges reached high over their heads, leaves flickering in the low sun as they turned the corner. Ahead lay Cringle Cottage, all thatched and squat, on its little knoll surrounded by an unruly garden.

'The old cottage?' Rose swallowed. How Krystof had loved it.

'You bet! They've given it to us. Do you like it? We've been whitewashing like I don't know what and it's nearly perfect. It was a bit shabby and a bit smelly, and a bit tired, but aren't we all these days?' Meg giggled. 'But now look at it. It's beautiful. A great place to start married life.'

Turning away, Rose burst into violent sobs.

'Oh, Ginge, listen to me go on,' cried Meg, mortified. 'I'm so sorry. I'm gloating. Oh, Ginge.'

'You were right,' she said, choking on her tears. 'My turn *has* come.'

'What are you talking about?'

'Like you said, first day we met. You told me so. The war will touch me one way or another. Well, here we are, and look at me now.'

'I was beastly to you. I was sick with grief.' Meg pressed her radiant face close to Rose's. 'But you have your baby. That's what's important. My mother told me that many women tolerate their husbands, just so they can have a family. Just think, very soon you will have your own little one.'

'But my mother will never see it.' She could barely speak.

Meg pressed on. 'Just because Betony's meadow is no longer there, we are the richer for having had it. You have to remember your parents as they were. As the lovely people they were.'

Wretched crying made Rose's words difficult to understand. 'But I wanted Krystof. I love Krystof. I've never loved . . .'

Meg put her arm around her shoulders but could not comfort her. 'I don't mean to be hard on you, Ginge. You are married to Will.'

'I can't go home tonight. I don't want to. I can't do it.' Rose was desperate. She shook her head over and over.

'Stay at Pengared then,' said Meg. 'Betony will love to have you. Give yourself time. You can't go on like this.'

Rose looked her friend full in the face.

'You look lovely, Meg. Look at your white suit, you are so lucky.'

Meg grimaced. 'Not sure I should actually get away with white, not with my reputation. But never mind that. I want you to be as happy as me. You've got to think about what you are going to do.'

Rose thought of what lay in the drawers in her husband's study; the filth that had invaded her life.

She said, 'I know already what I'm going to do.'

Rose woke early to the sound of Blossom clopping across the yard and Mutt and Jeff barking. For one blissful moment, she imagined herself back in time; that Meg was snoring in the bed beside her and Krystof was waiting by the gate. Then she was crushed by reality.

Creeping downstairs, she left Betony a note of thanks and departed swiftly, unable to bear brushing shoulders with the old life she had left behind.

The headland was as green and fresh as ever, with seagulls wheeling overhead and the gentle waves in the cove below. She ignored it all and set her sights on the rooftops of Trelewin.

She walked through the front door and straight into the sitting room. The French windows were open and Will was outside on the patio, smoking a Player. The radio was blaring with a thunderous BBC voice and irritating, mistuned static. She reached for the dial and switched it off.

'Hey, what the—?' Will yelled and swung round in his deckchair to glare at her. 'What are you doing? And where have you been?' He leapt up and walked to the radio to switch it back on.

She dodged around him and out into the sunlight, throwing her words back over her shoulder. 'I stayed at Pengared last night. I didn't feel like coming home.'

'Well, isn't that charming. My own wife doesn't want to come home to me.' He was grinning sarcastically.

'It was my best friend's wedding and I wanted to linger. It was too late to come home. What's a wife to do, when she has no husband to escort her?' She sat in a deckchair on the patio, exhausted from her walk. 'And can't you keep the volume down. That thing is hurting my head.'

He leant against the French windows, looking down on her. She sensed he was enjoying a feeling of power. 'You haven't heard, have you?' He cocked his head towards the radio in the room behind him. 'You simply don't know what's been going on.'

She looked at him, puzzled. 'What do you mean?'

'Pengared's isolated, I know,' he said, 'but it's not Timbuktu.'

'You're talking in riddles. What's going on?'

'Only the biggest-ever military operation in British history,' he crowed. 'They set sail before dawn yesterday. Old Churchill spoke at midday. I can't believe you missed it.'

She was dazed. 'Ted's radio doesn't work. We were all enjoying the wedding. We didn't hear . . .'

Will was warming up. 'Bombers first. Then the fleet. Thousands and thousands of them. They landed in France yesterday. Canadians, Yanks, the British. From Southampton, Portsmouth, Dartmouth, Plymouth.'

'Plymouth?'

'Mountbatten was just on; until you came and switched him off. Evidently, they've been planning it for two years.'

She bent forward in her chair, enfolding her swollen belly with her arms. She felt her jaw stiffen. Her voice trickled out of her. 'What have they done? Where have they gone?'

'Normandy.' Will's eyes were alive with anticipation. 'The BBC are calling it the Second Front. Shush!' He put his hand up to silence her, listening to the radio intently as he sucked on his cigarette.

She waited, holding her breath, shock seeping like melting ice through her bones.

He went on. 'Just as I thought: this is only the second day. Sounds like they've got a long way to go. Eisenhower said, you don't just walk to Berlin. This is it. This is the big one, Rosebud.'

Wild, empty questions flew out of her mouth. 'How? But what's happening? Why?'

'Sounds like the British are doing all right. But you know how cagey the news readers are. They talk about *air operations* all the time. What the hell does that mean? It's what they're not telling us that's important. They never tell the whole story. Could be the Yanks are taking a hammering.'

She blocked her ears with her hands. 'Shut up. Why don't you shut up!'

He looked over, aghast. And then with a caustic smile said, 'Ah, yes. Of course. He's with the Yanks, isn't he?'

She could not answer him. She did not know where Krystof was. How could she possibly?

'I've touched a nerve, Rosebud,' he jeered. 'Your little Slovac is out there somewhere, wading through waves up to his neck. You're my wife and you're hung up on some Johnny foreigner. Well, I'm not having it, I tell you. I looked after you. Bought you this damned house. I even gave you a chance to go and fuck him. And what do I get for it?'

'I never asked for anything, I never wanted any of it,' she yelled. 'And he is *Czech*!'

'You say *is*, there, Rosebud. I'd use the past tense if I was you.'

She hauled herself out of the deckchair and walked away from her husband and the alarming voice on the radio. She reached the garden wall and sat on it, but she could still hear the radio and smell his cigarette smoke. Her eyes darted to the sky, the grass, her hands. She was agitated, her body alive with shock. She whispered to herself, 'Yesterday, I sat here at first light, and at the same time, he was preparing, briefing his men, listening to the last rousing speeches. And all through the day, all through

184

the wedding and right through the night, while I slept at the farm, he was . . . he was . . .'

She rubbed her hands over her face and over her head. She pulled at her hair. 'How do I know? How will I ever know? Where will he sleep tonight?'

Easing herself down, she slipped off the wall and landed with a soft thump in the long grass of the graveyard. Her baby woke and kicked her hard. She meandered quickly through the sleeping graves, telling the baby, 'He told me that he could not kill another man. But he will have to. He will *have* to.'

Pushing open the church door, she was enveloped by the dusty smell of hymnbooks. How cold it was. How quiet, like a stone tomb shut off from the horrors of the living world. Flowers from Meg's wedding wilted on the font. She walked unsteadily up the aisle, treading on saints' faces, treading on the bones of Cornishmen. Sinking into a pew at the front, she turned her accusing face to the altar.

'So this is why all the men have disappeared.' Her voice cracked the silence, speaking to the cross, to a picture of angels beneath which Meg and Hugh took their vows. 'This is why all the men have gone from the pubs, the farms, the villages. All because of yesterday, today, tomorrow . . .'

Sinking to her knees in the tight confines of the pew, her flesh pressed the icy stones, the wood of the seat hard against her back.

'Dear mother and father,' she prayed, whispering into palms wet with tears. 'You were right, of course you were. Krystof has gone. But all this time, I thought that at least he was somewhere around . . .' she choked on despair, 'on Salisbury plain, fighting mock battles, training with the boys from the regiment. Now the battle is real. All too awful and real. And how in heaven, how on *earth*, will my soldier ever return?'

She waited, wanting a response. Wanting an answer.

'I love him,' she whispered to God.

Anger consumed her. She felt it rise like hot vomit.

As she struggled to her feet from the cold slabs, the baby objected with tapping little prods. 'Oh, it's not your fault,' she told it, hurrying back down the aisle.

Outside, she glanced at the clock on the church tower. Jack

Thimble's bus was leaving in ten minutes. Back at the house, she crept through the scullery door and slipped across the hall. A voice on the radio drifted from the sitting room and she caught sight of the back of Will's head, cocked to listen, whisky glass in one hand, a curl of smoke above his head. She went upstairs and padded into the office for a moment, scarcely able to breathe.

'What are you doing up there?' Will called out. 'I've missed breakfast. What about my lunch?'

She came slowly back down the stairs, her belly lurching in front of her.

'I need to go and buy some provisions.' Her false smile made her cheeks ache. 'I'm just going to catch the bus to Polperro. It will be here any minute.'

When she tried to pass him in the hall, he grabbed her arm. 'You had better give up on your Slovac chap.' He showed his teeth in a snarl. 'I don't think the news is very good.' His gaze penetrated her. 'Why do you look like that? You'd better not be trying to leave me.'

She held her handbag – containing the envelope of money pilfered from his office – to her chest as sweat trickled excruciatingly down her back. 'I'm overwrought, that's all, Will,' she uttered in the sweetest voice she could muster. 'It's quite a shock, isn't it, all of this. We can but hope for a good outcome for the troops.'

His face flicked from angry to jubilant. 'I think the German boys are going to give us a good kicking.'

She looked at him, at the sweat beading above his mouth, his eyes shifting back to the radio in the sitting room, straining to hear more of the battle.

She tried to sound warm and wifely. 'Do you want anything in particular from Polperro? I won't be long.'

He glanced back at her. 'Christ, you look like you're about to drop. Oh, just get me some Players.'

The cobbled streets were alive with anxiety. People leant on gates, gathered in groups, listened on doorsteps. Radiograms hummed in the warm summer morning. Faces were guarded, not wishing to believe. Could this be the beginning of the end? Or only the start of something far worse?

'Shush-shush, everyone,' a woman cried, 'the King is on.'

Rose kept on walking down the hill, and straight into the tiny police station sandwiched between the pub and the fishing-tackle store. The front desk was presided over by a young, flushed constable with sticking-out ears. He switched his radio down reluctantly when she walked in.

'Yes, madam, and how can I help you?'

She saw him turn pale when he looked at her. His eyes began to flicker with concern.

'I've come to report a crime,' she said.

Rose thought she had given it plenty of time. She waited in Polperro, had some tea and toast in the tea room, and walked for a while around the harbour, watching the people assimilate each snippet of news they heard. She breathed the sea air and listened to the gulls, trying to ease the crush of despair inside her head, the excruciating agitation of her fingers and toes. She was tired, so very tired. She rested on a bench, knowing she had to go back sooner or later. At least to pack a case and head for Pengared and the warm embrace of her friends.

Suddenly she felt a lightness, an exquisite feeling; and then, deep inside, a belt tightened hard around her middle.

'I need to get you home,' she told the baby, and began to trudge back up the cobbles to the bus stop.

But even then, after she had bided her time, the police car was still parked on the gravel in front of the Old Vicarage.

An officer approached her. 'Mrs Bowman? We'll need to take a statement from you, at some point.' He glanced down at her pregnant belly and back to her face. 'Perhaps when you are less indisposed.'

'Yes, I . . . of course.'

The young constable was loading boxes into the front seat of the car.

'Nearly done, sir.'

'Is that everything from the room upstairs?' his superior asked him.

'Yes, sir.'

The policeman turned back to Rose. 'We'll need longer to search the rest of the house, madam.'

'I'd better go to my friends,' she said, '. . . wait at my friends' . . .'

She glanced towards the front door at the sudden affray. Will appeared, flanked by two more policemen, his face white, his dark eyes fixed onto her.

'Just let me say goodbye to my wife, damn you!' he cried, indignant.

'One moment is all you have, sir.'

They released him, keeping a watchful eye from a distance, as he bore down on her, his jaw set, his eyes never leaving her.

He leant in close, and held the top of her arm in a tight, spiteful grip. She flinched with pain as he bent to plant a kiss on her cheek. He whispered, his spit hitting her ear, 'I bought you this house. I pulled your parents' bodies from the rubble, and this is what you do to me.'

She looked at him, frozen. His eyes, brimming with unexpected tears, penetrated her.

'And when these monkeys set me free, which they will, eventually, Rosebud,' he hissed deep into her ear, 'I'm going to come and find you. And I'm going to kill you.'

She heard the police car doors slam and the engine start up as she stumbled along the footpath, desperate to make it to the stile before another contraction split her body. Her legs buckled. Doubled over, she moaned in pain, muttering to herself. 'Got to get somewhere safe. Got to get to Pengared.'

Climbing the stile, she felt an enormous warm deluge fall out of her and splash over the path like a torrent. She rested on the bottom rung, unaware of the minutes ticking by, the sun shifting the shadows, the hour passing. And then, not knowing how, she found herself at the top of the headland. The pain came again. A hundred times worse. She fell to her knees and rested her head on the ground. She screamed into the long grass, feeling the cool, sharp blades stick into her mouth. Shaking violently, she pulled herself up and began to limp on. One tiny part of her mind told her how amazing she was, how astonishing it was that her body kept on issuing her with little explosions of strength.

She reached the farmyard gate and tried to call Betony's name but all that came out were stifled mews. As she opened the gate she thought, I've gone and let the dogs out. But, for once, Mutt and Jeff sat by obediently and watched her, ears cocked, tails wagging hesitantly.

Far away, the elegant shape of Betony, her hair in curlers, stood hoeing the sugar beet in the meadow. Rose lurched towards her across the yard. There was no escape, no mind, no thought; she simply had to reach the meadow. Only ten yards to go. Five. Four. Oh, the tearing agony. Was this the end of her life?

Rose fell screaming on all fours among the leafy tops of the sugar beet, her body sinking into a sea of searing, bloody pain.

Betony was by her side. 'Don't try to fight it, Ginge. You've got to go with it.'

Rose sunk her palms into the red earth, digging with her fingernails.

Betony's voice was over her, below her, shrill in her ear. 'Ted is phoning for the doctor. But why didn't you telephone from home? Where's Will? Why did you come all the way here . . . oh, Ginge, go with it . . . why didn't you stay put? The doctor can reach Trelewin easier than here . . . Oh, Ginge.'

Too many questions; too much commotion. All Rose managed was, 'He's . . . been . . . arrested.'

Ted's large smiling face came into view and his gentle words and strong hands tried to guide her to a more peaceful place.

'What is happening to me?' Rose whispered to Betony as she leant over her. Rose's fingers reached up like claws and sank into her friend's hair.

'My gosh, Ginge, the baby's coming quickly!' cried Betony. 'Ouch, what are you doing to my curlers!'

Black curtains closed in at the edges of Rose's eyes; all sound was muffled; all senses gone until a voice said deep in her ear, 'You've got a little baby girl.'

Rose lay on her side among the sugar beet, wondering why curlers and hair pins were scattered over the ground. Betony wrapped something in a towel and placed it next to her.

'There,' said Betony, kneeling down beside her. 'I was conceived in this meadow, and now your daughter has been born here. She's early, and she came quickly. The doctor will be here soon.'

Rose stared at the wriggling bundle. A red hand emerged and unfurled like a flower.

Rose looked up at Betony. 'I pulled all your curlers out.'

'And some of my hair. Never mind.' Betony smoothed Rose's own damp hair out of her eyes. 'Now, Ginge, what's all this about someone being arrested?'

Rose stirred herself and grabbed at her friend's hands. 'Have you heard? The troops? All the men? About what's happening in France?'

'Yes, yes,' said Ted. 'I fixed the radio at last. It's stupendous, hard to get our heads round.'

Betony said, '. . . but now, now you hush yourself. If you can move, let's try to get you into the house.'

Rose blurted, 'But Will Bowman's a disgusting Nazi.'

'Is he? Oh, dear,' said Betony. 'We always thought he was a complete rotter, an utter wrong 'un, but this really takes the biscuit.'

'I shopped him.' Rose began to laugh, then to cry.

'Ginge, you mustn't upset yourself. Can you stand?'

'And Krystof . . .' she murmured. 'Krystof is somewhere in France. Like in your book, remember, Betony?'

Ted's strong arms held her up. 'Whoa, there you go. Steady, Ginge,' he said. 'I can hear the doctor's car coming down the track.'

'Don't you want to look at your baby?' Betony asked, soothingly.

Rose lifted her head from Ted's shoulder and carefully parted the folds of cloth in Betony's arms.

'Why,' Rose said, 'she looks just like a little plucked chicken.'

Sixteen

PERCHED ON THE FARMYARD GATE IN THE MAY SUNSHINE, ROSE SAID, 'All right, Mo, if you like you can walk her over to the hedge. That's it. No further.'

She watched the young boy hold Nancy's chubby hand and take small, patient steps while the little girl toddled beside him. She was born early, and was now walking early. Rose thought, *She is certainly going to be precocious*. Her dark, straight hair had been cut by Betony that morning and it framed her pale face, emphasising her long-lashed eyes.

'Off you go, chicken,' she said to her daughter, whose pinched, troubled face looked back at her. 'You can go without me. Don't worry, I'll be waiting here for you.'

Mo's care and interest in her daughter was fascinating especially when there were days Rose could barely look at her: the colour of her hair, the length of her lashes constantly bringing her father into mind. Despite this, she felt a smile soften her face as Mo stopped by a froth of cow parsley to point out a tiny bouncing butterfly. Nancy, all of eleven months old, was mesmerised, her finger following its flight. He can't hurt us now, Rose told herself, for he is locked away in Bodmin jail.

Feeling the sun warm her shoulders, she listened to the comforting sounds of Pengared: birdsong, the cock crowing in the barn, Ted chopping wood somewhere, the dogs' friendly bark, the general whirr of nature. What had been Krystof's word for the month of May? She did not know, for she had never asked him.

She watched her daughter's progress along the lane with Mo through a mist of grinding regret. A year and a half had passed since she'd last seen Krystof and her heart was an aching void. Just when she thought she was having a 'good' day, misery would rise up to slap her in the face. And now, on this exquisite May morning, it did so again. She gripped the top of the gate to steady herself.

Then in the midst of the Cornish countryside, a new, unfamiliar sound. Her ears twitched and she cocked her head to listen. There came out of the blue a clear and joyful ringing. She looked behind her in confusion, and then upwards to the sky.

'Mo!' she called in excitement. 'Mo! Quickly! Bring Nancy back here!'

Could it be? Could it possibly be? The bells of Trelewin church, silenced for six years, were resounding across the headland. Betony and Ted ran towards her across the yard.

'Can you hear the bells, Ginge?' Betony cried, in disbelief. 'Is it really the bells?'

'This can only mean one thing,' cried Ted. 'By God! Is it the end?'

And then another sound made them all turn to look up the track. There was Meg, triumphant, sitting atop the throbbing, spluttering Allis.

'Hey, everyone!' she screamed, standing up in the seat and waving like mad. 'Jack Thimble just told me. Hitler's dead! He's done himself in. It's over! The war is over!'

Meg leapt down from the tractor and came running. Their cheers were dizzy with joy as they hugged and jumped together; the children, squeezed in their arms, were tearful amid the melee. Mutt and Jeff yapped around their knees, tails lashing in rapture.

'Come on, Ginge,' said Meg, breaking free and tugging at her hand, 'the day has finally come.'

Rose laughed, remembering her promise. 'Goodness, yes, but we'd better telephone ahead and warn Polperro.'

'If you're going on the tractor,' said Betony, 'leave Nancy here.'

Rose looked at her daughter's face, at the huge tears squeezing out of her wary eyes. The child weaved her little hands into Rose's hair. 'No, no, I want her with me,' she said, discovering a new compassion. 'She's coming with me.'

Meg cried, 'All aboard then.'

'Go carefully,' shrieked Betony.

'You're mad,' said Ted, 'you're both barmy.'

'Mad with joy!' cried Meg as Rose settled beside her and held tightly onto Nancy. Meg pulled the starter switch and the tractor rumbled up the hill, driver and passengers all waving with gusto.

'Just look at the day, what a beautiful day. I'll never forget this.' Meg's voice sang out as the tractor chugged on, faithfully negotiating the lanes, trundling through tunnels of green. Tall horse chestnuts shaded the way, the blossoms, like pink and white candles, swaying in the soft breeze.

'We're not getting very far,' said Rose. 'What's the top speed on this thing, anyway?'

Meg giggled. 'Well, it's not exactly the Chattanooga Choo Choo, is it? Can you sing that, Nancy? Come on let's sing: "Pardon me boy, is that the Chattanooga Choo Choo –"'

Nancy gurgled, pressing her finger to Rose's cheek.

Meg looked round. 'Oh, Ginge, you're crying.'

Rose wiped her face on the back of her sleeve. 'Disbelief, I suppose,' she sniffed. 'I never thought this day would ever come. It's a shock. It's been so hard. So long and hard and *bloody*. I was just wondering about . . . I wonder if . . .'

'I know, I'm thinking of everyone too. Ol' Kentucky from the dance. Did he make it? And that awful New Yorker who groped you? What about Joel? We haven't heard from him. Some lose the battle, some win.' Meg put her hand on Rose's knee and peered into her face. 'We're OK, aren't we?'

'We are,' she said, blowing her nose and holding Nancy tighter than ever. '*We*'re alive. *We* made it.' She felt inexplicable guilt. 'We must be thankful . . .'

The tractor came to a spluttering stop at the top of Polperro's hill. Meg killed the engine and they sat and stared in amazement down the street. All the way to the harbour, everywhere they looked, people were moving in a mass, singing, cheering, dancing on the cobbles. Couples kissed in corners, on doorsteps, in the alleyways. Music trumpeted from a gramophone and someone had wheeled the piano out of the pub and was bashing away on it, singing 'There'll Always Be an England'. The landlord stood at the window passing pints of beer out and children ran this way and that, screaming in delight. The happiness and noise surged closer and closer, drawing them in.

Meg cried, 'Joel! There's Joel! He's home!' and leapt off the tractor.

Rose held onto a fidgeting Nancy and watched Meg's curly head bobbing through the throng. She caught sight of the boy Joel, now a man in navy uniform, unlatch the two girls he had on either arm to embrace Meg. He had a patch on his eye. *Perhaps that was why he was home*, Rose thought. *No matter. At least he was alive.* Joel and Meg held onto each other, whooping and jumping up and down in the crowd. Meg turned and waved, her face split in two by her smile.

Rose waved back, indicating that she would stay put. It was wonderful to sit and watch and Nancy seemed happy enough to have her full attention, to sit on her lap. Someone handed her up a glass of lemonade, and someone else handed Nancy an orange. A group of boys strung the wheels with bunting. Rose felt the utter joy of the people envelop her, but inside her heart, sorrow sat like a lump of granite.

'Where's *my* soldier?' she whispered into Nancy's hair. 'Where can he be?'

The day that everyone had been longing for had arrived. But, now the war had ended, would they release Will Bowman? The memory of his last words to her still made her freeze in terror. She needed to be safe. She turned Nancy around on her lap and looked at her. The little girl bit into the orange, the first she had ever seen, and chewed the peel, wrinkling her nose at its bitterness. For so long Rose had avoided gazing at the little girl's face, but the sudden desire to take care of her was overwhelming.

'Oh, chicken, we'll be all right. I am here for you.'

She held the child, trying to draw some strength from inside her, trying not to be envious of the faces below her laughing, cheering, singing. Perched there on the tractor she felt marooned above the gaiety. The unbelievable news became more and more real and she could not fathom what it meant for her.

Rose's eyes were drawn to someone. He was very still, not laughing or singing, with cap pulled low. Not part of the crowd. She pressed her hand to her throat. No. It couldn't be. Not here, in all this commotion. It couldn't be him?

The mass of people surged and she craned her neck, searching for the face again. She lost it. She leant over, straining, nearly crushing Nancy on her lap. She saw him again: the curve of his face, the colour of his skin. He was standing there, by the lamppost. He was not part of the celebrations; he was trying to pass through.

'No,' she breathed, suddenly feeling crushingly sick. 'No!' she shouted.

She shuffled around on the tractor seat, holding onto Nancy, trying to plant her feet in the spoke of the tractor wheel, to get down without dropping her child.

'Oh, God, hurry,' she muttered.

She landed on the ground with Nancy clinging to her neck. A great stitch ripped at her side. She hoisted Nancy higher in her arms. The orange rolled away across the cobbles.

'You all right, love?' someone said. 'Go steady now.'

'I just need to find him. Oh, God, I've lost him.'

On the ground, the crush of bodies shielded him from view. She should have stayed where she was on the tractor and called his name instead.

She forced her way forward, pushing people aside. No one minded, everyone was laughing. She was desperate and Nancy, heavy in her arms, started to cry. She tasted metallic panic in her mouth. She'd seen him, and now she would lose him.

'Krystof! Krystof!'

She felt an elbow in her ribs and a brush of rough khaki across her face. She was lost and panic turned to anger as she thrust her way through. Desperation made her fierce. 'Please, please, get out of the way.' She screamed, 'Krys-tof!'

The people parted and he stepped into view. He looked older; his face was peaceful but lined; his eyes were weary but beautiful. They opened wide, and wider. He saw her.

'Ruzena!'

Her knees buckled when she heard him call her name.

He plunged through the crowd to her, his elbows pushing, his arms opening to her. She felt a rush in her soul, an uncontrollable lifting of her heart. Her body trembled as she took in his poise, his smile, the shape of his hands. The memory of his body – him bare-chested on the other side of the wire – that had lain dormant inside her was reawakened, suddenly, in a bubble of joy.

But he stepped back from her. His jaw dropped.

'Who is this?' he asked.

'My daughter. Nancy. Say hello.' She jiggled Nancy up and down. 'This is Krystof.'

He stared at Rose. 'You married him?'

'I did.' She lowered her eyes, suddenly feeling dreadful and ashamed.

He shook his head, his eyes empty and shielded by his lids.

Her voice was thin with panic. 'Krystof, what's the matter?'

'This proves it to me,' he said, his face blank, shut down, immovable.

'What? What do you mean?'

'I should have known better, and listened to the warnings in my head.'

'Krystof, please . . . this is hard enough . . .'

'You were engaged. I suppose you were stringing us both along. I was the idiot who lost out.'

'Oh, no, Krystof, you don't understand.' Her words blurted in a frenzied stream. 'I was beside myself. I didn't know where you were. No one told me. I didn't get your message. Betony and Ted couldn't find me. The day my parents died I was deranged. Mrs Brown didn't remember to – or simply didn't – tell me you'd come to Stanley Crescent until too late. I was broken. I couldn't cope. You were gone.'

'So you went ahead and married him anyway. You didn't try any harder than that.' His voice was cold. He turned swiftly to go. 'I was just a distraction.'

'Oh, no. No, you weren't. Krystof, please. You were *everything*.' She tried to grab his hand but he shook her off.

'Please don't go,' she cried. 'Please listen to me. Let me explain.'

'I can't listen to you any more. This is all I can give you. I have to go.'

She hurried after him, feeling the burden of Nancy, who now began to cry.

'I made a dreadful mistake, Krystof. But I was not myself.'

'No,' he snapped back, 'I have made a dreadful mistake.'

The people jostling around stared at them for a moment before continuing with their celebration.

Her voice was tiny, desperate, close in his ear. 'Don't leave me again,' she pleaded. 'Not now.'

Krystof wiped his hand over his face. His voice broke. 'I thought about you all the way to the beaches, all the way across Normandy, all the way to Paris. I thought that maybe I had been mistaken. That he was just giving you a lift somewhere. But the way that woman spoke to me . . . what she said to me . . .'

'Mrs Brown, she—'

'I wanted to marry you. I came for you.' He drew himself tall, standing to attention. His uniform formed a shield. 'I believed you loved me.'

'Stop, Krystof, please.' Rose set squawking Nancy on the ground, feeling her hands tug the knees of her trousers. She turned to Krystof. 'You should believe, because it's true. I love you. I always have.'

She embraced him, kissing him long, hard and deep, knocking his hat off the back of his head. She smelt him, tasted him, breathed him in. He wrapped his arms around her and she felt him press himself to her, succumb for a moment.

He pulled back. 'No, you stop this, stop this now.' He held her away from him. 'You need to take care of that child.'

'But it's me, Krystof.' She looked up at his cold face, her chest hammering with dread. 'It's your Rose. You love me. You're my boy. You're the one.'

'You have his child.'

She blurted, 'My husband is in prison. We are separated.'

He uttered, 'But of course, *married*.'

Rose began to shake with dismay.

Sensing someone at her side, she turned to see Meg who was saying in wonder, 'Krystof, you made it.' But Meg's smile dropped as her eyes darted between them.

'Meg, please take Nancy for me.' Rose's voice was weak. 'I need to talk to Krystof.'

Meg assented and gathered Nancy in her arms. She disappeared into the crowd.

Rose waited, head bowed. Krystof looked at her hard for a full minute and then took her hand. He pulled her up the street, striding quickly as she hurried behind trying to keep up.

'Let's get away from here,' he said, opening the door of his army car.

He drove at speed down the lanes, his eyes never shifting from the road. Rose turned herself sideways in the seat, silently imploring him to speak to her.

Eventually he whispered, 'Why, Rose?'

Tears streamed down her face. 'I don't know. I just don't know.'

'I came for you. I had our *marriage* licence ready.' His teeth were gritted. She had never seen him angry. The war had changed him. The war had changed them both.

The night at the maisonette returned to her. The shock and the horror of seeing her life destroyed that had altered her. How she had allowed Will to claim her. How she had punished herself.

'But you weren't there!' she wailed. 'My parents were dead. I thought I had lost you too!'

He drove on in silence.

'Krystof, look at me.'

She saw his lips twitch then realised immediately that he was trying to smile so that he would not cry.

'I can't look at you,' he said. 'It hurts too much.'

Krystof pulled the car up outside the church in Trelewin and marched off along the path to the cove. Rose hurried to keep up.

'That's your home, isn't it? That's where you live with *him*.' He broke the silence, nodding at the Old Vicarage. 'Hadn't you better be getting home?'

'I live at Pengared now,' she said awkwardly, sensing his bitterness. 'Officially it still belongs to him. I don't know what's going to happen to it now.'

Krystof shrugged. 'I'm sure you'll think of something.'

As they descended the ferny path to the cove in silence, she felt the cold and frightening space between them.

She sat on their rock, shivering despite the sunshine. Krystof walked to the wire, standing motionless with his back to her. How she had dreamed of this moment, being here at Trelewin cove again. Together. But not like this. Never like this.

'No need for this any more,' he said, giving the wire a half-hearted kick. He looked through it out to sea.

When at last he turned to her, his face was shining with tears. He walked over and sat by her side, reluctantly allowing her to take his hand. She felt once again the warmth of his skin, knowing that, once, she had believed she never would again. She felt her chest tighten in agony.

Into the silence, he said, 'You know I love you, Ruzena. God knows I love you . . . but . . .'

Her voice trembled. 'Don't punish me, Krystof. Now that we have the chance to be together.'

'What chance?' His voice was a hoarse whisper, still edged with resentment. 'I was on my way to find you when I stopped in Polperro. I was going to go to Pengared to ask where you were. I am glad I found you, for at least now you will know.'

'Know what?'

'I have to go away again. I've come all the way from liberated Europe, back here to England, only to be sent back home.'

Rose lifted her hands to cover her mouth.

He said, 'There is a trainload of Czech servicemen leaving Plymouth for Prague tomorrow. And I have strict orders to be on it. Now the war is over your government waste no time in sending us back. They don't need us any more.'

She felt as if he was choking her. 'Not again. Not this time, no, Krystof. Please tell me you are joking.'

'I can't even begin to tell you what hell I have been through in the last year,' he muttered, unable to meet her eyes. 'Utter hell.'

Krystof lowered his head and she watched his spirit breaking in front of her, his light extinguishing.

He said, 'I have not heard from my parents or brother in two years. I need to go back.' She saw the skin tighten over his face as he spoke. 'My grandmother, my Babička, will need me. If she is still alive. I have no way of knowing. I need to go. Understand, please, Rose. I have to go home to Prague.'

'But I've only just found you again,' she wailed. 'At times I tried to forget you. But that was impossible. I soon realised my mistake, marrying the wrong man. My life was cold. It just stopped. I have my daughter, and there are days when I resent her. But what has never changed, Krystof, through all of this, is that I love you.' She reached out with a trembling finger to touch his face. 'Not again. Please don't leave me again.'

He avoided her touch, got up abruptly and went to sit on another rock. His jaw was set, his eyes staring into the distance, his fists clenched. She could not bear him being so close, yet punishing her, almost hating her. She doubled over, her crying soaring upwards to mix with that of the gulls.

'All I wanted was to be with you,' she whispered to herself. 'Is it so much to wish for?'

Krystof looked over at her. Through her tears she saw him gather his thoughts. He took a deep breath and walked back to her. He knelt on the sand at her feet and rested his head in her lap. The hell he had spoken of, what lay behind his eyes, she would never grasp. She cupped his chin with her hand and tenderly stroked the face she had not set eyes on since their night in the barn.

He sat up and rested his forehead against hers, his embrace enfolding her.

'Oh, Ruzena, Ruzena,' he breathed. 'I don't want to leave you. I never want to leave you. I want to soak you up.'

She grasped his hands and drew them to her breasts. Lowering her head she kissed his fingers and held him close. They kissed, as if kissing was the same as breathing, as if it would give them life. Give them time. Give them each other. Anger surged through her veins. Her lips bit him; she pinched him; her fingers pulled at his hair. He let her. As if he needed her to. As if he wanted to feel the pain.

'You made it back to me, Krystof. The least I can do is follow you home,' she declared, her voice edged with new strength. 'If you are going back to Prague then I'm coming too.'

As they climbed back up through the shady ferns, Rose felt a glimmer of desire and expectation, imagining this was how the people in Polperro, in London, all over the country were feeling. Now she could join them.

'Do you know what you just said back there, Ruzena?' asked Krystof. 'Are you sure about it? There may be peace in Europe but there is also turmoil: battlefields, devastated cities. Your RAF did a good job in Germany, you know. Refugees, evacuees, starvation. There are reports emerging of dreadful horrors perpetrated by the Nazis. You will be travelling through all of this. Do you really think you can make the journey? What about your child?'

Rose swallowed hard on her fear. 'She will be safe with me.'

She held on tightly to his hand, nibbling his finger with her lips. She had no idea how she would make it.

Krystof stopped her when they reached the top of the headland, and sat her down on the shimmering long grass. She watched the gulls circling the cove, realising her life was changing with every terrified, thrilling breath she took.

'My friend Vaclav is shipping out tomorrow with me,' Krystof said. 'Remember him from the pub in Polperro? He married Mabel yesterday. Remember her from the dance?'

Rose nodded each time he mentioned a name she knew, her mind fixing on one thing: she and Krystof would be together, whatever it took.

'Mabel is going to go to Prague. It might take a while to sort out but you must travel on the train with her. It will be safer, the two of you. Safer for Nancy.' Krystof fumbled in his pocket for a pen. He wrote on the back of an envelope. 'This is my house. This is where I live, in Prague. You must find me there.'

She took it and thrust it in her pocket as clouds of tears began to blind her.

He stroked her eyelids with the tips of his fingers. 'You have to take extra care of yourself. I need you safe and well.'

'Don't speak any more. Just hold me, Krystof.'

'I haven't much time. I have to report back to Plymouth barracks. The curfew is six o'clock.'

'Damn these bloody orders! The war is over!' she shrieked. 'I can't say goodbye now. I just can't.'

'Then we won't say goodbye. I will simply look at you.'

He was deadly serious, holding her in his arms and leaning back to study her face. 'I see your green eyes, the little crinkles at the corner; your tiny dimples, see, when you laugh, although you are far from laughing now. I see the fire of your hair, your scar. Everything that makes you.'

She watched as he tried to say more, but seemed to choke on emotion.

'Your car is at Trelewin. And I have to go that way to Pengared,' she mumbled. 'So this is where we part.'

His eyes were hollows of sorrow. 'Ruzena, you sound so bitter.'

'That's because I am. We have moments, literally moments. And you have to go away again. It's too much to bear.'

'Are you going to book your ticket?'

'Of course I am,' she sobbed, her tears fat, hot and angry. 'I want to take a photograph of you, but I haven't a camera.' An abrupt shout of laughter burst from her. 'What am I saying? I've never had a camera.'

'Your face is in here.' He touched his chest.

'I can't bear it,' she said, then a movement caught her eye and she glanced at the sky. 'Oh,' she cried. 'A swallow, the first of summer. He's early! He must have heard – the war is won!' The sickle shape of the bird's wings switched back like a kite caught on the breeze. 'Oh, there's another one!'

She glanced back at Krystof but he was walking away from her.

'Krystof?'

Every few steps, he glanced back over his shoulder.

'We are not saying goodbye,' he called above the soaring sound of the waves, the calling of the gulls.

Aghast, she watched as his presence peeled away from her side like a bandage unravelling until his waving figure faded into the horizon.

'I will never say goodbye,' she screamed to the sky, to the earth, to herself. 'I will never say goodbye.'

Seventeen

THE PLYMOUTH TRAVEL OFFICE WAS BUSY WITH A LONG QUEUE OF people waiting. Rose sat beside Betony on an uncomfortable bentwood chair, crossing and recrossing her legs. On her lap sat her handbag containing the envelope of money she had filched from Will's study. The airless room was stifling; voices were pitched with anxiety; a typewriter tapped sporadically on her machine.

'Fill these forms in while you wait,' said a prim secretary, handing out sheets of paper. 'Seems like the whole of Europe is on the move.'

The woman sitting the other side of Rose asked, 'What did you do on VE Day? I stayed home and listened to Churchill's speech. When he was on the balcony and he said to the people, "This is your victory." And they all shouted back, "No, it's yours." Made me darn well cry, he did.' The woman put her hand to her cheek, shaking her head, remembering the pleasure. 'How about you, lovey?'

'I cried too,' Rose said. 'I cried a great deal. But I'm booking my ticket to be with the man I love. So, hopefully, no more tears.'

'Good for you, lovey. I like a happy ending.'

Betony tapped Rose on the sleeve and leant in to whisper, 'Are you sure you're doing the right thing, Ginge?' Her voice cracked with concern. 'This has been bothering me for days. It could be so dangerous going all that way. And little Nancy . . .'

'Nancy will be fine.'

'She wasn't that fine when we left her with Meg this morning. One little bit of disruption to her routine and she gets very upset. God knows what a three-day train journey across Europe will do to her. Have you seen the reports? What they're finding in Poland and Germany?'

'I'll be with Mabel. She will help.'

'Huh – that flighty piece. What use would she be? This is such an enormous thing you're doing, Ginge. Have you really thought it through?'

'Krystof fought in the desert. Krystof helped liberate Paris. All I am doing is travelling by train with silly Mabel across France and Germany to be with him. That's all.'

'Oh, but Ginge. It would be safer to stay at home.'

Rose took a breath. 'Will Bowman threatened to kill me,' she said. 'And so to get me and Nancy as far away as I can from him will be the safest thing to do.'

'My God . . .' Betony breathed. 'You must tell the police.'

'No, that will make it far worse. Me calling the police in the first place was what set him off. And they let that Mosley out eventually – and his Mitford wife. It's only a matter of time before Will is set free too. And then what?'

She looked at Betony, whose eyes were spherical with shock.

'We won't breathe a word of where you are if he comes back to Trelewin,' said Betony.

'Thank you, Betony. You and Ted, and Meg and Hugh, too, have been the best friends anyone could ever . . .'

Betony rummaged for her handkerchief in her bag and dabbed her eyes. 'But we won't see you again.'

Rose placed her hand on her friend's arm. 'We all only have one life, Betony,' she said, sounding braver than she felt. 'We must live it. Live for today.'

'Next,' barked the bald-headed man behind the desk.

Rose sat down in front of him and Betony took a chair behind her.

Rose opened her mouth to speak. 'I'd like a—'

'Wait a moment. Before we start, have you your passport? Your identity card?'

She handed them over. She waited. He studied the form she had filled in, shaking his head, tutting.

'A passage to Prague, Czechoslovakia?' He sounded incredulous. 'Not in any hurry, I hope. You'll hardly get there before summer's out, the rate things are going. I thought most people would be coming the other way. Getting out of the likes of there. Are you a war bride, then?'

'Yes,' she lied. 'I'm taking my daughter with me.'

The man looked dubious. 'Not many girls go east. Most go west, following the GIs. Two boatloads have left Plymouth already, and the war's not been over five minutes.'

Rose was impatient. 'Well, I'm not one of them, am I?'

He lifted an eyebrow and appraised her. He turned over the form. 'Right, er . . . Mrs Bowman, is it?'

'Yes.'

'Bowman, you say?'

'Yes.'

He narrowed his eyes. 'That doesn't sound like a very Czechoslovakian surname to me.'

Rose swallowed. She had just told this man she was a war bride and wanted to follow her new Czech husband back to Prague. And yet she was still married to an English convict and Nazi sympathiser. All her papers said her name was Bowman, Mrs.

Betony, behind her, let out a sigh of resignation and began to put on her scarf and gather her bag and gloves. 'Come on, Ginge,' she whispered.

Rose spoke up. 'I think – er, there has been a mistake – my married name is—'

A loud voice resounded behind her, making her jump: 'Pepper? Pepper? Is that Pepper?'

Rose turned. 'Oh, Mrs Pike. How do you do?'

The South Cornwall district commissioner's robust, energetic frame filled the space beside Rose, looming over her.

'My, my. You have grown into quite a young woman, haven't you? How long is it since I've seen you? Early '43 when you passed out of our college, wasn't it, Pepper? March, if I'm not mistaken. You girls were exceptional.'

The man behind the desk leant forward, his pate shining under the overhead light. 'Her name isn't Pepper any more, madam. It's Bowman.'

Mrs Pike smiled down on her, appreciatively. 'Ah, so you married. How lovely for you,' she boomed. 'I'm here to buy a ticket to Bristol to see my daughter. She's been working as a FANY up here. Haven't seen her in months. These wretched queues. Nothing changes, does it? And where are you off to, then? Didn't go and marry a GI, did you, girl?' When she laughed her jaw appeared more square-shaped than usual.

'No, I—'

'She married a Mr Bowman, says here,' chipped in the official. 'Now can you move on, please, madam. I have to deal with this young woman.'

Mrs Pike scrutinised the man through her round spectacles.

'Excuse me, Mr Jenkins,' she snipped, studying the officious name plaque on the desk. 'There's no need to be tetchy. We are only having a conversation.'

'And if you haven't noticed, there's a lot of people waiting. So if you don't mind—'

'I had noticed, but you can't use your usual excuse, that there's a war on. It won't wash any more. Try being civil instead.'

The man harrumphed and drew Rose's attention. 'That lady called you Pepper . . . ?' he said.

'That's my maiden name,' Rose said quickly. 'My married name is—'

'Not very Czech sounding at all,' he bleated, shuffling the forms. 'I smell a rat. You say you are a war bride. But you're not married to a Czech man. You haven't the paperwork. None of it matches up. These papers could be forgeries. This isn't going any further. Next!'

Rose stared at the man, hating his sweating forehead and long superior nose. 'If you please, sir . . . I can explain . . .' she faltered.

Mrs Pike's broad bosom leant in.

'Now, now, Mr Jenkins. No need for all this fuss,' she clipped. 'Just issue her with a ticket to wherever she wants to go. That's a ticket to match her passport, Mr Jenkins. And be done with it. Stop wasting everybody's time.'

PART TWO

Prague
September 1945

Eighteen

IT WAS LATE AT NIGHT WHEN THE TRAIN FINALLY EASED TO A HALT and let out a belching hiss of steam. Woken from her doze, Rose opened her eyes. Clouds of vapour obscured the windows, then evaporated to reveal a great gloomy vault of a station. Trains slept on platforms either side. Ironwork pillars, decorated with leaves and tendrils swirling like the frontispiece of her child-hood book of fairy tales, reached up into darkness. The rusty, battered sign told her she had arrived: *Praha*.

The grinding and juddering of her journey had ceased, but the voices, sounds, fatigue and the gnawing hunger (Mabel's food had run out long before hers and Nancy's so they'd had to share) remained with her like a bad dream. The sea-sickness on the ferry; the busy Paris streets through which they had hurried between stations; the refugees of Stuttgart shuffling among the flattened ruins through which the train chugged; starving faces; shattered lives.

Rose had distracted Nancy from the famished girl who had reached up to the train window at the signal stop outside Stuttgart, asking for *wasser*. When the train pulled across the Czech border and a brass band struck up, red-and-blue flags fluttering on trombone and trumpet, they had laughed with hysterical relief. Nancy had waved through the window this time, clapping her hands in delight.

Now, on Rose's lap, Nancy began to stir. Her pale cheeks were flushed, her brow was crumpled, her hands grimy. She began to cry.

Rose tried to comfort her. With her stomach flipping and her limbs tingling with sudden energy, she frantically smoothed down Nancy's hair. Rose's reflection in her hand mirror showed her own face covered with a film of dust. She was ashen with exhaustion, but there was a blaze of purpose in her eyes.

Mabel on the seat opposite applied powder and lipstick, her wedding ring flashing on her finger. 'Thank God that's over with,' she moaned. 'I never want to set foot on another train again as long as I live. These blessed seats are certainly hard on one's posterior. They said we didn't bomb Prague much at all, so I hope it's in a better shape than those awful German cities. Can't wait to see Vaclav. He'd better be there to meet me. And I hope he has learnt some more English, for I don't know any Czech to save my life.'

They disembarked, Rose clutching Krystof's address written on the back of an envelope, holding Nancy tightly, her suitcase wrenching her other arm. She was stooping with fatigue.

'Where's the porter?' asked Mabel. 'Hey, Ginge, do you know the Czech for "porter"?'

'No,' Rose said, then muttered under her breath, 'I don't even know the Czech for "please shut up".'

At the barrier, they gave up their tickets and were solemnly beckoned into an office by two uniformed officials. One sat behind the desk and flicked through their passports and visas, writing in a ledger. The other watched their faces. Rose held her nerve, standing passively. Mabel jigged from one foot to the other.

'I hope this doesn't take too long,' whined Mabel. 'Can't stand all this red tape. We're *British*, *English*.' She leant over the desk. 'Do you understand? *We* helped *you* in the war. They should just let us through. There shouldn't be any need for all of this.'

Please be quiet, thought Rose. We *have* to stand it.

The officials spoke in their inexplicable language, their straight faces giving nothing away. Rose strained to understand. She wrote down Krystof's address for them and they nodded indifferently. Mabel proudly showed them her marriage certificate. At last their passports were stamped and they were free to go.

'About time,' muttered Mabel.

Their train had been the last of the night. All the passengers had faded away and the empty echoing station concourse opened up before them. Rose felt utterly lost but wanted, more than anything, to leave behind the babbling voice of her travelling companion.

'What now, Nancy?' she said into her daughter's hair as she hoisted her higher in her arms. She had been wondering all along if Krystof would be there to meet them; wondering and hoping all the way across England, France and Germany. The station was deserted.

A man appeared by the entrance, his arms open wide. Suddenly, Mabel cried out and sprinted off, her joyous whoops of 'Vaclav! Vaclav!' resounding up to the roof. Rose slowly approached the couple and waited politely for the kissing to stop.

'I haven't seen Krystof in weeks,' Vaclav told her, extracting himself from his bride's embrace, his face covered with lipstick. 'He is on leave. Had to travel to his country home for some reason or another. You need tram number eight.' He raised his voice over Mabel's giggling. 'That will take you to the Old Town Square. It's easy from there. Go straight on, turn left, right, left . . . left again. Here, take this.'

He fished in his pocket and poured some coins into Rose's hand.

She looked down at the unfamiliar money, unable to read the value.

'Oh! That's very kind of you, but I still don't know . . . how do I . . .' she began.

'It's easy. You'll find it,' repeated Vaclav. 'We have just minutes to catch our last tram. I need to get this one home.'

He saluted Rose and took his wife's arm. They set off together, Mabel's short legs skipping to keep up with him.

'Good luck, Ginge. Bye-eee,' called Mabel, barely looking back, her high heels clipping away into silence.

The station clock struck a quarter to midnight as Rose hoisted Nancy higher on her hip and walked out into the empty street. Night had fallen like an inky cloak, hiding the city and its secrets from her. Gaslights glowed weakly at sparse intervals along the street and a solitary tram rumbled by, its lights feeble in the darkness. Clutching Nancy, she hurried across the cobbles to where she thought it might pick up passengers; but in vain. It did not stop.

She turned to the sound of a man calling. One of the officials, standing at the station exit, was gesticulating. Not understanding a word he said, but assuming he meant she should go towards the left, she raised her hand in thanks.

A wretched tiredness dragged her down. Her arms, holding both Nancy and her suitcase, began to burn. She contemplated the streets, some no bigger than alleyways greeting her with bottomless shadows, and felt herself pulled into a labyrinth. Buildings towered either side, shutting out the sky and the stars. Walls were pockmarked (bullet holes, she feared), bricks were crumbling, stucco peeling and ruined. Great studded doors were bolted to the night. Feeling Nancy's sleepy cheek against her shoulder, the suitcase tugging on her hand, she turned corner after corner. They were alone save for the accompanying echo of her own footsteps and the smell of cooking cabbage, damp and wood smoke. Lamplight showed itself sporadically through the tiniest gaps in shutters. From pitch-black lanes came the drip-drip of water and a dog howled behind a wall. Footsteps approached and then receded without ever revealing their owner.

Shaking with nerves, she walked under the arch of a mighty stone gateway, its roof disappearing into the black sky above. She found herself, small and shivering, on the edge of an acre of cobbles. Putting her suitcase down, she told a protesting Nancy to sit on it, feeling her own anxiety rising to match that of the little girl's. She wondered if this, indeed, was the Old Town Square. A streetlamp shed a vague gleam on a medieval hall rising like a haunted storybook castle at the centre. All around her loomed the enclosing edifices of grand buildings. Silence surrounded them. There was not a soul to ask.

Rubbing her aching arms, Rose gazed up at the wall of the old hall, to see, by the glow of the gas lamp, a peculiar clock. It had not one but three faces, overlapping like arcs in a mathematical drawing. Shimmering with gold in the grim darkness, its long iron hands reached to point out indecipherable moments in time.

'Look at that clock, Nancy,' she bent down to whisper to her daughter. 'See how beautiful and strange it is. I've never seen anything like it in . . .'

In the empty stillness came the whirr of clockwork and the hands shifted to midnight. Chimes struck up and, suddenly, a figure of a grinning skeleton squatting beside the clock face lifted a bony hand to brandish an hourglass at them. Nancy screamed.

Rose picked her up and turned her away. But over her daughter's shaking head she fixed her own eyes on the white leering skull. Her parents would be broken skeletons now, buried in St Budeaux churchyard.

'Oh Mother, Dad, help me!' she blurted. 'I'm so sorry. I did not come to visit you. I never said goodbye. I don't know where we are. We're so far from home.'

Another noise singed her nerves as a tiny door above the clock creaked open to release a parade of mechanical doll figures shuffling out to mark the passing of the hour. Their wooden eyes in blank faces watched her, haunted her.

She gripped the suitcase handle, gathered Nancy close to her, turned and ran. What was she doing bringing her little girl here? What was she doing in this strange city in the dead of night? Her chest was squeezed with fear and her legs propelled her, urging her to get away. Tears of panic burst from her eyes. She could scarcely breath. *What if Krystof is not here? What if he decides not to remember me? What if he turns us away?*

She blundered down a dark lane, confronted with corner after corner: this way or that? What had Vaclav said? Oh, damn Vaclav! Her neck was drenched with sweat, her feet were like lead. And a stitch tore open her side. Nancy was clinging to her neck, fear silencing her, while Rose moaned in terror. Twisting her ankle on a kerb, she stumbled. Streets became tighter and walls closed in. She met with dead end after dead end. Dripping walls; stinking drains. They were trapped.

A memory of Krystof's voice found its way into her head: 'I live by the monastery of St Clement near the river. My house is called *At the Clementinum*.' But how would she ever find it? The street signs were tiny, indecipherable, high up on the walls. Doorways were shaded; steps led to nowhere. There was no one to help her; no one to care.

She stopped, setting the suitcase down, hoisting Nancy higher, feeling the little girl's frightened heart beating fast against her chest. Then in the darkness a match was struck. A figure emerged from inky shadows. The man spoke, his words rumbling, his expression shielded by an enormous moustache through which he smoked his cigarette.

'Please help us,' she said, her desire to find Krystof overwhelming any fear she had of the stranger.

He looked at her and at the whimpering Nancy, who was hiding her face in Rose's neck. With shaking hand, Rose drew out the envelope on which Krystof had written his address. The man's eyes widened and his moustache lifted in what Rose believed to be a smile. He spoke again, his finger pointing to a porch set in a thick stone wall.

'Thank you,' she said.

'Ah, *Anglický*,' he said, his voice and his footsteps drifting away.

Not daring to breathe, not daring to hope, Rose walked over to the arched stone entrance and pressed the bell. A great dripping silence returned to the street. Agitated, she lifted the huge knocker and rapped on the door. After excruciating, breathless moments, she heard the rattle of the latch, the drawing back of bolts. The door opened a chink and she saw the face of an old woman. Rose found a well of strength. She whispered, 'Krystof Novotny? Do you know him?'

It was no use. Her words were futile. Deep wrinkles carved the woman's face and puzzled brown eyes glistened by the light of a candle. And then a crooked hand stretched past the door to touch her hair, then reach for Nancy's face.

'Ruzena?' came the deep voice, rolling the 'r' like a cat's purr.

Rose felt the woman grip her sleeve and pull her in. She stumbled across the threshold, supported by surprisingly strong arms encased in aged soft flesh.

The door was shut behind her and she was inside a small vestibule lit only by the candle that the woman held aloft. Mutely understanding the woman's gesture, she dropped her suitcase and began to climb the stairs, with Nancy's head lolling over her shoulder. At the top, her eyes swimming in the new lamplight, fatigue drained blood from her bones and she clutched the banister, not able to take another step. The woman extracted Nancy from her arms. Were there more stairs to climb, more corners to turn? Or was their journey finally over?

The woman spoke to Rose as she would to a child, coaxing

her into a room. Wooden panels glimmered in the light of a bank of candles and orange flames crackled in the fireplace. Thick ivy-green curtains shielded the windows and the polished parquet floor glimmered like a fish pond. In front of the window lay a divan; the sight of its cushioned, silken depths brought a groan to Rose's throat.

The woman led Rose to the bed and lay Nancy down. She made Rose sit, and in silence knelt to unlace Nancy's shoes. With trusting innocence, the little girl curled herself up on the bed and was, in one sigh, sound asleep. The woman turned her attention to Rose's laces. Sinking fast, Rose fixed her eyes on the top of the silver-grey head and the thick hair tied in a bun at the nape of her neck. She dug her fingertips into the sheets to keep herself from falling as the woman muttered a string of words to her. They rambled up and down, like an old tune; like unimaginable poetry.

'Krystof?' Rose asked again, her voice a shadow.

She realised she was in her underthings and a nightgown was being pulled over her head. The woman gestured that she should lie down but she knew that as soon as her head touched the pillow next to Nancy, she would be gone. And still she wanted Krystof.

A glass of wine was held to her lips and she gratefully sipped its sweetness, feeling its fire fill her head. Then softly, like the enfolding wings of an angel, sleep began to draw her down.

She heard snatches of songs as the woman stroked her hair. Bohemian lullabies? Slovakian folk songs? A pinprick in her mind dearly wanted to know. Where was Krystof? Were these his songs? Who was this lady? She tried to open her eyes to ask the question, but simply could not.

His voice came to her in the midst of a green velvet forest. It flickered in the embers of a banked-down fire and curled through the smoke of a dozen snuffed-out candles. She heard his footstep. She knew it was him, and she was sure that she smiled and reached for him, but her arms were heavy and her body numb. He left her once more. And then her mother and father also began to walk away from her. They turned their backs on her, holding hands, and walked into the depths, veiled by a whole season of falling leaves. She tried to call out, but she was in agony. This was the pain she had been meant to feel the first time they left her. A pain so deep, it melted the marrow of her bones. A pain so raw, it turned her heart inside out. The pain gagged her, turned her over and made her sleep once more.

Nineteen

ROSE HEARD THE DRAWING OF HEAVY CURTAINS AND THE CHINK OF a china cup and saucer. The soft morning light was the colour of butter. She opened her eyes. Krystof was standing beside the bed, his tawny hair gilded by the sunshine through the window. His grey eyes gazed into hers with intensity. His soft hands held hers and she felt his vitality seeping through her skin. She smiled sleepily. He was as familiar as her own self; his features belonged to her.

'Welcome home, Ruzena.'

He had opened a leaded pane in the tall stone mullioned window and the balmy breeze touched her face as gently as his fingertips smoothed her hair.

'The air is so soft, this time of year,' he said. 'I missed it when I was away. I missed it, but not half as much as I have missed you. It has been far too long, these last few months. Waiting for you to arrive. It has been an age.'

'Where's Nancy?' she asked.

'Babička is giving her breakfast.'

'Babička?'

'My grandmother.'

'Is Nancy all right?'

'Yes, yes. Better, I think, for a good night's sleep. Babička said she might well benefit from a bath.'

Rose sat up slowly, conscious of her head swimming with drowsiness. She stretched inside the voluminous nightgown, her hair tousled, her face flushed with sleep.

Krystof smiled at her. 'You made it, Ruzena.' His eyes were shining with disbelief, shining with joy. 'You look just like a child angel.'

She slipped her fingers into the palm of his hand.

'I don't feel much like an angel this morning,' she said. 'And I expect I was a sorry sight last night.'

'Come and breathe the fresh air. It will make you feel better.' He drew her up from the bed and she padded barefoot with him to the window. He pushed it wider and rested his arm around her shoulder, holding her close.

'Look, Ruzena. Drink in the first sight. It's always the best. It stays with you. Always.'

Her body close to Krystof's was tingling, emerging from deep sleep. The breeze caressed her skin beneath the nightgown, softened by years of laundering; it must belong to Babička.

'Last night your beloved city frightened me. Frightened us both,' she said. 'There was a strange clock, a skeleton, footsteps, and a man with a huge moustache who showed me where you lived. But . . .' She splayed her toes and stood on tiptoe, peering out the window. She couldn't believe her eyes. 'So this is Prague.'

Red-tiled roofs and creamy yellow walls were laid out before her; layer on layer; an illogical jumble of streets. The sun bounced over eaves and chimney pots, tipping beams of gold onto ledges and gutters. A honeyed light, captured by a single pane of glass, winked at her. Above the roofs grew a forest of spires and turrets, dark and epic in antiquity. Some were topped with gold stars, some with crosses, some with gilded spheres. Peering from the window she felt herself expand with the immense view. Krystof's hand was on her shoulder. She placed her own over it to keep it there.

'This is why I came.' She looked up at him and kissed him softly.

'And you are why I am here,' he said.

As they embraced, her terror, like last night, evaporated.

'Come and say hello to Babička,' he said. 'She is longing to meet you properly. She was worried you were outside for ages ringing the bell. It hasn't worked since the beginning of the war. If we're not too late, she may well have some breakfast for us, too.'

He wrapped a shawl round her shoulders and led her out of the room onto a landing. Stairs snaked downwards into the dark vestibule, where her suitcase still lay, and upwards into the light of a lofty skylight.

'How many floors have you here?' she asked as they walked up the stairs. Square patches on the gilded wallpaper indicated the ghosts of paintings long since removed. Above her head, carved plasterwork crumbled on the ceilings.

'Four floors. The narrow entrance downstairs, with my two shops either side. These I rent out: one is a café, one a tobacconist but that's boarded up. Then the bedrooms. One is mine, where you slept, the other Babička's. On this floor are the kitchen and salon. Above us are the laundry and the bathroom. Ah, Ruzena your face.' He smiled. 'You are looking like that quizzical angel again.'

'I have never set foot inside a house like this before. It's beautiful. I can't believe all of this is tucked behind that front door.'

'But Babička could not look after it properly during the war. And then of course, my mother, my father . . .'

'Oh, Krystof, what?'

'So many stairs! This will keep you healthy!' he cried. 'But first, Babička.'

Stung by his refusal to talk, she followed him into a room at the back of the house. Squares of sunlight through the windows lay over the surface of a huge table and set the red-painted walls on fire. Nancy sat on a pile of cushions, drinking some milk from a tin cup.

'Mama,' she called.

'Oh, my darling chicken,' cried Rose and rushed to pick her up.

At one end by the stove, knitting furiously, sat the old woman, dressed in black, her crumpled face soft under wings of grey hair.

Krystof said, 'Ruzena, this is Babička.'

The woman unfolded her stiff limbs, got up from the chair and bundled her work away, exclaiming in her sing-song way, 'Ruzena, Ruzena.'

'Her name is Lara,' said Krystof to Rose. 'My grandmother. Oh, she has some coffee. My goodness, we are to be treated.'

Lara's fingers brushed Rose's cheeks and then rested on Nancy's dark head, a glow of pride in her eyes. She bustled back to the range to set a coffee pot on the hob, her movements like those of a woman twenty years younger as she glided around her domain of table, dresser and larder.

Rose sat with Krystof at the long table, and set Nancy on her knee while Lara poured the steaming coffee into tiny cups.

'Go carefully,' said Krystof. 'Coffee may be scarce here and we have to be sparing, but don't drink it all.'

He added a dash of syrup to her cup and then a little to his own.

Questions tumbled through her mind as she glanced at him, wondering at his cheerful smile. He must have had news about his family. Vaclav had said he'd gone to his country home. What stopped him, just now, from speaking of them?

Lara brought black bread and a dab of butter to the table. She chattered away to Rose. Rose looked to Krystof for a translation.

Krystof told her, 'She says she is glad you have both arrived safely. She is glad you are here; that you are safe. She wants you to feel at home.'

Rose turned to Lara. 'Thank you so much for helping me last night,' she said. 'Krystof, you must teach me to speak your language. How do I say "thank you"?'

'*Dekuji ti*,' he said.

She turned back to Lara. '*Dekuji ti*, Babička.'

Rose sipped her coffee and wrinkled her nose: it was very strong and the syrup did nothing to take the edge off it. But she knew she had to show her appreciation. The warmth of the room, the welcome from Lara and the closeness of Krystof made her throat tighten with pleasure.

Lara picked Nancy up and walked with her around the room, jiggling her up and down, singing in her ear and blowing raspberries on her neck. The little girl laughed in delight. Rose watched her daughter, feeling satisfaction settle in her stomach. How far they had travelled to be here. And now they were safe from the fear and grief they had left behind them in Cornwall. She held Krystof's hand on her lap, sharing smiles with him.

Rose drained her cup and choked, instantaneously, her eyes huge and smarting with shock. Her lips were fused by a sticky mess.

Krystof and Lara laughed, shaking their heads at her. The bottom of her cup was silted with bitter grounds.

'Oh, Ruzena, you'll learn.' Krystof handed her a handkerchief, still laughing. 'Here in Prague, however rare it may be, even if it's the last cup you'll have in a long time, never *never* drink all of your coffee.'

Rose bathed at the washstand in the bathroom upstairs, where a window overlooked a landscape of attic windows and chimney pots. She took the tiny piece of scented soap, knowing how precious it was, from the china dish and lathered her hands. As she washed away the dirt of her journey she listened to the gentle purring of pigeons on the tiles above. She rinsed out her hair, brushing it as she sat in a faded old slipper chair in a stream of sunlight. Her toes sank into a Turkish rug and in the armoire, as intricately carved as a church altar, hung her and Nancy's clothes. As the golden Prague air puffed through the window, she breathed on it deeply, sensing a new beginning. A new life.

She heard Krystof call up the stairs.

'Come on, darling, hurry! I want to show you my beloved city.'

Outside *At the Clementinum* the streets were alive with mingling voices and faces. Such a contrast, Rose mused as they stepped over the cobbles, to the deathly quiet of the night before. She found herself constantly craning her neck to stare at the towering houses, each one snug to its neighbour, floor on floor up to the tipsy roof line.

Krystof took her past the sheer walls of the St Clement monastery which threw deep shadows across the narrow streets, and she became transfixed by the statues and carvings that filled every niche.

He laughed. 'If we stop and look at everything, we'll not get anywhere. Come on, angel Ruzena.'

'But there is so much to look at,' she cried. 'I have never seen such a city.'

Krystof put his arm round her and she strolled with him, breathing smells and seeing sights she'd never dreamed of. Suddenly before her lay the river and a cobbled bridge glimpsed through the arches of a majestic tower.

'This is the Old Town bridge tower, the Vltava river, and over it, the ancient Charles Bridge,' said Krystof.

'These carvings, are they kingfishers?' she asked, pointing to the stonework on the tower.

'Wenceslas's favourite bird,' he said.

'As in the Good King? I didn't know he really existed.' She laughed. 'I thought he was just the king with the poor man in a carol.'

'Our patron saint. Murdered on his way to church.'

They walked onto the bridge and the noise and huddle of the city melted away as she contemplated the wide, green river flowing gently beneath. Upstream, white water tumbled over a weir and a flock of swans glided by. A hill rose before her, crowded again with a muddle of the red roofs of houses and churches, topped by the serene castle. She smiled at the sunlight on her face, the freedom she felt in her limbs, the warmth in her bones, walking by Krystof's side.

'Where's that music coming from?' she asked.

'Halfway along the bridge. There, see?'

A trio of two violins and a cello were serenading the passers-by.

'It's beautiful,' she said, her spirits soaring even more. 'I have not heard music like this in so long. My father loves—' she hesitated and tears stung her eyes, 'loved – Mozart but Mother loved Glenn Miller even more, so she inevitably won.'

Krystof said, 'They say that whoever is Czech is a musician. But I cannot play a note.' He laughed. 'Everywhere you go in this city, in this country, you will hear music.'

'Like the band that played as the train crossed the border,' she said. 'They appeared from nowhere. It was such a sight, such a welcome! Oh, Krystof, I have so much to tell you about our journey. Some of it was very grim, but the beauty of Paris . . . the forests in Germany . . . the mountains in the distance . . . And you? What about you?'

She stopped, seeing his face close down.

'Krystof?'

He tried to distract her. 'Look around you here, Ruzena. Look at my marvellous city. There is so much to see here, right here.'

She glanced upwards. 'Oh, my goodness,' she cried. 'We're being watched.'

Perched on the bridge's parapets, surrounding her on either side, were statues of solemn men, black with age, in flowing robes, brandishing bishops' crooks and crosses. Eyes in tortured, frozen faces glowered down on her, scrutinising her.

She shuddered. 'Who *were* these men?'

'Saints and popes,' he said. 'Put to death, martyred. Like our Good King. And so preserved in stone for ever to remind us.'

'But it's as if they are being *paraded*, to teach us a lesson,' she said, seeing faces twisted in agony and, on the plinths beneath, carvings depicting warnings, predicting death.

But, walking along the line, she looked more closely and saw, alongside the torment, some of the carved faces fixed in religious rapture, gilded haloes and wreaths of golden stars.

She sighed. 'Such contrasts: day and night, ecstasy and agony. It's like a fairy tale.'

'We love it all,' said Krystof. 'We love the *drama*.'

'Will I ever get used to it?'

'We have all the time in the world for that.' He gathered up her hand. 'Come on, let's cross over the bridge to the other side. There's so much more than this for you to get used to.'

She linked her arm through his, looking up at him in his trenchcoat, with his neat trilby cocked over one eye.

'How handsome you are,' she giggled. 'I am so proud to be standing next to you. Walking next to you. How far I have travelled to see the sunlight on your face again.'

'Now, now,' he said. 'You must be delirious from lack of sleep.'

'But, I tell you, Krystof,' she insisted, playfully, 'I am perfectly all right, I . . .'

Suddenly, the beautiful music that had been drifting around them stopped. Rose glanced back to see the musicians holding their instruments close to their chests and the crowds around them sinking back. In the abrupt silence that followed, a rowdy group of soldiers started to cross the bridge towards them.

She held tightly onto Krystof's hand.

'What's going on?'

'I'm not sure, but we'd better blend in with the crowd,' he said.

He turned her towards the parapet and they leant over, watching the water flow beneath them as the rabble of soldiers in dirty uniforms came nearer. Some had slanting Slavic eyes, others were fair-haired. They were jostling, singing and laughing

– but only with each other. Everyone else crept out of their way. The intense smell of unwashed skin that singed Rose's throat as they passed by made her want to vomit.

'Russian soldiers,' Krystof whispered. 'Don't catch their eye. They're always trouble.'

He quickly led her down some steps on the other side of the bridge to the water's edge. They found a bench in the shade of huge chestnut trees, under leaves flapping in the breeze. A water wheel turned languidly in the sluggish millrace, separated from the main river by a small island.

'The Russians liberated us in May,' said Krystof, 'which is all well and good. But they seem to have outstayed their welcome. There are hundreds of them. Rather undisciplined, making a nuisance. Trouble seems to follow wherever they go, although I'd rather it was them than the Nazis.'

'But I thought the Americans liberated Prague?'

'Good old propaganda, it works for both sides, doesn't it? No, the Allies only got so far east into Germany, Czechoslovakia, Poland; they left the rest of Europe to the Soviets.'

She watched a flotilla of ducks quack past, dipping their heads in the water. 'But even so, Krystof. Better them than the Germans?'

'Oh, yes.'

She watched him carefully. 'Vaclav mentioned that you'd been to the country. What about your family—'

He broke in. 'The Russians! I don't care much for their politics. We hoped for a new start for Czechoslovakia. A new republic. A return to the golden age we had fifty years ago when Babička was a girl.'

She asked, 'How do the Russians affect you? You're still an officer in the Czech army?'

'On leave at the moment. You're right. I had been out of town for a few weeks . . . got back late last night.' His voice drifted. 'So I have been out of touch for a while.'

'But how does it work, with all these other troops here, pounding the streets?'

'It doesn't *work*. Why do you think you saw not a soul on your walk through the city last night? There isn't a curfew – yet – but the people of Prague are scared. They stay locked behind their doors at night.'

'Well, what does the government have to say?'

He forced a laugh. 'So many questions. The Czech government and the army have an *understanding* with the Russians. You must remember our army is very weak. Our country is very weak, after years under the Nazis. Look at me. I've been given a desk job. I don't even wear a uniform.'

She slid her eyes sideways to look at him. He looked bewildered.

'Please tell me about your family?'

Pain shadowed his face like a series of clouds moving across the sun.

He stood up and pulled her to her feet. 'Come and see my favourite church.'

Krystof pushed open the great door and they stepped inside. The cavern of the interior was silent, cool, pure and still. Their footsteps tapped out a delicate code as they crossed the flagstones. Rose's eyes grew wide as she took in statues of the Virgin dripping with gold; cherubs dancing with angels; the stupendous splendour of worship. Krystof stood behind her, his hand on her shoulder, to point out the jewelled altar at the far end as it captured the sun beaming down through monumental stained-glass windows. Then she recoiled when he showed her the rotting body of a saint inside a glass coffin. She gaped at the exposed bones beneath threadbare robes, black fingernails, the crooked crown atop the decomposing head.

'I have walked just one mile in this city,' she whispered to him, 'and everywhere I look I see images of pain and death. I think it will take me a long while to get used to *that*.'

Krystof put his finger over his lips and led her between immense pillars to a side chapel. They sat down on an ancient pew under a statue of a bleeding Christ.

'I feel I am being judged.' She lowered her voice. 'All these statues, these saints . . . and God looking down on me. They know I am a married woman. They know I have left my husband. They know . . .'

As if he wasn't listening, Krystof spoke up suddenly: 'We used to worship here. Every Sunday when we were up from the country, we'd cross the Charles Bridge twice a day to attend this church. But now . . . now . . .' He rested the side of his head against hers. 'I cannot understand why people continue with their faith. The war . . . the dreadful atrocities that are coming to light. All my faith is gone.'

She looked at him, frightened by the tremor in his voice.

He said, 'We are both orphans, Ruzena.'

'Oh, Krystof.'

She watched as his face drained of colour; his eyes turned sharp with pain.

'My mother, my father, my younger brother Tomas. Murdered by German soldiers.' He was whispering and yet his voice was enormous.

A coldness crept into her bones as he told her how Tomas had, a year before, married his childhood sweetheart and they were all living together in the farmhouse with his parents. When the soldiers stormed the village, he told her, the women and children were sent to the camps and all the men over sixteen were rounded up. Shot dead.

'Why? But *why*?' Rose's voice caught her in throat.

He told her that the village had been made an example of – punished for the assassination of an important Nazi. The Nazis – rightly or wrongly, it didn't matter – thought that the perpetrators were from there. Babička was in Prague at the time, visiting her friend in the Little Quarter – the only reason she survived.

'The village was bulldozed,' he said. 'Everything eliminated. They have sown crops over it. It no longer exists.'

Rose looked down at his hands; they were shaking. She tried to steady them with her own. She had lived with a man who supported these people. She had slept next to a man who condoned these acts. She had given birth to his child. Her stomach churned with revulsion.

'When did you . . . ? How did you . . . ?'

She caught his eye. It was opaque with anger.

'I found out when I returned a few months ago. Babička had been alone for three years, her family dead; she was terrified that the Nazis would arrest her if they discovered that she was from the village. She did not know if I was ever coming back. When I arrived she was nearly starving. She'd sold paintings, silver, our furniture on the black market to survive.'

However hard Rose tried, no words would form in her mouth.

Krystof muttered, 'I had to go and see it with my own eyes or I wouldn't have believed it.'

'Krystof, I know ... my home ...'

He looked up at the statues, the trappings of worship, the treasures of his religion. 'I can't pray any more. I am finished. I am angry, so *angry*.'

He gestured to the church and then, gently, touched her chin to turn her to face him. 'When I guessed that you were on your way to me, I found a reason to live. And Babička has blossomed in just the few hours that you have been here. You are a good thing for us, Ruzena. You and Nancy.'

She cradled his head against her shoulder, sitting with him under the unchanging gaze of the saints and the prophets.

'And you are my good thing, Krystof,' she said into his hair.

'Who is that man?' she asked, 'and why is he staring?'

They had walked back across the bridge and were outside *At the Clementinum*. Krystof was fishing for his keys.

'Everyone stares at you, Ruzena. It's your hair. Not many people in Czechoslovakia have such a red. Just like *Září*. The month that glows with colour. How apt that you should arrive here in September.'

The man in question was standing outside the café next door to Krystof's house, apron on, sleeves rolled up, big arms folded, a cigarette between large fingers. He grinned widely at Krystof, showing teeth under a huge moustache. He shouted a cheerful greeting.

Krystof glanced his way. 'Oh, that's Milan. He manages my café next door,' he said, calling back, '*Dobrý den*, Milan.'

'He's the man from last night,' whispered Rose. 'I thought I recognised him.'

Krystof walked over and shook Milan by the hand, as the man clapped him on the shoulder.

'Rose, this is Milan,' he introduced them.

'Please tell him thank you,' she said. 'If it wasn't for him, I'd still be walking the streets.'

Milan gazed at her hair, and then his eyes began to travel down her body.

Krystof told her, 'He wants us to step inside; he says he has some schnapps under the counter. I have told him, another time maybe.'

'I'm glad. Thank you,' she said to Krystof, avoiding Milan's eye.

Krystof opened his front door, waving away Milan's good-natured protests. As she shut the door behind her, Rose glanced back and saw the man's expression change. He was insulted.

They met Babička on the stairs. The old woman kissed them on the cheeks to say both hello and goodbye. She patted Rose's arm and pointed up to the room above.

Krystof said, 'She has given Nancy her tea and put her to sleep in her bedroom; she is going for supper at her friend's house across in the Little Quarter.'

Rose crept into Babička's room. Nancy lay abandoned to a deep, healing sleep, one arm thrown over her head, her pale face like porcelain framed by dark hair.

'Such a long way to bring you, chicken,' whispered Rose, kneeling down to touch her little hand. In her sleep, Nancy's fingers tightened around hers. 'But we are safe here; safe and loved. We are going to be fine.'

In the kitchen, Rose and Krystof sipped the pheasant broth and nibbled on the black bread that Lara had left out for them.

'How far is it to Babička's friend's house? Will she be getting a taxi back, or a tram?' asked Rose. 'I don't suppose she wants to be too late home?'

'Just over the Charles Bridge. I think she may well stay the night there.' Krystof looked at Rose and gently laughed. 'Didn't you see the little valise she was carrying? She is a wise old lady. She knows we would like to be alone tonight. Our first night.'

'*Oh?*'

'Now just look at your face, Ruzena. I want to show you!'

He walked her out onto the landing. In the speckled mirror Rose saw her own shocked face, her blushing cheeks and demure, downcast eyes. In the reflection, standing behind her, Krystof's eyes were shining with delight.

'Krystof,' she said, fully understanding his suggestion. 'We will be committing a sin.'

'I'm sorry, Rose, I know. I am not being a gentleman. But see how you try not to look at me, you are shy of me, and yet your eyes are alive. Your cheeks, they match your hair.'

She felt the euphoria of his infectious laughter, and tried to stop herself. 'Even so, Krystof. I am still married.'

'You are estranged, separated. Your husband is in prison.'

Immediately, the awful memory of Will Bowman in the dark maisonette bedroom flashed through her mind: the ticking of the alarm clock; the rumbling pipes; his breathing, hard in her ear. How utterly lost she had been. How mindlessly she had given herself away. And, now, how right being with Krystof felt. And yet, sex, in her mind, was connected only with her cold, dreadful husband.

'I need some time,' she said, swallowing hard. 'I am a little . . . can I just . . . I am *surprised*. Remember in the barn at Pengared, how you wanted us to wait to be married. And I knew deep down you were right. Why have things changed?'

'I was a good Catholic back then. I wanted everything to be right and proper. Now . . . so much has happened. So much has changed. All except me wanting you.' His eyes were huge and serious. 'You are here now. We are together. And now that you are safe in my arms . . .' Standing behind her, he held her belly and swayed her softly. His lips found the back of her neck. '*Miluji ty*.'

His smile fell away. She watched him drink her in through her reflection.

Rose turned to face him. 'What did you say?'

'You know what I said. *I love you*.'

Krystof's face was transparent with desire and she felt a fierce warmth rise up in her body as it had done at Trelewin cove and again in the barn at Pengared. Such bitter, tearful longing. She felt wild and free, and suddenly terrified.

She pulled herself out of his arms and walked away from him, up the stairs, opening the door to an empty room. She heard him call her name. She shut the door behind her.

The room was bare, save for a grand chaise longue in the middle of naked floorboards. Lara had had to strip the room to pay for food. Rose sat down on the chaise and leant forward, burying her face in her hands. What was she *thinking*? Krystof was everything to her; she had crossed Europe for him. She loved him but she felt paralysed by grief. Why could she not relax and let him love her?

After some minutes, she wiped away her tears. Patches on the salon walls revealed where paintings once hung and ragged, moth-eaten drapes at the windows were held together by remnants of gold thread. It must have been a wonderful room once, full of Babička's family and friends: glittering parties, conversation and music. She thought of her parents' back parlour and imagined the laughter there too.

Glancing up at the one remaining painting hanging over the fireplace, she turned cold. It was a wedding portrait. A man in a dark suit and smart moustache was seated, bursting with pride. Behind him stood a woman in a gown of eau de Nil, a certain confidence in her eyes – the same grey eyes as Krystof. Her forehead was as strong as Lara's and her tiny hand, captured brilliantly, was resting on the man's shoulder. The brushstroked date in the corner read 1923 – the same year her parents had married.

Rose sat transfixed by the painted faces, her tears drying in streaks. Krystof's parents looked so happy: they did not know how it would end.

Shivering with despair, she got up and walked to the window. Church bells were ringing in the fading light of the September day and birds had begun to roost on the rooftops. As the beautiful evening started to glow, she contemplated the chances she'd had, and the chances she'd ruined by trying to be good and proper, trying to please others. The man she loved was waiting for her downstairs. He had escaped occupation, fought a long hard war, only to return to find his family murdered. And now he was sitting there, snubbed by her prissiness.

Leaving the room with the portrait to settle back into its closed tranquillity, she quietly shut the door.

She found Krystof by the kitchen stove, drinking a tot of schnapps in the twilight. She reached for the light switch. Nothing happened. He glanced up at her, love and fear etched onto his face.

'Do the lights not work?' she asked.

'We haven't had electricity for six months, not since the last raid by your RAF boys. Some say it was the Germans sabotaging the power supply as they left. Wouldn't put it past them.'

'Never mind, I like candlelight.'

He smiled hesitantly. 'So do I.'

She sat in the chair opposite him and took his hand. She gently worked her fingers up to the crook of his elbow.

'Krystof,' she said, 'shall we light some candles in the bedroom?'

He closed the bedroom door and walked to the window to shut the casement and draw the thick ivy-green curtains.

'Leave them open a chink. That's it. And the window, just a little,' she told him. 'I want to breathe the evening air.'

Her hands trembled as she lit the candles on the mantelpiece. She began to laugh softly, her nerves fizzing. He stood behind her on the hearthrug and spun her gently to face him, cradling her in his arms.

'Why do you laugh, Ruzena?'

'I am in shock. I still can't believe that I am here, in this strange and beautiful place. Nancy is safely asleep next door. I am with you. Like this. This is my dream.'

A sigh of warm air through the window brushed her skin and she began to shiver.

'Don't be nervous,' he said.

'Not nerves. I'm ecstatic.'

Even so, she drank from the small glass of schnapps that he handed her. Then he took the glass and knelt down.

'Oh, Krystof, you don't have to propose.' She felt giddy, seeing his serious, enquiring face gaze up at her. She touched his hair as he pressed his cheek to her stomach as if to listen to her body, the thumping of her heart. His hands moved to the buttons on the front of her dress, pausing first to ask the question with his eyes. She nodded in silence and watched as he undid the buttons with such patient composure that she was blinded with tears.

She whispered, 'You know I have had a baby . . . my body is not . . .'

'Do you think that matters to me?'

They kissed to say hello. They kissed to bridge the void of time and distance that had kept them apart. His fingers found the clips in her hair and he tossed them one by one onto the floor; he found the fastenings of her underwear.

'I've never been naked in front of a man before,' she mumbled.

'Oh, but Ruzena, you are beautiful!' he said in mock battle-cry and scooped her into his arms.

They laughed together as he tottered towards the divan.

'You need to be naked too,' she giggled, and helped him undress.

She gasped at the breadth and beauty of his body. She nuzzled into him, unable to believe that she could be so happy. She let him guide her to a place where she could, at last, believe, and their laughter softened into sighs of wonder.

Rose lay in the circle of Krystof's arms and listened to his gentle, snuffly snoring. A sweet smile crept over her face. She thought, This is love. It has nothing whatsoever to do with marriage, pleasing others, conforming.

Watching the night sky through the chink in the curtains, she saw the dark roofs of Prague silhouetted against a dusting of stars and she heard, in the distance, the chimes of the Town Hall clock.

Twenty

'I THINK I'VE FOUND JUST THE THING,' KRYSTOF CALLED UP THE STAIRS. 'Ruzena, get up and come and look at this.'

She did not have a dressing gown, for there were still none to be found in the shops, so, instead, she wrapped one of Lara's shawls around her shoulders. The morning chill settled round her ankles as she descended the stairs to the vestibule. September had slid all too quickly into October and, although the days were still bright, mornings had a raw edge, hinting at the winter to come. Shivering, she opened the back door to see Krystof in the courtyard dressed for the office in his smart suit, tie and trilby, beaming at her.

'Hurry up,' he cried. 'I've got to report at the barracks before eight this morning. First day back so I need to make a good impression.'

'What's that you've got there?' she asked, folding her arms to fend off the chill and stepping tentatively over the cobbles.

'A pram for Nancy. Look. It might need a bit of oil. And you may want to brush it down a bit, give it a clean. She'll love it. Isn't it perfect?'

'It's wonderful, Krystof,' smiled Rose. 'Where did you find it?'

'In the shed under a pile of old sacks,' he said, laughing. 'Don't look like that. Just be thankful!'

She put her arms around him. Kissed him.

'Oh, I am. I am. It *is* perfect!'

'So what will you do today, while I'm working away pushing useless pieces of paper around my desk?' he asked.

'I will help Babička, as normal, with the chores,' she said. 'Then I will take Nancy for a walk in her new pram and post my letter to Betony.' She cocked her head at him, puzzled. 'Do you think it's strange that I haven't heard from her yet? She

233

hasn't replied to my first letter and I sent *that* the first week I arrived.'

'Not so strange,' said Krystof. 'Remember, the post will be in a very sorry state. Think how far that letter has to travel. Like you did.' He kissed the top of her head. 'Send another by all means. Do you think you will cope at the post office? Remember what to say?'

'Yes, yes. I've got to learn how to do it myself, without you always having to translate for me. I will be fine.'

'That's my good girl,' he said. 'Now I must be off.'

As she hugged him, she glanced at the top of the high garden wall to see a trail of cigarette smoke and Milan's dark head. He was standing in his own yard, as if he was waiting for something to happen.

Rose called goodbye to Babička, closed the front door behind her and pushed Nancy out into the chilly air. There were no tables and chairs outside the café next door today. A brazier burned inside instead, and men huddled around it, smoking and playing dominoes. She turned left and scooted the pram along the pavement, determined not to pass by the window and be noticed.

Grey clouds blew across the watery blue sky above the turrets and spires of the Old Town, and the weak sun winked at her occasionally from behind a rooftop. Woodsmoke was pungent and sour on the cold air. Rose hurried along the twists and turns, feet crunching over the first of the falling leaves and Nancy juddering as the pram wheels rumbled over the cobbles.

Market sellers in the Old Town Square were animated, dealing with long shuffling queues of people, all eager for the few loaves of bread on offer, the sparse, rotting vegetables. Carp barrels stood empty; potato sacks limp and discarded. Lara had already been out at dawn to buy their provisions. There wasn't much left now.

Inside the post office Rose joined the end of another snaking queue. She added up the people ahead of her, estimated how long each person took to be served and noted how many counter windows were open to work out how long she might be waiting. She reckoned she'd be there an hour. Shifting from one foot to the other and blowing on her fingers (for there was no brazier here in the post office), boredom stretched her nerves. Speaking to the people of Prague was a trial. She did not want to be misunderstood. Nancy mercifully slept, wrapped in her blanket, a knitted hat with ear flaps protecting her face.

Just like Prague station, the post office had a faded grandeur, hinting at the long-past days of the glorious republic. Now a film of dirt covered the elaborate carvings, the stained-glass windows and, Rose thought, each and every person as they trudged forward in line.

A telegram, she thought. I will send a telegram instead. It will be quicker than a letter although more expensive. She might hear from Betony sooner. In her head Rose repeated the words, over and over, practising what Krystof had told her to say:

'*Mohl byste to dat na postu?*'

At last she reached the service window. Queasy with nerves, she tried to speak but her tongue twisted the words and they came out tangled. The stiff-faced clerk looked blankly at her, shaking his head. She tried again but her mouth was desiccated. She sounded ridiculous. Swallowing hard, she pushed forward ten crown notes. Frustrated tears stung her eyes. She glanced over her shoulder to see the mass of listening people; sullen faces under headscarves, crumpled brows under sheepskin hats. Feet were being stamped against the cold; their impatience was tangible.

'Please,' she said to the clerk, 'I'm *Anglický*. Please help me.'

To her astonishment, he shrugged, glanced at his watch and pulled down his blind with a snap.

Furious and embarrassed, Rose spun the pram around and sped out of the building under the hard stares of the muttering people who immediately began to rearrange themselves into another queue.

She sat on a bench in the square, her shoulders sinking despondently, her stomach churning. Bright, brittle leaves, some as large as dinner plates, fell in a steady stream from the tall chestnut trees. Nancy woke and began to cry. Worried she was too cold, Rose picked her up and settled her on her lap, glancing around at the grand buildings and the medieval Town Hall. The leaden sky failed to bring life to the beauty of the city. Its spirit, like hers, was crushed by the gloom. Townspeople hurried by, glancing as was their wont, at her hair, which fell in a wave from under her hat. She noticed the holes in their shoes, the patched coats, and felt pity coiling in her belly.

She wondered about Mabel, who, Krystof told her, was living outside the city with Vaclav. Even a ten-minute chat with that irritating girl would perk her up, Rose decided. With a start and a shiver, she realised that without Krystof to talk to she was lonely. But his leave was now over and he had an important job to go to. She could not rely on him for everything.

A large black Daimler rumbled across the square, a red flag with golden hammer and sickle fluttering on its bonnet. She watched it park outside one of the larger old guild houses which had a brand-new sign over its portal. Rose marvelled at how perplexing the Czech language was, but at the same time, inexplicably, some words translated effortlessly into English. The sign said *Ministerstuo Bezpečnost*. So that must be the *Ministry of State Security*, she thought with a shudder. The car's paintwork shone; it was a stupendous sight on the medieval square. People stopped to stare as the car door was opened and a dignitary, in dark wool coat with large furry lapels, got out of the car and, flanked by soldiers in grey sheepskin hats, strode into the building.

'*Ruský*,' someone next to her said.

She turned to behold the dark eyes of Milan glinting at her from under his woollen cap.

'Oh, *dobrý den*,' she greeted him, crestfallen but trying to be polite.

He moved up the bench, shuffling closer. Her skin prickled with displeasure beneath her coat. Not wanting Milan to speak to or touch Nancy, she sat the child back in her pram and strapped her in.

The man said, '*Ruský všude*.'

She looked at him blankly, folding her hands demurely on her lap.

'*Všude*,' he repeated, sweeping his arm towards the Daimler and then to encompass the square, the whole town. He tutted with impatience.

She shrugged, shaking her head. She knew he had said *Russian*. What did he mean? That the Russians were everywhere?

He sighed and appeared to try something different, patting his arms and pretending to shiver. '*Studeny*,' he said.

'Ah,' Rose nodded, copying his actions. Was he saying he was cold?

'*Studeny nyni. Říjen*,' he insisted.

Relieved to have caught one word she knew, she said, 'Oh, yes. Krystof has taught me all the months of the year.' She spoke in English, not caring that he did not understand. '*Říjen* is October. The rutting season.'

Milan leant in closer and she smelt the tobacco on his breath; the stale smoke on his clothes. His eyes were bright with pleasure. He gestured with his hips, as if he was, himself, rutting. '*Říjen! Říjen!*' he cried, laughing at his crudity.

Rose tried to avert her eyes from the bushiness of his moustache, his thrusting pelvis. His bulky body was invasive, his thigh pressing against hers. She shrank away.

He held out fat fingers and counted off the months of the year for her. He pointed to the trees and the leaves, and fluttered his hands in front of her face.

'Ah, yes, *Listopad*,' she said, politely. 'Yes, next month is November, *Listopad*, the month of falling leaves.'

'*Listopad, studeny*, cold,' he repeated, then when he got to January, '*Leden*,' he began to shiver even more, as if he was in agony.

'Oh, yes,' she said, brightening a little, pleased to have understood. 'January, *Leden* – I know. It translates as *ice*. Very cold. Colder than this?'

Milan pointed a finger at her chest and said, '*Anglický*.' He gestured at his mouth and tapped the side of his temple. His eyes roved over the front of her coat and then latched onto her hair. She felt herself squirm. He was truly revolting.

'What are you saying, Milan?' She spoke carefully, shrugging again, letting her face fall in mock incomprehension. He kept on, pointing and gesturing, pressing himself closer, hostility in his eyes.

'*Anglický ucitelka!*' he insisted.

She understood him. She remembered her frustration in the post office, in the market place, talking to Babička. Krystof was helping her with some phrases to equip her for the shopkeepers and the delivery men, but she hated to burden him. She looked at Milan and thought, You are quite odious but I am a stranger here and I ought to be open-minded.

She took a breath.

'*Ano*,' she said, 'Yes. I'll teach you English, if you teach me Czech.'

He nodded, his tongue poking out through his moustache.

She said, 'We'll teach each other.' And yet, even as she said it, she felt her mouth curl with distaste.

Back at *At the Clementinum* Rose left Nancy with Lara, telling her she had one more errand to do. Lara's angry stare was like a slap in the face. As she slipped out of the front porch and opened the door into the café she was still shocked by Lara's anger. Was she cross about having to look after Nancy at short notice? Rose had no idea but resolved to make it up to her as soon as she got back.

At least the café was warm. The air was laced with the scent of strong coffee; a smoky fug issued from the cigarettes of the men huddled at the tables; the brazier glowed in the corner. Milan poured two cups of coffee at the counter and set them on a table, gesturing to her to be seated. The men, muffled in scarves and caps, stared at her before turning their backs and continuing to play dominoes, their murmuring punctuated by the clicking of ivory tiles.

Rose looked around her at the untidy crowd of tables and chairs which was reflected again and again by huge mirrors on the walls. Gas lamps glowed, highlighting advertisement posters of beautiful girls holding burning cigarettes or mugs of frothing beer. She remembered Krystof telling her about the Czechoslovakian 'land-girls', and here they were in all their glory.

As Milan sat down opposite her, she thought of Krystof. He will be proud of me, she decided, for I'm being independent. He will be pleased I am courteous to his tenant, and showing willing. I will learn Czech from Milan, and surprise Krystof and Babička.

Milan tapped her on the arm impatiently. The first lesson began.

* * *

Much later than she intended, and feeling guilty for leaving Nancy for so long with Lara, Rose returned to the house. Quietly shutting the front door behind her, she was climbing the stairs out of the darkness of the vestibule when voices reached her from the kitchen above. Lara's shrill, angry cry resounded through the house, stopping Rose in her tracks. Then, under this astonishing tirade, she caught snatches of Krystof's gentle voice: persuasive and apologetic.

'Oh, goodness, I have left Nancy with her one too many times,' Rose muttered to herself. 'And now Krystof's in trouble over it.'

As she reached the top of the stairs, Lara burst out of the kitchen door. Rose set her face into a smile of apology but was arrested by the utter fury of the indistinguishable words that flew from the old woman's mouth. Lara advanced on Rose in a frenzy, holding out her left hand and brandishing it in Rose's face. Rose stared wide-eyed in disbelief as the old woman began to tap furiously at the wedding ring on her own finger.

'What are you saying to me, Babička?' cried Rose, desperately trying to think of any useful words she might have learnt in the last two hours from Milan.

'*Kurva!*' Lara hissed at her.

The grandmother turned on her heel and stamped her way up the stairs.

Somewhere in the house, Nancy was crying and calling for her mother. Lara slammed her bedroom door.

'What's going on, Krystof?' asked Rose, her legs shaking as she walked into the kitchen. 'I am so sorry. I left Nancy with Babička this afternoon – obviously for far too long – but I won't be doing it again. She seems so *cross*. Have I offended her *that much*?' Hearing the odd Czech word tumble out of her mouth, she thought, I'm doing quite well, at least some of the time.

'Sit down, Ruzena,' Krystof said, pouring a tot of schnapps for her. His face was serious.

'What – what's happening? You look dreadful.'

'Have this. I'm having one. You might need it.'

'But first, I must go and see to Nancy. Is she all right?'

'Leave Nancy for a moment, please. Sit.'

Rose felt her heart hammering as she waited for him to speak.

By the light of the lantern his face looked ashen, his forehead twisting with anxiety.

She took a nip of schnapps. 'Why is Babička so angry? I have never seen her so . . .'

'As you know,' he began, a hard edge to his voice, 'my family is – was – devoutly Catholic. And Babička remains so. Myself, as I told you . . . I have no time for any of it now. But unfortunately,' he held out his hand and took hers to kiss it, 'Babička has just found out that we are not married. And that Nancy is not my child.'

Rose gasped, 'But we did not pretend. We never told her otherwise . . .'

'Well, what's true is we didn't tell her *anything* and she assumed that we are married, and that Nancy is our little girl. I know. I know.' His hand rested on her shoulder. 'She told me this morning that she was wondering about Nancy and how dark her hair was. No one in our family has that colouring.'

'That's why she glared at me earlier,' said Rose. 'She must have been dwelling on it all day.'

'And just now she asked me directly. I had to tell her. Nancy does not look anything like me. I couldn't lie to her. I just couldn't. You wouldn't want me to, Ruzena. You wouldn't want us to live a lie.'

'But you are like a father to her,' said Rose. 'You always will be. And I want nothing more to do with Will, you know that . . .'

'Yes, but Babička does not see it that way. In the eyes of God – her God – you are still married and we are living in sin. And she is angry. As you can see: very, very angry. It is an absolute affront to her.'

'So it seems. Goodness, I didn't imagine that was why she was so . . . I think she just called me a name out there on the landing,' said Rose. 'She literally spat at me.'

Krystof looked incredibly tired. 'We have to try to make amends with her. Somehow make it right.'

'It will help when I get my divorce, which I will try to sort out as soon as I can. I'm not sure where to start or how it will be possible, being so far from England.'

'But of course, for Babička, divorce is equally bad,' sighed Krystof. 'I don't know what else to say.'

'I will not allow my sham of a marriage to ruin our happiness!' cried Rose. 'We will have to think of a way to get round this. To help Babička understand why we have to be together.' She stroked the palm of his hand. 'She will come round when she knows how much we love each other.'

'Yes.' He sounded dubious. 'She will calm down soon.'

'I hope so. I have never seen anyone so furious. Apart from my husband.' She shuddered at the thought of Will and his bullying grasp on her. 'Babička kept holding out her hand to me, tapping her wedding ring. Oh, what was the word she used . . . she literally hissed it at me. *Kurva*, was it?'

Krystof's eyes widened in shock.

'*Kurva?*' he asked. 'Are you sure?'

'Something like that.'

'Good God,' he said, running his hand over his face. 'I don't believe it. I don't know if I can bear this. *Kurva* means prostitute.'

Rose stood up, wrenching her hand away from him.

'Well, well. So that's what I am.' Her voice was shaking. She felt sick with shock.

'Oh, but Ruzena . . . She can't mean it.'

'I think she did! And now I must go and see to my daughter.' She looked at Krystof, livid. '*Our* daughter.'

Twenty-one

ROSE LAY IN THE DEEP, DELICIOUS WARMTH OF THE BED BESIDE KRYSTOF. She could just make out the outline of the alarm clock, ticking away, through the grey dawn darkness. She squinted at it, unable to read the hands.

I wonder, she thought to herself, '*kolik je hodin?*'

And then she gasped and laughed, waking Krystof with a start.

'What?' he asked, rolling over. 'What's the matter?'

'I just *thought* in Czech,' she said, with delight. 'I was wondering what the time was and there it was: *Kolik je hodin? What's the time?*'

'If you're *thinking* it,' said Krystof, 'it must be sinking in.'

'At least now I won't have to spend so much time with Milan . . .' She shuddered. 'I'll tell him. I don't need his lessons any more.'

'What about his English?'

'I think Milan's up to scratch,' she said, feeling dismissive. 'I'd rather stop now, and spend more time with Nancy. It's hard enough at the moment without having to constantly ask Babička to look after her when she won't even look me in the eye . . .'

'I'll talk to her again.'

'You can try . . .'

Before Krystof left for work, as was his habit, he lifted the sleeping Nancy from her cot and put her in the warm hollow that he left behind in the bed. Snuggled like this, Rose drifted off again to be woken by the flapping of the letter box below. She hauled herself out into the frigid air of the bedroom and padded down the stairs.

'Oh, my goodness, it's for me!' she called out to herself in English, snatching the envelope up from the doormat. She thought carefully and then called out in Czech: 'A letter for me!'

Lara, crashing pots together in the kitchen above, ignored her. Rose was not in the least bit surprised: the old woman had hardly spoken to her since calling her a prostitute. Racing back up the stairs with the letter, Rose tried to put the ridiculous insult out of her mind. She bundled back into bed and cuddled Nancy to her, leaning against the pillows as she slit the envelope.

'At long last, Nancy, my first letter must have got through to the farm,' Rose told her. 'All those weeks ago and finally Auntie Betony has replied. I wonder how Ted is, and dear Meg. Of course, you won't remember them but . . . Ahh, a telegram no less . . . we are honoured.'

She pulled out the chit of paper, laughing at Nancy's bemused face.

And then her stomach dropped. She read:

Will Bowman released from prison STOP Back at Old Vicarage STOP To accuse you of kidnap in courts STOP We advise swift return STOP Cumberpatch.

She crushed the paper in her hands, her head sinking forward. Would he ever let her go? She breathed steadily, waiting for her nerves to calm before getting up and dressing herself and her daughter, tense in the coldness of the bedroom. Nancy clung to her, sensing her distress. Rose's fingers made hard work of her buttons.

'Oh, do keep still, Nancy,' she snapped.

Her world began to spin: she, too, wanted her own mother.

'He can't do this to us,' she told Nancy brightly to make amends for being cross, and also to convince herself. 'Kidnap. What a silly idea. It's not a weepy old movie, is it. This is real life. *Our* life. I will divorce him, and I will marry Krystof. He is your father, Nancy. And we will be happy. A family.'

Nancy chuckled and pointed to a pair of Krystof's boots.

'That's right. Krystof.' Then, unable to control her sarcasm, Rose said, 'Come on, let's go to the warm kitchen and see if Babička will smile at us today.'

* * *

Lara was in the midst of de-scaling a carp. The fish rested on a chopping board on the table and the old woman wielded a sharp knife, running it backwards down the fish's flesh, scattering wet silvery flakes all over her hands.

'*Dobrý den*, Babička,' Rose spoke in Czech, hoping to appease the grandmother. 'I wondered, as the sun is shining, shall we both take Nancy for a walk? Perhaps over to the Little Quarter, over the bridge. We could visit your friend . . . ?'

Silence.

'Or, if you like . . . er,' she searched for the words, 'You might like to take her by yourself. She loves the pram, you know. She loves to count the statues on the Charles Bridge.'

With a grimace, Lara turned her back to reach for a bowl of eggs on the dresser, clumping it down on the table and resuming her work on the fish.

Rose sat Nancy on her pile of cushions and poured her some warm milk, trying to remember a word Milan had said, the word for cold.

'Er . . . Babička, perhaps it is too *stude* . . . ?' She hesitated, knowing she had got it wrong.

Lara shrugged. The soft brown eyes that had once greeted her with such pleasure now glared hard at her across the room. She bent back to the fish, pressing the tip of the knife behind the head.

Rose fingered the telegram in her pocket. She needed to talk; she wanted this lady to comfort her, just as her own mother would have done.

'Can I help?' Rose tried again, walking to the table.

Lara gave a fierce shake of her head, then prepared to plunge the knife into the fish to slit it from neck to tail.

'I'd like us to be friends again, Babička. Please, for Krystof's sake.' She tried, searching hard for the right words. 'For Nancy's sake. I need your advice. Truth is, I've had some shocking news . . .'

Lara lifted her face and yelled, '*Skutečny*? Truth?'

'Oh, please, *prosím*, Babička.'

Lara struck an icy stare at Rose and in a flash, she took her eye off her task. The blade slipped.

'*Jezis-Maria!*' The old woman screamed in pain and clutched at her hand as blood oozed over the mess of fish scales.

Rose rushed over to her. 'Oh, Babička!'

The old woman flinched away, yelling angrily in a stream of incomprehensible words.

'Please let me help you,' Rose cried.

Lara hurried into the scullery.

Nancy began to cry but Rose, hearing bangs and crashes from within the little room, hurried after Lara. She found her trying to turn on the tap with her elbow. There was no water.

'*Sakra!*' cried the old woman.

Rose knew this meant 'bloody hell', for Krystof said this often enough whenever the electricity was cut off.

'Babička, perhaps this will help,' she said, rushing to fetch a bottle of vinegar.

Lara backed away. '*Ne, ne.*' She shook her head, tears of pain in her eyes.

The old woman wrapped a cloth around her finger and Rose watched as the stain of blood blossomed through the fabric.

'I know the vinegar will sting,' she said, fearing that the right words would escape her, 'but it will help clean it . . . It's a nasty cut.'

Lara stared at her. Hatred and disgust boiled in her eyes.

'*Kurva,*' she hissed.

Tears fell down Rose's cheeks. In her distress she cried out in English.

'Please don't say that to me. You don't understand. My husband was . . . I didn't love him . . . I didn't know what I was doing when I married him . . . My parents were dead . . . I was beside myself . . .'

Lara went back into the kitchen, cradling her injured hand. Rose followed, desperate to comfort her; to seek comfort from her. The old woman was standing by the table, staring hard at Nancy. The little girl sat cringing, her shoulders hunched with distress. Rose, issuing soothing words towards her daughter, gently touched the old woman's arm. Lara yelled and twitched away, flinging out her hand, sending the bowl of eggs crashing to the floor and marching out of the room.

Nancy's crying began again, reaching a new crescendo as Rose sank to her knees to try to retrieve the mess, knowing how valuable the eggs were. As she scooped yolks, whites and shattered shells with her hands, the liquid ran through her fingers.

'Please stop crying, Nancy,' she muttered, hiding her tear-stained face below the edge of the table. 'Oh, what a waste. What an utter waste.'

With Lara keeping to her room, not answering Rose's tapping on the door or her offer of the last of the coffee, Rose had no choice but to put Nancy to bed, press her finger to her lips and hope she stayed put, before slipping quickly out the front door. She went into the café. As she eschewed a table and walked straight to the counter she felt a murmuring among the patrons, their eyes flicking to look at her and then back down to their dominoes or beverage or schnapps.

Milan was leaning there, his large hairy arms folded in front of him.

'Find a table and I will serve you,' he grumbled.

'I don't want anything.'

'Ah, an extra favour today, is it?' he asked.

She heard a snigger from the table behind her.

'*Ne*. Not today. Or any day,' she said. 'I have come to tell you that there will be no more lessons. I think I am sufficiently fluent in Czech to get by, thank you very much. So I'm putting a stop to it.'

'Oh, no,' he said. 'That wasn't the deal.'

'What deal?'

'I am not *fully* fluent in English,' he said. 'So, you still have to teach me. The Party wants people like me. Translators. I want to be the best. And you. You should see it as your duty to teach me.'

'The party?'

'The *Party*.'

'No, Milan. There was never any deal. As for duty, I . . .'

She heard more chuckling and turned to see that most of the men were laughing surreptitiously at Milan, shaking their heads, wagging their fingers at him. Milan's face flushed red with fury.

'I'll give you double schnapps if you teach me now.'

'No, I don't want anything from you. I have to get back to my daughter.'

246

A customer nearby called, 'Hey, Milan's been put into his place by the *Anglický*. And not even a double schnapps will tempt her. He's losing his touch.'

'Did he ever have a touch?' someone answered.

'I doubt it,' someone else piped up.

Rose watched as Milan's embarrassment seemed to swell his frame, his mouth masticating with fury.

'Get out then,' he hissed, staring hard.

'With pleasure,' she said.

For the rest of the day, Rose busied herself in the kitchen, salvaging the carp and wondering if she could make an omelette with the smashed eggs. At last she heard Krystof's key in the lock below.

Rushing to the kitchen door to greet him, she cried, 'Oh, Krystof, I've had an awful day. I'm so glad you're home. I have had a telegram from Betony. It's awful, actually, and Babička – I – oh!'

She stopped talking when she saw him come into the lamplight. His face had the pallor of a corpse, his eyes were wide and shining with shock.

'Nancy in bed?' he asked.

She nodded.

'And where's Babička?' He was at the dresser pouring a shot of schnapps.

'Asleep in her room. I'm afraid she cut her finger badly on the fish knife. She . . . she said she wasn't feeling herself, she wanted an early night,' Rose lied.

She thought, I mustn't tell Krystof how bad the shouting was today.

With a trembling hand, Krystof knocked the liquor back. 'Well, I'm glad she's in her room, as I don't want her to hear this.'

'Krystof, what on earth has happened?'

He closed the door to the kitchen and pulled her to the table. 'Come and sit here.'

'What? What?' He was scaring her.

'I was walking back across the Charles Bridge, as usual, as I do every evening, when I saw two men walking towards me.' He was breathless. The schnapps had made his eyes water. 'You know how dark it is in the middle of the river when the gaslights aren't on. I thought they'd step aside, I tried to avoid them – God, I've just had a thought. Wait!'

He jumped up and hurried from the kitchen. Rose followed him to the landing window. He stood in the darkness and carefully tilted his head from side to side, watching the street below. Finally he backed away and drew the curtain.

'*Krystof?*' she whispered.

He gestured that they should go back into the kitchen. He closed the door behind them and leant on it.

'They're following me,' he said.

'The two men . . .' he said, finally, his words disjointed by shock. 'The bridge was deserted. I was about halfway across. They were coming towards me. I go one way, they go the same. I hopped to the side, they did likewise. Like a silly dance. I laughed and said, "Good evening, gentlemen. Please excuse me". But they stopped me with a hand to the chest. I looked down in disbelief. "Excuse me," I said again. I tried to keep my voice light. I didn't want to get into a fight. But I would have liked it to have been a fight, I tell you.'

Agitated, he got up and strode around the table, his eyes blazing.

'They asked me if I was Captain Novotny of the Tulka Regiment, Army of Czechoslovakia. I said, yes, of course I am. They introduced themselves. They said they were from the Communist Party. I remember looking from one to the other, trying to pick out their features beneath their Homburgs, wondering why they were trying to pass the time of day in such a way. It was so dark that I could hardly see their faces. And then they said, Would I like to join the Party. But it wasn't a question. It was a trap.'

Rose pressed her lips together, fighting her bubbling fear.

Krystof sat down next to her. 'I said, "No. No, thank you. I support the Social Democrats."'

'Of course you said no,' she said. 'Were they *Ruský?*'

'No, they were Czech. But they are under the influence of . . .'

She remembered the sleek Daimler with its fluttering red pennants in the square. She asked, 'What did they do?'

'One of them has followed me home.'

'Oh, Krystof.'

'Don't worry. I can't think why he bothered. They know who I am, where I work, where I live, my route to and from the barracks. All this *following* is just intimidation.'

'Even so,' she said, her voice shaking. 'What does this *mean*?'

Krystof sighed. 'It means our Russian friends are here to stay. As an army captain, I am useful to them. The forces are a very good place to start. They want the army, they need the army on their side.'

'Are you frightened?' she blurted.

He looked at her. 'Not as much as you seem to be, my darling Ruzena.' He gathered her hands in his. 'In a way, some people see it as a good thing. Now that the Germans have been booted out and the war has been won, our new government is desperate to get away from anything remotely right wing. I see their point, but I also see the whole of the East being eaten up by the Soviets. Everything that was blown sky high by the war is only just starting to fall back to earth. And who knows how it will settle?'

And here I am, Rose thought, *in the centre of this mess, waiting for the debris to fall*. The telegram from Pengared played on her mind, but she would not bother Krystof with that tonight. Instead, she gazed at him, feeling shy with the amount of love she felt for him.

To her astonishment, he suddenly laughed. 'One thing you can say,' he said, 'is that we've swapped one lot of occupying clowns for another. But at least the Germans had better manners.'

She joined in with his laughter, noting the edge of hysteria.

He put his arms around her and spoke into her hair. 'We'll be fine. We'll get through this. Just stay close to me.'

But then, as they held each other in the lamplight, she heard the telegram crinkle up in her pocket and a sick melancholy broke over her in a huge, queasy wave.

Twenty-two

GOLDEN LEAVES WERE FALLING IN STREAMS FROM THE TREES, GLINTING like jewels in the low sunlight as they descended between the tall houses, landing softly on the courtyard cobbles. Brown smoke from coal fires floated in a layer above the chimney pots. From the kitchen window, Rose watched as Krystof spun Nancy round and round in her pram, sending leaves flying back up into the air. The little girl shrieked with laughter and trusting fear, throwing out her hands to him.

Krystof bent to unstrap her and then hoisted her onto his shoulders. Their clouded breath merged in the chilly air as he jogged and jiggled her around, wincing with laughter as her shrieks pierced his ears.

Rose smiled and then her face dropped. On the other side of the wall, Milan was methodically sweeping up leaves in the café courtyard. With each drawing of his broom, he paused and cocked his head to the sound of Nancy's laughter. Rose thought that perhaps he was irritated by her daughter's shrieking. But then she drew in her breath as she saw him step to the wall, carefully slide a loose brick to the side and press his eye to the hole.

Rose turned to see Lara walk into the kitchen with the post and she began to gesture towards the yard below. With her usual sullen silence, the old woman ignored Rose and placed the letters on the table. Then she went to the window and craned her neck to watch her grandson play, a scowl of contemplation on her face. Glancing sideways at her, Rose noticed a thin smile twitch her lips.

After a while, the old lady turned to go, muttering to herself, 'She should learn to call him *Otec*.'

Rose felt hope rise like a bird as she realised, long after Lara had left the room, that she had said that Nancy should call Krystof *Papa*.

'We will resolve this,' she told herself as she picked up the letter addressed to her. 'Babička will come round.'

Then she frowned and turned the envelope over and over in her hands. It had been already been torn open and resealed. Her fingers shook as she ran her nail along the edge and pulled out the letter.

The folded sheet of thick, well-thumbed paper was headed with the name of a London solicitor.

Dear Mrs Bowman, she read, *Re: Bowman vs Bowman*.

Even across the thousand miles, Will had the capacity to reach her.

> ... *the very serious charge of kidnap will be brought to bear if you do not comply with our client's wishes and return to England with the child Nancy Sylvia Bowman ... our client will petition for divorce on account of adultery, desertion and unreasonable behaviour ... custody of the said child will be given to Mr Bowman ... return immediately ...*

She sat down at the kitchen table, let the letter fall into her lap and held her head in her hands. Betony had warned her in the telegram, but she had decided to ignore her. And now, just two weeks later, the full fury and cold patience of Will Bowman sat on her shoulders. The last words he said to her taunted her: *'And when these monkeys set me free, which they will, eventually, Rosebud, I'm going to come and find you. And I'm going to kill you.'*

'But what of his conviction?' she cried out loud. 'Don't these awful solicitors know anything?' She snatched up the letter again and scanned the lines. In her shock, she'd missed out a paragraph.

> ... *our client's contrition over his past misdemeanours stands him in good stead ... has stood before an appeal judge ... pardoned ...*

Rose heard the back door to the yard open and Krystof and Nancy bundle in, bringing a blast of cold air with them. She went to the top of the stairs.

Her voice was hollow with shock. 'Krystof, please put Nancy down for a nap.'

'Oh, she's too excited for that. I thought she could have some milk and a *zákusek* from Milan next door.'

'I haven't got time for pastries. Take her to bed!'

Krystof looked at Rose aghast. 'What's the matter? What on earth?'

Her jaw froze into a solid line. She handed him the letter and took Nancy from him. She held the child tight, feeling her cold little cheek pressing against her own.

'He has tracked me down,' Rose said. 'He wants me back or he will take Nancy away. Take her away from me.'

Krystof glanced at the letter, open-mouthed, and then looked back at Rose.

She turned to take Nancy up the stairs but the little girl began to wriggle and call for Krystof.

Rose's hand flashed out and slapped her hard.

'Stop your crying!' she shouted. 'You do as you are told!'

Krystof cried, 'Ruzena, please!'

Rose stared at him over the top of her weeping child's face.

'Read it,' she said. 'Then you will know why I just did that.'

Feeling equal amounts of guilt, resentment and love for her child, she held Nancy close and slowly walked up the once grand, now decaying staircase.

Unable to sleep they rose before dawn and, mindful of waking Lara and Nancy, crept quietly down the stairs. The night air in the street outside was so cold that Rose cried out, silencing herself with her mittened hand.

When they reached the Charles Bridge lined with its frozen statues, they turned left and walked along the embankment. The inky river slept in the darkness, its frigid depths unimaginable. The city was beginning to stir, and the first tram rumbled past them on its way to Wenceslas Square. Below the white froth of the weir, shivering boatmen cast their first lines of the day by the light of swinging lanterns. She thought of the fishermen of Polperro . . . the night she met Krystof.

They stopped at the next bridge along, the Legii, and leant on the parapet. From here, the Charles Bridge was indistinguishable from the black water, and the castle on the other bank was in deep shadow, like a sleeping giant on his side. But behind it, in the east, the veil of night was lifting and a pale greenness spread over the horizon.

'I can't believe it has come to this,' Rose said, feeling the cold air bite at her nose and settle over her shoulders like a heavy cloak. 'I am being accused of abducting my own child by the man I detest. He is being pardoned for his terrible crimes. And your grandmother thinks I'm a whore.'

Krystof, ignoring her, spoke with conviction. 'I want to marry you, Rose Pepper.'

'Is that really the answer? How can we even start to think about that!' She took a deep, despairing breath, feeling the air chilling her blood, sharpening her senses. The awful clarity of their situation revealed itself to her. She cried, 'Why didn't we think of this before – why was I so hell-bent on getting away from England?'

She stopped. One glance at Krystof's face told her why.

'I wanted my life with you to start as soon as possible,' she admitted. 'But I have been selfish. I should have waited and sorted out my affairs. I should have divorced Will while he was still in prison. I should have cited cruelty and threatening behaviour; the very fact that he was a *Nazi* . . .' She paused and shuddered. 'But I ran away. And, now, because of that, my chance of happiness with you is fading by the second.'

Krystof's arms surrounded her. He pressed his face to her hood. A church bell over in the Little Quarter tolled the waking hour.

'I *said*, I want to marry you, my blazing firecracker Rose.'

She lifted her face. Her eyes adjusted to the growing light and she saw the deep shadows in his eyes.

'I heard you, Krystof.'

He sighed deeply and let go of her. He was restless with agitation; he kicked the toe of his boot against the parapet wall.

'You have to return to England.' His voice cracked with reluctance.

'How can I?' she hissed.

'You need to set yourself free from this disgusting man. Show the courts you deserve custody of Nancy. Let them know of his appalling behaviour. Show them what a good mother you are.'

'But how can I leave when I have to be with you? I can't leave you.' She began to shiver, the cold reaching her stomach.

His whisper was edged with pain. 'But I cannot leave Babička.'

She heard the first stirrings of birds, waking in the half-light in the bare chestnut trees by the river. Poor little creatures, how do they survive this bitterness? She drew a shuddering breath as tears streamed from her eyes. How did they not freeze when all around her was cold, so cold?

'No, no, don't cry.' Krystof stepped closer and wrapped his arms around her, tried to stop her shaking. 'Perhaps we will find a way. I will speak to people. I will ask the right questions.'

Her eyes grew sharper as the daylight increased. Fragments of light were caught in the eddies of the river.

'But what can be done for us?'

'I'm thinking of people in high places . . . my superior at the barracks, perhaps.' Krystof's voice rose with hollow enthusiasm. 'People who can help us, so you perhaps won't have to leave at all. Even Lucenka the old lamplighter woman has contacts. You'd be surprised.'

'But why should these people bother with us?' She sensed his lack of conviction and her strength plummeted. 'It's useless,' she whispered. 'Krystof, you know it. There is no hope left. Nothing.'

'Don't you dare say that, Rose Pepper.' Krystof was angry. 'I will not hear it.'

But even as he spoke, she watched anger fade from his eyes as an awful realisation spread slowly over his face.

'If you leave Czechoslovakia,' Krystof said, 'the way things are . . . you may not be able to come back.'

'Then we do nothing,' Rose said.

As the sun pushed up into the stillness of the dawn, a sudden wind tore the last of the leaves from the trees, scattering them around their feet.

She said, 'I remember leaves were falling in my parents' garden when I returned to find my home bombed . . . the life I knew . . . over.' The breeze sent icy fingers down the back of her neck. 'I feel exactly the same now, watching these leaves fall.

A different country, a different time. But the same feeling. I am lost. Utterly lost.'

Krystof held her, pressing his lips to her forehead.

The golden stone of the Charles Bridge began to emerge from the gloom and the silhouetted statues appeared like a line of chattering old men.

Prague's beauty had never looked so transient nor so brittle.

Twenty-three

'ON DAYS LIKE TODAY,' SAID KRYSTOF, SCRAPING THE ICE FROM THE inside of the bedroom windowpanes, 'they say that birds fall dead from the sky. Frozen in mid-flight.'

Under the covers, Rose watched his breath cloud as he spoke. He knelt in front of the grate, poking at the damped-down fire to bring it back to life. Even in bed, her nose was numb, her toes icy, her eyelids chilled.

'Who says?' she shivered.

'Well, the good people of Prague do. Babička swears she saw it happen over the castle when she was a little girl.'

'I thought the kitchen at the Old Vicarage was chilly,' Rose's teeth chattered, 'but this is monstrous.'

'You will get used to it. *Únor* is the month of floating ice. Of course it's going to be cold. But at least the ice is breaking on the river. Just think, in a month or two, the glorious spring will return.'

'Get back into bed, Krystof. Quickly.'

He joined her under the fur cover made by his mother from rabbit pelts, hare and russet fox, all sewn together and backed beautifully with silk. She reached out a brave arm and pulled it over their shoulders, feeling its weight settle on them. His warm arms encircled her and slowly their combined body heat returned.

'And in the spring?' she asked, responding to the edge of hope in his voice.

'I will resign from the army. We will sell this place. We can go and live in a *chalupa* in the country. Get away from Prague and its prying eyes.'

'A *chalupa*?'

'A little country house. Perhaps have some chickens, a pig and a goat? What do you say, Ruzena?'

'I say *ano* to that. Yes,' she whispered, feeling a future for them all expanding before her.

'Nancy will love it. And Babička will agree, I am sure,' said Krystof. 'I take it she is giving Nancy her breakfast at the moment? Are things improving between you both?'

'She is being nice to Nancy,' said Rose. 'She can't ignore Nancy. No one can.'

'I do try to talk to her, every now and then,' said Krystof. 'The reason why you married him. How you made a mistake. That you are only human.'

'Human . . . yes.'

Krystof asked, 'Have you seen our friend recently?'

'Our man who stands and watches?' she replied. 'No. I think even the *Ruský policie* are finding this weather too barbaric.' She paused. 'Krystof, does Babička still not know about you being followed?'

'No, I want to protect her. She will be worried. Let her cope with one thing at a time.'

And yet, thought Rose, *I have to cope*. With a twinge of resentment, she rolled away from Krystof under the covers.

'Hey, come back here,' he laughed. 'You'll be in a cold patch.'

'I'm just getting comfortable,' she lied.

'Well, don't get too settled. I have a busy day. I want to fix that doorbell. We are civilised people. We need a doorbell that works,' he laughed. 'It is driving me *bláznivý*.'

'Driving me crazy too,' said Rose, 'but it's too cold to even think about stepping outside.'

'It won't take long. Half an hour at the most,' he said. 'Talking of things driving us crazy . . . I saw Milan yesterday and said hello but he just stood and stared at me and stroked his moustache.'

'I find the man frankly revolting. I avoid him at all costs.'

'Well, just think, when we move away, we can leave all of our troubles behind us. Including him.' Krystof's eyes sparkled at the thought. 'I'll even pass the café to him, if I have to, to keep him off our backs. He can have it, bricks, mortar, coffee pots and all.'

'I don't think he deserves to be given the café,' said Rose, grumpily.

'Another thing I could do if it wasn't so bloody damn cold is to fill that hole in the wall. But something tells me the cement will freeze before I can do anything with it. So that will have to wait, I'm afraid. I wonder where my tools are?'

Squinting up at the patches on the frosted windowpanes, Rose saw the grey frozen morning, and heard not a peep of birdsong. No birds would dare fly today.

Restless, Rose wandered the house, checking the fires in the bedrooms, making sure they were properly banked to preserve their warmth so that it lasted until the evening. The salon door was shut fast; there was no need to heat it, no reason to go in that naked room for another two months. Krystof had folded a rug and pushed it against the bottom of the door to stop draughts seeping through. Even so, the cold on the landing was breathtaking.

She walked to the landing window and craned her neck to see if she could spot Krystof working below. The porch blocked her view, but she could hear the faint tapping of his hammer.

She watched the street like a hawk; as she predicted, the cold had driven even the hardiest of spies indoors. But she would not let herself feel comforted. They could be watching from behind any window, hiding inside any doorway, listening through a hole in the wall. Shivering, her face stiff and her feet leaden, she knew she should go back to the kitchen and sit by the stove and watch Lara's stony face. It was too cold to stand there any longer.

Lara sat knitting, her mouth set in a pensive line. By her side, Nancy was having her nap in her cot brought close to the stove. As soon as Rose walked in, Lara stood up stiffly and poured some coffee from the enamel pot, punctuating the silence with a smattering of tutting and groans.

She proffered the steaming cup and Rose deduced from the mute gesture that she should take the coffee to Krystof.

As she descended the stairs to the dark vestibule, the frigid air enveloped her feet, her legs and her waist. The stone floor exuded a damp and clammy stagnation. Her head ached. She longed to breathe fresh air instead of the oppressive, smoky chill trapped inside the house. As she opened the front door a chink to call Krystof, the icy blast hit her like a blow. She smelt the rancid aroma of coal fires and felt the profound silence of the still day press on her ears.

'Krystof? Coffee for you. You must be nearly finished?'

His chisel and screwdriver were laid neatly on the doorstep; his stepladder propped against the wall.

'Krystof?' She peered around the porch, her expectant smile dropping a fraction, and then falling clean away. He must have popped away for something from the ironmonger's. Screws, perhaps? She pressed the bell. It still did not work.

At midday Rose, Lara and Nancy ate their soup in the quiet kitchen.

'Oh, isn't *Otec* a scoundrel?' she said to Nancy. 'I wonder where he's gone?'

Lara raised an eyebrow at her and Rose tried to draw a smile from the old woman but her mouth felt dry. He had been gone two hours.

Sitting close to the range, she held Nancy on her lap and read to her. The little girl patted the picture book with her finger, pointing at colourful drawings of a farmyard, a house with a red roof, chickens in the hay, while Rose enunciated the strange formations and accents in Czech, allowing herself to dream a little of their own *chalupa*.

The clock on the landing chimed three, and the sun began to sink. Glancing up, she saw that Lara was dozing.

Shutting the book with frustration and telling Nancy firmly to stay by the stove, Rose went back downstairs and opened the front door. She wanted Krystof to be on the doorstep, grinning, so that she could shout at him and drum her fists on his shoulder. But the doorway, gloomy under darkening skies, was empty. She folded up the stepladder and brought in his tools.

'How careless he is,' she muttered out loud as she closed the door. 'They might have been stolen.' But she was pretending: her voice was not her own.

'Krystof?' came Lara's despondent voice from the top of the stairs.

'*Ne*,' she told her.

In the shadows of the stairway, Rose saw lines of worry carve up the woman's face. She saw her wrinkled hands wringing in and out of her apron.

'Wait here, Babička,' Rose said, quickly bundling on her coat and hat. She went out into the cold.

Through the windows of the café she could see that all was dark and quiet. Chairs were upturned on tables and cloths covered the coffee pots. She took a deep breath and knocked on the door. There was utter silence, broken eventually by the tolling of the four o'clock bell in the monastery tower. She knocked again. Eventually, a light showed at the back and Milan came out from behind the counter.

He waved her away. '*Zavreno!*' he called. 'The café is closed.'

She shook her head at him, pummelled harder, rattled the handle. He came up to the door and stared at her through the glass, his eyes sharp under bushy eyebrows.

'Let me in!' she cried. She watched him comb his moustache with dirty fingernails.

Eventually he shrugged and unlatched the door. 'I was asleep,' he moaned. 'It's my day off. The café is closed.'

'Krystof has gone,' she breathed urgently. 'Do you know where? Did you see anything? He was there . . .' She gestured to the porch. 'Now he is gone. Oh, please, Milan, *prosím*, Milan.'

He regarded her briefly and then gripped her arm and pulled her into the café. He closed the door behind her.

'Sit down,' he grumbled.

In a daze, she sat. 'You know where he is? Are you telling me that you know where he has gone?' She felt panic rising in her cold, aching chest.

He regarded her with cruel control. She stared back at him, fighting her fear. But after some moments she had to avert her eyes and suddenly noticed that, behind him, in front of the Czech land-girl posters hung Soviet flags.

Milan told her, 'The *Ruský policie* came for Captain Novotny hours ago.'

'*Why?* Why didn't you tell us?'

He shrugged again. She wanted to slap his bristled face.

'His awful hammering stopped,' said Milan. 'It had given me a headache, so in the peace and quiet, I could sleep . . .'

'You stupid man!' she cried. She stood up abruptly; her chair crashed to the floor behind her. 'Why have they taken him? He's done nothing wrong!'

Milan's hand gripped her arm. He put his face close to hers. She saw his fat lips glisten as he licked them.

'Maybe he has.' His fingers tightened their grip; his other hand reached to touch her behind her ear. She flinched in disgust.

'I can tell you more,' he breathed. 'I know what's happened. If you teach me again, teach me more *Anglický*. . . If you stay here with me . . . tonight . . .'

With a murmur of fear, Rose whipped her arm away and fled from the café, feeling the roughness of his fingers still on her neck.

She stumbled through the front door to *At the Clementinum*, ran up the stairs and into the kitchen. Lara lifted her face, her eyes like saucers in the half-light, and then, seeing that Rose was on her own, covered her face with a trembling hand.

'Babička . . . Krystof has been arrested.' Even as Rose spoke, she couldn't believe her own words. 'By the *Ruský policie*. Milan just told me. They took him away this morning.'

The old woman sank down into a chair and rested her head on the table.

Rose woke, curled up in the centre of the bed. The dawn was sullen and unwelcome. She was stiff with cold and her head still ached.

In silence she and Lara ate a breakfast of old bread and warmed milk and then they buttoned up their coats. Rose pushed a grizzling Nancy in the pram, along the empty, misty streets, stepping over frozen conduits and iced-up puddles. Lara walked a few paces behind. Doorways and corners still held the shadows of the night and stone houses rose either side of them like ghostly giants, blackened by smoke. As they crossed the Old Town Square, the mist swirled away and Rose spotted the shapeless figure of a woman shuffling from streetlamp to streetlamp. She hoisted up a long pole to pull on a ring, shutting off the gas. A large hairy dog trotted beside her like a horrific doppelganger.

'*Dobrý den*, Lucenka,' called Lara, her voice cracking in the cold.

The woman lifted a ragged gloved hand as a greeting, grunting from beneath her deep fur hat. *So this was Lucenka*, thought Rose, *the witch of the gas lamps*. One by one, she snuffed the gas lamps out as Lara and Rose approached the Ministry of State Security, where Rose had seen the shining Daimler pull up all those weeks before. From each of its tall windows, floor on floor, hung two flags, flat in the frozen air. One, the Czech flag, the other, guarding it closely, was the blood-red Soviet banner.

Two guards in grey coats and square sheepskin hats stood to attention either side of the porch, rousing themselves at their approach. It was the end of a long, cold night shift. Their rifles crossed automatically in front of the great studded door and one of them barked a question. Lara answered, lifting her chin to look at him. In a smooth motion, the rifles were lowered and an arm reached out to open the door. They walked quickly. Rose could not bear to catch the guards' eyes; they looked younger than she did.

They stood in the entrance hall of what must have once been a busy guild house full of merchants and commerce. Parquet stretched to right and left; a wide staircase swept upwards into endless gloom. Above their heads hung a chandelier, covered in the ubiquitous film of dust. How drab it was now; how officious. But also, how warm; it was almost luxury.

Behind a small desk in the far corner sat a clerk in uniform with an angled desk lamp casting a pool of light at his elbow. Rose parked the pram by a wooden bench near the door and she and Lara approached the clerk, their footsteps ringing out across the parquet. He continued to ignore them, just as he had done when the great front door had swung open. They stood before the desk and watched him write in a protracted manner on a form. They waited. He lifted his head and Lara opened her mouth to speak. But he simply dipped his nib in a bottle of ink and continued to write.

Rose cleared her throat. 'Excuse me, sir.'

The man glared up at her, eyes like chips of steel.

'The ministry is not open yet,' he clipped.

'Can we wait, sir?' ventured Lara, her voice humble and hesitant.

He flicked his eyes to the old woman, pursed his lips and lifted his shoulders in a slow, insulting shrug. He settled back to his writing. He was not going to say another word. They walked back to the wooden bench and sat.

The guard's pen continued to scribble and the clock on the desk ticked like a hollow torturous metronome. A phone started to ring behind a closed door along the corridor. The ominous sound repeated over and over like an alarm until, abruptly, it was silenced.

Lara fidgeted, tapping her foot. Rose felt a gnawing in her stomach. She covered it with clenched knuckles and tried to soothe Nancy, praying that she would sleep, thinking again, *At least it is warm.*

Somewhere in the vaults of the building a door was shut with a sharp rap and footsteps clipped their approach along the corridor. Rose bristled with expectation and straightened her shoulders as a Russian officer appeared. He walked straight past, oblivious to them. The clerk got to his feet, his chair grating, and saluted. They spoke in staccato Russian, turning their broad backs on Lara and Rose. Then the officer retreated into an office and closed the door.

Rose heard Lara take a breath to speak out and swiftly placed a hand on her arm to stop her. In that instant, they stared long and hard at each other. Rose saw tears in the old woman's eyes, a fire of anger; and then a softening. Lara twitched her arm away and thrust her trembling hands back inside her gloves.

An hour dragged past and Rose felt her insides turn in agony. Suddenly, the man behind the desk looked up and addressed them.

Lara rose unsteadily to her feet and walked quickly towards him, straining her neck forward, propelling herself, crying, '*Ano, ano.* Krystof Novotny. Captain Novotny, Tulka Regiment, Army of Czechoslovakia.'

Hearing Krystof's name, Rose felt her heart pound. Surely, he must be here? Somewhere in this building? There must be news. It was all a mistake and they must let him go. Mistaken identity, just a warning. Please, let him go.

She rushed to Lara's side, fixing her eyes on the guard's disdainful expression. Then it came to her, in waves of sickening comprehension. Of course he was here. All these people knew: the young guards outside knew, this clerk, the officer who had marched through an hour before, knew. But that meant nothing. She glanced in pity at Lara's open, eager and trusting face.

The guard used the very tips of his fingers to leaf through a pile of papers on the desk beside him. He drew out a buff file, its cover printed with Russian words.

'Hmm, Novotny,' he muttered.

Rose felt herself shaking. She tried to swallow her anger.

'Ah,' said the man, as if alighting on some new piece of information. He paused as if to relish the moment. 'Ah, yes.' He looked them in the eye for the first time and said, 'You will be informed.' He spoke some more, his words clipped and few, and Rose's mind raced trying to pinpoint his meaning.

'What?' asked Lara, incredulous, her body sagging in disappointment, her bottom lip loose with shock.

'We must leave,' Rose whispered to her, suddenly understanding. The man's face was blank with inhumanity.

'*What?*' cried Lara, her thin voice cracking around the high ceiling. 'Where is he?'

Rose pulled Lara's trembling, frail figure away towards the door, and grasped the pram handles. Glancing back, she saw the guard had returned to his scribbling. His face broke into a smile.

As Rose walked towards the ministry the following day, she wondered which window might conceal Krystof. Her eyes travelled from the small attic casements, down past the grand windows of the main rooms to the arched basement windows that she glimpsed down the dank stairwells either side of the main door. These windows were blacked out. They had bars.

Again, she waited on the hard bench by the door. It was a weekday and there was a busier atmosphere. Orders were issued as officers strutted with paperwork and tightly coiffured women in grey suits marched stiff-backed, holding bundles of buff files. She sat alongside a weary man and a frightened woman on the bench. No one said a word, and no one paid her any regard until, after two hours, the desk clerk deigned to lift his head and call out, 'Novotny?'

She walked over with a trickle of hope, a glow of optimism

on her face. The clerk lifted a stamp and ground it into his pad of ink. Then with a whack he stamped a file.

'You will be informed.'

Lara glanced up from her knitting with a hopeful smile. Rose shook her head and then watched the old woman compress her mouth in pain and haul her stiff body from the chair. She began to pace the kitchen, panting in distress, wringing her hands.

Rose could not bear to watch. 'Babička, please, *prosím*. Please sit. Calm yourself,' she pleaded. *I must not cry. I must not cry*.

Lara pressed her hands to the sides of her head and began to wail. Goose bumps prickled Rose's shivering arms. Standing in the centre of the kitchen, Lara extended her thin arms and then shook her hands hard, again and again, snapping her wrists. She balled up her fists and brought them down onto her thighs, hitting herself over and over until, breaking down, she hurried from the room.

Rose found Lara sitting bolt upright on the chaise longue in the freezing salon, her face sagging, staring at the portrait of her daughter on her wedding day. Tears fell down the old woman's face. Nancy toddled in, following her mother, and reached out for Lara.

The old woman broke her gaze to glance down at the child and an unexpected compassion transformed her face. She pulled Nancy onto her knee and Rose watched her tears fall into the little girl's hair.

Rose went downstairs to fetch the fur cover from the bedroom. She draped it around the old woman's shoulders, enfolding her daughter with her inside its warmth. Without a word, she planted a kiss on top of both their heads and left the room.

Very early on the sixth bitter morning without Krystof, as Rose left for the ministry in darkness, she was stopped by an insistent rapping on the café window. She turned to see Milan opening the door and beckoning her.

'Come in here for a moment,' he hissed at her. 'I have some news.'

Cautiously, she did as he asked. He closed the door behind

her and pulled down the blind. In the dim light she saw his eyes glinting; his moustache was damp.

'You teach me English properly, like we agreed before,' he said, his voice reverberating, 'and I will speak with the Party.'

She took a step back, recoiling from the smell of his breath. 'Really?' she asked, her voice high with disbelief. 'Is it that easy?'

'I will help secure the release of Captain Novotny,' said Milan, reaching for her. 'And perhaps we can be *friends*.'

She felt his thumb massage her shoulder; his breathing on her cheek.

'Captain Novotny is a very brave man. A war hero.' Milan spoke deeply into her ear. 'He is my landlord, and I pay him good rent for this place. So he is rich. Richer than most.'

Rose frowned, struggling with some of his words. He spoke urgently, his voice pompous and crowing.

'They don't like him at the Party. He is bourgeois. They know how influential he is . . . at the barracks . . . with his regiment. They want him to mend his ways. But I can convince them that he is not a threat to them. They will listen to me.'

She dared to glance at him. She finally guessed his meaning. Krystof was in danger. And Milan could help him. But she said, 'No, Milan. I think you are causing more trouble for everyone.' She was surprised how clear and steady her voice was. 'Please leave me alone.'

'Yes, you *are* alone. There is no one in Prague to help you. No one in this whole country who cares about you. I am your only hope. They like me. I am new to the Party, with fresh ideas. I am eager to prove myself.'

She went towards the door. 'I'm leaving. I am already late. I have to report to the ministry, and see if I can get some real news on Krystof. Not this rubbish.'

'You're not going anywhere . . .' He gripped the top of her arm.

She bit her lip to stop herself crying out.

He leant into her, his spittle hitting her lip. 'You are *kurva*. Everyone thinks it. Everyone knows it. Even your blessed Babička knows it.'

She turned her face away.

'Don't pretend you don't understand me,' he snarled.

She watched in horror as he thrust his hips towards her.

'You remember,' he said, 'it's no longer the rutting season, but it can be if I want it to be. Come upstairs with me now to bed and you will see your captain home this evening.'

'I said . . . leave me alone.'

He gripped her shoulder, his eyes unflinching.

'No? So he doesn't mean that much to you?'

'Please, you're hurting!' She fought her instinct to struggle, to push him away, knowing it would make things worse. How could she deal with a man like this? His strength and belligerence were too much for her.

'You made a fool of me in front of my customers. I haven't forgotten that.'

'You made a fool of yourself, Milan.'

Inexplicably, he released her and stepped back; surveyed her.

He said, 'I tried to help you, silly girl. Just remember that. So it has come to this, then? Something else, then?'

'What?'

Turning to look over his shoulder, he shouted, 'Officers, if you please!'

Two men wearing black Homburgs and smart fur collars appeared from the back of the café.

'That will be all, Milan,' one of them said with a rumbling Russian accent. 'We don't need you any longer.'

The other approached Rose and held her elbow.

'Don't make a fuss and you won't be harmed, Mrs Bowman. You have to come with us.'

From the window, Rose could see the skeleton on the Town Hall clock. Twice now he had raised his bony arm and the chimes had struck. Two hours she had sat there, waiting. Two hours in dreadful, protracted silence.

The office at the ministry was frugal. Grey linoleum, an ordinary desk, wooden chairs, a metal filing cabinet, a radiator, a framed picture of Joseph Stalin. Beyond the closed door, she sensed, people, efficient people, were busy working. She heard typing. Incessant typing. And then, intermittently, the innocuous ting of the typewriter bell. But inside the room where she waited: utter quiet until the telephone rang, shrill and scolding.

Sometimes Major Ivanov, sitting behind the desk, ignoring her as he worked, would pick up the receiver and listen. Sometimes he'd just let it ring.

Rose shifted on the hard seat, her back sore, her shoulders hunched in apprehensive agony. Fear was taking a grip on her, fastening onto her spine. She fought it with all her strength, trying to clear her head, convince herself that this was normal procedure. That she and Krystof would be home for tea.

Suddenly, the major spoke to her. 'Your file, Mrs Bowman, is very interesting to us.' He was Russian but spoke in Czech with sinister authority. He opened a buff folder and extracted a sheet of paper, marked here and there with red pen.

She glanced up, surprised, and saw that he was holding a duplicated copy of the letter she had been sent by Will Bowman's solicitors: the letter that had been opened and inexpertly resealed. She swallowed hard. Her mouth was dry. She licked her lips.

Major Ivanov's hard face looked momentarily genial.

Lowering his voice, he said, 'Would you like some water, Mrs Bowman?'

How dry and hot it was in here. She was unused to such warmth.

'Well, I . . .'

'Perhaps some questions first.' He shuffled the papers in his hand, tapping them on the desk to align them. 'What have we here? Ah, yes.' He squared his shoulders under his uniform epaulettes, lifted his eyes and stared at her, his dark glare unflinching. 'Your husband is a Nazi convict. You have been accused by the British authorities of the kidnapping of a minor. You left England to be with your bourgeois lover, Comrade Novotny.'

'I'm sorry, what did you say?' She heard the words for 'British' and 'Nazi' and terror hit her in the stomach. His rumbling accent was turning her mind into knots.

'I repeat. You followed your bourgeois lover here to Prague. Is that not right?'

'Is Krystof . . . ?'

He barked, 'No, you speak when I have finished.'

Rose sank back in her chair.

Major Ivanov tapped the letter with his fingernail. 'This is not a very good start, is it, Mrs Bowman? Not a good start, for someone wishing to live here in our Soviet state of Czechoslovakia.'

'Soviet state? Is it already? I thought . . .'

'Silence!'

He shoved the papers back into her file.

'Very soon to be part of the glorious Soviet Union. Very soon to shake off the grasp of the heinous right-wing government, the greedy landowners, the capitalist money-grabbers,' he seemed pleased with himself. 'You will see, Mrs Bowman. Stop, I should say, Comrade Bowman.'

He poured water from a carafe into a glass and sipped from it slowly.

'Now,' he said, smacking his lips, 'we require your co-operation.'

She eyed the water. 'I just want to know that Captain Novotny is well. Is he . . . ?'

'No questions.'

She bit her lip. Tears filled her eyes. She willed them to retreat, to leave her, to not betray her.

'We only want the best for you, and your little . . .' he glanced back at the letter, 'girl. We only want the best for Comrade Novotny. The Soviet Union cares for you. Joseph Stalin cares for you all.' He nodded up to the portrait. 'He liberated this country from Hitler. Liberated Europe. If it wasn't for us, you people of little England would be speaking German now. And so would the Czechs, Poles, French. Don't you understand?'

She looked up at the portrait: at the dark, slanted eyes of Stalin; at the surprisingly friendly moustache.

'But where is Krystof? Please tell me.' Her voice was small, frightened.

Major Ivanov leant forward on his arms. 'He is downstairs, reconsidering his position.'

Frustration boiled under her skin like a rash. She glared at the man, hating his slicked-back hair, shield-like uniform and hard-set shoulders.

'I don't understand why he has been taken away from me.' She folded her arms over her stomach to stop the panic rising, to hold herself together. 'He is a good, loyal citizen. He fought for his country. He, also, helped in the fight against the Nazis. Is this how he is to be repaid?'

'Comrade Bowman, you are too sensitive. Too in love. I can see it in your eyes. In your whole . . . body.' He glanced at her and she saw a brief softening. 'Comrade Novotny is an enemy of the state. He knows that . . . now . . . after a few days in our care. He knows, now, that Soviet workers unite against the likes of him.'

'But he gives a livelihood to many people. He did so, on his farm in the country before . . . At his café. He provides a job for Milan, and the—'

Major Ivanov replied, as if reading from a script, 'He is an owner of property. He is bourgeois. He is also a commanding officer in the Czechoslovakian army, and we have to be careful. We have to rein him in. Keep him in our sights. It is for his own good. For the good of the Party.'

She turned and looked at the window to disguise her blazing anger.

'Fools,' she muttered.

'You are mistaken, comrade . . .'

She faced him. 'Your people starved. Your soldiers died in their thousands at Stalingrad. They were dispensable. Krystof fought against the Nazis. He was on your side. And you do this to him.'

'It is for his own good. As I said before, Comrade Bowman. We care. The Party cares.' He stood up and walked around the desk. He stood close behind her. His authority radiated towards her like a fierce heat from a fire. Even though he was not touching her, she fought the revulsion, fought the desperate desire to flinch away.

'Now what are we going to do with you? You are a renegade. You are rather unconventional. Not our usual idea of a sweet English rose.'

'Why don't you call me a *kurva* and be done with it,' she snapped. 'Krystof's Babička thinks it. Milan thinks it. He thinks the whole of Prague knows it.'

'Milan is a stupid, self-important individual. We deal with Milan.'

'He is . . . ? He is . . .'

'As for *prostitute* . . . I do not believe it for one minute.'

Her shoulders slumped under a wave of gratitude and relief.

She looked up at Major Ivanov, trying to see the human underneath the uniform.

'But, Comrade Bowman,' he said, 'how do we know you are not a spy?'

'A spy? A *spy*! That is ridiculous!' Her mouth gaped with the horror of it. Her feet, suddenly, washed with cold, cold fear. She felt her heart collapse. 'I am just a girl from Plymouth. I worked on a farm. I—'

'But, like so many others, we also have to deal with you. We have to watch you. We have to be careful the Nazi sympathy has not infiltrated here.' He reached out and tapped the side of her head. It felt like a violation. She wanted to cry with frustration.

'I hated it. I hated my husband. I should never have married him. I had no idea.'

'What drove you to leave your home and drag your child across Europe to be with Comrade Novotny?'

Rose turned to face him, her eyes swollen with fear. The answer was ludicrously simple.

'Because I love him.'

'Ha!' Major Ivanov strode back to his desk. He tidied more papers and put her file away.

He walked over to the filing cabinet, extracted a new buff folder and sat back down. Ignoring Rose, he began to leaf through the papers, his ink pen scoring out lines, marking paragraphs, circling words. The dragging silence returned.

She swallowed hard, her heart knocking at her ribs. Was the waiting to start all over? Would they ever let her see Krystof? What was going to happen to her?

The skeleton raised his arm again; the cadaverous skull grinning.

'Oh.' Ivanov looked up. 'You are still here?'

'I don't know . . .'

'You are free to go, Comrade Bowman. You have always been free to go.'

She slammed the front door shut and leant back against it. As shock finally enveloped her, hitting her with cold, hard violence, her scream froze in her throat and, instead, an unprecedented shout of laughter bubbled out.

Ashamed, she stared up the cold stairs. The pram was gone from its usual place in the vestibule. Babička must have taken Nancy out for a walk. Rose walked up slowly into the empty house, opening doors to empty rooms. She crept into Krystof's empty bed, contemplating a life without him.

Twenty-four

ROSE SAT AT THE KITCHEN TABLE, WHILE LARA DOZED IN HER CHAIR by the stove. The old woman had turned in on herself, shrinking down with worry; her head had sunk to her chest as she slept. The lamp was low and spluttering; the oil nearly spent. The dark corners of the room grew closer. Nancy was curled up under a fur muffler in her cot by the open stove door where red-hot embers disintegrated into black.

Rose thought that they would be safer in the kitchen; perhaps they should all sleep here. She knew she did not want to go back to her cold empty bed. The rest of the house, behind the closed door, was like a vast, icy cave.

Ear bent to the wireless, she chanced upon the World Service. The broken tones of the shipping forecast, as they crackled around the kitchen, gave her a crumb of comfort: Finisterre, Dogger Bank, Plymouth. She wanted to hear some news. English voices. As she turned the dial, radio waves crackled and, occasionally, the precise enunciation of a BBC man floated forward for a moment, just as hope did, to recede again into an unintelligible hiss. Sighing, she switched off the radio set and listened to the hum as the last of the electricity coursed through its wires.

Woken by the silence, Lara jerked, her eyes focusing on Rose. There was a grunt of realisation that the other chair was still empty. Her face crumbling with misfired anger, Lara took herself off to bed. Nancy, snuffling in her cot, slept on, blissfully unaware. Rose had never felt so alone.

She settled herself into Lara's still-warm chair and gazed down at her daughter.

'I'm sorry I brought you here, to a place where you might not be safe,' she whispered to the sleeping child. 'But when you are older, I hope you will understand why.'

The words she spoke to the major at the ministry came back to her: *Because I love him*.

Dozing then, she did not hear the rattle of the latch below or the muffled thud of the door closing. She did not hear the shuffling footsteps as they mounted the stairs; the kitchen door opening imperceptibly.

Her eyes popped open. 'Who's there?' she hissed, thinking of Milan. Had he come to claim her? Do her harm?

The atmosphere in the kitchen changed in one breath and, as she sat rooted to the chair, an intensity swept towards her. In the darkness, she saw a haggard figure in the doorway, hanging onto the handle with both hands.

She gasped in fright; then cried out in disbelief. And then flew from her chair towards him.

'It's me, it's me,' came Krystof's voice deep in her ear as she took him in her arms and pressed her face to his neck. Engulfed by the cold he brought in with him, she smelt the fusty rot of his clothes, his neglect and his terror. She drew herself away and looked him full in the face, plucking off his cap and unravelling his scarf, desperate to reveal him. She tried to mask her reaction. His face was puffy and unshaven, his eyes dull. There was no smile. Above his eyebrow, his skin had swollen angrily around a deep cut. Bruises in varying shades of grey and yellow, denoting the time passed since the blows were inflicted, blossomed over his cheeks and chin. His hands were raw. She gingerly held him and guided him to the stove. He cringed and recoiled with every laboured step.

'What have they done to you? Oh, Krystof, what has happened?'

'A Russian jackboot happened,' he exhaled in a groan of pain. 'My foot is broken. They stamped on it.'

'Oh, God!' She turned to the dresser, poured him a tot from the bottle of schnapps.

Krystof, with shaking fingers, his nails black with grime, tipped the liquid back into his throat. His face screwed up in a grimace of despair and he doubled over, regurgitating the lot onto the floor.

'Sorry, so sorry.' He wiped his mouth with his hand. 'I am in pieces. Ah, Nancy . . . is she well? Is she warm?'

'Don't speak, don't try, oh, my love.' Her mind was wild with questions, but she knew she must wait. 'I will get you into bed. You must lie down and sleep.'

'Sleep? I have not slept,' he said. 'They would not let me.'

She raked hot coals into a warming pan and went to put it in their bed. When she came back, she recoiled: the sight of him sitting by the stove, crumpled and broken, shocking her once again. She knelt in front of him. He closed his eyes, and tilted his head away as if he could not bear her to look at him.

'Oh, my love,' she whispered again, her eyes brimming with tears. She dashed them angrily away. There was no time for her emotion. 'We must fight them. They can't win.'

He shook his head, wincing. 'I haven't the strength.'

'But you are going to be all right?' Suddenly she was panicking. Her Krystof seemed remote, unrecognisable.

He drew a deep, raw breath. His eyes were two dark slits. 'Am I going to be all right? I don't think so, Ruzena. This changes everything.'

She lay awake all night, her hand on the back of his head as he slumbered and dreamed; as he called out, twitched and shuffled. As he wept. He was delirious.

She held his hand as he muttered, 'I shot a German boy.' He turned in his sleep, wincing through unconsciousness.

Hours later, he spoke again: 'He was just a child in a Panzer uniform. He was combing his hair. He put his cap back on. I shot him. Him or me. East of Caen.'

In the morning Krystof turned to face her. His eyes softened and opened wider. She could see their true colour, and a minute glimpse of the real Krystof.

He whispered, 'I am the enemy. I am bourgeois. Because of my property. Because I am an army officer. I am a threat to the state. They will make our lives a misery, until I join the Party.'

She opened her mouth to speak. She wanted to tell him. She knew already.

He placed a shaking finger over her lips. 'Ne, ne, Ruzena. There is nothing we can do. They want to strip the army of its powers, of its men, of its weapons. In case we rise up against them. They will put us in prison.'

He shut his eyes and slept.

Rose got up and knocked on Lara's bedroom door. 'He's here,' she said. 'He's home.' Lara burst into tears and rushed to see for herself. She opened the door a crack and peered in at her grandson, shaking with disbelief, wiping at her wet face, unable to speak.

When Krystof woke, Rose sat on the bed and gave him a bowl of porridge.

'"You piece of filth," they called me, with every blow. "You stupid bourgeois traitor."' He took a mouthful of porridge, tried to swallow. 'They told me you and Babička wanted nothing more to do with me, because I am an enemy of the state. The cell was two metres by three. I paced it out before they broke my foot. It was deep underground, there was no air to breathe. I think it was an old wine cellar.'

Rose told him, 'I came to the ministry. We both did. We tried to find you . . .'

'My head thundered from the cold and lack of fresh air. They watched me through a spy hole in the great iron door. Every day, staring at four blank walls.' He chewed a little, tears in his eyes. 'Every night, lights went out at eight. Two hours later they hauled me to another cell. This one was a bit bigger. Questions, then. Interrogation.'

Rose saw that he could not look at her, for fear of frightening her. But she knew. She already knew.

'I was returned to my cell at four in the morning. Imagine. Two men holding me up. Lights went on at six. No sleep. They took away the mattress and left me with a bare wooden bench. Kept me awake.' He dabbed at the porridge with the spoon. 'They made me stand in ice for hours. I dreamed of you in snatches. Daydreams. Fantasy. I dreamed you'd gone. You'd left Prague. I dreamed you loved me, I dreamed you didn't. I heard the cries of other men through the walls.'

He stopped speaking and gazed beyond her shoulder. Lara was standing in the doorway, listening.

'Some were weeping for their mothers. They were driven mad. Sleep starvation *is* starvation.'

Lara sat on the bed and Rose jumped with surprise as Lara held her shaking hand, clutching Krystof's with her other.

'Sometimes,' said Krystof, 'I was taken to a normal office, with daylight. Overlooking the square. The commander . . . Major somebody . . . sat under a picture of Uncle Joe Stalin. "Why don't you save yourself all this trouble?" he asked me, his pen poised over a confession they'd cooked up. A confession of bourgeois behaviour and an application to join the Party. All I had to do was sign.'

'Krystof, I know,' whispered Rose. 'Did you hear the type-writers? I never thought such everyday machines could sound so ominous.'

'He had a file on me, and I asked if I could read it. He laughed. He had spectacularly good teeth. Ten days, Ruzena. I was alone, without sleep. I lived and died a hundred lifetimes. I dreamed you did not love me. But still I did not sign.'

She held her handkerchief to his face to dry his tears.

Picking up the spoon, Lara tried to feed her grandson.

Rose whispered, 'We came every day. They expected us. They ignored us. Every day. They just said, "You will be informed."'

Krystof said, 'They cleared my desk at the regimental office. They have taken my passport. They showed it to me and then put it in my file.'

So, Rose thought, her terror disabling her, This means we can never leave.

Krystof pushed the spoon away. Lara gathered up his porridge bowl and left the room.

He shuffled back under the covers. Rose lay down beside him. He drew her very close, as best he could with his shattered body. His lips touched her ear, his breath was hot on her neck.

'They are watching us, Ruzena.' He spoke deeply into her ear. 'They are listening. Every person is our enemy.'

She cried silent tears as cold flashes of fear engulfed her body.

'We trust no one.' His voice was thick, unreal. 'From now on, we pretend. We buy ourselves time. We buy ourselves a life. But I will never sign.'

Twenty-five

THE THAW WAS ALMOST COMPLETE; THE DRIP-DRIPPING OF DRAINPIPES
and gutters perpetual. The Vltava swelled with new water beneath
the Charles Bridge. March had finally arrived.

Puffs of soft air from the west boosted Rose's mood as she
walked out on an errand. Turning up the collar of her coat
against the cold spring drizzle, she crossed the steep cobbled
lane in the Little Quarter. She allowed just one bubble of thought
about their new life in the country to pop into her head before
contending with the matter in hand: Krystof was fighting an
infection in his foot and someone at his regiment had some
penicillin on the black market. She was on her way to find his
house under the shadow of the castle. Every other shop front
she passed was boarded up or closed: there was nothing much
to sell. Sparse bits of gold and silver glimmered dully behind
dusty glass; all second-hand, all pawned. Lara's wedding ring
had recently joined the haul to pay for the medication. People
were selling what they had for food, for medicine; but who had
the money to buy trinkets?

Something up the street caught her eye. The blonde hair was
faded and hanging in rat's tails, the hat was dented and pulled
down too far, as if to hide her face. But it was unmistakably
Mabel.

'Hello, Mabel!' Rose called, stepping over a conduit and its
sluice of debris, cursing the treacherous cobbles as her foot
slipped.

'I'm sorry,' she told a man with whom she bumped shoulders. '*Prominte*, sir.'

Mabel hurried up the hill, keeping her head down, turning
into an alleyway. But Rose was quick on her feet, and her long
strides soon ate up the ground.

She called again, 'Mabel!' as she dodged a man pushing a cart of scrap iron, her foot splashing a dirty puddle up her stocking.

'There you are!' She put her hand on Mabel's shoulder from behind, feeling the thinness of her coat and the bone underneath.

Gone was Mabel's red lipstick, the powder. Fierce blotches covered her neck.

'I thought it was you,' said Rose, breathless, feeling the fine rain soaking her coat. 'We haven't seen each other – not since the night we got off that blessed train. I heard that you and Vaclav were living on the outskirts of the city. What brings you here to the Little Quarter?'

Mabel stared at her as if she did not know her. Her once-pretty eyes protruded. A defensive shield settled over her pale features.

At last she spoke, reluctantly: 'Rose Pepper, isn't it?'

'As was.'

Mabel's eyes brightened a little. 'I'm surprised you're still here. I'm on my way to see some bloke to buy my ticket home. Sold this.' She held up her wedding ring finger. It was naked.

'Oh . . . ?'

'Vaclav left me.'

'Oh, gosh.'

'There's no need for sympathy, Pepper.' Mabel linked her arm. 'Or don't they call you Ginge? Come on, let's get out of this bleeding rain. It's perishing. Have you any crowns? Good. In here.'

Mabel led her through a small doorway into a dim vaulted room under the rock of the castle. There were a few battered tables, stained with water rings, and a dusty counter.

'Two schnapps,' she told the proprietor.

In the half-light, Mabel's fair hair seemed to glow; she looked half pretty again. 'That's the only Czech I seem to have picked up,' she said, 'but I find it's the handiest. That and the word for food.'

Rose sat down and removed her gloves. It wasn't warm enough in that grubby dank place to take off her coat.

'As I said,' Mabel went on, grasping her shot glass, 'Vaclav left me. The pig. He just vanished. I'm renting now with an old biddy in the Jewish quarter. Place is like a ghost town. It was completely empty after the war. But new people are moving in, snapping up the houses. I have no money left. I keep selling what I can. I suppose this is the last straw. But good riddance also.' She indicated her ring finger again. 'Now I can afford my ticket out of here.'

'Mabel . . .'

'My parents warned me. They said don't trust Johnny Foreigner. How right they were.'

Rose slid her eyes to the floor, not able to think of her own parents, and what they said about Krystof. And what it made her do.

'I trailed all the way out to this godforsaken place for that man,' said Mabel. 'And he's gone and left me. God, it's still so cold. Even their so-called spring is freezing.'

Rose squared her shoulders. 'Did you actually see Vaclav leave, Mabel?'

'No. He just didn't come home one day. No one knows where he is. Or if they do, they're not telling. I tell you, if he's living with a tart, I'll kill him.'

'Oh, Mabel, Krystof also vanished . . .'

The girl's eyes widened with pleasure. 'See! Just as I thought. These Czech men are all the same!'

'But Krystof returned. He had been interrogated, tortured. By the Russian state police at the ministry in the square. I wonder. Vaclav might be there?'

Mabel picked up her shot glass to sip her liqueur. Her fingers were trembling. Rose could see tiny blue veins beneath her skin.

'Interrogated?' Mabel repeated. She wouldn't look at her.

Rose lowered her voice. 'Are you really going to leave?'

'What else can I do? The rent the old witch is charging is killing me. Awful woman. She's the lamplighter. Thing is, she smells worse than her dog.'

'That's Lucenka. I know who she is.'

'One good thing about her is that she knows who I should go to to get a travel permit quickly. She has her contacts.'

'Who is going to sell you a ticket?'

'Some man at a café near the monastery. Milan someone. Lucenka says I may have to give him more than these crowns I've got to secure the deal. If you know what I mean. I tell you,

I'll do anything. I can't possibly stay in Prague. Truth told, I want my mother.' Her bottom lip trembled and was then bitten. 'My bastard of a husband has left me.'

Rose put her hand on Mabel's arm. 'But Mabel, I don't think—'

Mabel snatched her arm away. 'And I would do the same if I were you, too. Go home. Get back to Blighty.' Mabel took another sip, grimacing at the strength of the liquid. 'Hey, were you *not* married, or something? That will make it easier for you: being still classed as English. I am tarred with being Mrs Vaclav Budova. A Czech citizen, I suppose. Not so easy for me.'

'Mabel, you must go straight to the ministry. See if you can trace Vaclav. It might be that they are—'

'Ugh,' Mabel shuddered. 'Those awful Communists. I couldn't bear to. They're everywhere now, aren't they? I can't keep up. Are they the government now, is that it?'

'Well, they are . . .'

Mabel squinted at her. 'You're *not* married, are you?'

'I *am*,' she said. 'To someone else.'

'Jeepers, and where does your husband think you are?'

'He knows I'm here, unfortunately.'

'Of course. Your daughter. She's your husband's child, isn't she?'

'She is.'

Mabel whistled. 'You were the quiet one, as well. Compared to me and Meg. Us wild girls. And look at you now – a *mistress*? What are you still doing here?'

'I can't leave Krystof.'

Mabel looked at her as if she wanted to ask why not. 'Well, I've had enough. I can't cope with the language, for a start. Isn't it like someone is spitting-angry with you the whole time? And the food? Give me fish 'n' chips in a warm English pub any day. Even rationed dried eggs would be better than the gruel I eat every day. Hey, have you heard from that minx Meg? She bagged herself a goody, didn't she? That handsome farmer. How are they all?'

As Rose sipped her own schnapps, Pengared slipped into her mind. The windy Cornish clifftops. The cove at Trelewin. The gentle, benign waves reaching across the sand.

'I haven't heard . . .' she began. She drowned her words in a mouthful of alcohol.

Mabel squinted at her. 'So . . . Krystof came back to you?'

'Yes, I told you. He was released.'

Mabel wasn't listening. 'That's because he loves you. He fought his way out of there. You are very lucky. Vaclav the pig just wanted me in the bedroom. Well, he can get that now with his tart.'

Rose rallied, suddenly. 'Mabel, perhaps Krystof knows about Vaclav. Perhaps he knows where he is. He might have heard. I mean, he is still rather ill at the moment and hasn't mentioned him . . . but he might know something. Would you like to come to tea?'

The girl laughed, her thin face wan, her cheekbones sharp and her teeth showing too much gum. 'Oh, Pepper, you are a hoot. Tea? Tea! Are you telling me you have *tea*?'

'No, no, I mean come to my home and have something to eat. We can ask Krystof together.'

Mabel shrugged her shoulders and drained her glass. 'Home? You mean your lover's four-storey mansion? Haven't the time, Pepper. I have to get me to this damn Milan fellow. See if I can't score a ticket home. Oh, how glorious that sounds. A-ticket-home.' She knocked her glass on the table.

'Mabel. This man, Milan. I know him. He runs the café next door to us. He is not to be trusted.'

'Look, dear, I don't care about trust. I actually don't care if Vaclav is in the ministry of God-knows-what. I just want this ticket home. This girl can take care of herself, you know.'

Rose gripped her thin arm. 'But, Mabel . . .'

The girl stood up. 'Thanks for the drink, Pepper. It'll keep me warm.'

Out in the blustery street, Mabel said goodbye. Outside, her hair matched the grey of the stone walls, the pewter of the sky.

'I would come with you to Milan's café, for moral support,' said Rose, her fingertips on the money for Krystof's medicine in her pocket, 'but I have an urgent errand. I'm sorry.'

'No matter.' Mabel shrugged and then eyed Rose's hair. 'You always were striking. All the men liked you. All those GIs . . .'

'Heavens . . .'

'But as my pig of a husband once told me, there was only one man who ever loved you. He wouldn't let you go. Would not stop talking about you all the way across Normandy, all the way to the Rhine. Drove his mates crazy, he did.'

'Mabel . . .' Lost for words, she stumbled, 'Please take care of yourself. Watch out for Milan. Don't trust him.'

'Goodbye, Rose Pepper, as was,' cried Mabel. 'Good luck.'

'You too,' she called, as the slight figure of the girl disappeared around a corner. 'You too.'

Twenty-six

A RUDE HAMMERING WOKE THEM. THE NIGHT BEFORE, KRYSTOF HAD opened the bedroom window a chink to let in the fresh air. Now, from the street below, a hubbub of noise on the cobbles, hard voices, Russian voices, filtered through the casement.

'Open up, comrades,' came the cry. 'Open up in the name of the state.'

Krystof swore, '*Jezis-Maria.*' He hauled himself out of bed and limped to the window, pushed open the curtains and peered out.

Rose screwed her eyes up to the morning light, sat up and held the sheet to her chin, watching his face. How miraculous was the healing balm of time, she thought. Two months after his traumatic experience, she very nearly had the same Krystof back with her. The bruises had faded; but what of his memories?

The banging and crashing from below was a wicked assault on her senses. Nancy in her cot stirred and sat up, rubbing her eyes and whimpering.

'What's going on, Krystof?' asked Rose.

'There are so many of them. Did they have to send so many?' muttered Krystof. 'Get dressed, Rose. We have visitors.'

'But what do they want?'

She did not like the look on Krystof's face.

'Wake Babička up.' He shrugged his shirt on. 'Second thoughts, she must be awake anyway, but keep her calm. Tell her to take Nancy and stay in the kitchen. Make her stay in there, for she is not afraid of them. And that could prove a problem.'

But Rose's own fear made her annoyed with him. '*Who* are they? Tell me!'

'Red Army,' he said. 'But try not to worry. Think of them as chimps working for the organ grinder.'

Flinging on her trousers and buttoning up her blouse, she managed a laugh. 'Krystof, it's *monkeys* and the organ grinder.'

'You English. So precise.'

She felt a smile stretch her face.

'How I love you,' she said.

'Shush. Go on.'

She made sure Lara and Nancy were safely installed in the kitchen, whispering urgently to the old woman to lock herself in, before Krystof went down to the vestibule. Rose watched, resting on the banisters, as Krystof opened the front door.

Immediately Krystof was flung aside and the door slammed back against the wall as the soldiers surged in. A dozen men with grey peaked caps set on the backs of their unwashed heads and brandishing old-fashioned rifles tramped up the stairs, bringing with them their noise and smell. Rose winced as they passed her, looked her over, their boots denting the parquet. Then they set to: barging from room to room, peering behind doors, sprinting up to the upper floors.

Following in protest into the salon she watched, aghast, as they scuffed the floor and tugged at the old curtains, discarding them as rags. A soldier bounced on the chaise longue before lying down on it, boots and all, and then set his sights on the painting of Krystof's parents. He was poking at it with the tip of his penknife as Krystof limped up the stairs and stood close to Rose, speechless, with his hand on her shoulder, a muscle flinching in his cheek.

One of them tried the kitchen door, which Lara had locked from the inside. Rose could hear her shouting through the door:

'Touch anything of mine and I will stick your rifles up your arses!' she shrieked. 'Then I will kick you in the trousers!'

Major Ivanov brought up the rear of the rabble, walking slowly up the stairs in a long grey coat, his hands behind his back.

'Good morning, Comrade Bowman.' He bowed to Rose and then turned to Krystof. 'Comrade Novotny, we have been instructed to assess this house. We have come to confiscate your property in the name of the state.'

Krystof fixed his face with good humour. 'It's *Captain* Novotny, actually.'

'Not any more. We both know that. We've been through all

of that,' said the major, taking out a clipboard. He licked his finger and leafed through the paperwork attached to it. 'How many floors do you have here?'

A soldier interjected, out of breath from checking the cellar. 'Four, sir, plus a cellar.'

'What's up there?' Major Ivanov pointed up the stairs.

'Two attic rooms, sir,' said another dirty-faced boy-in-uniform, eager to please. 'A *bathroom*.'

'As you have been made well aware, comrade, during your stay with us at the ministry,' the major turned to Krystof, 'all property is theft. The state will not allow all this space for just two people, a child and –' he indicated the shut kitchen door, 'and the old woman who I believe is locked in that room.'

'My Babička,' Krystof corrected him. 'And by locking herself in there, she is protecting you all from the full force of her fury.'

The major ignored him. 'It is a crime against the people for you to have all of these rooms. You will live with your mistress, her child and your grandmother up there in the attic. The rest of this house now belongs to the state.' He wrote something on a form on the clipboard. Then barked an order to his men. 'Clear these rooms.'

Krystof went to the kitchen door and spoke softly through it to Lara. She opened it and let him in. Rose saw him wrap his arm around her to stifle her anger, taking her into a corner. Immediately, avid-faced soldiers followed him and began to count the china on Lara's dresser, knocking the coffee pot off the stove, treading over the shards. She saw Krystof pick up a white-faced Nancy and try to comfort her.

Rose held back on the landing, clinging to the banisters, watching, with increasing bewilderment, the plundering of Krystof's home.

Feeling her anger rising uncontrollably, she walked up to the landing where the major had spread his papers on the windowsill and was filling in his paperwork.

'Perhaps you can enlighten me, major,' she said. 'If we are to live upstairs in the attic, what will happen to the rest of the house?'

'It will be shared among the people,' he clipped, knowing his doctrine. 'Shared among the workers. The proletariat. Have you not read the manifesto?'

'This is Captain Novotny's home.' She spoke bravely. She felt she knew the major. That he knew her. 'It has been in his family for over a hundred years. You know that he fought in the war against the Nazis. We both know what that means to this country. To your country. To mine.' She lowered her head and looked up at him beneath her brows. 'And now you are taking it all away from him. It's hardly fair.'

The major corrected her. 'Not taken away, Comrade Bowman. It will be *shared*. Equally. I am glad you decided to talk to me for I have more questions. Now, to recap: who owns the café downstairs?'

'Captain Krystof Novotny.'

'The boarded-up *tabak*?'

'Captain Krystof Novotny.'

He flicked his pen to get the ink running and then wrote something laboriously. He began to laugh, a cold, hollow laugh, saying, 'I know you mean *Comrade* Novotny but I am tired of constantly correcting you. You will learn. Anyway, the café will be confiscated by the state, also. It will become a people's café. Run by the people. You will be sent the appropriate paperwork.'

'His passport's been taken,' she blurted in panic. 'What do we do?'

Major Ivanov's eyes swept over her and the hardness in his bearing faded. A watery sun filtered through the landing window onto her hair that coiled around her shoulders like ropes of auburn silk.

He deliberately fixed his eyes onto hers. 'As I told you before, at the ministry, you are free to go.'

Her lips wobbled. She felt a pulse in her temple. 'I cannot leave him.'

'Then I cannot help you.'

She turned her face away. 'Please tell them to leave the painting. It's all he has. His parents, they . . .'

The major took a breath, leant over the banisters and yelled in Russian to his men. Rose glanced down to see one of them sheepishly walk back into the salon with the painting under his arm and rest it against the wall.

Major Ivanov turned back to her. 'It is good to meet with you again, Comrade Bowman. But I wish it was under different circumstances.' He twitched his head a degree and she saw, briefly, the man beneath the uniform, the tight collar and coat. 'It does not have to be like this. All you people have to do is comply.'

As he licked the end of his pen and began to write again, a loud thud and a crash drew her back to the banisters. She looked down the stairwell to see the pram in the vestibule buckling under the weight of a lead money chest that the soldiers had decided to steal.

Krystof rushed from the kitchen and looked down, aghast. 'You bastards,' he muttered. 'Nancy's pram.'

Rose ran down to his side and peered over for a better look.

'The chest must have slipped from their hands when they got it down there,' she said. 'They're too greedy and too hasty.'

'There is nothing in it, you fools!' called Krystof. 'The reason it weighs a ton is because it's made of lead, not full of crowns. I suppose they could pawn it if they wanted. Let them take it. But we need that pram. It was my brother Tomas's. We've had it in the family for years. It's worth far more to me than that stupid chest.'

Rose put her hand on his arm, to try to console him. 'They have no respect. None at all.'

Krystof gestured to the soldiers. 'Go on, take the chest,' he called. 'We don't care any more.'

Lara appeared on the landing and, seeing the pram with its frame twisted and one wheel fallen off, she cried out, '*Ne, ne.* The pram! The pram!'

Rose tried to console her. 'I know, Babička. It's such a shame.'

'But it was for the little one! The *děť' átko!*'

'The baby?' asked Krystof.

'What are you saying, Babička?' asked Rose. 'For Nancy? We know it's for Nancy.'

Lara spluttered through her handkerchief, her head shaking. '*Ne. Ne.* The *little* baby.'

'The baby?' Krystof persisted, alarmed by his grandmother's raging tears.

'Tomas was coming to collect the pram,' Lara wept. 'He never made it. The Nazis . . . came to the village . . . before he left . . . before he . . .'

'Collect it? Collect his own childhood pram?' asked Krystof. 'What on earth for, Babička?'

Lara's sobs reached to the ceiling.

'For his own *dět' átko*. His own little boy.'

'Tomas had a son?' said Krystof. 'I had a baby nephew?'

Lara's voice was muffled with grief. 'They didn't even have time to christen him. I don't even know whether he had a name.'

Rose glanced up and saw Major Ivanov gazing down at them, his face twitching from bewilderment to sorrow, his eyes drifting, not able to catch hers.

Twenty-seven

AN ENORMOUS MOON WAS SUSPENDED OVER PRAGUE, LIKE A FAT WHITE cheese against a velvet navy night sky. It spilled light onto the Vltava, onto the statues on the Charles Bridge, over the jumbled landscape of red roofs, making silver pathways for rats and cats. The forest of chimneys and spires cast moon shadows over tiles and over cobbles in the streets where dogs trotted silently, stopping occasionally to sniff the drains.

It was a strangely tranquil night. The middle of May. The month of *Kveten*. The month of flowers. Their spring had come, thought Rose, watching from the attic window, and yet their future had not yet started. As she gazed along the roof-scape, her strong love for the city was crushed with each alternate breath by her utter loathing for it. What was being whispered behind those shutters over there? What was being said around the hearths behind closed doors? Were people listening for the sound of radio sets through their neighbours' wall? Were they keeping a record of times, dates, visitors, voices?

'Are you all right, Ruzena?' asked Krystof. He got up from the bed and came to stand beside her, his bad foot making him flinch, ducking his head under the sloping ceiling. She was wearing only her nightdress as the room was still warm from the sunshine of the day, and yet she needed his arms around her to stave off the chill she felt creeping through her bones.

'Where's Babička?' she asked, holding him.

'She is just at her toilet. She won't be long.'

Rose glanced around at their accommodation. The rescued portrait was leaning against the wall. They had been allowed to bring up two beds, which they had pushed up against each other, and two chairs. Their clothing was in the bathroom next door. They had to share the toilet, and the kitchen downstairs, with whoever was going to move into their old home. In the meantime, the soldiers were garrisoned below and a commotion of footsteps and a bevy of drunken, laughing voices came sporadically up the stairs.

She watched Krystof's face tighten with anger as he listened to the racket.

He said, 'First I lose my family to one kind of evil, now I lose my home and livelihood to another.'

She pressed her body to him, feeling a constant wrench of frustration.

'We have each other,' she whispered. 'I will be strong for you. We have our Nancy and our Babička. I don't want to ever be apart from you, Krystof.'

In the light from the lamp, she saw that his face was serious. 'I might not be able to give you much of a home, Ruzena, but remember that I love you. I always will.'

His tone made her question him.

'What do you mean? I know that you love me. But you sound unsure . . . What are you saying?'

'You have a home elsewhere, remember. Where you and your little girl can be safe?'

'Do you mean it's time for us to go to a *chalupa*?' She felt excitement fizz, her world opening up. 'Do you mean we can really get away from here? That we can have our farm?'

'No. That's not what I mean.' He looked down at her, gravely, tilting her chin with his gentle finger. 'What I mean to say is, you have another home. You have Pengared.'

'No!' she hissed, turning away from him. 'I will not hear of it. I will not go anywhere without you.'

He caught her and held her tight. 'Not so fierce, Ruzena. Not tonight. I don't want to have this conversation tonight. But we may have to have it, one day. I want you and Nancy to be safe.'

She lifted her chin, defiantly. 'I will only ever feel safe when I am with you.'

Slowly, he unbuttoned his shirt and took it off, his body drawing her knowing gaze. He plucked at her nightgown and exposed her shoulders. His lips pressed enquiring kisses over her skin, up her throat. He lifted her hair and found her precious skin there. Kissing it, he sighed.

She whispered, 'But Nancy?'

He glanced to the cot in the corner. 'Fast asleep.'

'And Babička?'

'But I want you.'

'She is only next door.'

'She will knock.'

'What about them downstairs?'

'They can rot.'

She felt his heart thumping under her hands. She whispered, 'We will never be apart again, Krystof.'

'I won't let it happen,' he said, his mouth in her hair.

They made love briefly, tenderly, and with as much intensity as to last a lifetime.

As she lay curled in his arms, she watched the tension melt from his jaw, a light return to his face. He leant over her, stroking her cheek. 'Remember the Polperro dance, Ruzena? Remember the haymaking?'

She smiled lovingly, thinking of the Cornish sunshine. 'One day,' she told him, 'we will sit on our rock again, and watch the gentle waves of Trelewin cove.'

'And we will not watch them through the wire.'

'No, the wire will be well and truly gone then,' she said. 'And what's a confiscated passport got to do with anything anyway?'

A smile curved her face and then fell away. She tried to laugh, but she began to weep. He carefully dried her eyes.

'We have jumped the wire once and for all,' she said, trying to be brave for him, for herself.

But as she watched him drift off to sleep, she knew that the wire was still there, tightening around them, the rusted barbs cutting their flesh.

She whispered to herself, to the ceiling, to the night outside, 'Whatever happens now, whatever we do, we do it together.'

Rose awoke suddenly. Someone had whispered her name.

The moon was higher and the attic bedroom was soaked with pure white light. Krystof was gently snoring next to her, but there, in the other bed close by, Lara was sitting bolt upright against her pillows, her silver hair shimmering, her eyes brown pools in her face.

'Ruzena,' she whispered.

'What is it, Babička? Are you all right?'

The old woman whispered back to her, but her words tumbled in Czech; a dialect Rose had not heard Lara speak before. She struggled to understand. She nudged Krystof awake. He groaned and turned over, propping himself on his elbow.

'What is it?' he asked.

Lara began to speak.

Krystof sighed, rubbing his face sleepily. Half-awake, he said, 'Babička wants to tell you all about her days as a young lady . . . fêted in the gas-lit ballrooms of Wenceslas Square . . . Hosting her own parties here, downstairs in the salon. During the *fin de siècle* . . . Her *belle époque* . . . She dined . . . she played cards . . . she drank schnapps . . . everything glittered . . . it was Czechoslovakia's golden years.'

'Your golden republic?' asked Rose.

'Yes, and she says how you would have loved those days . . . the laughter . . .'

Lara chuckled deep in her chest, playfully wagging her finger at Krystof.

'I just told her,' said Krystof, 'that the winters were still bloody cold in those days, never mind the social whirl, but she says she never felt the cold. She was young and foolish.'

'She had a beautiful time?'

'She did. There was so much music, so much singing.'

Rose imagined the laughter tinkling down the hallway, the lamplight reflected in oil paintings, cards snapping over polished tables. She watched Lara's face in the semi-darkness, trying to imagine the young girl whose long life had come to this: most of her family dead; billeted in the attic of her own house.

Krystof turned back over in the bed. 'I am tired, it's time we all slept. It must be way past midnight.'

All was quiet below. The soldiers obviously slept, but Rose could not. She, too, sat up against her pillows and gazed at Lara, whose smile suddenly struck her with its unexpected warmth.

How Rose wanted to tell her about her own life, her friends, her parents, her own beautiful time as a young girl in the days before the war in her little Plymouth suburb.

'*Dobrou noc*,' whispered Lara.

'Goodnight, Babička,' Rose returned, understanding the settlement between them; the start of forgiveness. She snuggled down under the covers next to Krystof.

But the old woman stayed sitting upright and, as Rose drifted off to sleep, once or twice she opened her eyes to see Lara watching over her.

Rose came to, to the sound of jackboots and riotous shouting from below.

'What now?' she murmured, her face in the pillow.

She heard Krystof say, 'They are simply carrying out their morning ablutions.'

'I wish they'd be quiet about it.'

She rolled over in annoyance to see Krystof standing on the other side of the two beds, his face fixed. Lara was still sitting upright.

'Oh, Babička, have you been there all night?' she asked. 'Couldn't you sleep . . . I'm not surprised. What with that awful lot downstairs . . .'

Krystof was shaking his head, unable to take his eyes off his grandmother's face.

Rose squinted, and cocked her head to the side.

Lara's face sagged down, her chin rested on her shoulder. Her hands were folded over the covers, her deep brown eyes wide open. She was dead.

Twenty-eight

ROSE WATCHED THE MEN BRING LARA'S COFFIN DOWN THE STAIRS, bumping door frames, taking chips out of the banisters, as warm sunshine fell in long shafts through the high landing windows. Krystof, his face pale and haunted, cradled the head end, giving gentle instructions to the unusually decorous soldiers. No one else spoke. Dust motes floated upwards in the void of the stairwell, sparkling and spiralling in the light. The day was far too beautiful for a burial.

The hearse was waiting outside on the cobbles. Customers at Milan's café rose from the tables and removed their hats as the soldiers slid Lara into the open back of the car. Rose caught sight of Milan standing at the café window, his moustache moving with silent ruminations of his mouth. Not wishing to linger under his gaze, she quickly encouraged Krystof into their waiting taxi. The small crowd of onlookers parted as their taxi pulled away and followed the hearse, rumbling along the crooked lanes towards the river.

In the back of the taxi, Krystof held Nancy on his lap and she clung to his neck, sensing, Rose decided, his distress. But what of her own? As the taxi pulled out onto the main road and the river lay beside them, Rose turned her head to gaze at it so that Krystof could not see her face. Clasping her gloved hands on her lap, her fingers began to shake as her shock at Lara's death, suddenly, became edged with other, more selfish, emotions.

Ahead of them, further along the river bank, the steep cliff of Vysehrad Hill loomed up, topped by Gothic ruins and the twin spires of a church. Up there, amid the tall trees lay the cemetery where they were to bury Lara and where Krystof was to leave her. Feeling the bitter sting of relief that they *could* leave his Babička there, Rose took Krystof's hand and leant towards him, tears of shame in her eyes.

The tiny funeral cortège shuffling around the open grave included Lucenka and her dog. Rose took a step towards her, to welcome her as Lara's old friend, but Krystof pulled her back and whispered in her ear, 'Ignore her.'

'Why?' Rose whispered back. 'Might she not help us one day?'

'Exactly.' Krystof glanced around him at the gravestones in the crowded cemetery. 'But we don't know who is listening.'

Rose shivered in the sunshine. *Only the dead are listening*, she thought. *Only the dead.*

The priest finished and Lara was lowered into the family plot next to her husband, Krystof's grandfather. Rose could not take her eyes off Krystof as he flinched at each clod of earth hitting the coffin. Something about that sound – hollow, final, dismal – thudded through her head and she was struck by the memory of her parents' funeral that, up until then, had been a merciful blur. She was being escorted by – held up by – Will and guided through it as if she was disabled. And now, as the tiny congregation turned away from the grave, to get on with life and leave the dead behind them, her pain returned with such speed and intensity that she felt her knees give way.

She cried out, 'Krystof, I . . .' Then she felt her mouth snap shut. She couldn't tell him this and trample all over his grief.

He looked at her, understanding. 'Come, let's walk,' he said, hoisting Nancy high in his arms.

They picked their way through the crowded city of graves and monuments, passing the marble faces of weeping angels, losing themselves among the ruins that populated Vyšehrad Hill. When they reached the edge of the cliff they stood and gazed down at the river snaking on through the golden-stone houses, chimney stacks and spires snoozing in the sunlight.

'This is a lovely spot up here,' Krystof said. 'I feel that we're outside of the city, able to breathe fresh air again. It certainly gives me a new perspective of Praha.' He sighed. 'I haven't been up here for many years. Not since Dedecek died. I was a boy. That was a long time ago . . .'

'Your grandfather? . . . now your grandmother, oh . . .' Rose's tears fell unchecked; her legs began to tremble.

'Hush, now,' soothed Krystof. 'Babička's in a better place. She's with . . .' he hesitated, 'her family.'

Rose tried to dry her eyes. 'I'm sorry for crying. I'm selfish. Thinking of my own . . . my parents' funeral . . . Remembering when I *hadn't* remembered. When I hadn't been *there*. I was there in body. Not in spirit.'

Krystof tried to soothe her. 'You told me. You weren't yourself.'

She cried out, 'Oh, I want to be in Cornwall again. I want to be home.'

Krystof led her to a bench and they sat. They let Nancy toddle to a patch of grass where she knelt and pushed her fingers into a forest of daisies.

Krystof made Rose look at him, his face deadly serious.

'I told you, the night Babička died,' he said, peering into her eyes. 'Your home is Pengared.'

'But, how can I . . . how can we . . . ?'

He grasped both her hands and shook them gently, bringing them to his lips.

'I think now . . .' he said, wincing in disbelief at his own words and gazing out over the city, 'now we are free to go.'

'Free?'

'In the sense that Babička . . .'

'Oh.' Rose hadn't wanted to acknowledge what Lara's death meant to them both. And, she knew, neither had he.

'I know it's what you want,' Krystof said. 'I see it in your face every day.'

Rose felt a surge of hope. 'And when we get back to England, I can settle my divorce.' She spoke quickly. She tried to brighten the situation, which they both knew held such unspeakable danger. 'Then we will be truly free.'

Krystof's eyes glazed with tears. 'We will be free,' he repeated.

They sat in silence and watched Nancy play, plucking white petals and scattering them over the glistening grass. Tall trees swayed in the breeze, leaves whispering above their heads.

'I will talk to Lucenka,' said Krystof. 'I was pleased to see her here today. She had known Babička for a long time.'

Rose felt guilt tap her on the shoulder. 'Krystof . . . are you sure we can leave? They took your passport.'

297

'When I look at you and Nancy, I know we have to try. When I look at the view over Praha it always strikes me with utter, stupendous grace. This place is truly beautiful . . . but it holds no beauty for me now.'

'But your passport?' Rose insisted.

'Lucenka is the only person who can deal with something that serious. She will get me the correct visas, documents, whatever. She knows the right people. She has the right contacts, not made-up ones like Milan.'

'Oh, hang that man,' muttered Rose. 'I forgot to tell you. While you were ill, after your release from the ministry, I bumped into Mabel over in the Little Quarter. She told me she was renting a room at Lucenka's house, and that Milan was getting her some paperwork so she could leave. Oh, Krystof, I didn't tell you about Vaclav. I thought you'd be too weak, too ill to take it. Mabel told me: he was missing. That was in March. Two months ago now . . .'

Krystof shook his head, resting it in his hands. 'He was probably in the next cell to me. Do you know if he was ever released?'

'I have no idea. Mabel wouldn't believe me. Wouldn't believe he could possibly have been arrested. She thought he had left *her* and was living with another woman. She was ready to leave Prague. Past caring. She's probably back in England now.'

'But with Milan's useless documents?' Krystof said. 'I doubt it very much. I would not trust him to get me a fake library card, let alone a visa. I don't understand why, if she already knew Lucenka, that she went to Milan? I would not trust Milan with my *life*.'

The café manager's face loomed back into Rose's mind's eye. She shuddered, stood up and walked over to where Nancy was playing. Sitting on the grass, Rose pulled her daughter onto her knee and looked up at Krystof.

'You were too weak for me to tell you before.'

'Weak?'

'When you were ill after your ordeal, your arrest.'

'Tell me what?'

'What he tried to do. What he suggested. He tried to . . . He called me . . . that word.'

She watched Krystof's face crumple.

She pressed on. 'He said that if I . . . slept with him, then he would ensure your release.'

Krystof slammed his hand hard onto the bench, his eyes ablaze with anger. 'How dare he!' He gritted his teeth. 'How dare that man think he can even speak to you!'

'I told him to get lost. But of course . . . they still took me in.'

Krystof stood up, agitated, pacing the grass. 'It's my fault. All my fault. I should have been firmer with Babička. Made her apologise to you. I should not have let it happen, let it go so far. I should not have let these people think that of you. Speak like that about you. You're right, Ruzena. I was weak. But not any more.'

'But it's not your fault,' she cried, aghast at his distress.

'To think!' he yelled. 'I was going to leave the café to that weasel. Well now, he'll see what Communism really means. I don't have a café to give him. Let him rot on the streets and see if his Red friends help him then.'

Nancy, jolted by Krystof's rage, began to cry. Rose scooped her up to comfort her, speaking to Krystof quietly over her head, 'And I say we keep quiet. We say no more. Leave him to it. Walk away.'

Arriving back home, Krystof hesitated outside the front door.

'I see two very tired girls in front of me,' he said, lightly. 'You take Nancy in. Have a rest. Take a nap. I won't be long.'

Rose squinted at him, registering his false smile.

'Krystof, what are you doing?'

'Just some unfinished business. I won't be long.'

Rose laid a sleepy Nancy on the bed.

'My goodness, chicken,' she said. 'It's nearly your birthday.'

She tucked a lock of her daughter's dark hair behind her tiny ear.

'To think, nearly two years ago, Krystof was heading for Normandy, I was with . . . that man. And now here we are.'

Nancy snuffled, dozing, not hearing her mother's words. Rose was pleased.

'We can't do much for you this year,' she whispered, 'but we'll celebrate your third birthday, I promise you.'

She heard Krystof come up the stairs. He was right about not being long: she had barely had time to change out of her old brown suit.

'The soldiers didn't heckle you today?' she asked, buttoning up her summer dress. She noticed he'd already undone his tie; his shirt was dishevelled.

'No, they're being very respectful today. I think they liked Babička's spirit; the way she yelled at them. They remember her fondly,' Krystof said. 'But I'm surprised you didn't hear them cheer?'

'When?'

'Just now.'

She looked at him. 'Krystof, what have you done?'

'My business concerning the café is now finished. *Kaput*. Over with. Ouch!' He rubbed his fist, flexing his fingers, massaging the joints. 'I was just paying my respects to Milan.'

'Oh, Krystof. I said, *walk away*,' she scolded, suddenly understanding.

He grinned. 'You knew I couldn't do that.'

'Did it hurt?'

'Yes.' He shook his hand, examining the knuckles. 'But I think it hurt him more. It's not good for Milan to be socked in the face by his ex-landlord and find himself sprawled on the cobbles in front of a group of jeering soldiers.'

'Even if they are his comrades?'

'Especially when they are supposed to be his comrades.'

Twenty-nine

KRYSTOF TOOK OUT THE FRONT DOOR KEY TO *AT THE CLEMENTINUM*
from his trenchcoat pocket and slapped it against his palm.

'Won't be needing this any more,' he said. He took a step back
and craned his neck to look up at his home, shielding his eyes
from the sunshine that washed the stone facade with creamy
gold; the pinnacles of the roof line were hard against a pure blue
sky. The bells of the monastery rang out clearly as he dropped
the key down a drain.

Hearing the plop deep below the street, Rose looked at Krystof.
'That's the only spare?'

'Yes. That should annoy the commandant for a while.'

'We're really doing this, aren't we?' she said.

Krystof nodded, the depths of his grey eyes searching hers.

'We are. We are mad fools, but . . . Are you feeling all right?'

'No, but I will be once we are on the train.'

She followed his gaze up to the attic window.

'Are you thinking of the portrait?' she asked, imagining it up
there, its face turned to the wall, at the mercy of whoever
commandeered their home.

'It's the only thing I regret leaving behind,' he said, shaking
his head.

Rose distracted him. 'Now look,' she said brightly. 'I've packed
as little as possible, as if we're going on holiday, in case we're
searched.' Then, just as quickly, her spirits plummeted. 'But our
tickets and visas are for Paris. That will draw attention, surely.
Oh, Krystof . . .'

'Forgeries from Lucenka.' He sounded immensely confident.
'You can't have one without the other: a ticket without a visa.
Permission has been granted from a higher authority. That's
what it will look like to the "monkeys" at the station anyway.

Remember what I said about the organ grinder?' He tried to make her laugh.

'I just want to be on that train,' she snapped.

'We will be fine. They'll just get out their rubber stamps and wave us through.' He paused, and looked at her. 'You and Nancy will be fine, but if there's a problem—'

'Krystof!'

'We have been through this,' he said, his words clipped, his nerves making him cranky. 'If for any reason they stop me getting on the Paris train, then there is the other plan.'

Her stomach lurched with nausea. 'Tell me again . . .'

'I take a local train that goes somewhere near to the Austrian border. I leave the train – throw myself off it if I have to – I will stay undercover and sneak across the border. I will make my way to Vienna, and then on to Paris. I will find a way.'

'I can't even think of it,' she hissed. 'My nerves are in shreds.'

'I will find a way to follow you.' His voice was grave with promise. He picked up his suitcase. 'Goodbye, *At the Clementinum*. Goodbye.'

Glancing round, Rose saw Milan standing at his café window, arms folded, stroking his moustache. His black eye was turning a nasty shade of yellow.

She hissed under her breath, 'He's watching us again. We shouldn't be standing around here in full view of everyone. Let's get going.'

'Don't worry,' said Krystof. 'Don't let him see we are concerned. That's it, Nancy. Smile and wave.'

As the little girl flapped her chubby hand in the direction of the café, a black shiny Daimler rumbled over the cobbles towards them, a Soviet pennant fluttering on its bonnet. They stood still and stared.

Major Ivanov wound down the window and beckoned them over.

'Good morning, comrades. What a fine day.'

Krystof straightened his tie with nervous fingers and spoke reluctantly. 'Good morning to you.'

The major got out of his car and waved his driver away.

Rose saw Krystof's hands clenching into fists. She could not look at his face. She held tightly onto Nancy's hand, stroking the top of the little girl's head.

'I want to say how sorry I am for your recent loss,' said the major. He stood tall, hands clasped behind his back. His authority was tangible; the quality of the fabric of his grey coat highlighted by the sharp sunlight. 'Your beloved Babička. May I offer my condolences.'

'You may. Thank you,' said Krystof.

They know *everything*, thought Rose in wonder.

The major noticed the suitcases. 'Oh, so you are off somewhere? Visiting someone?' He knelt down so that his face was level with Nancy's. Rose watched a kindly uncle-like smile stretch the Russian's face. 'And where are you off to in all this glorious sunshine, young lady?'

Nancy shrank away, hiding her face in Rose's skirt.

'She's a little shy,' chattered Rose, holding Nancy's hand tightly. 'She doesn't really understand Czech – yet. Only English words so far, . . . she . . .' Rose stopped, realising she was talking too much. 'Say hello to the nice man, Nancy. Can you say *dobrý den*?'

'I won't keep you if you have a train to catch,' said the major, straightening up again.

Nancy peeked out from the folds of Rose's hemline, and spoke her first – and only – Czech word: '*Chalupa*,' she burbled.

'Is that so?' asked the major, smiling down on Nancy. He turned his attention to Rose. 'So you're off to your *chalupa*? I wasn't aware you had one.'

'Nancy doesn't mean that—' said Krystof.

'It's – it's the property of friends of ours,' stammered Rose, catching Krystof's eye. Even as her words left her lips, she cringed at her mistake.

'Yes,' said Krystof, half-heartedly, stepping forward and hoisting Nancy up into his arms, turning her face over his shoulder as if to remove her from the conversation. 'Friends of ours.'

'After the death of your beloved grandmother, I certainly understand,' said the major. 'And you, Comrade Bowman, you look like you need a good rest. Some fresh country air. Who might these friends be? Could it be Comrade Vaclav and his lovely wife Mabel?'

Rose opened her mouth to say no, but Krystof interjected, 'Yes, indeed. My old friend Vaclav.'

The major paused. 'Where might their *chalupa* be?'

'Moravia,' said Krystof.

Rose could not look at him. She knew that he regretted every word he uttered.

'Well, now that it's summer,' said the major, breezily, 'I hear it is lovely in that part of the country. So green and pure. Such a change from the city.'

'Indeed,' said Krystof, settling his trilby uneasily onto his head.

'Have a good journey, comrade. And you, too, comrade.' He bowed towards Rose.

Frantic to get away, her nerves on fire, Rose stared in astonishment as Krystof prolonged the conversation.

'Please make sure your men look after *At the Clementinum* for us, major,' he said. 'I would hate to see it starting to fall to rack and ruin even if we are gone for just a week.'

The major looked at him, amused. 'I give you my word, Comrade Novotny.' He clicked his heels and strolled over to the café. Turning once more, he called, 'Have a good trip.'

As Milan rushed outside and began to fuss with a chair and table for the major, Krystof gripped Rose's arm. They walked sedately away, heads held high. But as soon as they turned the first corner, they began to hurry, racing down the cobbled lanes, through the twists and turns. Nancy was giggling, enjoying the bumpy ride in Krystof's arms.

At last they broke into the open air of the Old Town Square and Krystof, his face drained of colour, blurted angrily, '*Jezis-Maria.*'

Rose panted, 'Oh, Krystof, what have we done? What have we said?'

'What was *I* thinking?' His voice cracked. 'What made me mention Vaclav? We have no friends. And to say it was Vaclav of all people?'

'Are we done for, Krystof?' she asked, out of breath, trying to keep up with him. 'Ivanov knows. I could see it in his face. Should we just give up, go back?'

'No, no. That might make matters worse.' He tried to smile at her. 'I think he is playing games. I think he pretends. To scare us.

He may not have even heard of Vaclav. Unless he sends a minion straight away to check up on us . . . we have time. The train leaves in half an hour. We have time to be on it, before anyone finds out that there is no *chalupa*. That Vaclav . . . oh, God . . .'

'What, Krystof?' Her voice was sharp with nerves.

'What an *utter* fool I was to mention Vaclav. If he *is* under arrest, then why on earth would we be going to stay at his country home?'

Rose felt a surge of bravery, a desire to convince herself.

'Now come on,' she rallied. 'It could be that Vaclav and Mabel invited us to stay there whenever we wanted?'

'It's all lies,' muttered Krystof, 'lies on top of lies.'

Over Krystof's shoulder, Nancy smiled at her mother and Will Bowman's blue eyes were laughing. Rose had to look away.

Oh, Nancy, she thought, as they lengthened their strides and headed for the station, one word from you . . . one word from you.

They skirted the edge of the Jewish Quarter and hurried past the end of a small winding lane. Sunlight sliced down through crooked buildings, catching the water drops from a leaking drainpipe, catching Rose's eye and making her squint as she glanced sideways. The lane was filled with Russian soldiers. They were banging on a door.

'That's Lucenka's house,' said Krystof, barely stopping.

'Oh, poor woman,' cried Rose. 'What do they want? And . . . what?'

Suddenly, with a crash, the door was forced open and soldiers pushed their way in.

'This is serious,' said Krystof. 'But we're not going to wait around to find out why.'

He turned to go, then stopped, a quizzical twist on his face.

They both heard, clearly, the strains of an English voice from behind the front door, asking with edgy indignation, 'What *do* you think you are doing?'

'Oh, God, that's Mabel,' said Rose, turning back to the lane. 'She *hasn't* left yet. I wonder why? What's going on?'

Krystof gripped her hand and pulled her on. 'Come on! We've no time for this. Sounds like Milan has acted true to form, and she tried to use his dodgy papers. Or perhaps they have news about Vaclav?'

'I don't think there need to be that many soldiers for that,' muttered Rose. 'Bashing down the door seems a funny way of . . .'

Through the balmy morning air came a high-pitched scream. And then, muffled, one, two, three shots.

'Oh, God!' cried Rose.

Krystof blazed at her, 'I said, come on! We have to keep going. We cannot waste our time here.'

'But it's Mabel. What's happened to Mabel?'

'We have a train to catch.'

Fear rose like a hand tight around her throat to choke her. This fear was real, so different from the make-believe horror of the first night when she ran from the wooden figures and the fake skeleton on the Town Hall clock. This terror was crushing, cold and mortifying. She believed this terror would kill her.

'If something goes wrong . . .' Krystof said, marching her on.

'What – what could go wrong?'

'I will make it, Ruzena. Listen to me. I will make it. I will follow you.'

She failed to believe him. Every ounce of her body was stretched, every weak breath she took she had to use to hold herself together. Somehow, her legs kept going across the treacherous cobbles.

Out of breath, she swallowed, 'They've just killed Mabel.'

'We don't know that.'

'Well, what do you think that was?'

'I won't hear it, Rose.' His voice was deep and grave, profoundly sad. 'Just keep going. Keep going.'

They hurried on, breathless. A stitch began to pull Rose's side apart. Her hand, drenched in sweat, slipped on the handle of her suitcase. Not long now, she told herself. Not long now. The station was just around the next corner.

'Ah,' said Krystof, slowing down suddenly, 'If it isn't Lucenka.'

The lamplighter woman was sitting at a table outside a café, smoking a pipe. Her great woolly dog sprawled on the cobbles, its hairy sides moving like bellows as he slept.

'*Tabak*, Novotny?' she offered him a pouch.

'*Ne, ne*,' said Krystof. 'We are in a hurry. But I just have time to say, Lucenka, thank you for coming to Babička's funeral. It meant so much. And thank you for everything else you have done for us.'

Passively puffing on her pipe, the woman listened to what he said but made no response. Rose smelt her unwashed flesh, saw her black, snagged teeth and felt repulsed to her stomach.

Krystof ventured, 'Did you know that there has been some trouble at your house?'

Lucenka shrugged and turned her mouth down. Her eyes were like those of a dead fish. 'Yes, yes,' she muttered. 'That girl will not listen to me. I told her Milan was no good.'

'I think you had better get back there,' said Rose, her lip curling, her voice quivering with disbelief at the woman's indifference.

'They told me, those *Ruskýs*, to give them half an hour,' said Lucenka. 'So I wait here, smoking my pipe, for half an hour.'

Rose looked at Krystof aghast.

'Are you sure you won't smoke?' persisted the old woman. 'Either of you? You look like you need one.'

Krystof merely saluted the old woman.

'No, thank you, Lucenka,' he said. 'Goodbye.'

They walked on in stunned silence.

Announcements reverberated from speakers, echoing around the high arched ceiling of the station. Rose felt tiny on the concourse. Krystof, holding Nancy, faced her. They stood close; she averted her chin one way, he the other. She knew that if she spoke she would give herself away. How her nerves would pull them out of the crowd and reveal them as fugitives.

Idling engines hissed contentedly beyond the barriers while people criss-crossed the area, going about their daily business, catching their trains. She tried to concentrate on the ironwork pillars, trying to distract herself with the beauty and madness of the city beyond.

'We should be laughing,' Krystof said quietly. 'We are going to our *chalupa*.'

She glanced at him. He looked back at her. Desperation on his face softened into adoration.

She said, 'I can hardly speak, let alone laugh.'

'Then let me tell you a story about Lucenka. I once saw her

coming out of an alleyway with a face like a slapped arse, adjusting her clothing.'

'That old witch.' She longed to smile, but it felt painful to do so.

Krystof went on, 'And who should follow her out, buttoning himself up? Some young Red, who looked like *his* arse had been slapped.'

Her false smile made her face ache; her stomach twisted into knots.

'Now we know why,' he said. 'Now it is all falling into place. Although why anyone would want . . .'

'Krystof, I think I'm going to be sick.'

'Look, you hold onto the tickets, I want to take this off.' He handed the folded paperwork to her, then removed his trench-coat and laid it over his arm. 'It is rather warm for the beginning of June, don't you think? Pity you will never see high summer in Prague. It gets very hot in the city then. Did you know the month of June translates as *Cerven*, the month of the colour red? Don't let the irony be lost on you.'

Her nerves fizzed to the surface. 'Krystof, be quiet, I can't stand it.'

'Come on now,' he tried to soothe her. He traced the line of her cheekbone and over her lips.

'Is the train in yet? Is it ready? Have they announced it?' she rattled. 'They're announcing just about everything else. I can't make out what the man is saying; his accent is too strong. I just want to be on it. Once we're on it, we are halfway there.'

'Not quite, angel,' Krystof smiled indulgently.

'In my mind we will be,' she snapped.

'Ah,' he said, looking at the indicator board. 'It's just come up.'

'Thank God. Come on, Nancy. Let's go to the ticket barrier.' Her teeth chattered with relief. 'At last. At last.'

They each held one of Nancy's hands, each carrying a case in their other hand, Krystof with his trenchcoat over his arm as they walked towards the ticket barrier.

'We're going to make it,' she said and smiled up at Krystof.

She put her hand in her pocket for the tickets.

'Almost there, Ruzena,' Krystof said. 'Almost halfway there.'

'Comrade Novotny.' The voice was behind them.

Two Red Army guards stood shoulder to shoulder, a wall of grey uniform, a smattering of red stars on lapels, caps and collars.

Turning good-naturedly, Krystof said, 'Yes, comrade. How can I help you?'

Rose, looking from one stony face to the other, felt herself shrinking with dread. She picked up Nancy and held her tightly, willing the child not to babble.

'We'd like a brief word with you,' said one guard, his Czech not very good. 'Before you go to your *chalupa*.'

As her eyes flicked between them, her stomach tightened. She wanted to shout with laughter at the horror of it all. How did *these* men know that they had told the major that they were going to a *chalupa*?

'A word, comrade?' Krystof repeated.

She knew that he was buying seconds; seconds in which he could *think*.

'Yes, it is about your property.'

'Do you mean *At the Clementinum*? Oh, I see. I do apologise. The key? It was a bit of a prank, you see. I threw it down the drain outside, a little misdemeanour, I'm afraid. I am sorry. I realise the major might want a spare while we are away. But my . . . my wife here has another one.' He turned to her. 'Your key, Ruzena. Your key.'

She plunged her hand into her pocket. Her fingers were trembling as she held it out.

The guard took it, barely looking at her.

'Thank you for the key, comrade,' said the Russian. 'Please come to the stationmaster's office for a moment. We need you to sign it over.'

Krystof said, brightly, 'But I'm *giving* you the key, comrade. Please, take it.'

'We need to complete some paperwork, comrade.'

Rose saw Krystof tilt his head back for a split second to survey the guards' faces. Then she watched his face change. She saw his eyes narrow, and his good-natured smile fall away. The look on his face made her heart freeze. Krystof was frightened.

'Ruzena.' He turned to her, his eyes searching her face. 'Would you be so kind as to hold this for me while I talk to these gentlemen?' He handed her his folded trenchcoat. 'I shouldn't be a moment.'

'The train leaves in ten minutes,' she said, addressing the guards, more than Krystof. Her mouth crusted with panic.

The voice of one of the guards rumbled at her. 'You must get on the train with the child.'

She glared at Krystof. 'Did they say we can leave?' she blurted in English. 'Did they say we could get on the train . . . and that you *cannot*?'

'No, no,' Krystof cried, his agitation making him harsh, 'you're not quite grasping the translation. A Russian speaking Czech to an Englishwoman is not the easiest to understand . . . Get on the train. I am to follow, they say. I will follow.'

The guard cracked his rifle butt on the ground and bellowed, 'In Czech, please!'

Rose recoiled in shock, clutching Nancy to her. The guards moved forward and quickly gripped Krystof by the elbows. They walked off across the concourse: a trio of men with Krystof limping in the middle. They went into the station office and the door was shut behind them. The blinds came swiftly down.

Clutching the trenchcoat, her suitcase and Nancy's hand, Rose made her slow way to the ticket barrier, not wishing to hurry, wanting Krystof, as always, to be by her side. When she drew out her ticket and visa she realised that Krystof did not have his. She handed the collector all of the paperwork and managed to make him understand that the gentleman delayed in the office would follow shortly. And that this was *his* ticket. The collector clipped her ticket and waved her through. She walked to the train and stood on the platform outside the first carriage she came to. Porters were hurrying with baggage on trolleys; families were embarking; businessmen got into first class; some soldiers got into third. She stood her ground staring towards the office, the door of which she could just see, willing it to open.

She gazed up at the train. This could be their private compartment, theirs alone, all the way to Paris. This was where they would make their plans for the future. This was to be their sanctuary. They were nearly halfway there.

The whistle blew long and urgent. She glanced nervously back to the concourse.

'All aboard. All aboard,' cried the train guard.

A railman walked the length of the train, slamming doors shut. The engine was building a head of steam. The noise assaulted her ears and a great belch of billowing smoke filled the great curved ceiling above.

On reflex, Rose climbed up the steps to the carriage, installed Nancy on a seat, folded the trenchcoat next to her and put her suitcase on the rack, making ready for when Krystof joined them. She closed the door and pulled down the window. She leant out, craning her neck.

'Come on, come on, Krystof,' she muttered, as the final passengers hurried down the platform.

Nancy knelt up on the seat, her blue eyes huge in her pale face and her finger pointing to the window, to beyond the train.

'Yes, darling. Your *Otec*, your Krystof will be here in a moment,' Rose told her, surprised at how calm she sounded.

She peered from the train window again, muttering to herself, 'It's just stupid bureaucracy about a stupid key. Stupid Communist time-wasting. Thank goodness we won't have to deal with that sort of—'

Suddenly she saw him. 'Krystof!' she screamed, waving as hard as she could. 'Quickly, Krystof! Here we are! We've got a compartment!'

He emerged from the office, flanked by the Red guards. He stood still and stared down the platform. She saw his eyes find her, but she could not read his expression.

'Krystof, here!' she called. 'Your ticket is with the collector. Oh, do hurry!'

The whistle sounded again. She felt the great wheels shudder beneath her and the platform seemed to move.

'Krystof!' she screamed. 'It's going! We're moving! Krystof!'

He remained motionless.

He mouthed, *I will follow.*

'No, come *now*. Get on the train!'

Rose watched with horror as the ticket collector gave the Red guards Krystof's papers. The soldiers were pressed either side of him, still holding his elbows. Then she saw that his arms were pinned behind him. He was in handcuffs.

'Krystof!'

The hiss of steam silenced her as the train pulled away. She opened the door. Krystof shook his head with such violence, his eyes piercing her with such passion, that he stopped her from leaping off the train. Again, he mouthed, *I will follow.*

His tawny head was still visible through the smoke and steam but he grew smaller and smaller, fading from her view as she was hauled away down the line.

'This isn't about a stupid key,' she breathed in pointless realisation.

She stared hard at the spot where he stood until her eyes began to burn. She tried to pin him with her eyes, to make him follow. The tracks merged behind the train to a point of infinity, and the platform, the station and Krystof disappeared.

She slumped back into the seat next to Nancy, bending double. Krystof's trenchcoat was bunched up on her lap. She pressed her face into it, smelling Krystof's scent. She buried her face, opened her mouth in a silent cry, feeling the dry cloth against her teeth. *Now he will be cold*, she thought.

There was something heavy in the folds of the material. Puzzled, she lifted her tear-streamed face and began to unwrap it. She found the deep pocket inside and moved her fingers, burrowing until she alighted on the smooth, cool steel of his gun.

She sat still, her mouth gaping in shock.

Clever boy. You knew. You gave me the coat. At that moment. You knew. You were so brave. My clever boy.

Rose leant forward to look out of the open window, allowing the fresh air to dry her tears. The city had faded into green countryside dotted with the red roofs of farms and *chalupas*.

If the guards had found the gun, they'd now both be dead; shot dead on the concourse. And what would have happened to Nancy?

No time to explain. No more life.

I will follow, he said.

Thirty

A WEEK LATER, ROSE BOUGHT RED ROSES FROM THE FLOWER SELLER at Gare d'Est. How appropriate they seemed and how frivolous they were. The room she was renting for herself and Nancy near the station was cheap but the crowns that she had found in one of Krystof's other pockets – now exchanged for francs – were not going very far.

She had left Nancy with the kindly *madame* at the hotel, and found a bench to sit on. The arrivals board indicated that the weekly train from Prague was due in half an hour. Agitated, she tapped her shoe on the ground. To try to calm herself, she traced her fingers over the delicate curling petals of the tightly packed rosebuds and felt a sad disappointment that they did not have a scent.

A crocodile of schoolchildren, headed by a nun, flowed across the concourse; a woman dripping with furs and leading a little trotting dog, strolled by and gave her a disdainful look. She shrank inside her clothes: her old brown wedding suit, well past its best, sagged over her narrow frame; the colour was drab in the Paris sunshine. The shoulders were too wide, the waist too high. Already, a year after the war ended, the women of Paris were revived: hats were tiny and feathered; lipstick was brighter than ever; waists were nipped in over wide swishing skirts.

She watched the people to pass the time: hurrying passengers, dawdling couples, the dark-haired girl in the ticket booth, the waiter at the café, the newspaper man. She bought *Le Figaro* and conjured up her schoolgirl French to read about the Nuremberg trials. Churchill, she read, had simply wanted to get it over with; to shoot the Nazi war criminals out of hand. She folded the newspaper.

As the minute hand on the station clock eased itself towards the hour, every nerve in Rose's body singed and twitched.

The voice on the tannoy announced the train and she gathered herself together. Shaking hands straightened her suit. Clutching her roses, she flashed a smile as she passed the ticket booth and the girl behind the window smiled back. She wanted to laugh out loud at the wondrous, warm excitement suddenly washing away the nerves. Her cheeks burned with pleasure; her strides were long and bouncing.

At last, the great train eased to a halt. Doors slammed and the crowd of alighting passengers – people, like her, leaving the East – surged through in a mass of drab greys and browns, dressed, she thought wryly, just like her. Her eyes flicked from one face to the next, her neck straining, to catch a glimpse of his hair, his cheek, his eyes. She waited, jostled; the poor roses were crushed. People bumped her shoulders, eager to begin their new life beyond the realms of the station. She waited and the stream of humanity grew less and less. It petered out to nothing. And, still, she waited.

A week later, Rose was hungry and hunger made her cold. She wore Krystof's trenchcoat, tightened the belt and relished the warmth of it. She couldn't stretch to flowers this time. Surely, by now, they would have finished with him; surely, this time, he would have made the train.

Holding back, she watched the crowd alight from the Prague train and file through the ticket barrier. Twice, she thought she saw him: a handsome man, confident and thoughtful, looking around for someone he knew. But both those men melted away into the city; both those men were free.

A thought suddenly blinded her: he might not be coming on the Prague train. He might have done what he said he might do: escape by leaping from a train in Czechoslovakia and crossing the border. Her eyes frantically scanned the arrivals board: Zurich, Vienna, Amsterdam? How could she know? How could she possibly guess?

With head lowered and drooping shoulders she moved away from the barriers, thinking of Nancy waiting for her in the dingy room; the endless hours stretching ahead of them.

The girl behind the ticket-office window caught her eye and tilted her head in sympathy. Rose walked on by.

* * *

A week later she was right on time. Unfailing hope made her buy roses again. But as she handed over the last of her francs, she felt her heart pounding with dread and futility.

She heard a tapping sound and looked round to see the girl in the ticket office knocking on the window, waving her over. Rose's eyes widened. Perhaps the girl had news? Maybe there was a message left for her? Perhaps he had arrived on a different train and had asked this girl to look out for her and . . .

'*Mademoiselle*, would you like *du chocolat*?'

Rose stared, speechless. She bit her lip, feeling tears brighten her eyes and stop, suspended, at her lashes.

'*Mademoiselle*?'

The girl was wearing a pink blouse with a lace collar and her dark hair was dressed back in a bun, like a ballerina. Rose had never seen such a pretty blouse. A veil of brilliant emotion paralysed her. She had not had chocolate since before the war.

She whispered, '*Oui, merci.*'

Handing her the steaming chocolate in a china cup and saucer, the girl said, her English as exquisite as her tiny face, 'The train is a little delayed. Due in ten minutes.'

Rose could not thank her, for if she did, she would cry. She held the cup and sipped.

'Would you like to come in here and wait?' the girl asked. 'It is a little more *privé*?'

Rose shook her head and watched the girl staring at the silent tears streaming down her face. She lifted the cup again and drank from it to shield herself, to protect herself from the tenderness she was being shown.

'*Merci beaucoup*,' Rose said as she heard behind her the train coming to rest on platform *deux*. She handed the cup back, unable to look into the girl's dark eyes.

Hope drained the strength from Rose's limbs. She could barely pick her feet up as she walked over and stood in her usual place. She tilted her chin up and waited.

The shuffling, weary passengers filed by and the ticket inspector clipped away. Moment on moment, her head sank down and her heart crumbled. She tossed the roses into a bin.

Thirty-one

THE TYRES OF JACK THIMBLE'S BUS SPLASHED OVER PUDDLES IN THE lane; through the windows blew the damp, woody smell of fallen rain, fresh from the moors. Going around the corner into Trelewin, Rose saw the blue slice of the sea and something inside her cracked. Oh, she had seen the Channel at Calais: a flat, wide mirror – a barrier to cross. But it had not been her beloved Cornish waves.

'All change. Last stop Trelewin. We go no further!' came the cry from Mr Thimble.

Wobbling with fatigue, Rose got to her feet. She felt burdened by the distress she had absorbed; the distress that she did not want to show Nancy. They could have waited in Paris for the next train, and the next, but something inside Rose had urged them to go home – or starve.

'Welcome back, miss,' said Jack Thimble, pipe clamped between his teeth. 'You all right with that suitcase? You all right with the little one? You all right to walk over the headland?'

'Yes, I am all right.'

'Telephone's working now,' he said, nodding towards the red box behind the hedge. 'You could call ahead to them Cumberpatchs.'

'A good idea. Thank you, Mr Thimble,' she managed.

With Krystof's trenchcoat tightly belted, she walked with Nancy across the triangle of grass that marked the centre of Trelewin. Sunshine showed itself around the clouds like a yellow beacon; gulls wheeled overhead, their keening cries stabbing her with nostalgia.

How peaceful it was, here in Trelewin among its quiet cottages, after the rattling of her journey, the unsteady lurch of the ferry, the continuous unease of travelling. But there, behind its high hedge, loomed the Old Vicarage with its neglected garden and missing roof tiles. A plume of smoke from the chimney indicated its owner was home. She dared not look for too long and hurried to the call box. It really wasn't a good idea to have got the bus all the way to Trelewin. She should have alighted at Polperro and called the farm from there.

Turning her back on the house and tensing her shoulders, Rose took out a penny.

Lifting the receiver, she spoke: 'Polperro 254.'

'Connecting you.'

After an empty pause and some static, the cheerful ringing tone struck up and Betony's gentle voice suddenly filled her ear.

'Pengared Farm.'

Tears began to flow, to choke her. She could barely speak. 'It's Rose. I'm home.'

Betony said, 'We'll come and get you. Stay where you are. Shouldn't be too long. Oh, Ginge.'

'I left him. I left him behind.'

After the stuffiness of the phone box, Rose's face was suddenly full of sea air. Down below lay the gentle cove, the whispering waves, the rock where they sat. She rested her suitcase down by a bench and sat, holding Nancy tightly, burying her face in the little girl's hair.

A village woman with her child walked towards her from the direction of the church, and, not recognising her, gave her a pitiful stare. Rose turned her face away, knowing she looked a fright; like a refugee.

Suddenly, as they passed her, the little boy pointed towards the Old Vicarage and said, 'Mummy, isn't that the Nazi's house?'

'Hush, Paul,' scolded his mother. 'That's enough.'

A burst of anger, like white lightning, flashed through Rose's head. Her grief returned, rising like bile in her gut.

She picked up Nancy and marched across the road, an incredible energy pumping through her blood.

'He'd better be home,' she muttered, crunching over the gravel towards the front door. She hammered on it. 'I want him to *know* how much this hurts. I want him to *know*!'

Breathing like a steam train, she waited. And waited. And then she hammered again.

She wanted to scream out her grief, enunciate her fear and frustration; spit in the face of the man at the root of it all. A full two minutes passed. She raised her fist again. The front door opened.

'What?' Will Bowman asked, his bleary eyes not registering. He slouched, rubbing the dark stubble over his chin. He was barefoot, his shirt untucked. She smelt alcohol fumes.

Suddenly, his eyes widened.

'Rosebud?'

'Will Bowman,' she said.

She pushed past him through the door and into the hallway. Immediately she was revolted. The air was damp and putrid. Piles of rubbish and old newspapers filled the corners. She saw mouse droppings by the wall.

'I see you've kept the place nice.' Her sarcasm grated angrily. She saw plates of old food in the kitchen; clothes strewn on the carpet in the sitting room; overflowing ashtrays; and a pair of ladies' stockings bundled behind a cushion.

'Is this my daughter? Is this Nancy?' A crooked smile softened Will's face into a pathetic mask. He took a step closer and reached for the child.

'Don't you dare touch her!' Rose cried, flinching away with Nancy in her arms.

'I have a right to hold her.' He fumbled for his packet of cigarettes in his pocket, his hands shaking as he struck the match. 'She is my daughter, after all. So you tell me.'

Before Rose could muster her answer, he demanded, 'What are you doing here, anyway?' He blew a stream of smoke to the ceiling. 'I thought you might be dead.'

'It's been touch and go,' she hissed.

'Then if you're not dead,' he said, 'aren't you supposed to be with your lover in Prague?'

'I had to leave,' she retorted. 'Haven't you heard what's been going on in Eastern Europe? Perhaps the BBC doesn't know half the truth.'

'And your lover? Has he come too?'

She slid her eyes to the floor, suddenly wondering what she was doing here, at the Old Vicarage, in the presence of the man she truly hated.

Will's eyes lit up as he took another drag on his cigarette. 'Your silence speaks volumes, Rosebud. So, your lover has left you.' His eyes narrowed as she stared at him. 'Well, well. You've got a nerve showing your face here. After what you did to me; and after you took my daughter away. Before I ever clapped eyes on her. Do you know, it was months before the screws at Bodmin jail even told me what you'd had – boy or girl.'

Will came closer, exhaling smoke, making her skin crawl. She moved away from him, holding onto Nancy tightly.

'How come they let you out, then?' she asked, agitated and thirsty for answers.

'They always release the likes of me eventually,' he said. He threw the cigarette onto the Victorian floor tiles and ground it out. 'Political prisoner. Has a romantic ring, doesn't it? I have to report to the police station every week for a year. A slap on the wrist, really. The threat's over. It's the bastard Communists now.'

Thinking suddenly of the major, she turned on Will. 'Don't you realise that your dreadful politics put me in danger? Put your own daughter in danger? They opened your solicitor's letter to me. They open all post, you know, you fool. They knew you were convicted of being a Nazi sympathiser. And they, rightly, abhor the Nazis. Your actions were more far reaching than you think. And to accuse me of kidnap . . . well!'

He took a step closer and reached for her hair, his voice unnaturally soft. 'Rosebud . . . Rosebud . . . I am sorry. But it's had the right effect. You've come back. Back to me. You've brought our daughter back to me . . .'

She batted his hand away. 'It stinks in here,' she retorted, shifting herself away. 'How on earth do you manage to entertain the ladies when it smells like this? It's revolting.'

'Let me hold her. Please. Just let me hold my little girl.'

Something coiled in Rose's heart. He was Nancy's father after all. But as she passed Nancy over, the little girl's shoulders flinched with shock, her eyes full of confusion.

'There we are, now, my own special girl.' Will lifted Nancy up high above his head and swivelled around, hoping, Rose suspected, for some laughter. Instead, the little girl began to cry.

'She is shy of strangers,' Rose told him.

'*Strangers?*' The look on Will's face brought a cold sweat to her scalp. 'She is my daughter. We will no longer be strangers.'

'Give her back to me,' Rose said, her voice shaking.

'Oh, no,' he said. 'She is here to stay, aren't you, Nancy? Now stop your crying. I am your daddy. This is your home.'

'No, please, Will. Please give her back.' Rose held out her arms, thinking, Nancy thinks that Krystof is her *Otec*. 'Can't you see how upset she is? She's had a long journey, and wants to go to bed. I'm taking her over to Pengared . . .'

'If you stay with me, Rosebud,' he said, moving towards the stairs and placing Nancy on the bottom step, 'If you come back to me, I will drop all charges of kidnap against you.'

Nancy shuffled around on the step and began to climb up the stairs.

'That's right, Nancy,' he called softly, 'you go up there. We'll sort out a nice bed for you.'

Rose leant against the wall, suddenly exhausted, unsure how much further her unsteady legs could carry her. Noticing, Will walked over to her.

'You just need a little comfort, too, don't you? A little lie down? Perhaps I don't have to be a stranger any more,' he cooed, reaching to touch her hair. 'Perhaps we can be a family again. All forgiven. All forgotten. I feel sorry for you, Rosebud. Off you went chasing a fantasy in a foreign land, chasing that Slavic conscript. And now he's shown his true colours – ha – that would be Red.'

'No, Will,' she said, feeling her fists tighten. Her heart beat with wild rage as she lifted her eyes to look at her husband standing over her.

'Just look at you.' Will drew himself back. His eyes roved up and down her figure. 'That coat is a bit big for you, but I know what lies beneath. I remember that cold winter here, our first winter together. You kept me warm all through the night, even though you rarely gave me your all. You've got a lot of making up to do now.'

'No, Will.'

'And your eyes – God, I have never seen such a green. I always told your parents, how beautiful you were. They liked me . . .' He reached for the belt on her coat. 'They wanted us to be together.'

'Take your hand away,' she spat, stretching her neck to remove herself from the tobacco smell of his breath, to avoid his leering eyes.

'Ah, that's my fighting girl. We're still married, you know.'

Fear crystallised her thoughts in a sudden rush. 'All I want is to live in peace with my daughter,' she hissed. 'I am the one who looks after her. She belongs to me.'

'Let's see, shall we,' he said, his fingers working their way over the buttons on her coat. He glanced up the stairs. Nancy had reached the landing. She sat there, hugging her knees, her eyes opaque with fear. 'Let's both call her and see who she goes to.'

'Don't be flippant. You know what I mean. Nancy, come here. Come to Mummy!' Rose broke away from him and raced to the stairs. Will caught up with her, grabbing her, his two hands on her shoulders. He wrenched her around, using his weight and strength, forcing her against the banisters. The rail pressed painfully into her spine.

'Listen, you,' he hissed, spit flying in her face. 'I gave you everything. I rescued you when your parents died. I identified their bodies at the morgue. What bits of them they found, anyway.'

She turned her head away, screwing up her eyes. The bomb that had obliterated her parents' lives had found her finally, detonating over her head in an almighty explosion.

'Look at me, Rosebud. That's right, look at me. Look at me!' he bellowed.

She opened her eyes.

'I put this roof over your head. Gave you a home. Gave you that child up there. And you repay me with nearly two years in prison, while you run off with your lover. Do you know what that does to a man?' He shook her hard. Her head rapped against the banisters. 'Remember what I told you, Rosebud, the day you grassed on me? Remember what I said I'd do?'

She felt the end of his finger trace the scar on her cheek. Her mouth curled up in revulsion. She could see the veins in his eyes, the spittle on his mouth.

'You remember how I loved you?' He was laughing close in her ear. He lowered his hand and slowly traced the curve of her body through the coat. 'Deep down, you love me,' he whispered, 'or you wouldn't have come back. You left your lover and you came back.'

'I didn't . . . He couldn't leave . . . I don't love you,' she managed to say, her throat constricting with terror. 'I never have. You know that. I already told you.'

She breathed in his hot breath and it seared her throat.

'Tell you the truth, I'm past caring,' he said. 'Same as your lover now, I expect. Now you've walked out on him. Out of sight, out of mind.'

'Get off me!' she screamed, struggling as he moved his face to kiss her. 'How dare you mention Krystof. *My* Krystof.'

He latched onto her, wrapping his arms around her, bending his face to her neck. He pushed her down onto the stairs, her backbone crunching against the steps.

She wriggled and struggled, gritting her teeth. 'I-said-get-off.'

'*Your* Krystof?' he grunted. 'How pathetic.'

His weight was on her. Rose thrashed and jerked, trying to escape. His force was crushing the breath out of her. She could no longer scream or speak to him, reason with him or plead with him. In a moment, he could take her. Her little girl was waiting upstairs on the landing. Rose wanted to live for her; she wanted her life back. She twisted her wrist, bending her elbow. She felt her way into the pocket of the coat and pulled out Krystof's gun. She pressed it to Will's chest.

He stopped and hoisted himself up, looking down in surprise. 'What on earth . . . ? Good God.' His eyes sharpened with fear, and then softened with a trickle of respect. 'My, my, Rosebud. You are a dark horse.'

He stood up and backed away across the hall, holding up his hands in the way she had seen villains do at the picture house. His eyes flicked from Krystof's gun to her face and back again.

'What are you doing with that thing?'

Rose stood up, training the gun on him with a shaking hand. 'It's a long story, and you're not worthy enough to hear it.'

He went to laugh but the smirk fell from his face as she jerked the gun higher, aiming it between his eyes.

He said, 'It's probably not loaded.'

'There's only one way to find out,' she said. She held firm, supporting her wrist with her other hand. She took a step towards him, feeling powerful, brave and complete.

'Now, Rose, come on.' He tried to make himself sound reasonable but his face registered blind fear. 'All right, all right, if it has come to this, say something. Anything. Come on, what do you want?'

He moved sideways towards the sitting-room door and stumbled. Sweat washed over his forehead and into his eyes; he tried to brush it away, his eyes darting brightly. She kept him in her sights.

'What do I want?' she asked. She cocked her head, listening to herself. *What do you want?*

She moved towards him, taking a firmer grip on the gun. It was heavier to hold than she had expected, but small, smooth and neat. Krystof's gun felt good in her hands.

'I want you to leave this house and never come back. I want full custody of Nancy. I want a divorce, a fair divorce. I want you to leave us in peace. I want *peace*.'

It was all she had ever wanted. As she spoke, she felt a tide of emotion rock her core. She had to hold herself together, to stop the tears. She could not show him her tears. This man looking down the barrel of Krystof's gun had put her and Nancy in danger, put Krystof in danger, had prevented their happiness, prevented their peace.

'Well, Rosebud, what a tearjerker.' Will shook his head, making a tutting sound. 'You've seen too many bad movies.'

She watched him lean against the doorpost and fold his arms. His hateful face twisted into a sarcastic smile as he said, 'That's my daughter up there, sitting on the stairs watching us, too, remember. You won't have peace, not from me, not for what you did to me. I will never leave you in peace. Not after this.'

'What about what you did to me!' she screamed. 'You brain-washed me and my parents into thinking you were a decent man. You took me away from the man I should have been with. If you hadn't taken me away from my bombed-out home he would have found me. He was coming to find me . . . I wouldn't have married you . . . I wouldn't have had – oh!'

'Aha – so you wish you hadn't had Nancy, is that it? Well,

that's about right, isn't it? I bet she's a burden to your lover. I can't even be bothered to remember his name.'

'It's Krystof!' she yelled. 'And I love him. He loves us both.' She glared at him, fixing him with all her hatred. 'I hate you! You have ruined my life.'

'I never thought you had it in you,' he said, firing off his sarcasm. 'All this ranting, all this bravado. Just put the gun down and give me a kiss, like a good girl.'

'Enough!' she screamed. Both hands holding the gun began to shake. 'I've had enough.'

She squeezed the trigger.

An inhuman force kicked her back, lifted her hands into the air. The retort hit her eardrums with a hard suck of air. The bullet exploded into Will's shoulder and flung him back against the wall.

He started to scream as blood oozed out of the wound. His hands twitched over it, his mouth agape with horror. He sank down the wall, his knees buckling. His eyes began to glaze in pain but the snarl was still on his lips.

'You bitch,' he breathed, choking. 'You little whore bitch.'

'What did you call me?' she screamed.

'You little—'

She lowered the gun two inches and fired again. And again. And again.

There came a hammering, an awful, insistent hammering. Ted was calling her name. He sounded urgent. He sounded angry. *But how could he be angry already?* thought Rose. *He doesn't know what I've done.*

She pulled herself up from the hall floor, unfurled her quaking body and walked unsteadily to the front door. As she reached her hand to unlock the latch she heard a whimpering sound. Looking back at Will's crumpled body, she saw that his open eyes were like glass, his legs in a peculiar position. She felt frightened of him, even with four bullet holes in his body. She glanced up to the top of the stairs. Nancy was crouched there, clinging to the newel post, her eyes wide and dark, her mouth square with shock. There were no tears, just a horrified whine.

'Oh, Nancy,' she whispered. 'I'm so sorry.'

Her shaking fingers fumbled with the latch. Betony, Ted and Meg burst through the door.

'We wondered where you were. We thought we'd better see if . . .'

'Are you all right, Ginge?'

'Good God, what's happened here?'

Rose stood in the centre of the hallway, beseeching her little girl at the top of the stairs. 'Come here, Nancy, come to Mummy. Mummy is so sorry. I am so sorry. Please come here for a hug.'

Out of the corner of her eye, she saw Ted kneel carefully by Will's body. Betony and Meg were cringing, holding onto each other, their shouts of horror growing louder and louder, filling the room.

'Please,' Rose whispered, beneath their screams, stretching her arms out to Nancy. 'Please come to Mummy.'

The little girl got to her feet and ran down the stairs, straight to Betony, who picked her up on reflex. Nancy curled her legs around her waist and buried her face in her shoulder.

'Nancy, I'm your Mummy,' cried Rose, horrified.

'Take her out of here!' came Ted's gruff bellow. 'Both of them, take them out!'

Rose felt Meg put her arm tight around her shoulders and move her towards the front door. Rose looked back. Ted's quick, efficient hands were wrapping Krystof's gun in an old towel that had been lying in the corner. He stopped what he was doing and caught her eye. She saw a grimace of pain on his face, his eyes dark with shock. He nodded at her. A tourniquet seemed to compress her brain, preventing her from feeling the horror of what she had just done.

'Keep walking,' said Betony, her face in Nancy's hair, their feet plodding over the gravel. 'Just keep walking. We'll be back home soon.'

Meg was crying. 'You should never have come here on your own, Ginge, knowing that man as you do. What have you done?'

'It's pretty bloody obvious, isn't it?' snapped Betony. 'Now shut up, Meg, just keep her moving. It will be all right. Don't look back. Keep going.'

But Rose could not pull her eyes away from Nancy's crumpled little face staring blindly at her over Betony's shoulder.

Rose didn't know how she made it along the footpath, past the post box, over the stile, following Betony and Meg onto the headland. High up on the clifftop, she caught up with them and embraced Betony, wrapping her arms around the child in her friend's arms. She gently touched the knit of Nancy's cardigan, letting her fingers alight secretly on the back of her soft head, becoming aware of the tug and crash of the waves below in the cove. A sigh from deep inside broke away from her.

'I won't be long, Betony,' Rose said. 'You go on.'

The wire had been removed. All traces of the crude wooden props and the cruel rusting spikes were gone. Rose had never seen Trelewin cove look so naked and natural.

She found their rock and sat on it, looking out to sea. Gulls cried overhead and nested in the cliff side; the little rock pools shimmered in the afternoon sunshine. She wasn't alone: a family had been picnicking, taking their chances on such a changeable summer's day. Now they were rolling up their blanket, packing their basket, putting on their jumpers. There were two children: little girls who would not leave their rock pool, despite the mother and then the father getting cross. They were fascinated by the life below the still, bright surface of the water, dipping their fingers and giggling, egging each other on to probe a little deeper. Eventually they were dragged away. After a minute of tears, it was all forgotten. She watched the parents tenderly hold each child's hand and walk back along the beach, picking their way over shells, pebbles and seaweed. Their fading chattering and laughter reached her on the breeze.

'I wish you could see it like this,' she said to the sky.

She was left alone with the tumbling waves as they hissed, spent, across the smooth sand. The sound seemed to cradle her, soothe her. It found the blackest, deepest part of her and forgave her. The waves set her free.

It was nearly dark when she made her way back up the ferny path. She wanted to get back to Pengared, to see Nancy, to hold her tight and tell her everything was going to be all right.

Something caught her eye and she hesitated. There was a light on at the back of the Old Vicarage. The rest of Trelewin was sleepy and deserted; curtains were drawn. Birds were roosting, winding down their evening song. The granite church tower stood out pale against a benign navy sky.

As she drew nearer she heard a clump-clump sound, a chink of metal against stone, a satisfying thump of spade penetrating earth.

Over the garden wall by the stile she saw Ted in the semi-darkness, his shirtsleeves rolled up, digging in the nettle-chocked corner of the garden next to the churchyard. She hitched herself up onto the wall and sat very still, tightening the belt of Krystof's trenchcoat to the increasing chill of the June evening.

Ted would not look at her as he worked, sweat beading his ruddy face, his ever-present trilby clamped tight on his head.

When the hole was deep enough he eased himself upright, rubbing grubby hands into the small of his back. He leant on his spade and glanced in her direction. She waited, her eyes growing huge in the twilight.

At last he spoke, his voice monotone as if he had been practising: 'I am very sorry to tell you this, Rose. Your husband has left you. He is going to divorce you for adultery, desertion, kidnap and cruelty, because of your flight to Czechoslovakia and back. But you have negotiated with his solicitors and you now have custody of your child. You are satisfied with the outcome. You are satisfied that he has absconded. You have no idea where he is gone. He left no forwarding address.' Ted stopped for a moment, breathless. 'You are relieved that it is all over, and that you can get on with your life.'

The hole was so deep that she could not see what was at the bottom of it. Silence settled around them as the dusk deepened. Many minutes passed before she could trust herself to say a word.

'And what are you doing, Ted?'

'I am planting you a nice flowering cherry, Rose, right here by the wall.'

'A flowering—?'

'I was going to plant it in the orchard at Pengared but I went and fetched it. I think it will look better here.'

'You called me Rose,' she said. 'What's happened to Ginge?'

He looked at her and cocked his head. 'I think the girl we knew as Ginge has gone.'

She turned away, tears blinding her. She pointed to the spindly sapling that leant against the wall. 'Is that it?' she asked, her words choked.

'I know. It looks small at the moment, but it will grow good and strong,' Ted said. 'The bark will be lovely, glossy and smooth. In springtime you will have blossom, in summer you will have cherries, and in the autumn you will have falling leaves.'

Thirty-two

NOW THAT THE EMPTY NAZI'S HOUSE WAS TO HAVE A NEW OCCUPIER, the villagers of Trelewin grew very generous. There was relief that they didn't have to put up with such a person in their midst any longer. It was a bad influence on the children; it was, frankly, an embarrassment. They were pleased he had been flushed out, and his young wife and daughter could be left in peace. They gave Rose a bed, new table and chairs; the vicar's wife had pressed on her blankets and sheets; Jack Thimble's wife a stove that needed just one small repair. Betony made curtains, and Ted splashed some paint about. Meg promised her the fireside chairs from Cringle Cottage, so that she could start nagging Hugh for some brand-new ones.

It took two weeks to clean the Old Vicarage from top to bottom. Even so, Rose knew that it would take a long time for her to be able to touch the walls, banisters and door handles without feeling a slippery revulsion. Not weeks or months, or years: maybe for ever.

Betony asked, 'Do you really want to move in here, Rose? Don't you want to live a long way away? Start again, somewhere else?'

'How can I?'

They were standing on the doorstep, watching Ted unload the suitcases from the back of his truck. Nancy was clinging onto Betony's hand. Her little face had closed in, her eyes were guarded. Only Betony was able to give her any comfort. Only Betony and Mo, who remembered his playmate tenderly from before and would not leave her side.

'No one else can live here. I can't let that happen,' Rose told Betony. 'Not with that thing in the . . .'

'You mean the cherry tree.'

329

The look between the two women was exquisite with a meaning which could never be voiced.

Rose rallied, trying to be practical. 'I can't impose on you for ever at Pengared,' she said. 'I need to be alone with Nancy, in our own home. I want to make amends for everything she has had to go through. Be a good mother.'

'Perhaps she won't remember what happened,' whispered Betony, brushing the little girl's hair with her finger.

Rose suddenly felt incredibly brave. 'I also want to be where Krystof can find me. I need to keep an eye on the post box. I need to be here just in case . . .'

'And, of course,' said Betony, her eyes shining with tears, 'you can make it into a nice home to bring up your new baby.'

Instinctively, Rose brushed her hand over her stomach. She felt a warm swaying inside herself. 'His baby.'

'Baby?' Nancy asked suddenly, looking up, her eyes round in surprise.

Rose squatted down and held her chubby hands. 'Yes, my darling. We are going to have a little baby. A little brother or sister for you.'

But Nancy would not look at her. Instead, her eyes roamed around the gravel on the drive, over the mossy steps, up to the front door of her new home.

'But where is my *Otec*?' she asked. 'Where is my Krystie?'

PART THREE

Prague
September 1992

Thirty-three

ROSE MANAGED TO SHAKE OFF HER TWO DAUGHTERS. SHE LEFT THEM sampling some budvar in the hotel bar, with a promise to meet later at a café near the Clementinum monastery.

'Try not to be late, Mum,' Lara said. 'We have a surprise—'

Nancy nudged her sister fiercely in the ribs. 'Hush, don't spoil it, Lara,' she said.

But Rose was not listening. A café? There must be lots of cafés near the Clementinum. They can't possibly mean . . .

'Mum? Don't forget, will you?'

Suddenly noticing their thinly disguised concern, she smiled broadly at them.

'I'll be fine,' she said.

What sort of surprise had Lara meant, Rose wondered as she walked along the river bank. The great pile of the castle rose up in front of her, surrounded by the familiar, indecipherable jumble of red-tiled roofs and spires either side of the curving green river. Smiling, she absorbed the city as if she was greeting an old friend who she had fallen out with; who had not been in touch for a long time.

She walked across the Legii Bridge, towards the Old Town side of the river, watching a father and son fishing from the island below under the shade of the chestnut trees. Even though she could no longer see that far, she knew that downstream on the Charles Bridge throngs of tourists would be shuffling under the glowering stares of the statues.

She found the spot where she and Krystof had stood that bitterly cold dawn to contemplate their fate. She remembered how the chestnut leaves had fallen around them, and how the cold had penetrated her bones, staying there for nearly fifty years.

There was a bench there now, far too appropriate to be ignored, and so she sat, resting her handbag on her knees, registering the nagging stiffness of arthritis in her joints. Thinking of Krystof's three letters safe inside the bag, she rested her fingertips nervously on the clasp. In a moment, she thought, in a moment.

People strolled past her, their chatter comforting. She gazed short-sightedly through dark sunglasses down the river. She was just one more elderly visitor in peach trousers and cream blouse. Just a little old lady sitting on a bench. Who would guess at her story? Who could imagine what she had done?

She thought how she had come to be here in Prague again, at this very spot on the Legii Bridge. How she had thought it might never be possible. The early years had been surprisingly easy. She'd received recompense from the government for the bombing of her parents' home; was able to sell the newly built property in Stanley Crescent. After seven years, Will Bowman was officially declared dead, his disappearance glossed over by everyone she spoke to. Her daughters grew up, oblivious. Nancy, whose dark hair and often guarded eyes were a constant reminder; and Lara, whose bright innocence never left her, despite her own disastrous marriage and hasty divorce. The people of Trelewin closed ranks around Rose and her family; never questioning, never commenting. The estate was settled. The Old Vicarage was hers.

She did not want the house. The years grew longer, harder; the passing of time less able to be borne. Slowly, her friends died: Ted, then Hugh, then Meg. And now only Betony remained, loyal and silent to the truth. The truth of what made Ginge disappear, and of who Rose Pepper became.

Rose opened her handbag wide and stared into it. Pulling out the bundle wrapped in the silk scarf, she carefully loosened it. The first letter was postmarked *Praha 9 June 1946*. She looked away, trying to recall. She and Nancy had been in Paris, waiting for the first train.

Her arthritic hands with their swollen knuckles shook, irritating her, as she tried to place her thumbnail in the envelope slit. She could not do the job fast or well enough. At last she tore the delicate paper and pulled out a folded, almost transparent sheet, looped with the faded ink of the hand she had loved for so long.

Fumbling again, she fished out her magnifying glass. A sharp breeze suddenly flapped at the letter. She held the glass as steadily as she could over the page, trying her hardest to be calm, and to keep breathing.

His English was as perfect as ever:

8 June 1946, Mirov prison, Czechoslovakia
Darling Ruzena,

How are you, my love? How I miss you.

This is where the Soviets have put me. Those Red Guards who spoke Czech so ill at the station soon made it clear where they were taking me.

Imagine an old castle stronghold in the middle of the countryside. It is now a labour camp. There is a concrete exercise yard in the middle, barbed wire all around. We are all the same here: ex-Czech servicemen, all of us, and now enemies of the state. Enemies of socialism. We are counted in, counted out: a roll call at every juncture of every tedious day.

They worry that we will rise up and fight them – but there is no need. There is not one man here, apart from me, fit enough to put on his army boots again. Vaclav is here. He has been here for months. He is very poorly. I cannot bring myself to tell him what happened to Mabel.

My Ruzena, when I think of the danger we were in, I am glad you got on that train. At least I know you and Nancy are safe. And please do not worry about me, for I am strong, very strong, knowing you love me.

This will reach you in Pengared where you will be safe. And you will know that I love you. You have always known that, haven't you? Your Krystof.

Did he know? she asked herself, sitting on that breezy bench forty-six years later. Did he know full well that the Red Guards were coming for him? That he'd be arrested at the station? That, like the major said, she was free to go? That he had to get us on that train? So that we could be safe? So we could live a life? Without him?

16th June, Mirov prison, Czechoslovakia
My Ruzena,

A week on and I know you must be definitely safely home now, with Nancy and all your friends. I hope you have managed to negotiate with her father and somehow start to make arrangements. I think of you every moment. I think of the sea, the little cove, the sound and the smell of it. We will see it again together one day. Until then, hold on tight to our dream.

We march, file in, are counted, fall out. Then we start work. Making string, sewing postbags. So, I think, I fought Rommel in the desert, and fought my way to Paris and Berlin for this? It makes me laugh, Ruzena, it makes me laugh.

They at least have allowed me the privilege of one letter a week. I have begun to feel unwell, some irritating cough. I suppose I am out of shape and it doesn't help being cooped up here.

Please don't worry, my love. But don't write to me, for anything you say may be used against me. They are a tough, unscrupulous, unflinching lot here. But enough of them. Speak to me in my dreams instead.

God knows we love each other and that one day we shall be wife and husband, mother and father. God help me to make you happy, darling, and God help you to make me happy. You see, my faith is returning. I pray to God again these days. When we are old, my true love, we shall look at this piece of paper and see how our wishes and prayers have been answered. Goodnight, my sweetheart.

Krystof.

Eyes misting, grief solidifying her blood, Rose grasped the third, and last, letter and tore at the fragile envelope. She was frantic to read more, desperate to hear again Krystof's voice in her head.

She unfolded the single piece of paper. Shaking her head in confusion, she lifted her glasses to brush tears away from her eyes. Krystof hadn't written it. It was in someone else's handwriting. In Czech. Panic gripped her; she wanted to scream. And all the time people strolled by in the sunshine, admiring the view down the river.

'I can't read it!' she cried out loud.

A man looked over, concerned.

Glad of her dark glasses to hide her pain, she smiled and waved her hand, hoping he would think her a silly old woman. She picked up the shreds of the third envelope, on which, she saw in confusion, Krystof had written her address.

She sat, stupefied and helpless. And then noticed the time.

I must go, Rose thought, I've got to find Nancy and Lara. Tell them the truth. They should know. We should all know.

Setting off through the labyrinth of streets, her feet tripped over bumpy cobbles as she dodged the rumbling trams. She had no time to devour the golden churches, arched windows, the monumental skyline. She saw the tourists filling the Charles Bridge like ants around sugar, and still, she was lost, frantic and late, hurrying down alleyways and turning blind corners, just as she had done on her first desperate encounter with the city.

'Three weeks!' she hissed to herself. 'I waited three stupid weeks. If I had just gone back, straight back to Pengared, I might have got the letters. And Will Bowman would never have got his hands on them, and stopped me knowing. Knowing the truth he stole from me,' she cried out loud. 'He stole the truth. Three weeks led to forty-six years.'

Rose hurried past a crowd of people gathering under the Town Hall clock, all eyes on the little door above the clock face, waiting for the show. She glanced up quickly to see her old friend the skeleton begin his party piece.

Heads in the crowd turned as she hurried past muttering, 'But at least he didn't open them, read them. At least he didn't destroy them. Oh, imagine if he had. Imagine . . .'

Lara and Nancy were sitting outside the café, next door to *At the Clementinum*. Tables and chairs were arranged in the sunshine on the cobbles. The doorway to her old home was freshly painted and had a bronze plaque on it. It was now a hotel.

'Is this the surprise?' Rose asked, her imploding emotion making her bitter and vile. 'Dragging me back here?'

'You're late,' said Nancy.

'Sit down, Mum,' said Lara. 'Calm down. We thought you'd like to see the old place you've told us so much about. How convenient – it's still a café! We've ordered coffee.'

'I think, by the look on your face, you may need something stronger,' said Nancy. She beckoned a waiter over and asked for some brandy.

Rose sat, stupefied, watching the aproned man scoot back into Milan's café door, circular tray poised on his fingertips.

'I suppose the doorbell to the hotel works now,' she muttered, looking around her at the little street, at the perpetual cobbles, and up to the lofty tiled roof in the attic under which she and Krystof spent their last night together. Where they left the portrait.

'Are you OK?' asked Lara, dipping her head in concern. 'Oh, no, you're not. You've read the letters, haven't you? I thought you were going to wait for us. Oh, Mum. Is everything all right?'

'Everything all right?' Rose looked at her daughters. Nancy was moulding her hard face into an expression of concern; Lara's eyes were wide and frightened. She had taken to wearing her fair hair in a ponytail since her divorce, and it took years off her. 'No, it is not all right,' Rose said. 'I can't read the last one. It's in Czech, and it is such a bloody hard language. I could only ever speak it. *Think* it. I can't *read* it. Not now.'

'Mum,' Nancy leant forward, her dark eyes scrutinising, 'there is someone here who can possibly help. This is our surprise for you, Mum. We hope you don't mind.'

'What? Who? Who can help?'

'He's just been to the gents. He'll be here in a minute.'

'*He?*'

'Let me explain, Mum,' said Nancy, straightening her shoulders, gathering command. 'Myself, Mo and Lara had contacted the Red Cross to try and trace Krystof. They put us in touch with the Prague university students, you know, who were doing a study on the experience of ex-servicemen after the war. They were very kind to us, they . . . Ah, here he is. Karol. Karol, over here.'

Rose lifted her head and saw Krystof walk out of the café. His tawny hair was a little longer, and his frame a little taller, but the way he moved, the way he slowly smiled over to her told her it was him. His grey eyes were as soft as they had ever been, shining deeply with his love. *I will follow,* he had said.

Rose gripped the table and tried to stand. The deep-freeze of her heart burst at last and her face dissolved into a dreadful hot tide of tears. She began to choke as she called his name, 'Krystof! Krystof!' as if she was still screaming at him from the train window.

'No, no, Mum.' Nancy's voice was in her ear. 'Please sit down. Brandy, waiter, hurry, please!'

'Drink it. Oh, Mum, we're sorry.' Lara was on Rose's other side, supporting her as her knees buckled.

Rose felt the fire of alcohol on her lips and finally opened her eyes. He was still there, looking down on her.

'Mum, this is Karol,' said Nancy, holding the glass for her, letting her take tiny sips. 'Karol, Krystof's nephew.'

The man sat down next to Rose. He took her hand. Even the sound – the quality – of his voice threatened to break her heart.

'I am Tomas's son,' he said. 'I never knew my uncle, but I did find out a little about him. How he fought in the war. I understand he used to live here. This was our family home.' He glanced over to the hotel.

'But – but . . . how did you?'

Nancy said, 'We tracked him down by chance when we were making enquiries at the university before the trip. The students were a great help, they—'

'No, no,' demanded Rose, turning on Karol. 'How come *you* are here? How come you *exist*? Are alive. You're *alive.*'

'I was plucked from the atrocity. I was a tiny baby, born just days before. I was – how the Nazis put it – *Germanised*. I was adopted by a family of the Third Reich; brought up in Moravia. When I was eighteen I left. I tried to track my family down. I tried to find survivors. I don't think there were any.'

Rose plunged her hand into her bag and pulled out the third letter.

'Please read it for me,' she said, her voice tiny and vanquished. 'Read it, please, and you may well find out.'

Karol moved his chair closer to her and unfolded the letter. Nancy and Lara sat back and sipped their coffee, listening. Rose watched Karol's face, unable to take her eyes off him even though it was as if she was staring into the sun.

Karol said, 'The letter is written by nurse Koste, at the Mirov prison infirmary, dated 20 June 1946.' He paused. 'Would you like me to read it, Ruzena?'

Twentieth of June? I was still in Paris; that was the week before I murdered my husband.

Rose nodded. Tears were pooling over her top lip. She licked them off.

Karol cleared his throat.

Dear Ruzena,

I am very sorry to inform you that Captain Krystof Novotny passed away today. He suffered from pneumonia, but the end was mercifully quick. He was able to give me this envelope, for me to send a letter on to you. His last words to me were about a wire, to tell you about jumping a wire. I am sorry but I don't know if I have that correct. My condolences, madam. He was a very brave, a very gentle man.

Epilogue

Cornwall
November 1992

STANDING ON THE STEPS OF THE OLD VICARAGE AT TRELEWIN, ROSE watched the taxi come to a halt on the gravel. Karol got out and paid the driver. He folded his raincoat over his arm and stooped to pick up his suitcase.

Behind him the sky was a deep astonishing blue; the late, slanting November sunshine was pure gold. Leaves – red, orange, burnt yellow – were spiralling through the air. *Listopad*, she thought. It was the season of falling leaves.

Rose breathed the damp air, smelling the salt of the sea. She closed her eyes for a moment to see a man, naked from the waist up, take a run and then a jump, clearing the wire with a cry of joy.

A wet leaf had stuck to Karol's shoe.

He smiled over at her and she tried to compose her face.

She heard urgent footsteps behind her, racing across the hall, and Lara sprinted past her, her arms outstretched, calling Karol's name.

Rose's daughter greeted her cousin with a hug, and a cry of delight, her ponytail bouncing just like it had done when she was a child.

Acknowledgements

Our Auntie Ginge is something of a legend in my family: we love to hear how, during the war, she met and married her Czech soldier Jan Chlebek and how, after his enforced return once peace was declared, she left on one of the first trains across Europe to be reunited with him in Prague. However, as a captain in the Czech army and a supposed enemy of socialism, Jan soon became a target for the new Communist government and it began to be imperative for them to return to England. Ginge packed a suitcase as if she was going on holiday so as not to arouse suspicion; Jan threw himself off a moving train to make it to a refugee camp in Vienna, and finally to England. Their story is incredible and inspired me to write *A Season of Leaves*, singling out critical episodes: Ginge's train journey, the hardships and tensions of post-war Czechoslovakia, Jan's gun in his coat pocket.

Once they had settled back in England, Jan anglicised his name to John Charlton but sadly died in 1965. Ginge (Gertrude Elizabeth Charlton née Robinson) passed away in November 2007 at the age of ninety-four, knowing that she and Jan were the inspiration behind my novel. I am indebted to their sons, Zdeněk (Robin) and Eduard Charlton, for being graciously accepting of my desire to commandeer parts of their story.

In the novel I married my protagonist Rose to the terribly patient and totally fictitious Will Bowman, but the sentiment and romance of the story belongs to Ginge, who followed her dream in the face of dreadful danger and uncertainty.

*   *   *

I am also grateful to Eva Melichar for telling me the equally amazing account of her family's escape from Eastern Bloc Czechoslovakia.

Like many writers, I am inspired by everything around me: a view from a train window, glimpses into living rooms, snatches of conversation, music, films, books and people at large. I wanted to create authenticity in my writing and make the events of long ago ring true in the present, so spent many hours soaking up the atmosphere and hard, brutal facts at the unparalleled Imperial War Museum, London.

I also immersed myself in the following books and stories: *Forgotten Voices of the Great War* by Max Arthur; *Forgotten Voices of the Second World War* by Max Arthur; *A Land Girl's War* by Joan Snelling; *Stasiland* by Anna Funder; *For the Love of Prague* by Gene Deitch; *Wild Mary: A Life of Mary Wesley* by Patrick Marnham; *Dark Blue World*, a film by Jan Sverák and Zdenék Sverák.

I would like to thank my brilliant editor Rosie de Courcy for coaxing the best out of me, and the Black Sheep design team for creating the cover of my dreams. Thank you, too, to Mary Chamberlain for her meticulous eye and attention to detail. Special thanks to my agent Judith Murdoch who has believed in me through many manuscripts bound for the shredder with the patience of a saint, and without whom none of my words would be read.

To my parents, step-parents, brothers and sisters, all my family and my wonderful friends – thank you for all the support and encouragement over the years.